Rooted

Rooted

Emma Golding

Emma Golding Writes

ISBN-13: 979-8-8693-9882-6

For my favorite pirate

From Cupid's quiver full of shafts two arrows did he take
Of sundry works: one causeth Love, the other doth it slake.
That causeth love is all of gold with point full sharp and bright,
That chaseth love is blunt, whose shaft with leaden head is dight.

—Ovid, "Apollo and Daphne" from *Metamorphoses*

Summer 1612

*Her running made her seem more fair. The youthful God therefore
Could not abide to waste his words in dalliance any more.*

1

MARGARET, STILL LADY Sherman, sat at her vanity depositing vials and pots into the individual compartments of a travel box. Her jewels, such as they were, spilled out of a smaller box. Her sister sat a few feet behind her, packing Margaret's clothing into another, much larger box.

My husband is in a box, Margaret thought.

"Will you sail to France with Aunt Crane?" Her sister tossed another folded skirt neatly into the open trunk from an arm's reach away.

"Would she brook refusal?"

"It will be good for you." Hearing Margaret's scoff, Elizabeth patted the paunch under her bodice. "If you had my excuse, it would help in more ways than one."

Margaret made eye contact with the face in the mirror's foreground, its pale skin ghostly against the black of its garments, a red band of hair between its forehead and its white coif. Predictably, the mirror girl rose to the bait. "Sir John was not in good health, and he was often away. Would you have had me enlist the aid of his son?" She played it off as a scandalous joke. Relating news of Robert Sherman's actual campaign to take his father's place in Margaret's bed would be too cruel, even for Margaret.

Once Elizabeth had recovered from the shock, she grunted. "I do not blame you for failing in your duty to Sir John, but you must agree it would improve your situation."

"I do not agree," Margaret lied. "A child would only complicate matters. In its absence, I may use my part of Sir John's estate as I see fit."

"Until you remarry, of course."

"Not so. My widow's third is mine as long as I live, married or not."

"That cannot be true. Robert will want it back when you have no more need of it."

Margaret wrapped a strand of pearls in a scrap of velvet and stayed silent. Her sister's refrains were tired. *Such masculine interests…* Or *your queer obsession with…* Or *what man will want a girl who…* Correcting her would only trigger another lecture.

"The right thing," Elizabeth went on, "would be to remarry and give your dower back to Robert. Poor man, to lose his father, God rest his soul, and a third of his property in one stroke." Elizabeth paused in her folding to make the sign of the cross with one hand.

Margaret followed belatedly, waving her own hand in a blasphemous zigzag across her torso. Poor Robert, with his title, his house, his properties and investments—not to mention his youth, beauty, and charm, which would secure him an excellent marriage. What about poor Margaret, childless and husbandless and homeless, returning to her father's house with her head hung in shame?

She changed the subject. "I do not relish the idea of traveling with Aunt Crane, but I am told the French are easier in their ways."

Elizabeth narrowed cold blue eyes at her sister. "Too easy, I hear. Protect your virtue carefully until you find another husband. The gossipmongers will be waiting for you to make a false step."

Elizabeth was about to launch into the Unfortunate Tale of the Wanton Widow, so Margaret hurried to disrupt her. "Why must I fear, with Alinor Crane as my protectress?"

"True. She will certainly limit the number of beautiful young men who try to woo you with poetry and songs."

"Why should they not?" Margaret swiveled on her vanity stool to face her sister. "Why may I not be serenaded and flattered and have verses written about me? Why this dogged belief that love has no place in a marriage?"

Both women had seen little of romance in real life, but Margaret owned a library of love stories. Tristan and Isolde, Helen and Paris, Guinevere and Lancelot were her childhood idols; each new play and poem published by Master Shakespeare added more to the list. Why would the poets write of love if it never happened to ordinary people?

Elizabeth tossed another dress on the pile. "'Tis not so easy as the poets make it seem. When we have naught to offer besides breeding and beauty, the water in which we cast our nets is but a pond. To find a man of wealth, with a title, who is respected, who is neither a traitor nor a heretic, who is not known to beat his servants, *and* who loves you?"

Margaret stacked the jewelry and cosmetic boxes and carried them toward the waiting pile near the door. Tomorrow, these relics of her married life would follow her back to her father's house. Her great-aunt had prepared her for the day she would leave her childhood home to join her husband's household. Nobody prepared her to reverse the trip.

"I cannot give it up, this notion that I might compel a man to disdain propriety and convention in the name of love. That I may be worth such a thing."

"That is a child's notion, I fear."

"It happened once before."

"Well, you were a child then." Elizabeth's slender fingers gripped the edge of the trunk's lid, and she let it fall with a sharp crack. "And that was not love."

Margaret remembered it differently. But eight years had passed since their story ended, and in that time, she cultivated the rosiest memories and trimmed away the ones best forgotten. It wasn't an epic tale, but it was hers.

"Something to eat?" Elizabeth said brightly.

Margaret's reserves were spent. "I hoped to wander down to St. Peter's. I will ask Cook to make you something before I go."

"Surely matins is finished by now."

"Then I will conduct my own matins."

Elizabeth frowned. "As you will."

Matins was indeed over by the time Margaret arrived at St. Peter's. She settled into the Sherman pew anyway, watching the shards of colored light melt across the stone floor. She had a meeting with Sir John's steward in the early afternoon; this was as good a place as any to wait.

Before she married Sir John, Margaret could only name the saints with the most memorable feast days. When she needed an excuse to escape her husband or his son, though, the old cathedral in town gave her one. She liked the music best, and the ritual of reciting the familiar words. After the services, she would greet her neighbors and her husband's tenants, then walk home alone down the tree-lined avenue. She would gather peace into her, storing it up to get her through another day.

She knew God was often busy, but she would talk to Him nevertheless. She told Him about Sir John's snoring, and the other revolting bodily noises he emitted whenever he was at home. She told Him about Sir John's loud laugh and his drinking, about the nights she laid beneath him as he attempted admirably to give her a child.

If she thought for a moment God answered prayers, Sir John's death would not have come as such a surprise.

In spite of it all, there was much she would miss about Bristol. This ancient church where she had claimed sanctuary so many times; the adorable Silver Starling Inn, of which she now owned one third; the ribbon of the Avon hurrying toward the Severn and the sea. Even the road to Sir John's house was the setting of a fairy story. Not that her father's seat at Duntsford Priory wasn't beautiful. There were churches and inns and solitary walks there also, along the same estuary, in fact. Several features of her childhood home, though, were short of idyllic.

The first was Alinor Crane. Margaret could imagine her father's aunt lying in wait, salivating and rubbing her palms together at the prospect of marrying her off to the first Frenchman who greeted them when they docked in Rouen. Then there was Elizabeth, less meddlesome but equally condescending, who would visit with the family before returning home to her husband and her young son.

Finally, Robert. At the moment she had been about to shake him off, he clung on for a few weeks longer: Alinor had invited him to stay and enjoy Lord Donwell's hospitality until she and Margaret left for France. No one would call Margaret worldly, but Robert could hardly be described as subtle: they both knew hospitality wasn't all he hoped to enjoy.

In the background of this tapestry loomed the specter of Lord Donwell. Her father was a stranger she had known all her life. He appeared at important moments—to bury his wife, to present his daughters at court, to marry them off to whichever old man offered the most gain—then receded into the shadows again. Not physically, for he was always there, sharing meals and sitting with the family in the evenings. In twenty-three years, Margaret resisted making a place for him in her heart. He would not have returned the favor.

The bells in the tower creaked, then clanged, startling her as they always did. She could lose whole hours, sitting in silence, tracing the pew's wood grain with her eyes, while inside her head, thoughts chased each other across a cluttered tournament field, clashing and fracturing and skittering. Often she worried this was proof of something broken in her. A slipping gear. A missing piece.

Sir John's steward was expecting her at the house soon. She stood and stretched and trudged back down the avenue. The warm yellow rays that flowed around the silhouetted trees buoyed her spirits, and she slowed her steps, gathering peace into herself and praying it would be enough.

Her late husband's office was cramped and dusty, lit by a wall of windows facing out onto the drive. Thomas Chauncey, a compact little man with a round face and a kind smile, greeted her at the door to the study and showed her to the desk chair, the most comfortable seat. Robert was already there. He stood when she entered, then sat back down on his stool.

Master Chauncey fussed with a sheaf of papers. "Now," he began, "there is only the matter of Lady Sherman's dower to discuss. You are entitled to one-third of the income from Sir John's real property while you live. It will be accrued quarterly. Who will have the managing of the account?"

"I will, Master Chauncey."

He didn't blink at Margaret's pronouncement. Under his tutelage, she had spent her lonely marriage learning about Sir John's assets and expenses, admiring the tidy ledgers and quizzing the steward about the enormous sums Sir John sent the king for the honor of being a baronet. He was the reason she knew as much as she did about her dower—not an inheritance, but a sort of insurance. It blessed her with an income after burying her primary means of survival in the local churchyard.

In her periphery, she sensed Robert fidgeting on his stool. "It would be better managed by a man who understands such things, would it not? With no husband or son to aid you, pray entrust it to me."

Now the little man blinked. "Sir Robert, I—"

"You need not trouble yourself, Master Chauncey," Margaret said, looking at Robert. "Sir Robert honors his father by offering advice and protection when he owes me neither. I may not rely on his kindness any longer."

"You are the only family I have, Margie, and you shall ever have my affection." Her family's pet name irritated her, but at least he didn't embarrass her by calling her "stepmother" while he fixed her with that magnetic gaze.

The steward cleared his throat and moved his finger down the page. "You, ah, leave for Gloucester on the morrow, and France after, do you not, my lady?" At Margaret's nod, he gestured to a coffer in the middle of the desk. "I have counted out the amount you requested for travel expenses."

The business finished, Robert and Margaret walked down the corridor together, the coffer tucked under Robert's arm. She held the door of her bedchamber open, and he set the coffer on the vanity before surveying the sparse room. "I will be sorry to see you go," he said. "You have been a good friend."

"I am a usurper. My place belongs to your Lady Sherman. I will toast your bride's health at your wedding feast, but she will not be me."

He stepped towards her into a beam of light tumbling in from a nearby window. It gilded the curls of his shoulder-length brown hair and bounced off his ruby ear bob. Two charming dimples decorated the slow smile that stretched between his high cheekbones. "Tomorrow you take your winnings and flee to your father. Are you so cruel you will not grant the wish of a poor orphaned child?"

Margaret snorted. "Robert, you are neither poor nor a child. Are *you* so cruel? Do not forget that in the eyes of the law, I remain your father's wife."

"Surely 'tis not cruelty for a man to seek what he wants."

"Apollo sought Daphne."

In the dozen times she had made this argument, he refused to consider Apollo's pursuit of the nymph as anything but romantic. Poor Daphne transformed herself into a tree to escape him; Margaret only prayed Robert would not make her so desperate.

"You truly envision yourself as Daphne, do you? Beholden to this idea of virtue? You would sacrifice your freedom and happiness simply to be… *good*." He frowned as he spat out the last word. "You do not see that you have a choice."

He had the story all wrong. Daphne fled Apollo because she didn't love him, because she was cursed to despise him. Margaret yearned to be so cursed.

"What choice? My dower may keep me clothed and fed, but the rest cannot be bought. I must safeguard the love of my family and the respect of my peers. Why do you beg me to endanger this?"

"None of that is in danger! Countless men have allowed their father's wife to remain in their household. There is nothing shameful about it."

"Do not twist it, Robert. You do not wish me to remain in your household as your stepmother."

"I want you as my *wife*."

"Which cannot be, not while I mourn your father! What, am I to endure ten months of playing your stepmother for the world while I play mistress behind closed doors? Not a soul will be fooled."

"What matter? 'Tis known a widowed woman has earned a certain degree of privacy in her personal affairs. She may engage in activities fatal to the reputation of an unmarried woman. After all, once a woman has experienced the act, it would be cruel to deprive her of it for the rest of her life."

How like him to cite a widow's cliche promiscuity as a benefit to her status, rather than a detriment. "'Tis crueler still to speak so to the woman whose only such experience was with your own father!"

"I care not. Others may be prudish—"

"The whole of England is prudish! What you are suggesting is not done, and I will not sacrifice my good name for your pleasure."

She quivered, heart racing, feeling like she had accomplished a heroic trial. For months, he had worked on her, wooing her just as she told Elizabeth she deserved to be wooed. She rebuffed him, rebuked him, laughed at him, employing every weapon she possessed to carve out the tumor that had been growing in her belly since he began his assault.

Daphne's curse was so… uncomplicated. To flee a man one despised, to be reminded of one's immutable purpose with each step? Margaret would have traded this torture for that clarity in a second.

"Pity, O Daphne," he said. "Pity a man in love."

She recognized the words of the song he often sang for her when they whiled away the long, solitary nights. *Pity, O Daphne, pity me*, he would croon to end the verse, brushing his elegant fingers across the strings of his lute with a lover's touch.

He stepped close, and she felt the back of her knee bump the vanity stool. "Did you not see it? Every morning you woke beside my father, my heart bled. Every time I addressed you as Lady Sherman, I wished I had given you that name. To linger near you was such sweet agony." His gaze drooped to her lips. "Pity me and end my torment."

There it was, the fever, the ache, the symptom of the disease. It struck her whenever he gave her that look of distracted hunger. It wasn't love—she didn't even *like* him most of the time. When she had been in love as a child, it had never felt wicked. But this… It had to be a sin to feel this way, to fall asleep imagining his lips on her skin, to entertain the voice wondering how vital *were* the Commandments, really? She had been on the precipice long enough to make a home there. Soon, Robert would topple her, but only she would fall.

"How stands the hour?"

He froze, inches from her face, then sighed and backed away, looking at the watch pinned to his doublet. "Two of the clock, near enough."

"I am needed at the church." She wasn't. She had already wrapped up her charity projects, and the evensong service wouldn't start for hours. But St. Peter's was as good a place as any to wait.

2

DUNTSFORD PRIORY WAS a squat stone building that sprawled across the manor like a sleeping mollusk, with far-flung wings and winding passages providing the perfect playground for an imaginative child.

Now, though, the shadowy corners and tall garden hedges were hazards, not havens. The spectacle of Robert was unnerving and out of place, a firework in a cathedral. This was her sanctuary, and it had been infiltrated.

A fortnight into his visit, the family whiled away the evening in front of the fire in the sitting room. Elizabeth sewed clothes for the new baby while Alinor worked on her tapestry, both women's industriousness making Margaret feel slothful. Her father had installed himself at the table behind her, a goblet of wine in his hand and an open ledger and some papers scattered in front of him. Robert strummed his lute, outlining a series of too-familiar chords that had her nerves on edge. For her part, she buried her nose in *A Midsummer Night's Dream,* part of her collection of plays from London. She assumed she had plucked it from the shelf by random chance, but with Midsummer only a few days away, it must be some Delphic sign.

Hundreds of evenings had passed in this way. Robert was new, of course, but the rest was the same. Had she really floated through a sea of mundanity bordering on misery for three years, picking up dark thoughts like barnacles, only to end up back where she started?

"You haven't asked about my tapestry." Alinor looked up at Robert through her thinning white lashes, a flirtatious expression that might have been effective fifty years ago.

Robert dampened the lute strings with his palm. "An unforgivable offense, Lady Crane, but committed unwillingly." He laid the instrument on the chair and moved to her side. "What are you working on?"

"The figure here is Lord Crane, God rest his soul." Her gnarled hands made the sign of the cross at the mention of her dead husband. "These are his men, of course, and this…" She flicked a piece of lint from the crimson eye of the monster in the picture's foreground. "This is the demon beast that unhorsed my lord husband."

It was in profile, one fiery eye glowering at the flat image of Lord Crane with all the hatred several threads could muster. With its muscular haunches and grotesque tusks dripping with foam, the nightmarish creature was a sad old woman's interpretation of the wild boar that widowed her.

Margaret would never dream of asking, but Alinor must have a sizable dower as the widow of a baron. How much of it did she give Margaret's father to cover her living expenses? How much did it cost to keep a single woman fed anyway?

"I shall finish this one by the time we sail," Alinor told Robert, who hovered over her shoulder as if enraptured by the image. "Methinks I will bring the loom and the supplies for the making of another. It will not be too cumbersome, I hope?"

"I shall carry whatever burden you require, Lady Crane. Think of me as your willing pack mule."

Margaret watched them, feeling strange. "The servants and porters will do that, certes," she said.

"What need, when I will be there every moment to anticipate your commands?"

The longer she held his gaze, the easier it was to recognize the strange feeling as dread.

"Close your mouth, Margie. You are not a fish." Alinor's pink-rimmed eyes were bright and cold.

Margaret closed her mouth, only to open it again. "You will be where?"

"I have asked Sir Robert to escort us to Rouen," Alinor said.

"He cannot go to Rouen." Margaret transferred her panicked gaze to Robert. "You cannot go to Rouen."

"How may I refuse such a kind invitation?"

"Who did you think would accompany us?" Alinor said. "We cannot go *alone*."

Such nightmares were common when Margaret slept, but she had no experience dreaming awake. France was to be her means of escape—not heaven, but at least one circle of hell removed from wherever Robert resided. She heard Alinor's brittle, excited tones as she prattled about the upcoming trip, but she couldn't heed her. Her mind kept performing dramas starring Robert. He haunted her as she moved around the ship, he demanded every dance at the lavish French parties, he drew her into a secluded grove and…

"You do still have them, I hope, Margie." Her great-aunt's gaze was sharp, as if she knew Margaret's wicked mind had drifted. Alinor was asking about her clothes, the ones she wore before she was forced to don her widow's weeds.

"Of course, madam. They are packed away, but they are easily found."

"Excellent well. 'Twould be impractical to bring mourning attire. No one wants to marry a widow."

Margaret glanced to where Robert perched on the arm of a chair. *The dead man's son is right there!* she wanted to scream. Aloud, she said, "I cannot cease being a widow."

"Of course you cannot, but you do not need to crow about it. Why do you think I am taking you across the Channel? They will not know you are still in mourning."

"Still? I have scarce *begun* mourning!"

"You will not raise your voice." The cold, foreign sound of her father's voice lanced into the center of the room from his seat at the periphery. Everyone was silent, Margaret most of all, forgetting to breathe or to allow her heart to beat. She shrank, reduced to girlhood by the spell of his rebuke, and closed the book in her lap as a reflex.

Robert, immune, stood and held up a hand. "Be easy, Margie, and do not trouble yourself on account of my father. He would rather you be a blushing bride than a dour widow."

"Well spake." Alinor's prim sniff sounded to all ears like a full stop. The old woman jabbed her needle into the weft of her tapestry and hoisted herself from her chair, using the arm for leverage. "I am to bed."

Elizabeth threw down her work. "I will go with you."

Margaret closed her book and began pushing herself up off the couch, but a voice commanded, "Be seated." She sat without hesitation and looked over her shoulder. Her father was half-smiling at Robert as he added, "By your leave, I have some business to discuss with my daughter."

"God give ye good rest, my lord," Robert said, bowing as he followed the ladies out the door.

The phenomenon of Donwell's venerable aura fascinated and amused her, whenever she wasn't subjected to it. He was only a baron, not the archbishop, but those who encountered him gave him more deference than he deserved. It was partly out of fear, partly as a reaction to how he comported himself, as if he manifested the awe he required and no one dared to question it.

"Come."

She stood before him at the table. There was another chair, but he wouldn't invite her to sit.

Her father's dark eyes, shadowed and brooding, had terrified her as a child. The lines bracketing his mouth and the one splitting his brow gave him a perpetual frown. Aside from his hairline, nothing about the man before her now differed from the man in her childhood memories. It fooled her into thinking she was not much changed either.

"Why have I received no payment from your dower?"

She froze like a dog caught with his teeth around a roast duck. But why did she feel guilty when she had done nothing wrong? "This is the first we have spoken of my dower. You have received no payment because I arranged no payment."

"Who is managing your affairs?"

"Sir John's steward will manage the account while I am abroad, but I mean to take it over when I return."

"Absurd. You will write to him and transfer the dower to me." He gripped the chair's carved arms with casual strength and leaned back, a sultan on his throne.

Conceding would mean relinquishing a path to independence she couldn't bear to sever. Refusing would mean summoning a version of herself that didn't exist. She licked her chapped lips. "Aye, sir. If you would only inform me what amount would cover my room and board—"

"What is this? Nay, Daughter, this is not a negotiation. I will have the managing of your affairs in the absence of your husband."

Margaret nodded, hating them both. "Aye, sir."

"Excellent well. Sign this." He slid a paper across the table. "It informs Master Chauncey that I am to be custodian of your affairs, and that any further correspondence is to be sent to Duntsford Priory."

She examined the paper, chest tight with despair. No, this wasn't a negotiation. It was an ambush. The paper shook as she looked up at him. "I-I must have something to live on while I remain in mourning."

"I will grant you an allowance until I secure you a second husband, someone of greater consequence than your first. Lady Crane believes she will find one in Rouen, but the marriage must not take place until next Easter, when your mourning is complete."

He wanted a better match than her first? That ruled out the only suitor she had. "May I not have the choosing of my next husband?"

"'Tis not for you to trouble over. Business concerns should not weigh on female minds." He held the pen out to her, a drop of ink quivering at its tip.

She took it from him and tried to read the words on the page, but her vision swam. What did a woman know of accounts and titles and land and dowers, anyway?

He was blotting the wet ink and sealing the message before she realized what she had done.

3

A FRAGRANT BREEZE blew in through Margaret's open window and scattered the petals of a crushed rose across her vanity as she dressed. It was an innocent spell, one all the girls of her acquaintance used to cast on Midsummer's Eve. Placing a flower under one's pillow was said to summon visions of one's future husband, and although she had eschewed the tradition for the last three years, this year she was desperate for a glimpse of her fate.

She had been avoiding Robert all week, afraid she would reveal what her father had said. *Someone of greater consequence…* It was ridiculous to feel disappointed. Robert never listened to her, never respected her wishes to be left alone, disregarded her concerns and argued against her morals. But on occasion, he caught her in the right mood, chanced on the right turn of phrase, looked at her with those brown eyes, and that mortifying, electrifying feeling unfurled in her. In those moments, she begged him to push her beyond her breaking point, willed him to take her in his arms and silence her protests with a kiss. It was madness.

Yet she depended on that feeling, that jolt of pleasure. No one had made her feel so desirable, so reckless, so wanton, not for eight years. She was pretty, by her own estimation, although her red-gold hair frizzed and tangled, and her pale cheeks were susceptible to freckling, and her eyes were too close together and were a watery non-color between blue and green. Elizabeth's face and figure were more elegant, but Margaret's future husband would be pleased enough.

Could she desire him, though? Robert had the beauty of an Italian sculpture, which balanced his irritating behavior enough that she could imagine kissing him—and had, many times. Sir

John was so old and fat and crude, it didn't matter how much he desired her; she couldn't shake off her disgust. What sort of man would Alinor and Donwell approve? Was there a young, handsome, wealthy marquis in Rouen who would forgive Margaret's awkward widowhood?

Avoiding Robert was lonely business, so she headed to the kitchen, a reliable source of distraction. The door was ajar, releasing the clank of pans, the scent of pastries, and the burble of a cauldron boiling over the fire. A cheerful whistle wended its way out the door, but it stopped the moment she slipped over the threshold.

The startled kitchen staff sprang to attention. Ayda, the cook, put her hand to her breast and squeaked. "Mistress Mar—Lady Sherman!"

Margaret joined Ayda at the worktable in the center of the room. Two rows of berry tarts already covered half the table, proof the staff had been working since sunrise. A kitchen maid adorned each pastry with a sprig of cornflowers selected from a heaping basket. A ball of dough waited on the side. Margaret went to work flattening it with the heels of her palms.

Ayda shooed the kitchen maid away and leaned on the table beside Margaret. "Are you well?"

"Well enough."

"Tellin' falsehoods has ever come easy to you, if you don't mind my sayin' so."

"'Tis not a falsehood, 'tis a half-truth."

"Those come twice as easy, I vow." Ayda toddled to the hearth, where she drew two fresh tarts out of the oven using quilted pads.

Margaret felt her Robert secret bubbling up in her. No one could offer her advice or consolation; telling Elizabeth would result in the tongue-lashing of the ages, and slandering Robert to Alinor wasn't an option.

"If you had married..." Margaret pressed her thumb into the dough and regarded the indentation. "Would you have preferred a comfortable home with a respectable man who did not love you, or would you have given up everything for a man who adored you?"

Ayda paused, two hot tarts in her hands. Then she sucked air past her teeth and dropped the tarts to the table with a clatter, throwing down the thick pads. "'Struth, Margaret, you always catch me off my guard."

She examined her fingertips, pinker than they were before, and used them to swipe a hank of gray hair away from her damp forehead. "A safe match or a love match? Can't say, can I? Haven't had neither. But I know as well as any woman that richer is better than poorer."

Margaret peeled the disk of dough off the counter and set it in an empty tart dish before starting on another crust. "But how much would you give up for love? What trials would you suffer?"

"Suffer?" Ayda lifted Margaret's malformed crust out of the dish and flattened it with a wooden roller. "Why should I suffer? What man is worth such sufferin'?"

Ayda was missing the point. What about the romantic epics, where the lovers endured such hardships to be together? "Think of Helen and Paris," Margaret said.

"Who?"

"Guinevere and Lancelot?"

With a hand at her breast, Ayda cast her eyes to the ceiling. "Poor King Arthur!"

Margaret sighed, wondering how to make her understand. "Let us imagine a man loves you, but to be with him is to make a great sacrifice. Would you choose him over any other?"

"I'm thinkin' I would choose the man I could most respect," she replied. "If he treated me ill, 'twould not matter if he had all the gold o' the pharaohs—and my family's approval, which I wager is worth even more." She quirked an eyebrow.

It was chilling, that look, as if Ayda knew already what Margaret was so careful to conceal. Margaret lifted a flower stem from the pile and brushed the tender petals with her fingertips. "Are not love and respect the same?"

"You might love a man, but it don't mean he's the respectable sort. Pardon my askin', but what's brought this on so sudden?"

"I have been… considering my future."

Ayda frowned. "Is he back in the county, then?"

"Cry pardon?"

"I thought you…? Yer not speakin' of Matthew Kent, then?"

Margaret's blood turned cold, as it always did whenever anyone alluded to that time.

Seeing the horror on her face, Ayda laid a doughy hand on her sleeve. "Oh, my love, I cry yer pardon…"

Margaret focused on the drooping cornflower in her fingers and took in a breath. It made her furious she couldn't govern her emotions when Matthew's face appeared in her mind, even after all these years. "I'll find you some more flowers." Margaret skirted the table and shoved open the exterior door.

Gulping the early summer air to stem her anxiety, she hurried down the kitchen garden's gravel path. She had been doing an inordinate amount of escaping recently.

If only she could escape the feeling of panic lurking in her abdomen since Sir John died, growing by the day like the son she should have had. A dowager had one purpose: to safeguard her son's inheritance until he was of age. Sir John's assets would have provided for her and the baby, and her son would have supported her in her dotage. He would have made her respectable. Margaret could defend her childlessness to Elizabeth all she wanted, but her sister was right: a son would have fixed everything.

Only when her muscles began to burn did she realize she was climbing the hill with the oak tree, her favorite place. Each ancient, gnarled branch ended in a shimmering, sighing bouquet of new leaves. She settled herself in the Y of its roots and gazed out over the priory grounds, where patches of villagers set up tables and wove garlands and hung lanterns from tree branches for the feasting later.

Midsummer was a season of renewal for all but Margaret, for whom it was cursed. On Midsummer's Eve eight years ago, her dashing darling, a farmer's son, agreed to run away with her. Then, at dawn on the solstice, at this very oak tree, he failed to appear. She waited for Matthew until the sun was at its zenith, the tree's spidery shadow inching across the hill hour after hour. Later, she would learn he was long gone by then. She had been fifteen years old.

What had possessed her to sit beneath the same tree on the anniversary of that day?

She rose, brushed off her skirts, and descended the hill, feeling foolish for worrying about something so far removed from her present. Ayda thought she meant Matthew when she spoke of Robert? Ridiculous. The circumstances were nothing alike.

The feast was merry and the dancing was lively, though Margaret's dark clothing and black mood kept would-be partners at bay. As dusk darkened to night, the revelers lit the lamps and set a torch to the straw at the base of the bonfire. When the first foolhardy youth leapt over the mounting flames, it was Margaret's cue to go to bed.

Her path took her through the formal garden, past the rose bushes where she found the component for her dream spell. She stroked the petals of a white bud and inhaled its sweet scent.

Gravel crunched behind her. Shadows obscured his face, but she recognized Robert's form and groaned. "Not tonight."

"What troubles you?"

"Naught that can be remedied."

"Are you certain? I ken a remedy that never fails."

"What magical cure is this?"

He took her face in both hands, and she froze. The scorching trails he thumbed across her cheeks made her shiver. Was she unable to move away, or unwilling?

Accepting her hesitation as consent, he kissed her.

Her fingertips tingled from holding her arms ramrod straight. She was stone, body and mind. She stared at his lashes, long and black, resting against his cheeks as he kept his eyes closed. How foolish he looked, eyes closed in ecstasy while he kissed a marble statue.

The warm ache sparked in her belly, familiar, unwanted. Her eyes fluttered closed. His kiss was nothing like Sir John's. His lips were sweet with ale, not bitter with spirit. He smelled of perfume rather than stale sweat. She felt herself relax moment by moment as she realized what she felt was not nausea, but pleasure.

He tilted his head, angled his mouth, deepened his kiss. Lust flared, and she knew she was damned, but she pressed against him, touched her fingers to his jaw, parted her lips and descended into hell.

"Let me come to you tonight."

The words were muffled when he breathed them against her lips, his voice low and rasping, and they doused the flames curling in her abdomen. If only he would go on kissing her, holding her, making her flush and shiver at the same time, instead of demanding the one thing she couldn't give him.

She put a palm on his chest, feeling the rapid beat of his heart as she pushed him away. "In my father's house?"

"What of it? Does he lock your door at night?"

"Be not a fool!"

"Do not deny me, Margie, I beg you."

"Enough of this." She shook her head to free herself from his magnetic pull. "I will share my bed with none but my husband. You must not ask it of me again."

"Be mine tonight, and I will marry you the day you come out of mourning."

If only it was so simple; if only the distant promise of marriage was enough to absolve adulterers in the eyes of God and men.

Not that it mattered. "My father will not sanction it. He has told me so."

A tilt of his head had his eyes catching the moonlight, an eerie flash. "But you are not beholden to him. You have the means to make your own choice."

Her throat tightened. "No longer, I fear."

"What is your meaning?"

"I know naught of taxes and investments—"

"Margie—"

"Besides, I cannot expect to live here on my father's charity—"

He gripped her arms. "Tell me!"

She had been babbling, nonsensical, justifying her mistake while she distracted herself from her tears, but now she calmed and looked down at their feet. "I could not refuse. He is my father."

"Your dower?" She nodded. His grip on her arms tightened, and he clenched his jaw, breathing through his nose. "When?"

"A few days ago. He will have sent the order to Master Chauncey."

He released his hold on her with such force she stumbled back a step, and her stomach dropped at his burst of anger. What did he have to be angry about? The lost income was hers, the fault was her own. "It is of no consequence," she assured him. "I will have an allowance—"

"No consequence? I depended on that income!"

"How? 'Twas not yours to depend upon."

"It *was* mine! You would have made the estate whole again when we married—or before, if you had heeded my advice to allow me the managing of your dower."

A flame reignited inside her, hotter and more volatile than any desire she had felt for him. "Heeded your—?"

"The baronetcy honors come due this year. How am I to pay them?"

"That is none of my—"

"You may yet correct this. Only a few days ago, you said—you can write to him and belay the order. Better yet, meet him in Bristol before we sail. Nay, 'tis too long to wait… You must do both. Write to warn him of your coming—"

"Why would I do such a thing?"

His brow melted into a theatrical look of woe. "Prithee, Margie, you must get it back. Lord Donwell does not need it as desperately as I do."

"Was this your plan from the first?" Her hands trembled at her sides. "How long have you considered my widow's third to be your inheritance?"

"Margie..."

"I denied you until my face went blue, and you persevered because there was treasure to be had?"

"Peace! You cannot think me so cruel. I wanted you before my father died. You were supposed to stay with me until we could marry without scandalizing the county."

"It did not deter you, then, the hundreds of times I refused?"

"You are hard, I grant you. But I beg you, be not cruel. The timing is awkward. There is hardly enough money in my father's estate to pay the king and maintain a widow. What am I to do with only a portion of my inheritance at my command?"

Sympathy was the typical response to this sort of appeal, and if she loved him, it would be easy to summon a little. But his flash of anger, his overconfidence, and his pitiful performance were a firm shake, and she awoke from her mystical slumber. Perhaps he was earnest about both needing her as a lover and as an asset. She wanted him for neither.

"You are to be pitied," she said, her voice gentle, "but I doubt not you will raise the money somehow. Mayhap in Rouen you will meet a wealthy *mademoiselle* who is too stupid to see what you are."

Later she would regret saying it, wondering if he deserved it, but she savored that feeling of triumph all the rest of that Midsummer night.

4

THE IMMINENT VOYAGE to France was a miserable prospect, now Margaret and Robert weren't speaking. In a desperate ploy to secure one night of peace, she convinced Alinor to change their lodging arrangements for the night before they sailed. Robert's house was so far from town, she explained. An inn near the docks would be much more convenient. The Silver Starling was clean and comfortable, and the innkeeper made the best beer outside of London. Margaret would pay for the room.

It had felt like a child's tantrum, as unequipped as she was to argue with her betters, but in the end, Alinor agreed.

The Silver Starling was the pride of Bristol's docks district. The guest rooms on the first floor were clean and well appointed, and the meals served in the ordinary on the ground floor were the best in town. Since Master Chauncey had the unwelcome task of collecting rent, Margaret was free to visit the innkeeper and his wife, Stephen and Anne Brown, whenever she couldn't rationalize another visit to the cathedral.

"Well met, Lady Sherman!" Anne Brown's voice greeted them as they entered the dining room. Only a few of the dozen tables were occupied, with a party of travelers perched at a table in the front, some rowdy locals near the bar, and two men in the back corner who rudely wore their hats indoors. A trio of musicians fussed with instruments by the window, setting up to play during supper. The caramel yeastiness of fresh bread mingled with the savory steam of roast chicken, and both battled the wood smoke drifting from the hearth on the east wall.

Anne bustled over to the newcomers. "We're right pleased to see you again. Sir Robert," she added, curtsying.

"May I present to you my father's aunt, Lady Alinor Crane, the dowager Baroness Crane d'Arnesby?"

Anne melted into a lower curtsy. "Welcome to the Silver Starling, my lady. Come and sit. What might I fetch for you to drink?"

"Wine," Alinor demanded. "I fear I will never recover my strength from the journey downriver. The waves were as tall as horses." The old woman shuddered and sank into the chair Anne offered. "I abhor boat travel."

Margaret shared a glance with Anne. If she were lucky, the ship to France would be beset by pirates before she had to put up with much more of this.

"Shall I send my man to bring your things in?" Anne said.

"They are being unloaded now from the barge. Lucy can show your man." Alinor flicked her hand at her maidservant, who leapt into action.

Robert did not sit when the ladies did. "If you have no need of me…"

"Nonesuch!" Alinor's eyes flashed. "You will not abandon us so cruelly!"

"Let him go, my lady," Margaret said. "You may enjoy his company all throughout the voyage. I will entertain you until he returns."

Robert bowed before he moved toward the back of the room, fishing a handful of dice out of his purse as he went. He addressed the two strangers at the corner table, one wearing a black broad-brimmed hat, the other yellow, and their brims dipped as they agreed to play. She couldn't have asked for a better outcome: Robert would gamble for hours. Now she only had to get rid of Alinor.

Anne brought the wine, and Margaret matched Alinor sip for sip, hoping a cup would be enough to make her retire for a nap. Instead, she chatted about lost friends and old grudges, modern fashions and Tudor customs. Margaret fidgeted with her cup, her muscles tight and alert. It was getting late.

A sudden commotion at the dice table turned her head. By the agitated gestures of Robert's companions, it was clear he had won another game. She half wished it would become an all-out tavern brawl for the novelty of it. When they settled, she returned to fading in and out of Alinor's conversation as she watched the inn fill up with people.

The Starling's reputation for entertainment was unmatched. Margaret would come as often as she could and bring the memorized melodies home to puzzle out on her flute. It would have been indecent of her to perform with a band, but that didn't keep her from fantasizing. *Here, Lady Sherman, here is a spare flute for you to use. Play us a sad one, an it please you.*

The lute player picked out a sweet, unhurried melody. The fiddler joined on the repeat, and the flutist laid his instrument in his lap to sing. It was a melancholy air, telling the story of a woman whose true love went to sea to seek his fortune. When the chorus returned, she hummed along, committing the tune to memory: *"So I'll lay in the heather on the cliffs all alone, where the waves there echo on the purple stone, till my true love's vessel shall bring him home."*

By the last round of it, her throat was too tight to swallow any more of her beer. It was the man's plaintive voice, surely, and not the subject that so moved her. After all, she was hardly a war widow. The boy she had waited for had not gone to sea with promises to return. He had just… gone.

"Such sentimentality." Alinor wrinkled her nose. Hope, bright and buoyant, leapt up into Margaret's throat. "'Tis not to my liking. I will retire." Alinor peered at Margaret and added, "You had better come to bed also."

"I will anon. I would enjoy the music."

"Very well. Do not linger too late and sleep too long. The ship will not wait for one slothful woman."

Margaret clenched her teeth behind her smile. "I share your bedchamber tonight, madam—if I am tempted to lie abed, Lucy would wake me, certes."

Alinor scowled and waved Anne over to show her to their room. The moment the women mounted the stairs, Margaret rose from her seat. A glance in Robert's direction showed he was still at dice with one of the men, though the other had gone. The stranger looked up at her from beneath the broad brim of his yellow felt hat. She didn't care if he saw her go, as long as Robert did not.

Torchlight bounced across the inn's plaster facade, flanking the door and illuminating the painted wooden sign above it. She set a brisk pace along the road, dodging the muddiest puddles and offering tight-lipped nods of greeting to the folk she passed. The letter she had sent Thomas Chauncey the day after Midsummer gave a date, but not a time, since she didn't know when she would be able to slip away from her travel companions. She had asked, therefore, to meet him at home, despite the irregularity and impropriety of it. It couldn't wait until she returned from France, she wrote, keeping the subject of her concerns vague.

Robert had been the impetus. Before he suggested it, it hadn't occurred to her she could rescind her approval of her father's scheme. Maybe she couldn't, and this covert trek through the dark city was all for nothing. But she had to try.

For nineteen years, she had forced herself into the mold of a virtuous woman, a diligent wife, a nurturing mother. For three years she did her duty, all while being subjected to the humiliation of the marriage bed. The pain of it, the reek of her husband's body, the disappointment every month blood spotted the sheets. Now she was expected to do it all again.

Robert was a stumbling block, making her doubt her own feelings, pushing her into the role of the wanton widow as if it was an inevitability. Because those were the only two paths forking in front of her, weren't they? Dutiful wife or shameful hussy.

One thing was certain: she would leave Robert behind and take her chances with the devil she knew not. Her dower, a nebulous something glowing in the distance, would afford her some relief while she charted her course.

She just had to get it back.

Margaret made it as far as the high street when a voice close behind her said, "Lady Sherman."

No one had spoken to her since she left the Starling, so the sound startled her. When she turned, instead of finding someone she knew, she found a man in a yellow broad-brimmed hat.

He had followed her all the way from the inn. Had Robert sent him to fetch her—or worse, to spy on her?

He was well dressed, a merchant or some other man of business, his clothing fashionable and tailored to his lean proportions in a pleasing way. He had a dark beard, but in the light seeping from the window of a nearby building, she couldn't make out the features of his face under the hat. It was as if he was trying to hide from her.

"Pray do not struggle."

What a strange thing to say.

Then she understood. A hand clamped onto her arm from behind. There was a point of pressure at the back of her waist, where her bodice met her skirts. Her breaths came shallow as she turned her head.

The man in the yellow hat took a quick step forward. "Look at me." She obeyed, unblinking. He reached toward whoever held her and came back with a heavy piece of dark fabric—a cloak. He stepped close to drape it around her shoulders. "There is a blade at your back," he murmured. "Come quietly, and my friend will not use it."

His voice was smooth and cultured, his demeanor calm, a businessman who specialized in terrorizing women. This close, she could at last examine his face. Thick brows were pulled together over dark eyes and an elegant nose. The short beard and mustache hid his age, but not the serious slant of his lips. With no gray in his facial hair, she guessed him to be younger than thirty. A pearl dangled from his ear, and the collar of his doublet and shirt both gaped open in the style of the moment.

"Who—" She interrupted herself with a gasp as the pressure at her back increased. If not for the heavy material of her bodice and stays, she would have felt the blade's sharp tip. How much pressure would it take to pierce her organs?

The man in the yellow hat flicked his eyes to the presence beside her, then gave her a grim smile. "Quietly, madam." With both hands, he drew the cloak's hood over her head and arranged it to hide her face. Now she could only see his legs and feet, dark blue stockings disappearing into tall black leather boots, the toes gray with scuff marks. Boots? An unusual choice for a fashionable gentleman, which meant they were more practical than aesthetic. A faraway voice reminded her to focus on escape, but her panic-mad mind couldn't hear it, and she continued to calmly list the reasons a man would wear boots. Travel. Animal slaughter. Sailing. Abducting women at knife-point.

He led them back the way they had come. She shuffled along with the man at her side, whose face she hadn't seen, but whose hat brim brushed the side of her hood as he swiveled his head side to side. He had an unfamiliar scent, briny and acrid, and his hand on her arm was hot and bruising. Every few steps, the tensing of her muscles against the threatening knife yanked her from the oasis of her mind, and she struggled against reality. A child, half-asleep, reluctant to rise.

The streets were quiet, most folk at supper. When they passed someone, the man's grip tightened in warning under the cloak. To passersby, it would appear she was being escorted home. That must be what was happening. She would tell Robert how displeased she was to be dragged back to the Starling in such a way. Or had it been Alinor who hired them? She pictured the old woman in the corner of a smoky alehouse, conferring with thugs over cups of beer, and she wanted to giggle.

The knife poked into her back, and she wanted to cry.

They reached the river port, where a handful of ships and barges bobbed and creaked in the dark, their lamps gilding the black waves. One of those barges held the luggage of those bound for France in the morning. It would ferry them to the transport ship waiting where the Avon met the River Severn.

Down the road, the warm glow of the Silver Starling's windows beckoned her. A step in that direction had her tripping on her captor's feet, and he hauled her back up against him. The man in the yellow hat looked back at them but kept his path down toward the docks. She slowed her steps, certain there was some mistake, but the man beside her prodded her toward a rowboat rocking beside the far dock.

The simmering terror bubbled over, dissolving the protective film of disinterest her mind had created. She was in terrible danger. Somehow she knew if she got in that boat, she would never return.

"No, I pray you," she whispered, dragging her feet.

Beside her, a huff of annoyance. The man was tugging her forward as she struggled backward, and she could see him now, the brim of his black hat obscuring the top half of his face, his jaw sharp and white as marble. Her eyes sought the yellow hat, and there he was, a few yards away, muttering orders to the four men who were already in the boat.

Tears spilled down her cheeks, and in a broken voice, she pleaded for her life. "My father is a peer of the realm… He will give you whatever you want…"

"Aye, that he will. Now get in the pinnace, there's a good lass," grumbled the man in the black hat, his Irish accent all hard R's and bright vowels.

"Have mercy, I beg you—"

He tugged her forward with force enough to wrench her shoulder, and in one movement he had her flush against his front, the knife in his right hand pressed under her chin. She ceased breathing. The Irishman's flint-sharp eyes narrowed. "You'll get in the boat, or I'll give you a fine red ribbon to wear about that dainty neck."

A hand came between them and brushed her chin as it pinched the knife blade. The Irishman sighed and lowered his weapon, stepping back to reveal his stormy-faced companion. Her eyes flicked between them as they communicated silently for a terse moment. Could she bolt while they were distracted? Not with the Irishman's hand around her upper arm and his knife unsheathed.

The hand gripping her released, and the Irishman hopped into the waiting boat with practiced grace.

Now was her moment. But before she could take one step, she was captive again, this time held by both arms. The bearded man's grip allowed no more than an inch of movement in either direction as she tried to shake him off. "I will not harm you," he said, a new edge of frustration to his voice, "but neither will I release you until my purpose is complete."

"What purpose? If 'tis a ransom you seek, I will fetch it. You need not take me."

"You may climb into the pinnace under your own power, or—"

"I will not go with you. I… I will scream!"

"You will get in the boat, or I will summon my mate to compel you."

"I am not afraid," she lied, wondering where the mad impulse to talk back to an armed thug had come from. "You said you would not harm me."

"I said *I* would not harm you. Come, we must away."

One last glare of defiance, one last battle of wills, and the man grappled her around the waist and hoisted her over his shoulder, knocking his hat off. She was too stunned to resist, too precarious to squirm lest he drop her. Was she more afraid of falling than of being abducted by men with knives? Why could she not make herself fight him?

When he lowered her again, it was into the waiting boat, and several pairs of hands reached out to steady her, then to hold her down. A rib in the floor of the boat dug into her tailbone, and when she planted her palms to try to push herself up, she recoiled from the damp. She looked around, frantic, seeing only the blurred fibers of the hood over her eyes. Her heart hammered against her ribs as if it would no longer be contained, and her lungs refused to fill. She would die now; if she didn't lose consciousness from lack of air, the man with the knife would reach down and open her throat.

There was a heavy hand on the top of her head to keep her low in the boat. A slight shudder as someone hopped aboard, then a high voice, a child's voice, saying, "Your hat, captain." The hand left her head, and another voice rumbled above her, "Good lad."

The waves beneath her fell into a rhythm as the rowers pulled away from Bristol.

5

THE TABLE WAS bare except for a single candle in a pewter dish. Its flickering light summoned things out of existence and banished them again: the unglazed gray pitcher in its shallow basin on the washstand, the bucket in the corner she had already been sick into twice, the balled-up cloak beside her on the bed, the black iron door latch—locked from the outside, of course. That was all there was to see in this tiny, empty space.

She had inventoried the room a few hours ago, but somehow she kept rediscovering it. Letting her mind drift and forgetting what was happening, then coming back to herself with a sickening jolt. Already the memories of the endless boat ride, the harrowing climb up the rope ladder, the grim face of the man with the knife as he deposited her in this cabin were tinged with gray, blurred, like they belonged to someone else. All she could make herself focus on was the nauseating rolling of the ship, but whenever she did…

The door opened just as she raised her head from the stinking bucket, more full than it had been a few retches ago. A handkerchief, formerly white, fluttered an inch from her nose as a masculine voice said, "Here."

She took it and wiped her mouth, then sniffed and swiped the backs of her hands under her watering eyes. With a sigh, she sagged against the wall and looked up.

She knew that face.

"Better?"

Margaret shook her head, dazed. She was feeling better, in fact, but the question didn't register. All she could do was stare at him, a boy with brown hair curling out from under a gray knit cap, his face narrow, his reddish stubble catching the candlelight. His apologetic grimace reminded her of a little boy under an oak tree on a hill, brandishing a branch like a sword, defending her from the black knight whose arms encircled her waist.

"Luke Kent?"

A dimple appeared in his cheek. "So my mother called me."

"You look like—" She swallowed the sour taste in her mouth. "You look like a man." His face had lost the prepubescent roundness she remembered, and the life of a sailor made him lithe and weathered. The resemblance to his older brother was unsettling.

"You've not changed a whit." He had one knee braced on the floor to bring himself closer to her level.

The presence of Luke Kent was proof she was dreaming. Obviously, the drama involving Robert had dredged up latent feelings about Matthew, and because her subconscious could not face the older Kent boy, it supplied the younger in his place. It was as good an explanation as any, and far better than accepting the truth: that she really was here, the prisoner of ransomers.

"Do you know why I have been taken?"

For the instant before he spoke, she was certain he was behind it somehow, that he had offered her up as an easy target. It was too great a coincidence otherwise. But he shook his head. "All I know is the crew's not to speak to you."

"What are you if not a member of the crew?"

"Oh, I'm one o' the crew." He gifted her a lopsided smile. "And sure to be whipped if I linger."

A distant part of her was touched he had risked punishment to comfort her, but it was a part of her she couldn't access through the residual fog of terror.

"Made a friend, wee Kentling?"

Luke bolted to his feet, standing straight as a rod, eyes fixed ahead. The Irishman from before, divested of his black hat and knife, framed himself in the open doorway. He peered at her where she sat in a pile on the floor, then turned back to Luke and waited.

"She, uh…" Luke nodded at the bucket in the corner. "Again."

"And listenin' at the door's not breakin' the captain's order to keep away from the officer's quarters, is it? I hope 'tis worth the lashes, Lancelot. Take care o' that as you go." The man jerked his head at the bucket, and both it and Luke were gone before Margaret could react. In a carrying voice, the man added, "And ring the bell!"

Arms crossed, the man leaned in the doorway. "How now, your ladyship?"

Margaret struggled to her feet, clumsy in her skirts. "Who are you? What ship is this?"

The sharp clang of a bell caused her to jump, although the man didn't flinch. It clanged again as he spoke. "Hush, lass. You're safer here than anywhere else, I promise you. No one would dare harm a hair on your head."

The bell was still ringing. She tried to count the sharp tolls, nothing like the deep thrum of cathedral chimes, but his speech was distracting her. In the end, it was as if she had heard neither. "What hour is't?"

"Midnight."

There had not been twelve bells, she was sure of it. Feeling unsteady on her feet, she lowered herself to the bed. The straw mattress crunched.

As if on a breeze, the man's words belatedly floated through the brambles of her mind. *No one would dare harm a hair on your head.* Did holding a knife to her throat count? She looked up at him. "If I am not to be killed, then you seek a ransom for me."

"Aye."

"How long until I am freed?"

"Not long now."

He seemed unperturbed by the situation, friendly, even. This man was difficult to reconcile with the one who had dragged her away from her family by force.

"I've come to ask if there's aught you need. Drink? Some'n' to eat?" She shook her head. "Just as well. You look a mite green."

The nausea had begun to subside as she grew used to the movement of the ship. "I have not sailed for years. I forgot about this part."

"You're doin' grand, Margie."

That name in a stranger's mouth delivered a shock, and for the first time since her adventure began, anger displaced fear. "That is not my name. Call me Lady Sherman or do not address me at all."

With an expression of mock chagrin, he held up his hands. "Cry pardon, lass. 'Swhat your husband called you. I meant no offense."

They thought Robert was her husband? Was that why she was safe, because a man would not hesitate to pay his wife's ransom? Each drip of information cleared another swath of the picture. She was desperate to reveal the entire image, but imperious demands seemed to have no effect on this cheery, casual mercenary.

Forcing her tense shoulders down, she tried another tack. "Forgive me. I am tired and frightened. May I know your name?"

He introduced himself with a name that sounded like "Pawdrick," and she was too embarrassed by her unworldliness to ask him to repeat it. "Captain ordered us not to tell you our names, but what's the harm, I say. You'll ne'er meet us again, and 'tis not a story you'll be wantin' to tell anyway, I reckon."

He rambled for a few uninterrupted minutes, teaching her about the three-masted brigantine they were aboard, describing the varieties of fresh food and drink they had picked up in Bristol. She struggled to follow the way he rushed and cascaded from one sound to the next, the English words behaving like submerged rocks for the stream of his rapid cadence. There were thirty men on the crew, he explained, all eager to be paid whenever the second mate could be bothered to get around to it. They were bored sitting here in Bristol Channel, all itching to get back out to sea. They were denied shore leave because this was meant to be a quick stop, but then the plan changed.

"Because you gambled with Robert," she interrupted, glad to have regained her hold on the thread of the conversation. "He must have seemed to you an easy target. How much did you demand of him?"

His eyes flicked to the dark corridor outside her cell, then returned to hers. "T'ree… hundred pounds."

"That cannot be." She was doomed.

"He agreed to it. Desperate to see you safely returned, he says."

"I know Robert's worth to the last shilling. He cannot pay such a sum." It was an exaggeration—she only knew what Chauncey allowed her to see—but three hundred pounds was a third of his annual income. Half, in fact, when another third was set aside for her dower. He didn't have three hundred pounds of silver sitting around in case he needed to pay a ransom.

Suppose he did, she thought. Or suppose he had used these few hours to move assets around, solicit friends and neighbors, sell priceless heirlooms. The feelings of love he had admitted must run deeper than she realized, and the idea of it warmed her.

Then a thought struck her. "He has already agreed to your demand? So soon?"

The man shrugged, looking away. He was no longer interested in chatting.

She listened to the sounds of the ship. It had been years since she had sailed, but it was quieter than her recollection. No feet pounding the boards as men worked, no waves slamming against the hull, no ropes and masts screaming with the force of the wind. Robert's first action when he learned of her abduction would have been to summon the bailiff, maybe even the lord mayor, and set every available ship in the port to the task of catching the criminals, yet they hadn't attempted to flee.

"The ship is yet in the channel." Disbelief pitched her voice higher. "You do not fear discovery?"

It didn't make sense. Either these men were foolhardy or brave. Or they knew something she didn't.

She stood and raised her chin. "I wish to speak to the captain."

"He does not wish to speak to you."

"He ordered my abduction and he is now responsible for my life. If he possessed an ounce of honor, he would look into my eyes and tell me what is to become of me, rather than hiding behind you like a coward."

The Irishman's stature grew, his shoulders broadening, his chin tilting up, and she felt tiny—breakable—in comparison. It was lunacy to speak like this to a man who knew how to wield a knife. Before she could pay for the insult, though, the creak of an opening door caught both of their attention.

"Padraig."

Looking toward the end of the corridor, the Irishman raised an eyebrow. "You said no names."

The low voice came again, raising goose pimples on Margaret's arms. "Do not play the fool. How thick do you think this door is?"

A few soft footfalls, and then the bearded man filled the doorway. Without his yellow hat, waves of black-brown hair curled over his forehead. The same color hair tufted his chest in the deep vee of his open doublet and shirt. He made the fashion indecent, like something a widow in mourning shouldn't be allowed to see. It was clear from his shadowed eyes he needed sleep, but instead of appearing disheveled and cranky, Margaret saw him as carelessly dangerous.

He bowed, touching his fingers to the curls on his forehead, a sarcastic but elegant version of the courtly honor she was used to. "This way, madam." He straightened and extended an arm in the direction he had come.

Margaret edged past him out the door and moved unsteadily toward the lamp-lit room at the end of the short corridor.

The captain's quarters were paneled with old, dark wood. A tidy but not pristine bed was built into one wall, with a washstand secured adjacent and a table nailed to the floor in the center of the room. Storage cabinets and a wardrobe hid any clothing and personal clutter, revealing only that he was fastidious. The reek of unwashed sailor she had expected was conspicuous in its absence, or it was covered up by the subtle fragrance of perfumed oils, the sort a vain man would massage into his beard and hair. His yellow hat was on display, hanging from a hook.

She whirled to find the captain's fingers gripping the edge of the door, about to shut her in with him. "Nay!" Her hand shot out to stop him.

His mustache twitched, as if her behavior amused him. "You do not wish to be shielded from my crew's curiosity?"

It wasn't the crew she was worried about. "Most would find a closed door more curious than an open one."

He looked at her for a long moment, then released his grip and glanced at Padraig, who lingered in the hall. "No one comes near," he said to him. Padraig took up a post at the mouth of the corridor, where quiet sounds of movement and chatter reminded Margaret there were thirty men out there.

The captain pulled a chair out from under the table. "I pray you will do me the great favor of keeping your voice low. As you are aware, voices carry even with the doors closed."

Instead of sitting at the table with her, he stood between her and the door, his weight on one foot in a relaxed lean. With his arms crossed and his steady gaze fixed on her, he exuded the confidence of a seasoned commander despite his age. Sir John had been forty when he was given his first ship.

They regarded each other for a moment until he broke the silence. "I have no desire to rush you, my lady, but the women who have requested my presence in the past came straight to the point."

She bristled at his mocking tone. "Your lieutenant's answers only left me with more questions. I would have the full account from your own lips."

"Padraig speaks for me. I have naught to add that would be of interest to such a refined lady as yourself."

"Did you demand three hundred pounds for my return?"

"Aye."

"And Sir Robert Sherman has agreed? The deal is all but completed?"

"We have only to set you back ashore."

"Then why have you not done it yet? Each moment that passes gives Robert more time to commandeer a ship and rescue me."

"Is that something he is like to do?"

"What sort of man are you, who takes innocent women by force and sells them back to their families in revenge for losing some foolish game?"

"Revenge? I assure you, my lady, there is yet honor among thieves."

"You must know Bristol is lost to you after this. Sir Robert owns the inn of the Silver Starling and others besides. He has the Lord Mayor's ear. Your life will be forfeit if you dare enter the Avon again."

The captain waited for her monologue to wind down before he responded, a patient smile on his face. "I did say the details would not interest you, did I not? Let us speak no more on it."

Why could she not reach him? She clenched her hands into fists in her lap. "How dare you use Robert so ill! To be beaten in a fair game and then to pry your losings back by coercion? Despicable behavior from a man who fashions himself a gentleman!"

"Have a care, madam. You know me not—"

"I have no wish to!"

"—And neither do you know your Robert, I wager."

"A pox on you!" she shouted with tears in her eyes, beyond rationality. "Robert is one hundred times the man you are. You may bow like one and dress like one, but you are nothing but a worm in hose."

He was silent, and the smile was gone. When he spoke, his quiet voice held a dangerous edge. "None may speak to me as you have done. Yet I will not seek satisfaction from someone in so pitiable a position as you."

"Pitiable?"

"Aye, most pitiable. You are ignorant both of the circumstances of your abduction and the character of the man who arranged it, and I promise you, your anger is misplaced."

"Pray, do not enlighten me. I know all I wish to about your character, sirrah."

"I do not speak of myself." He took two steps toward her and braced his hand on the table, leaning over her. "Shall we discuss gentlemanly behavior? By your leave, I present the behavior of your beloved Sir Robert."

She jumped to her feet and ducked to get past him, unwilling to hear what he had to say.

The great room was too small to escape him, and with a single step, the captain cut off her exit with his body. "In faith, he did win a good deal of coin off me, but as the hour grew late and his flagon emptied, he proposed a different sort of bet."

She wanted to silence him, but his earnest gaze held her captive. He was too close, almost as close as he had been when he clasped the cloak around her neck. She stepped backward, a coldness creeping up from her fingertips. "What sort of bet?"

"If he lost, he would return every penny he took from us. But if he won, we would make you disappear for a time while he raised money to pay your so-called ransom. *And* we would get our coin back."

The words were all easy enough to understand, but she would have comprehended his meaning just as well if he spoke Portuguese. "You lie."

"I have been called a rogue, my lady, and worse things besides, but I am not so cruel as that. What cause have I to lie? I have no loyalty to this man."

"But what of the ransom? The three hundred pounds you demanded?"

"I made no demand. I imagine he will set whatever ransom he believes you are worth."

The coldness in her fingers had suffused throughout her body, rendering her numb, causing her to tremble. She felt tears well up, and she turned her face away so he wouldn't see her cry.

The captain was still speaking, oblivious to the crash as Margaret's world crumbled around her. "He seemed to think your father would pay a little. Rather cold to prize money from his father-in-the-law, but..."

She ignored him, conscious of only one truth: Robert was the architect of her terrifying ordeal. Desperate for money, mad with disappointment, he found a way to raise a few pounds and take revenge on both her and her father in one stroke. Strangely, it was not the news of Robert's cruelty that upset her the most. It was the fact she didn't question it.

"He is not my husband." Her voice emerged tiny and strangled.

There was a distinct change in his posture, an uneasy alertness at odds with his hitherto commanding presence. "You share a name." It wasn't a question, but his wary tone sought an answer.

"He is the son of my late husband."

"I do not wonder why he failed to mention that fascinating detail."

"You prefer to believe he ransomed his wife, rather than his widowed stepmother?"

"Were he one of the legion of men who regard their wives as property, I could at least begin to comprehend this distasteful commission. That he had no claim on you…"

"I am no man's wife, nor no man's property." A tear spilled down her cheek and she swiped it away.

"Lady Sherman…"

"I hate that name." She kept flicking away her tears with frenzied motions as though he couldn't see her hiding them.

"Maggie, then." He offered a smile someone must have told him was charming.

A sound somewhere between a laugh and a sob escaped her throat. Her back hit the wall, and she slid down it to land in a cloud of skirts on the floor. Her face and eyes would be red and puffy, but she gave up trying to hide her misery.

The captain surprised her by lowering himself to the floor beside her. He extended his left leg out in front of him and bent the other so he could rest his elbow on his knee. Wasn't he worried about dirtying his beautiful breeches? She cried harder; if she was concerned about clothes at a time like this, she must be going mad.

He leaned his head back against the wall and gazed up at the ceiling beams, the ship's bones. "Forgive me, Maggie. I ought not to have told you." He turned to give her a conspiratorial wink. "But you did call me a worm."

She had a feeling he would keep joking with her to cheer her up, but she wished he wouldn't. No amount of joking could undo Robert's betrayal. What devil could have possessed him to concoct a plan like this? He put her life in danger, conspired to steal from her father, all because she had refused to fall in line with the plans he made for himself.

Vaguely, she wondered if there was a second motive, a consequence that would sweeten the pot. If she returned to Bristol ignorant of Robert's treachery, would she have softened toward him for saving her from brigands? For becoming the Menelaus to her Helen? She remembered the brief surge of warmth she had felt earlier. How long before the feeling would have dissipated? Long enough for him to get what he wanted from her?

"Maggie."

His gentle voice reeled her back in, and she realized her eyes were dry as she stared at a knot in the opposite wall. She drew the cabin's perfumed air into her lungs. "Pray, forgive my behavior. You did not look for such a spectacle when you took me."

"'Tis just the spectacle I looked for, though I expected it hours ago. You were kind to come along without much fuss."

She snorted. Was she really joking with her kidnapper?

"I have done you a service," he went on, in the soothing baritone one uses on a skittish mare. "I shudder to think you would never have known the sort of man he is."

"I had a notion." Turning her head to look at him, she asked, "Why did you tell me the truth? Why did you not cleave to the ransom story?"

"Because I find his treatment of his father's wife abhorrent."

"You told me before you learned of his relation to me."

The stiff fabric of his doublet scraped the wooden wall when he shrugged. "I tired of your insults."

"Methinks not."

"Indeed?" The corners of his eyes betrayed his amusement. "If you know the answer, I wonder why you ask the question."

"Do you understand what you have done? By agreeing to this cruel scheme, you have indulged a fancy that should never have been spoken aloud. How can I go on, knowing what I know? Knowing the… *depravity* of which he is capable? I sail to France with him in a matter of hours—how can I?"

"You will not call him out?"

"Who will believe me? Would you, if I told you my stepson hired pirates to ransom me to my own father?"

He laughed at that, a full-throated sound that rang in the close room, before her expression silenced him. "Forgive me, Maggie. I do not laugh at your distress, but I agree your story is risible."

Her thoughts swam in a jumbled mess, but somehow she latched onto one. One that didn't even matter.

Maggie. A name no one had ever called her. A version of her she hadn't met. Was that the person the captain saw when he looked at her? She took him in—his dark hair, his elegant profile, his fine clothing, his nonchalance—and wondered what he called himself. Everything pointed to arrogance, shallowness, a man who demanded to be called Captain. But then he sat with her, dirtying his breeches. And even though he didn't have to, he told her the truth. It didn't absolve him of his part in her misadventure, but it raised him far above Robert in her estimation.

How could she go back to that nightmare, where it would be his word against hers? Where his stature would aid him in shaking off any punishment? And now she knew how low he would stoop, how long until he stooped further in retaliation?

On the other hand, if she said nothing, Robert would be crowned the hero and she would despise herself for not speaking up when she should.

The captain sighed and got to his feet. He held out a hand to help her up.

Margaret stared at his calloused palm and had a desperate thought.

"Let me stay aboard."

He looked down at her and raised an eyebrow. "We cannot keep you. 'Tis counter to how this transaction works, I fear."

"Marry, you will get your money." She struggled to her feet, ignoring his proffered hand and tangling herself in her skirts as a result. "Return me for your lost coin, then let me sneak away and sail with you. I cannot stomach the notion of returning there. Let me earn my keep here. I… I play a little, and I sing. I could help cook and clean and serve. Of course, I would not receive the same pay as your crew, but in exchange for meals and a place to sleep, I would be at your command."

"At my command?"

She blanched, realizing how foolish the choice of words had been. What could she say to turn his mind in another direction?

"Your crew have not been paid," she said, snatching at a snippet of Padraig's rambling soliloquy. "Whoever manages your crew's accounts is like to be overworked on a ship this size. I read and write, and I am good with numbers and sums. I know how to run a household and balance accounts. I could help your…"

"Purser?"

"I could help your purser!"

"I have no purser."

Her heart sank. Of course he wouldn't need her. Stupid girl, to get her hopes up. To imagine for a moment that a ship's captain would hire on a twenty-three-year-old woman who had no experience sailing and only a wife's education.

But the captain hadn't moved, his thoughtful expression hadn't changed, and she realized she had misunderstood. He didn't have a purser; therefore, he needed one.

"Tell me what I have if I take four pounds, seventeen shillings, and sixpence from twelve pounds, nine shillings, thruppence."

Hope flared anew, distracting her. This was an inopportune time for her mind to go blank. "Nine pence… eleven shillings… seven pounds."

His mouth was a thin line beneath his mustache.

Her heart dropped. "Is it not? I am certain I could figure it on paper."

"The better test would be one to which I know the answer." He rubbed his beard with his hand and looked at her for a moment in silence. Then he heaved a laborious sigh, his brow low over his eyes in defeat. "You will bring all your things. Any item immaterial to your survival will be traded for your board. You will maintain an orderly space and do any task I or my officers ask of you, without argument and without delay."

She nodded, stared, refused to speak lest she break the spell.

"This is lunacy," he added, apparently to himself. "Half the crew already think you bad luck, and you have only been aboard a few hours."

She didn't know how to respond to that, but he didn't require a response. He lowered his voice, his eyes boring into hers. "The boat will wait for you for one hour, not a moment more. *And if you go to the bailiff...*"

"On my life, I will not!"

"On your life, indeed. I have avoided the gallows for nigh on thirty years. I will not be undone by a game of dice with a lovesick madman."

She felt the beginnings of a laugh bubbling up in her chest, despite the captain's serious expression. This was what she had waited for, for years, without knowing it. Here was her way out at last.

"And Maggie—"

She held her breath.

"You will speak of this to no one until we are out of Bristol Channel."

6

THE CITY APPEARED by degrees in the distance, rooftops frosted with pre-dawn light, as four rowers pulled the pinnace toward the waking town. Margaret leaned out over the gunwale as if those few inches would make the miniature people on the wharf more distinguishable. Alinor likely remained abed, but she expected Robert to meet her, at least. He was the playwright of this farce, after all.

The boat tipped a fraction, and Padraig dragged her back to her seat with a rough hand on her shoulder.

It had been the captain himself who steadied her as she descended the rope ladder into the pinnace. With his face close to her ear, he had said, "Methinks your courage will forsake you when your feet touch land." He had planted one knee on the deck as she climbed down, putting her in mind of a soliloquizing thespian.

She had paused to find her footing, then looked up at him. "Is there aught I can bring you from town?"

Padraig's displeasure was a tangible presence for the hour it took to row upriver, but Margaret was happy to ignore him, too. There was too much to do, too many plans to make and worries to assuage. When they arrived at the far wharf, away from prying eyes, she still didn't know exactly what she was going to do with Robert.

He was waiting there when they arrived. Beside her, Padraig pulled something out from near his hip. She looked between him and the familiar knife blade. "Just a precaution," he muttered, glancing away.

They slid alongside the wooden planks of the dock. Robert rushed forward. "Hands," barked Padraig. Robert stopped short and held his palms face out. Padraig nudged her with his elbow, and she wobbled on her feet until Robert reached down to help her out of the boat.

She looked back at the Irishman, who nodded once. The captain had given her one hour to complete her business on land, and the countdown had begun.

The sun cowered below the horizon, but folk were moving about the street, already at work. She let Robert lead her back to the inn. It wasn't difficult to feign exhaustion; her feet were sluggish, and she hung onto his arm to keep in a straight line. He didn't speak. Another man might have asked what had happened on the ship, how the kidnappers treated her, whether she was hurt or misused. Robert was not an accomplished playactor.

"I hope my aunt was not worried," she said.

"I saw no reason to wake her. The shock would have distressed her."

His hubris made her furious. To be so confident the plan would work that he didn't bother telling Alinor? "I cannot conceal such a thing if we are to be always together on the voyage."

"Then we will tell her when she wakes. Will you take some rest first?"

The Silver Starling was dark aside from a single sconce in the dining room to light the way to the stairs. Thumps and clanks coming from the back of the building meant the kitchen staff were the only ones awake. Upstairs, Margaret hesitated. In normal circumstances, she would go straight to the room she would have shared with Alinor. But she had a plan for Robert, and she needed to get him alone.

Before she could decide how to proceed, he tugged her elbow. "Here." He pulled her two doors down. "Let Lady Crane sleep. Besides, I refuse to let you out of my sight. I will watch over you."

Her uncharacteristic willingness didn't seem to surprise him. She hovered in the center of the room as he lit a candle from the coals in the hearth, unsure how to begin. He was so certain he had triumphed. How much higher could she raise him to make his fall all the more delicious?

"Robert," she whimpered, reaching out a hand.

He was upon her in an instant, arms wrapped around her, face buried in her neck. "Sweetest, I was so afraid for you." He kissed her neck, below her ear, along her jaw, as he blurted out whatever sweet nothings came to mind. "I did not know where you had gone. When they sent word, I pleaded with them to send you back to me—" His breath was hot in her ear as he pressed his lips to her earlobe. "Whatever the cost."

She set her teeth and suffered his clumsy assault. It made her want to shed this corrupted skin like a snake, but with effort, she could experience the moment as if from afar, looking at him as an observer would. Did he think she would melt in his arms? Did he not hear the inane drivel coming out of his mouth?

"Last night made one thing clear." His arm was tight around her waist, pressing them together from knee to breast. "I never want to be parted from you."

He declaimed his lines like a character in a romance, like a Romeo, and her breaths came shallow as her courage waned. What if this was not a rehearsed speech? What if this had all been a misunderstanding, or a drunken mistake, or a lie told by a stranger on a ship?

She ducked her head as he moved in for a kiss. "How much was the ransom?"

"What matter? You are here with me. Let me taste your honeyed lips again."

"Tell me how much you paid for me, so I may know how much to thank you." She knew nothing about flirtation, only what Robert had taught her, and it felt absurd to trail her fingertips down his chest.

Again she dodged a kiss, and instead he pressed his lips to her jaw as he took in a shuddering breath. Her fumbling attempt at seduction worked better than she could have hoped. "God's blood, Margie." His hands roved over her gown. "I would have paid anything."

"How much?" Disgusted at how easy it was to play this part, she combed her fingers through his hair as he slathered wet kisses over her collarbone. "Ten pounds? Twenty?"

He raised his head and chuckled, his eyelids heavy with satisfaction. "Nay, my dearest one. You are worth ten times that, and they knew it. They demanded two hundred pounds, and I gave it without a thought."

Liar.

Her heart skipped to have it confirmed. The captain told her the truth; Robert was a monster. For a moment she froze in his arms, jubilant and devastated, and he swooped in to take her mouth in a fierce kiss.

She wrenched her face away and shoved him. "Fie!" she spat, wiping her mouth with the back of her hand. Fie on Margie Sherman, the gullible child, and fie on the soulless villain before her. She looked him in the eye and reveled in his bewilderment. His arms hovered in midair as if they still encircled her. "Twenty shillings, prithee, and I will tell no one what you have done."

"I do not understand. A few kisses… Surely there is no lasting harm in a little lapse of propriety."

"Do not be a fool. One pound is nothing if you have asked my father for two hundred." She held her hand out, palm up. "I should tell you, the mercenaries you hired valued me at three."

His face went pale, and she could have laughed at how long the realization took him. When he solved the puzzle, he glowered at her and her outstretched hand. "You are mad."

"It would not do for both of us to be lunatics."

"I will not pay to silence you. Who would believe you?"

Now she was bluffing, but she frowned and used her fingers as a tally. "My lord father, my sister's lord husband, Master Brown and your other tenants, Master Chauncey, the bailiff, of course…"

His eyes were dark with rage. He tugged open his purse strings, snatched a handful of silver coins from the bag, and dropped them one by one into her waiting palm like a petulant boy. She transferred them to her own purse and held out her hand again. "And another pound for Alinor. 'Twould be most ungenerous to deprive you of a fully funded trip abroad."

He froze. "Are we still to sail?"

"I see no way of begging off without telling her why. I shall have to endure it. And you." She hoped her condescending performance was convincing, so he would believe all she wanted was money, not revenge.

He looked warily at her. "You give your word?"

"If that means anything to you, then aye, I give my word."

He sprinkled another handful of coins into her palm. When the payment was complete, he relaxed, as if relieved the ordeal was over. She closed her purse and strode to the door.

"I made an error of judgment, Margie. I am most grateful for your forgiveness."

Her hand on the latch, she turned back and tilted her head. "Is that what you think this is?" Heart bursting, hands trembling, she swept from the room, leaving him ten percent poorer.

Time was slipping away. She didn't know how much of her precious hour the blackmail scheme had consumed, and there was more to do. She slipped blindly into Alinor's darkened room and felt around for the jar of spills above the fireplace, but when the side of her hand connected with it, it tumbled off the mantle and shattered on the floor, scattering the twisted papers.

A shape bolted up from the nearby bed. "Who goes?" the old woman shrieked. A head and shoulders appeared over the far edge of the bed, and Alinor's maid, Lucy, rubbed her eyes.

Margaret ground her teeth in frustration. "Only me, Aunt." She felt around for a spill, pricking her finger on a ceramic shard. She managed to get the spill lit, then transferred the flame to a candle. "I am sorry to wake you."

The old woman was an eerie apparition, all white from her chemise to her nightcap. "You dressed in the dark?"

Margaret planned not to tell her; after all, Robert had paid her two pounds not to. She sucked on her bleeding finger to give her time to think.

What did she care what Robert thought? In half an hour, she'd be gone. So she sat on the edge of Alinor's mattress and told her a tale.

Lucy and Alinor listened in horror. "Mercenaries?" the old woman gasped.

"They did not harm me, and Sir Robert met their ransom demand without delay. Although…" Margaret lowered her voice. "I overheard one of them say the ransom was three hundred pounds, and Robert told me he gave them two hundred. 'Tis my mistake, methinks, yet… what if he did cheat them? What if they return seeking satisfaction?"

Alinor's rapt eyes glittered in the candlelight. "Nonesuch. The barge departs within a few hours. We will be gone before they discover the money is missing." She swung her bony legs over the side of the bed. "We must board the barge at once. You will be safe there."

Lucy leapt into action, throwing back the lid of Alinor's travel trunk to help her mistress dress. Margaret found her own things, a bag and a cosmetics box. "I will have Robert escort me to the barge." She hooked the edge of the door with her foot and dragged it open. "Meet us there when you have broken your fast."

Alinor waved her away, and Margaret floated down the stairs, light as a feather.

7

PADRAIG REFUSED TO speak with her, and the four rowers only stared, so Margaret fixed her gaze on the ship ahead and told herself she hadn't made a horrible mistake.

It was not as grand as the ship that would have taken her to France, but it was beautiful. The hull at deck level and above was painted forest green, with golden yellow trimming the railing and the bowsprit. The colors repeated in geometric patterns up each of the three masts. Small, square windows were scattered along the wall of one of the stern decks, and there were more square cutouts in the hull for guns—ten on the near side, probably the same on the other. She was well armed, but she needed to be if kidnapping was a common activity.

Margaret's favorite detail was the carving of a bare-breasted woman emerging from the bow. Her torso ended in a sinewy fish tail that wrapped around the near side of the ship. It was expertly carved and carefully maintained, boasting the sort of vibrant colors that belied a fresh coat of paint. She must be a source of pride.

"What a beautiful mermaid," she murmured to Padraig, forgetting he was in no mood to chat with her.

He humphed. "Merrow."

The word snagged on a memory. She could name a handful of sea captains—Raleigh, Drake, Sir John Sherman's fellow war heroes. They were known to pillage enemy ships in the name of the queen, but others, such as the infamous Dermot Moran, were pirates through and through. Moran had been at the height of his celebrity when she was eight or nine, and for a whole summer, she had played at pirates in the garden, swashbuckling with the rose bushes. Moran was executed a few years later.

"Not Dermot Moran's *Merrow*?"

"Not anymore."

Yes, this had been a horrible mistake, she told herself. But when she tried to dredge up regret or despair, all she came up with were memories of Robert's behavior—and regret that she hadn't struck him in the face.

With practiced grace, the rowers slid the pinnace alongside the *Merrow*, and the rope ladder dropped down to meet them. She didn't relish climbing it again, but at least this time she could see it. With a smug smile, Padraig gestured for her to go first.

At the top, she hesitated until a pair of scuffed boots appeared at eye level. "Your ladyship." The captain crouched, offering her a hand, and she let him take hold of her arm as she used her other hand to hike her skirts away from her feet. When she was finally aboard, she looked around.

Everyone was staring at her.

Beside her, a cluster of men waited to haul her belongings out of the boat. Across the deck, Luke and two other boys stood frozen, jaws slack. A man peered down from the ratlines, another from the main yard. There were at least a dozen, maybe twenty, all watching her. It was useless pretending she wasn't ludicrously outnumbered.

The captain released her arm. "Welcome aboard the *Merrow*. How did you escape?"

"I came to an understanding with Sir Robert and then bribed a pair of sailors to transfer my trunks from the barge to your longboat."

"Pinnace," he corrected her. "Smaller than a longboat. No rigging."

Behind her, Padraig crawled one-handed over the gunwale with her bag over his shoulder. Meanwhile, the sailors had rigged a pair of pulleys to hoist her trunks up to the deck. They had worked quickly, dropping the heavy hooks down as soon as the pinnace bumped against the *Merrow*'s hull. A square-shouldered, sandy-haired sailor on deck was already unhooking the first box.

"Let us get underway before someone comes looking," the captain said to Padraig. He shifted his focus to the gathered crew. "Take these things to my cabin."

The broad-shouldered man who hovered over her trunk looked sidelong at her and sneered.

The captain's hand shot out and gripped the sailor's collar, jerking him off balance. "Another look like that one, Driscoll, and you will be looking with but one eye." Every sailor on deck became enraptured with his own work as the captain roughly released his grip.

Margaret knew what the look meant, and she didn't blame the man for hearing something lurid in the captain's command. "To your cabin?"

"I need you out of sight and out of the way until we're safe at sea. Kentling!" He called over to the group of young men, and Luke dashed to the captain's side. "You two are acquainted, methinks. Escort Lady Sherman to my cabin and help her choose which of her possessions to keep. Only what she needs, mind. And do not allow her to wander the ship, no matter how prettily she asks." At this, he glanced at her. "I will send for you when you're needed."

As Luke led her across the deck to the officer's quarters, she let out her held breath.

The parade of sailors carrying her things into the captain's cabin gawked at her. No one spoke, although one short, balding man smiled.

Luke eyed the heap of bags and trunks with distrust. "I know not a fig about what a lady needs. Just try not to keep too much. There'll not be room for it, anyway."

She opened the cosmetics box and rifled through it, selecting only a comb and a box of hairpins. "Where is my berth?"

"Mayhap you'll find a dry corner like the rest of us."

Margaret had never slept on a floor. She could get used to it; people did it all the time. The lack of privacy, though, would be harder to overcome.

Pulling spare underthings out of the trunk and stuffing them in her bag, she tried to make conversation. "Do you have a particular job on the ship?"

"Just a seaman. Been sort of apprenticin' Merry, though. He mends rope and such. Methinks I could have another share if I become a master rope-maker. About time, anyway."

He grumbled the last few words, and she looked up at the sudden change of tone. "About time you were a master?"

"About time I had another share. Been here longer 'n some. Pratt gives me ship boy tasks as if I'm not an able seaman."

"Is that why they call you Kentling? They think you a ship's boy?"

He shook his head. "'Twas easier."

"Easier than what?" It seemed like a mouthful to Margaret, when both his names were made of such short, simple sounds.

"Than havin' two lads with the same name. We cannot both be called Kent."

Her hand hovered over the lid of the next box, but she forgot her task.

Both. They were *both* here, Luke and Matthew. How could she have been so stupid, so focused on her own selfishness, that she hadn't fully considered the possibility? Of course they would both be here—wherever Matthew went, Luke went, too.

Horrible no longer adequately described her mistake.

Her flustered fingers fumbled with the box's latch. "And Matthew…?"

"Aye, I gather you did not part on the best of terms. But 'tis thanks to you we got out of that godforsaken house, so I've no quarrel with you."

What butchered version of events had he told his little brother? She wanted to hear the story. Even if it were a fiction, it would be an improvement on her current understanding. She spent eight years questioning what went wrong that day and could find no answer.

The memory of that time, how despondent she had been, had only recently begun to lose its sting. She turned her sadness into disdain for her younger self, choosing not to cry, but to roll her eyes instead. *That poor fool,* she would say. Yet on occasion, the heartbroken girl would break through, and she knew coming face to face with Matthew would prove too much for her. How could she avoid it on a ship this size?

She responded to Luke's polite inquiries with short answers, worried he would hear her turmoil in her voice, and focused on her task. After examining her belongings and weighing each item's usefulness, she kept an extra shirt, two pairs of stockings, a spare muslin coif, her cloak, and a quarto of Shakespeare sonnets she couldn't bear to part with. The fine gowns she had packed for France would fetch a few coins for the crew, and her most serviceable gown was already on her body. Her jewels held no sentimental value, and the scant bottles and pots devoted to her toilette would be a waste of space. She only needed one pair of shoes and one hat.

It was strange and more than a little sad to see how much she was left with, but no sadder than realizing how many unnecessary bits of frippery she had hitherto relied on. Parting with them was so easy, she wondered why she had ever had them in the first place.

Footsteps in the corridor set her heart thumping. She glanced up, bracing, but it wasn't Matthew. How many times could she expect to enjoy this jolt of panic before the awful reunion?

The man in the doorway had a bulbous red nose in the middle of his grizzled face, and lank hair he didn't cover with a hat. He brushed his forelock politely. "Jim Pratt, mistress. Bos'n. Cap'n sent me to fetch you."

She shoved the last item in the oiled canvas bag and slung it over her shoulder as she followed Pratt back out onto the deck.

Below, the captain stood in the morning sun, his dark hair tousled by the same wind that had carried them out to sea, conversing with Padraig and another man she didn't recognize. Pratt deposited her at the captain's side.

With a glance at her single bag, the captain nodded his approval. "I must needs explain your presence to the crew, but these gentlemen requested an introduction first."

"An explanation would do just as well," said the unfamiliar man in a wide northern accent. He was short and solid, with gray-streaked brown hair that receded from his forehead. He had his arms across his chest in the traditional pose of distrust.

"You well know my decisions require no input from you," said the captain.

The man flexed his shoulders, not changing his posture. "Aye, sir."

"This is John Osborne," the captain told her, "my second mate. He is the best navigator on the seas." Out of the corner of her eye, she caught Osborne's chin tilt up. "He also acts as the ship's purser."

"And makes a right muck of it," Padraig muttered.

The two lieutenants shared a look, but just when she thought fists would fly, Osborne nodded. "'Tis not my calling," he told her, still glaring at Padraig.

The captain went on. "You will assist him in his work keeping the ship stocked, valuing cargo, and making sure the lads are paid fairly and on time."

"That is quite a lot to ask of one person," she said. "Yet Master Osborne must act as navigator as well?"

Her compliment went over just as she hoped with Osborne, who puffed up his chest. She caught the captain suppressing his smile before he continued. "You will also help Lloyd in the galley before and after dogwatch. Mayhap you will be so kind as to provide some music during supper as well—you said you sing?"

She wished she hadn't said that.

"I need not remind you that you are no sailor. You need keep no watch, nor you need not answer to Pratt, who manages the crew. You answer only to me, Osborne, or MacCraith." He nodded to his lieutenants as he named them, and she committed it all to memory: Padraig MacCraith, John Osborne, and Captain…

She didn't know his name. She had chosen him over Robert, he had seen her cry, and she didn't know his name. "What am I to call you?"

With a flourish, he gave her a beautiful courtly bow, far too regal for a sea captain. "Allow me to introduce myself to you, my lady, as Captain Richard Moran, master and commander of the ship *Merrow*."

A relative of the late pirate captain? Unlikely. He was too old to be Dermot Moran's son, too young to be his brother, and too well bred. Besides, he looked less Irish than she did.

Despite her much higher rank, she dipped into a curtsy to humor him. "Well met. At what point may I be trusted with your real name?"

Padraig snorted while Osborne blanched, and both men looked back and forth between their captain and the presumptuous landlubber they were now saddled with.

The captain offered a tight smile. "Moran is the name under which I conduct my business."

"If an alias, why could I not know it before?"

"Because abducting noblewomen isn't the sort of business I want associated with my name."

Should she be relieved to know they didn't make this a habit, or worried to think they might start now?

"Shall I also adopt an alias, lest the missing Lady Sherman be discovered aboard your ship?" she said.

"An it please you."

A new name, something to keep her safe. A fortification.

"Let it be Bailey," she said, then made an impulsive addition. "Maggie Bailey."

The captain turned to his lieutenants. "Mistress… *Bailey* is a civilian who is now under my protection. She has no claim to an officer's berth, but I thought the navigation room a fair compromise." Padraig nodded and Osborne frowned. "Show her to her quarters," he said to Osborne, then added to Padraig, "All hands."

Osborne beckoned her with a jerk of his head while Padraig glanced about for someone to relay the "all hands" order to. While she followed Osborne back up the steps, a young boy darted past, taking the steps two at a time. His hair was a dirty brown and his patchy clothing was too big for him. The boy paused below the bell bolted to the wall and gave it at least a dozen hearty clangs. She felt each one in her teeth.

There was a low rumble as twenty-odd pairs of feet tramped up from below or dropped down from above. Osborne hurried her up to the next deck and ushered her through an open door.

She was in a cramped room lined with shelves and cubbies. A map and some navigation instruments were laid out on the table in the center of the room, and a row of windows along the back wall let in dusty sunlight. Osborne cleared some maps and other items off one shelf and deposited them on another. He gestured to the empty shelf for a moment before she realized he meant for her to put her bag on it.

"Tha may move the table to lay out thy bed, but at first light, or whene'er I say, this is my domain."

He was just taking control of a frustrating situation, and she felt for him. "I will be in your way here, certes."

"Aye, I like it not."

"Why here? I do not deserve a cabin, but I am told the rest of the crew sleep wherever they can."

He narrowed his eyes as if trying to decide if she was joking. "Aye, lass, they'll sleep where they can. If 'tis thy wish to let 'em snuggle up to thee, I can speak to the captain…"

Her face burned. "Nay, I am most grateful for the privacy."

"Th'art not in much danger. Men go mad betimes, but for all we're a rough lot, we none of us wish to lose our place." He cleared his throat, his amusement fading. "Captain has a rule—I wager he's remindin' the lads of it now. No fornication. No loose women brought aboard, nor no dalliances betwixt mates. They're to do their duties and nowt more—save love and lust for shore leave, as it were. Mates caught… *ruttin'* aboard the ship are put off."

He was thoroughly uncomfortable by this point, a patchy blush blooming on his thick neck and big ears.

He paused, then pointed to a shelf. "Ledgers," he said gruffly, changing the subject. "Tha mun stay here awhile 'til the captain finishes his address. May as well acquaint thyself with the accounts." He tapped a blunt finger on the map-covered table. "Tha'll not touch my charts." Then he left.

Margaret faced the closed door, both mortified by Osborne's speech and confused by the captain's arbitrary code of morality. Gambling and kidnapping were permissible, piracy was required, but he drew the line at amorous liaisons?

She turned toward the ledgers Osborne had indicated and pulled a hefty book from the shelf, bound in expensive green leather. The *Merrow* was in passable shape, judging by what she could decipher of the untidy accounts, but the tame nature of the cargo disappointed her. There was no gold or treasure listed, only a boring manifest like any other: gunpowder and cannonballs, weapons, sail- and rope-making supplies, remedies, cloth, food, and water.

Margaret worked her way backward from the most recent logs until she ended at the first page, which explained why the ledger was so innocuous: it must belong to another ship. Instead of reading *Merrow*, the ship was named *Phoebus*, captained by someone called William Stokes. Perhaps it belonged to a ship they had seized. They *were* pirates, weren't they? Where was the evidence?

She replaced the ledger on the shelf and touched the spines of a few others, wondering what all their purposes were. On a high shelf, a little book bound in soft, natural leather and tied with thongs reminded her of her Shakespeare sonnets. Was there another poetry lover on the ship? She pulled it down and untied the straps.

It was not a book of poems, but another sort of ledger. The writing was cramped, but her eyes snagged on names she knew: James Pratt, boatswain. Padraig MacCraith, first mate. Matthew Kent, helmsman. Curious, she dragged the green ledger down again and opened to the most recent entries in both. They were identical.

No, not identical. Some sums were higher in the smaller book. It listed foreign-sounding names. It mentioned gold. And in the front, it read "MERROW. Richard Moran, Captain." This was the real ledger. The green one must be a decoy, sanitized for the casual observer, reflecting the accounts of an innocent merchant vessel called *Phoebus*.

She compared the names—Richard Moran, a ruthless mercenary, versus William Stokes, an unassuming merchant—and developed a theory.

The navigation room door swung open, admitting the red-nosed, thin-haired Pratt. "I'm to take you to the galley for a bite," he said.

Her stomach rumbled at the mere mention of food, and she followed him down the two sets of stairs to the main deck. They turned at the bottom to duck through the entrance to the galley. Several sailors sat at tables eating a cold lunch of bread and cheese, each with a mug in front of him.

Two were standing up to leave as Margaret and Pratt entered. The one who faced her was the same man who gave her the ugly sneer when she arrived, the one called Driscoll. He might be in his forties, with thinning blond hair atop his oddly square head. The sneer seemed to be a fixed expression. He smacked the shoulder of his companion and gestured with his head in Margaret's direction, as if to say, *Look what just walked in.*

His friend turned, and Margaret met his gaze. It happened just as she knew it would: her breath caught in her throat, her heart plummeted into her bowels, and her legs threatened to fail her. Eyes wide, she took in the man's face.

It was a *man's* face. Matthew had been eighteen when she last saw him, still with the youthful roundness of a child. He had grown taller and broader in the intervening years, and his hair was lighter and longer, pulled back from his face into a tail at the nape of his neck. He had been in transition then, but he was fully formed now.

She saw flashes of him as he had been, dashing and daring and jovial, playing at sword fighting with his little brother, joking with her as they explored the land her father owned and his father farmed. Her fingers tingled at the memory of his hand in hers.

The moment passed in slow motion for her, but no one else seemed to notice. Pratt moved forward, ready to introduce her to the cook. Driscoll kept his eyes on her as he passed her on his way out. Matthew blinked, then walked out into the sun without a backward glance.

She was grateful she didn't have time to dwell on it, because Pratt was already speaking. "Andrew Lloyd, this is Maggie Bailey."

The cook was chopping vegetables while a red hunk of meat waited on a board nearby. He wiped his hands on his apron. "Maggie! Well met. News spreads fastest in the galley, and I have been most eager to meet you."

Lloyd was gray-haired and thick-bellied, evidently fond of the food he cooked. He spoke like a man who had received an education—a gentleman's son, perhaps—but his English was sweetened with a faint lilt.

"Hungry? The lads come down for a quick meal around this time, either coming off forenoon watch or preparing for afternoon watch. But we two may eat when we please. Speaking for myself, that is oftener than it should be!" He patted his round belly and laughed, which made Margaret laugh as well.

"I fain would eat whatever you put in front of me. I have had naught to eat since supper last night."

"Zounds! 'Tis no wonder you are naught but skin and bones. Sit yourself down and let me fetch for you."

"Nay, Master Lloyd, I would help! The captain has tasked me with aiding you."

"So you shall, but not on an empty stomach." He pulled a pewter trencher from a stack nearby and busied himself with slicing bread and cheese.

After she had eaten, Lloyd released her until it was time to prepare for first dogwatch, the four o'clock supper shift. He instructed her to listen for four bells, which marked the halfway point until the next watch. "You'll get used to it," he assured her.

Impatient to get back to her examination of the ledgers, Margaret trotted back up to the sterncastle deck, the level that housed the navigation room. She sat with the logbooks while the bells marked every half-hour—two at one o'clock, three at half-past one. When she counted four bells, she closed up her work and emerged into the fresh sea air.

A sailor was climbing down the middle mast's ratlines, and he surprised her when he dropped onto the deck in front of her. Matthew stood perfectly still and stared.

She thought about what Luke had said earlier, about how they had parted. Matthew seemed to feel just as awkward about this sudden reunion as she did. But enough was enough.

"I am glad to see you well," she said.

"Are you?" His voice was richer and deeper than she remembered. "I should have thought seeing me was the last thing you wanted."

He was right, of course: she had long ago cauterized the wound he left, and she had no desire to reopen it.

Would he tell her, at last, why he abandoned her under the tree on the hill on that Midsummer morning? Would he admit what she knew, but couldn't prove—that he had snuck into the house while she waited outside and emptied the jewelry box she shared with her sister? Would he beg forgiveness for any of it?

No. He only stared.

"Have you been aboard the *Merrow* all this time?" she said.

"Anythin' was better than home."

"How strange that we ended up here after all. Delayed, of course."

"The difference is that you would have been with me." The words were so quiet she struggled to hear them over the waves. "But you're the captain's lass now."

"His lass?"

"'Tis no secret."

She wondered what important information she wasn't privy to. "I am no such thing."

Heavy footfalls and the creaking of stairs made them both jump. The heads of the captain and Osborne rose into view. The deck suddenly felt far too small for all four of them, and she had the instinct to press herself against the wall behind her to put as much distance as she could between herself and Matthew.

Seeing the stern look on the captain's face, she was sure he suspected something. He looked first at her, then at Matthew.

"Are you on watch?" he asked Matthew.

"Aye, sir."

"Then 'tis a wonder you have leisure to enjoy our Maggie's company."

"I was—"

"Dismissed."

"Sir." Matthew hurried down to the quarterdeck, giving the captain as wide a berth as he could while he passed.

The captain kept his eyes on Margaret as Matthew left, as if he ceased to exist once their conversation concluded. She did her best to hold his gaze, but part of her felt like a guilty child about to be chastised.

"My crew understands there is no… *mixing* aboard my ship." He lifted his eyebrow at his choice of word. "They may enjoy all the recreation they desire when they are on land, but fraternizing between mates is forbidden. Though you are not a member of the crew, this applies to you also."

She blinked, sure she was blushing all the way to her toes.

"Do you understand my meaning, or must I assault your delicate ears with bawdier language?"

"Master Osborne made me aware of your rule, but I assure you—"

He waved a hand to stop her. "Aye, my lady, you are the very picture of female purity. Nevertheless… what sort of captain would I be if I did not protect my crew from danger?"

Osborne snorted. She side-stepped to let them into the navigation room, shrinking with mortification. Had he implied that she was some kind of siren?

Mortification transformed into indignation.

"Captain Stokes!"

He turned his head, his hand on the door latch. He waited for her to continue.

She waited for him to correct her.

"Nothing, sir," she said.

8

ALL THE NEXT day, Margaret—or Maggie, as she was known—wandered the ship, poking around where she wasn't wanted and startling unsuspecting sailors. Men worked, lounged, or slept on every deck. All the secret hideaways had been discovered and claimed. For someone who habitually responded to minor irritations by escaping behind a closed door, this was a consequence of her impetuousness she hadn't foreseen.

She had made a horrible mistake. How many times would she shout those words over the din of dread and euphoria battling each other in her mind? Euphoria that she was *free*, in control of her own destiny, to an extent she had only ever imagined. And dread, the unshakable impression that she had leapt from the burning ship only to drown in the fathomless sea.

To silence the noise, Maggie distracted herself with work.

One of the purser's duties was to manage the ship's stores, collecting requisitions for food, equipment, and other supplies from the men who oversaw specific areas of the ship. Organizing those supplies, though, seemed not to be a requirement of the position—at least, not one Osborne cared much about.

Installing herself in the cargo hold, she surveyed the chaos. One would think the needles and twine should be on the same shelf, and razors should go with razors and lamp wicks with lamp wicks. As she tidied, she pretended to ignore the four dice-throwing sailors with whom she shared the hold. Judging by their hushed conversation, stifled laughter, and covert glances, they were not pretending as diligently.

Two hours sped by, and somewhere along the way, a series of eight bells signaled the changing of the watch. The gamblers went back to work, and no one appeared to take their place, leaving

Maggie alone. It wasn't silent—there were footfalls above her, the occasional slam of something heavy on the deck, shouted commands, and the ship's creaking and shifting—but it was serene. She no longer had to devote half of her attention to the men nearby, wondering if she was disturbing them, wondering if they disliked her, wondering what they had been whispering about her. She slipped into comfortable efficiency, caring only about the task at hand.

A noise caught her attention, a muted thump too near to be a footfall abovedeck. She twisted to look behind her across the hold, into the dim cavern on the stern end where the largest cargo was kept. Something white flashed in the shadows between two shipping crates.

Curious, she wandered toward the other end of the hold, keeping her footsteps light. She edged around a stack of ale casks and squeezed between two barrels to get a closer look. It must be some kind of animal, but the sound hadn't been the scrabbling of mice, and she had never seen a white rat. She would almost have thought it was a stoat, something bright and slinky and fast.

When she reached the stern wall, she discovered there was nowhere left to go: the top layer of cargo had shifted to create a tunnel too narrow for a human to crawl through. Not content to give up, she lowered herself to a crouch and peered into the darkness.

A pair of round, golden eyes caught the dim lantern light, and the creature hissed.

Maggie scrambled back and shot up, thumping her head on the edge of a box balancing above her. She winced and pressed her fingers to the sore spot as she hurried back into the safety of the open space.

"You are well?" The sing-song voice startled her as much as the hissing had. She recognized the man by his tall frame and long, white-blonde hair, but she had yet to meet him. In one palm, he held a dirty handkerchief tied in a neat package.

She rubbed her head. "Aye, gramercy. There is some sort of animal back there. Gave me a fright."

The man chuckled. "Is only cat. He is fearful, but he is tame." He crouched down and laid the handkerchief on the floor, unfolding the corners with care. It held a pile of salt pork, cut into bite-sized pieces. The man scratched the floor with his fingernails and sang, *"Hermelin, kom hit! Hermelin!"*

A pink nose and white, triangular ears emerged from behind the crate. The cat froze as he assessed the situation, then slunk out of the shadows, padding across the deck in a straight line from his hiding place to the food. He glanced up at Maggie with eyes of mottled green and gold, like polished marble. Disregarding her as a threat, he turned his head away and ducked down to sniff at the meat.

As he ate, Maggie lowered herself inch by inch until she knelt on the deck. The cat's shoulders stiffened as she moved, then relaxed when she settled. "What did you call him?" she asked.

"Hermelin." He stroked the cat's soft, pristine fur. "When I first see him, he reminds me of *hermelin* in the woods." At her bewildered expression, he put his hands up behind his head to pantomime pert ears and made a high-pitched "eek eek" sound.

"A rat?"

He shook his head, frustrated. "Nay, *hermelin*. Like… snake with hair."

"Oh! Ermine—stoat! Aye, 'tis just what I thought. He moves so quick."

The man picked up a few morsels of meat and held them out for Maggie to take. "He likes food. He is good mouser, but he will like you if you will give him food."

She laid her hand on the floor, palm up, the moist treats sticking to her skin. The cat ignored her while he finished what was in front of him, but when it was gone, he picked up his nose and looked at the blond man. He shrugged and pointed to Maggie, conducting a silent conversation with the cat: *Don't look at me. Ask her.*

The cat swiveled his head to stare at the food in Maggie's palm. His eyes rose to meet hers, and she saw the calculations that must be occurring in his little white head. Then, one step at a time, he approached. Every movement took time and patience, but in the end, he lapped up the food from her hand, scraping his rough tongue against her palm. He even allowed her to stroke the top of his head.

"Well met, Hermelin," she said, in the sweet tone reserved for children and animals. "What a bonny lad."

He raised his head to push against her fingers, and she scratched his ears and under his chin. Now her other hand was empty, she stroked both sides of his face until a low purr began in his chest.

"You see? He is good cat." The man gazed with pride at the feline and tucked the handkerchief into his belt. "You are friends now."

"Does he live down here?"

He nodded. "In false wall."

She turned to follow his gaze. "False wall?"

"For smuggling." Of course a pirate ship would have somewhere to hide stolen goods, she thought, feeling foolish. "This is where food is. No rats above."

Hermelin rubbed his teeth against her knuckles. "There were cats all around at home, but my mother and my aunt insisted they were dirty."

"You see his hair?" He patted the cat's white rump. "He is not dirty."

"My aunt is not here. I may pet as many cats as I please." She stroked the length of Hermelin's spine, and he arched his back to meet her. She had guessed at some of the new experiences she would look forward to on the ship, but sitting on the floor of the cargo hold petting a cat had not been on the list.

A stair creaked as someone descended into the hold, and Hermelin disappeared into the maze of cargo with a flash of white. "Where's our wee lad?" a voice boomed. The man trotted down the steps and glanced around him.

"You frighten him," the blond scolded. "Always you frighten him!"

"What's he got to be frightened of? Best fed cat on the seas." The newcomer looked past his friend for the first time and smiled broadly. "How now, Maggie?"

She remembered meeting him in the galley yesterday, a short man with a round, red face, bald except for a fringe of mouse-brown fuzz circling his head from ear to ear like a laurel crown. As with the others who had stopped by to get a glimpse of her, she had forgotten his name immediately.

The trick was to get someone else to renew the introduction. "I am well, gramercy," she said, then turned to the gangly blond. "I pray your pardon. I do not know your name."

He pressed his palm to his chest. "Gude Engberg."

"Is there a 'Bad' Engberg?"

"Ha!" the shorter one said. "'Tis one o' my favorite jests!"

"He tells this yoke always at taverns and ordinaries where we play," Engberg explained, looking fatigued. "You meet Davies?"

Davies. She silently blessed Engberg for supplying the name. "I met Master Davies yesterden," she said. To both, she added, "You say you play?"

"Aye, oft as we can," Davies said. "Brings in a bit o' coin when we're on leave. This one plays the hurdy-gurdy, and I do the rest—stories, songs, japes. And the flute, when they've tired of my angelic voice."

"The flute! I play a little—I *did* play a little, at home."

"And you'll play again! Few o' the lads meet for first watch the nights we're at leisure. I'll lend you my instrument."

"O'Flaherty will not like," Engberg said darkly.

Davies scoffed. "Show me aught he *does* like."

O'Flaherty, a surly Irish fiddler, did *not* like playing host to the new landlubber that evening, and in protest, he led them through the fastest, trickiest songs he knew. The flute Davies lent her was old, the wood around the finger holes shiny and smooth from use. Its sweet, airy sound was less precise than that of the instrument she left behind in Gloucester. Maggie made herself lightheaded trying to find the correct placement of it under her lip. The whole experience left Maggie winded and flustered—and determined.

By the end of her first week, Osborne relinquished the most tedious purser tasks to her, which was to act as shopkeeper and banker for the ship. Whenever a man needed a candle or a few yards of fabric, she subtracted the cost from his pay. The illiterate crew was suspicious of this process at the best of times, Davies told her, and now a strange woman was performing it, Maggie would be fighting an uphill battle to earn their trust. On odd-numbered mornings, before wandering down to the galley to help Lloyd with luncheon, she sheltered with her new friends as if seeking out a tall tree in a lightning storm.

On even mornings like today, though, she was stuck with the opposite watch. Driscoll, the man with the permanent sneer, directed his friend Leigh to clean the guns, supervising from his comfortable seat on a crate. Two decks above, Matthew stood at the helm, steering the *Merrow* as it patrolled a swath of water off the coast of Belgium.

Matthew's silence had unnerved her for two or three days, but they soon settled into a comfortable routine of ignoring each other. His accusation that first day had hurt initially, but now she was only confused. What did he care if she was the captain's "lass"? He forfeited the right to an opinion eight years ago.

Maggie sat beside Luke as he spliced ropes together with red, calloused fingers. The wind carried her wrong notes and imprecise tone out to sea as she practiced the tune Davies had taught her the night before. The longer she puzzled it out, the more irritable she became. Soon she gave up and switched to another song, childlike in its simplicity, her sure fingers covering each hole in sequence.

A few notes in, Luke began to hum along. "I've not thought of this tune in years."

She lowered the flute. "You remember it?"

"You made me learn it by heart."

Had she really been such a tyrannical child? She remembered composing the tune after bringing home a copy of *Romeo and Juliet* from London, the beginning of her collection. Fourteen-year-old Maggie was so desperate to see the play performed, she taught young Luke a few speeches—and yes, perhaps she had been a trifle demanding.

"'Twas only on account of your willingness to learn it," she said. "And your brother's unwillingness."

"Unwillin'? He played Romeo a dozen times, at least. I remember you weepin' o'er him as you gave Juliet's speeches."

Although he had no interest in learning lines, Matthew had readily agreed to lie on the ground and let Maggie, as Juliet, kiss the poison from his lips before pantomiming her violent suicide. The deceased hero should not have been able to kiss her back, but she gave up correcting him.

"I should like to see it on a stage one day," she said, eager to steer the conversation away from the topic of kissing Luke's brother. "Or any of Master Shakespeare's plays. My father would bring home copies when I asked, but I have not been to Town since my presentation at court. My husband spent most of our marriage in London and never brought me with him."

"Is he a lord, then, your husband?"

"He was a baronet. One of the first to be dubbed so."

"He's not one any longer?"

"He died in April, God rest his soul." She crossed herself reflexively, and Luke did, too. Neither knew what to say after that, so she put the flute back to her lips to ward off the awkwardness.

Footfalls behind her made her miss a note, then a whole slew of notes as she turned to catch Captain Stokes drag his shirt over his head and toss it on top of the doublet he had already taken off. Half nude, he reached for the mainmast ratlines to begin his daily calisthenics.

"Does he always do that down here? In the way?" she whispered over the flute's mouthpiece.

"'S his ship."

"I suppose he removes his shirt as often as he can as well. Do you all show off for each other, then?" She nodded her head at Luke's friends, Hale and Whip, who were also bare-chested as they worked.

"All the lads were a mite more modest before you came aboard."

"Captain!" The shout came from a distance, and Luke snapped his gaze up to the top of the mainmast. The lookout, Cadogan, was up there in his solitary nest, hunting for quarry.

Captain Stokes scurried up the starboard ratlines with impressive agility and twisted his body to peer across the water. Maggie stood and craned her neck, but all she could see was a dark spot on the horizon. He swung back down from his vantage, making the deck shudder as his boots slammed on the boards. "Hale—All hands!"

Hale, one of the two shirtless boys, sprang into action, dashing up the quarterdeck stairs to ring the watch bell.

"What is it?" she asked Luke.

"Spanish ship, most like."

It was ridiculous, the sudden shiver of eagerness that ran through her. What lunatic would be *eager* for the prospect of violence and larceny?

The entire crew swarmed onto the deck to the sound of the watch bell clanging, the air buzzing with fragments of frenzied conversation. Davies caught Maggie's eye and flashed her a grin.

There was her answer: these lunatics.

Some took their places at the cannons on this deck while some scurried below to man those on the orlop deck. Others jeered from the railings, waving swords and muskets. Burney, the scrawny ship's boy, was pulling at a rope, hand over hand, and a solid black flag skittered up the mainmast.

Maggie dodged the bustling sailors until she reached the entrance to the galley, as out of the way as possible while maintaining a decent vantage. After a week of accounting and kitchen chores, no one could keep her from her first glimpse of real piracy.

Stokes strode across the deck in front of her, now clothed and wearing his yellow hat. The speckled plume sliced through the air as he swiveled his head, ensuring each man was at his post. When he saw her, he changed direction.

"Stay out of sight, prithee." He glanced down at her waist and tugged her eating dagger out of its sheath, handing it to her handle-first. Without another word, he continued his path toward the forecastle deck.

She gripped the tiny knife in one hand and Davies' flute in the other, not sure whether to be pleased with his concern, or insulted that this was the weapon he gave her with which to defend herself. What could she do with this blade if the time came to use it? A distant part of her wondered if he was teasing her, frightening her with the threat of hand-to-hand combat. Surely the Spanish would not come aboard.

She gripped the knife tighter.

Now she could see their target. The ship flew a white flag with a jagged red cross, over which was a coat of arms too far away to make out. She was smaller than the *Merrow*, with fewer guns and a more limited crew, and she could not match the *Merrow* for speed with how low she sailed in the water. There was no doubt she was a merchant ship, heavy with cargo.

Soon, that cargo would belong to the *Merrow*.

A decent person would feel a pang of shame for standing by while brigands looted an innocent ship, but Maggie didn't even feel ashamed of not feeling ashamed. Piracy had been legal, more or less, until about ten years ago. Privateers such as Raleigh and Drake had committed acts of piracy for years during the war with the blessing—and the financial support—of the Queen. It was the source of Sir John's fortune; it had paid for the gown Maggie now wore.

Some sea captains continued the tradition now during the hard-won peace. Most ports were friendly to English pirates, and merchants didn't fuss overmuch about what ship their imports may or may not have fallen off of. Spain might be England's friend on paper, but a treaty couldn't alter the memories of an entire kingdom.

Stokes's yellow hat provided a sense of occasion as the *Merrow* raced toward the Spanish ship. Padraig stood beside him awaiting orders, and the crew who were on deck shifted their feet like restless horses.

"Ready cannon one." The captain's voice was clear and loud over the splashing waves. Driscoll repeated the order from his position beside the foremost cannon, and two sailors hurried to load it with powder and an iron ball. They waited for the next command.

For a while, nothing happened. "They intend to ignore us," she heard Stokes say. "A warning shot, an it please you, Driscoll."

Driscoll sighted down the gun's gaping barrel and nudged it into the correct position. He stepped back and shouted, "Fire!" It exploded with a deafening boom that had Maggie covering her ears.

The shot landed in the water only yards from the Spanish ship. The *Merrow* was close enough they could see movement on deck and hear a few faraway commands. Stokes raised his hand, about to order another round of fire, but he froze as a white flag skipped up the other ship's mast.

The crew cheered.

Maggie emerged from her hiding place and spotted Davies and Engberg clapping each other on the shoulder. "Is that all?" she said. Where was the drama? The fight? Her knife dangled in her slackened grip.

Engberg shrugged. "No one wants hole in hull."

"Or a hole in me skull!" Davies added.

Maggie lingered in the galley entryway while the crew went about their next tasks. Stokes wandered across the deck and raised his eyebrows at her. "Your first plunder. You were not frightened?"

"Of what? A cannon?" She sheathed her knife, forcing herself to appear more cavalier than she was.

"'Tis not always so easily won." He watched their progress as they slipped alongside the smaller boat. "Go with Osborne to see what they carry."

"Go… to the other ship?"

"Padraig will take a skeleton crew over and force the Spaniards off. You will be safe."

"You are taking the entire ship?"

"Ships are costly. The hold may have gold, silks, spices, wine… but the ship itself is also valuable. If one can sell it." He grinned. "Which I can."

There it was: a tiny moral pang. "Where will the crew go?"

"'Tis a short distance to Flanders—harder in a row boat, but not impossible. Methinks they are not too much worse off than before we found them."

"But they have no way to return home."

"They will manage with the aid of their Dutch allies." He tilted his head. "My dear Maggie, you must needs become more mercenary if you wish to stay aboard my ship. We have no love for Spain."

She stammered, rushing to her own defense, but someone shouted, "Ready, captain!" They both turned to find the Spanish ship tied alongside the *Merrow*. The Spanish captain stood on his deck with his hat pulled low over his eyes, his sword lying on the boards in front of him.

Pratt selected six men, three from each watch, to go with Padraig to the waiting ship. Matthew and Engberg went first, and Stokes himself brought up the rear. Maggie hung over the rail to eavesdrop on the conversation, but the wind caught most of it and carried it away. She wondered what language he and the Spaniard were using to understand each other.

Somehow, Stokes persuaded them to lower their pinnace into the water. They rowed to shore, stormy-faced, while the *Merrow's* skeleton crew explored their new ship.

Osborne came up to stand at the rail beside Maggie. Stokes waved up to them both. "'Tis time!" Osborne sang, his face bright as a child with a new toy. "Let us see what makes this beauty sail so low."

The Spanish ship was built like the *Merrow*, but with a foreign flavor. Peaked arches topped the doorways, with elegant patterns carved into the wooden beams. The hold was stuffed with crates, barrels, sacks, and casks, most with painted labels. Her Latin was passable and her French was excellent, and she used them both to guess at the contents, identifying wine, iron, weapons, and a great deal of food. A medium chest contained silver, and another contained gold dust.

"From the New World," said Osborne when he saw Maggie's big eyes. She had never seen gold in any form other than coins or decoration. In its original shape and color, it seemed too humble to be worth much.

Osborne scratched notes in the little brown ledger, taking a rough estimate of the amounts of each item. When he finished, he cocked his head toward the stairs. "To the master's quarters. Always somethin' worth findin' in the master's quarters."

Sure enough, when they entered the opulent state room, they spotted the captain's private coffer on the floor near the bed. Osborne ran his hand through the gold and silver coins.

"We'll tek this with us. The rest can stay aboard." He lifted the coffer with ease and held it out to Maggie with one hand. She underestimated how heavy it was by at least twenty pounds, but with a few flailing movements, she kept it from falling to the floor. Osborne snickered, delighted at the distress his joke had caused. She glared.

Out on deck, Stokes stood with Padraig. The captain's face broke out in a grin when he saw her stumble from the crew quarters. "Need a hand?"

She gritted her teeth. "I can manage."

"Are not wealthy baronet's wives accustomed to carrying around heavy coffers of gold?"

"We have people to do that for us."

With an undignified snort, Stokes took the coffer from her. "Your servant, my lady."

The *Merrow* sailed north. Every few hours, Maggie wandered to the stern to watch the figures move across the deck of the Spanish prize ship: Padraig strutting about as the ship's deputy master, Matthew bracing his fists on the wheel, Engberg and the others swinging up into the rigging. On the *Merrow*, the loss of a half-dozen sailors becalmed the usual bustle and noise to which she had grown accustomed.

Her own mind quieted as well. Without the threat of Matthew lurking around every corner, she felt free to let her guard down. Her tasks became easier. The ship became roomier. Even her flute playing improved when she ceased worrying Matthew could hear her wrong notes.

However nonsensical, she cared what he thought of her. When they were children, she hung on his every word and heeded his every command, desperate for his approval. It had been his idea to elope; he had chosen the time and the day.

When he failed to show, the first person she blamed was herself.

Then she blamed Elizabeth, who had started the row that inspired Matthew's drastic action. It must be her sister's fault Matthew left without her instead of following through with the plan. It served her right Matthew broke into the jewelry box. There hadn't been much in there, just a few chains and one or two pretty gems.

The rest was on the hill under the old tree, hidden inside Maggie's clothing. Her dowry.

Time and wisdom dulled the pain and made the details hazy. They had both endured a decade of drifting apart, of growing and forgetting.

Osborne set a course for the River Thames. It seemed like madness to bring a stolen Spanish ship straight to the King's doorstep, but when she asked Davies about it, he assured her London was the safest port.

The captain behaved as he always had, keeping to his irritating routine of exercising in the middle of his crew's work area. Maggie's spare shirt had a tear under the arm, so in the morning, she brought her mending out into the sunlight on the sterncastle deck, forgetting what time it was. The flash of movement at the mainmast ratlines caught her attention.

He was hanging a yard from the deck, his chest and shoulders bronzed by his daily exposure to the relentless sun. She watched as he pulled himself up and swung onto a higher rung of the rope net. Just when she began to fear for his safety, he let go and dropped with a thud into a graceful crouch. He swung his arms forward and back to stretch his tired muscles.

She usually looked away. Other men on deck were working half-naked, and she had the decency to keep her eyes averted from them. But Luke had implied they were all showing off for her benefit, and if that were true—if Captain Stokes's manly display was for her—maybe it was only charity to watch.

His drill complete, he trotted up the quarter deck stairs toward his cabin, catching sight of her on the deck above. Her instinct was to turn away, to pretend she had seen nothing, as a gentlewoman would do. But wasn't that only to avoid embarrassing both parties? This activity of his was so self-indulgent, so arrogant, there was no chance it embarrassed him. So why should it embarrass her?

She held his gaze and raised an incredulous eyebrow.

Stokes grinned, then bowed. It was a beautiful, graceful performance, something that wouldn't have been out of place at King James's court. He swept one arm out and brought the other hand to his bare chest, pointed his toe like a dancer and bent his back knee. Even with velvet and jewels, he would not have been more regal.

What business did a common sea captain have bowing like that? The thought of him practicing the moves in his cabin was too funny.

He picked his head up to catch her reaction. Maggie schooled her expression as quickly as she could, but it was too late. He had seen her laughing at him.

9

AHEAD, THE SHIPS crowded together, as dense as the buildings lining the Thames. Maggie feared they would lose the little prize ship in the fracas, but Stokes was as calm as ever as he gave his orders. He called Luke, Hale, and the ship's boy, Burney, to him, and she struggled to read his lips from her position at the starboard rail.

Osborne strode up next to her and looked over the side, searching for something in the water.

"What is the captain telling them?" she asked him.

"They're to run messages to our contacts." His posture changed as he found what he had been looking for. He waved his arm over his head and shouted, "Ho!"

A tiny rowboat, able to transport only six or eight men, bobbed in the water twenty yards away. The boat's owner cupped his hands around his mouth. "What can I do for thee?"

"How much to take four to the Tower stairs?"

The man peered up the river toward the Tower. "'Tis a bit of a crush."

They shouted back and forth until they had negotiated a fee. Maggie watched with interest as the boatman pulled his craft up to the *Merrow's* hull.

"A brave man to linger in the middle of the river," she said.

"'Tis a maneuver that takes time as well as skill. Most stay out of the way. But a penny's a penny."

"Are you to go with the lads?"

"I'm to find our customs officer friend at the Pool and arrange for the cargo to be unloaded, then sell it."

"Will they not ask questions?"

He shook his coin purse, and the money inside jangled. "This tends to answer them."

The three boys, having memorized their instructions, met Osborne at the railing. They swung down into the waiting rowboat one at a time, making it look effortless. She watched the boat weave around the waiting cargo ships toward the north bank.

"That expression tells me this is your first trip to London." Stokes appeared at her elbow, catching her by surprise.

"I have been to London twice, but never like this."

They both leaned on the railing. Stokes pointed to the immense stone structure looming upriver. "That is the Tower," he said.

She turned her head to confirm he was teasing, and he smiled innocently back at her.

"That steeple there is St. Paul's. Ahead is London Bridge, of course. Over there…" He turned around and nodded at the south bank. "That is Southwark, where many of the lads spend their coin when they have shore leave. Southwark is known for… exceeding friendly barmaids."

She wished she didn't still blush at such things. "Where is Whitehall Palace?" she asked, eager to change the subject.

"Where the river curves. You will see it when we pass under the bridge. And that…" He pointed at the spot on the river between the bridge and the Tower, where a forest of masts obstructed the view of anything beyond. "That is the Pool."

It looked like an insurmountable obstacle. How many hours did it take to get through the throng of ships jockeying for position at the quay?

"We are not to go in there, are we?"

Stokes nodded upriver. "There is a wharf past the bridge where we may restock and give the lads a few hours' leave while Osborne and Padraig shift the prize." He looked at her. "Word of your disappearance may have reached Town by now. If you wish not to be found, I advise you to stay aboard and out of sight."

It didn't sound like a command. Maybe it was a test, an out, to learn if she had changed her mind. "Aye, captain," she said.

For a moment, she imagined her answer pleased him, even if she was another mouth to feed, even if she was bad luck, even if she was a landlubber who made his crew's job more difficult. It was a nice thought.

Maggie lurked at the galley windows all morning, wishing she could go ashore but taking the captain's warning to heart. Around eleven o'clock, Osborne and the boys returned, pulling a cart behind them. When they arrived at the dock, each boy hoisted a heavy bag from the cart and carried it up the gangway, with a beaming Osborne bringing up the rear. "Ey up, Maggie!" he called. "I've a task for thee."

A half-hour later, neat stacks of gold and silver coins decorated the navigation room table. Maggie had never seen so much currency in one place—seventy-five pounds sterling.

"Is it always this much?"

"Often enough. 'Twoulda been more, but Bisset gave me another of his stories… Anyway, 'tis a fair payment for the tarnishin' of us immortal souls."

He opened the ledger to the roster, where a number followed each man's name: his shares, based on seniority. With the lowest, Burney, getting one share and the captain getting ten, the total number of shares was one hundred twenty-six. Maggie picked up a quill.

"Now the part I dread," said Osborne. He scooped some coins into his hand and began placing them in neat rows.

She watched him for a moment, puzzled. "Why do you do it like that?"

"How else would I do it?"

"By dividing the total coin into one hundred twenty-six."

"Aye, so I am."

"With a pen, I mean." She dipped her quill into the nearby ink pot and scratched the figures into the margins while Osborne stared, transfixed. Numbers were always imprinting themselves on Maggie, ordering themselves into neat patterns. She manipulated them like bobbins of lace-making thread, weaving and untangling them to suit her needs.

When she was done, she tapped the result with the tip of the pen. "Twelve shillings per share."

He shook his head and pushed the ledger away, returning to his work.

"But what of the unites?" Three shiny gold coins stamped with King James's face gleamed from the corner of the table, too dear to be included in Osborne's piles.

"They'll be put aside 'til they can be changed. Good enough, yer ladyship?"

The inefficiency of his system infuriated her. His buyers had paid in every denomination of English coin, and he had also mixed in the coins from the Spanish captain's coffer. It took an age to match up the correct number of shillings to *pesos* and pennies to *reales*. Why could he not think in values rather than pieces of eight?

However, since this was a losing battle, she left him to it. She busied herself instead with putting pen to paper to work out each man's total pay. She couldn't help the twinge of envy that Stokes would receive six whole pounds. Even the ship's boy got twelve shillings—twelve more than Maggie.

Every night she counted the coins in her purse, praying a penny hadn't vanished since the night before. For now, she was under Stokes's protection. What would she do when the *Merrow* docked for the winter?

Osborne was still laying out coins when she finished, so she scooped up her own handful of silver to help. In the end, the piles shimmered like scales all over the table.

Maggie stretched her aching shoulders. Osborne leaned back and gave Maggie an "I told you so" look.

"Eleven shillings six," he said.

"But if you divide these unites and add back in the leftover coin..." She did the math on the paper. "Twelve shillings altogether." She saw his face and faltered. "Methinks."

He glowered at the page for a long moment, and her face burned. She knew the figures were right, but she didn't have to be so insufferable about it. She had wounded his pride, a man who could navigate by the stars but who failed to grasp the intricacies of long division.

No man liked to be bested by a woman.

"Cap'n was reet about thee."

She knew better than to ask what the captain was right about.

"Off wi' thee. I'll finish up here."

"Master Osborne—"

"Lloyd'll be lookin' for thee." He put his palms flat on the table and bent his head, intent on the coins and the ledger. She was dismissed.

At least in the galley, there would be no risk of besting Lloyd at cooking.

Boxes and sacks of fresh meat and produce made the galley look more like the hold. Lloyd was already hauling ingredients out of their containers, and the scent of roasting meat made Maggie panic briefly, afraid she had lost all track of time.

"'Tis scarce half one!" she said.

"Festival day." He overturned a bag of turnips onto the worktable, and they bounced and rolled. "'Tis the captain's natal day," he added. "We've a feast to prepare."

She spent the entire voyage down the Thames toiling in the galley with Lloyd while the crew brought every chair and table out onto the main deck, transforming it into a labyrinth of sharp corners and trip hazards.

By dusk, they were clear of the river, far enough from the English coast to let the dark shape of the land melt into the black of night. The lanterns dotting the tables fended off the descending darkness, encapsulating the *Merrow* in a cheerful bubble of warm light.

The lads were in high spirits as Maggie served them roast beef, mashed turnips, hot salad, and spiced bread and butter pudding. As she scooped out servings to the waiting line of sailors, a minor commotion caught her attention.

"Oy, Driscoll, back of the line."

Driscoll appeared in front of her, cutting off everyone who waited behind. She couldn't tell who had taken offense to it, but it didn't matter to Driscoll, who waved the comment off. "I'm fair starvin', and these fairies move slow as treacle." He tossed his head to the two men behind him.

The lookout, Cadogan, created two white-knuckled fists, and his friend, Finch, laid a calming hand on his arm. Maggie caught Lloyd's eye, and he shook his head to say it wasn't worth getting involved.

She laid her hands on the table.

Driscoll stared at her, confusion flashing across his face. "I was mistaken," he said, tossing the words over his shoulder. "This wench moves slower than you two do."

"Forgive me, I am learning the way of things," she replied. "'The first man to arrive is the first man to be served,' is what I was told."

A few sailors chuckled, but Driscoll's face grew red. "You've no power to hold back a man's food rations."

Maggie glanced down the line, worried she would find Captain Stokes's glare of disapproval. Instead, she found Matthew. She looked away, wishing he didn't put her so off balance.

"I have no desire to," she told Driscoll. "There will be plenty for everyone, and they will receive it in the order they arrive."

"You should have a care when speaking so to your betters."

Maggie made a show of scanning the deck before she replied, "I see none about, but I thank you for the advice."

Driscoll only scowled. She watched his mind chug and whir as it struggled to produce a fitting retort, but Matthew strode forward from his place in the line and laid a broad hand on Driscoll's shoulder.

Driscoll transferred his scowl to Matthew, who beckoned with a jerk of his head. Both men glanced at Maggie, then at each other, and at last Driscoll relented.

Supper continued quietly, with Cadogan and Finch offering her uncomfortable smiles as they received their food, but the rumbling chatter resumed a few moments later and the awkward altercation was forgotten.

Driscoll didn't meet her gaze, only held his hand out to snatch a trencher from her. When Matthew stepped forward, she kept her lips tightly closed, afraid to let slip all the caustic remarks his friend had inspired. How Matthew could be friends with someone so rude was a mystery that would remain unsolved, at least for tonight.

As she dolloped turnips onto his trencher, she heard him mutter, "Luke says you're a widow."

Her hand paused, the wooden spoon hovering over the mound of turnips, as she wondered whether he had actually spoken or if she had imagined it. She glanced up, forgetting to brace herself for the flood of memory his eyes triggered. His face and body showed the years that had passed, but his eyes were the same, brown as barley wine. How could a decade disappear in a moment?

"Was it so bad being a baron's widow that you chose *this*?" A tiny smile flickered across his lips.

His right shoulder jerked as the person behind him gave him a gentle shove. Matthew grabbed his trencher from her frozen hand and moved away.

Disturbingly, what should have filled her with righteousness only filled her with doubt. He had no right to tease her after what happened—he shouldn't even be bold enough to say a single sentence to her that didn't contain an apology. Yet if he deemed it safe to be friends, was she clinging to her grudge unfairly?

No. She was the wronged party, and her bitterness was justified.

Then again, it had been less than a fortnight. His apology could still be forthcoming, and she was desperate to hear it.

The atmosphere was warm and convivial. Jolly sailors filled every seat on the deck, forcing the youngest lads onto the stairs. Stokes took the seat of honor by the galley entrance, flanked by

Padraig and Osborne. Maggie looked about, feeling out of place, until Davies waved her over.

"Rest your feet, lass," he said, offering her a chair he had saved for her at the table he shared with Engberg and their friend, Gillies. "You've worked hard as any man here, and 'tis time to take your leisure."

"You will be celebrated, methinks," Engberg said around a mouthful of turnips, as if his accent did not already make him difficult to understand.

"Celebrated? I just mashed the turnips."

"Nay, I speak of pay. Pratt says we are paid on the morrow. So soon!"

Davies emphasized this with a wave of his mug. "Aye, I heard it too. Osborne takes an age to split up the prize money. Sounds like you managed to split it."

Her eyes darted to the officers' table, where Osborne appeared in good spirits. If he told Pratt the lads would be paid tomorrow and Maggie was to thank, he must not have been as angry as she thought.

Around ten, Davies pushed back from the table and rose unsteadily to his feet. "'Tis a mite quiet for a festival day!" he called, his reedy voice interrupting the comfortable chatter. A few faces tilted up, but the majority ignored him. "A merry tale in honor of our captain." He swallowed, preparing his oration.

A groan came from one of the diners—a man called MacLoughlin—followed by the terse command, "Shut yer hole, Sam Davies, by Jesus!"

A chorus of agreement rippled across the deck. Davies looked around, his face turning red, then dropped back into his chair to pout.

"Give us a song, wilt thou, Maggie?" Inwood called from his table.

"You'll have a song from 'er, but not a peep from me, is it?" Davies shot back.

"A t'ousand times over, yeh windbag," said MacLoughlin.

The little red-faced Davies jumped to his feet, his chair tottering on its back legs.

"Peace, lads," Captain Stokes said, his commanding voice carrying easily. "We will grow as weary of Maggie as we are of you, Davies, have no fear. But until then, I will be pleased to have a song, if she will be so good."

A familiar hitch tugged at her insides, something like fear. It came upon her the handful of times they had asked her to perform for them at supper. But unlike fear, this was a feeling she didn't shrink from.

She wiped her hands on her apron and stood. "What tune will you have?"

"A Dowland, if you have one," the captain replied, inspiring a few grunts of agreement.

There were too many to choose from, but a festive occasion called for something lighthearted. She heard the first few notes in her head, selected a comfortable starting pitch, and sang, *"Come again!"*

They tapped their mugs on the table, pleased with her choice, and by the second verse, she had half of them singing along, neglecting their suppers, their eyes bright with merriment. The third verse was their favorite, full of innuendo. She performed for them, letting each hidden joke play out on her face.

A good woman would show reserve, but Alinor was leagues away and Maggie was enjoying herself too much to care. She spared a sidelong glance at the captain, wondering whether he approved. He had never come down to watch her sing in the galley. She expected him to quash the buzzy, heart-pounding feeling that filled her whenever she performed, but the disturbing hunger for approval only increased under his gaze.

When she finished, he clapped his hands along with the crew. "Gramercy, Maggie. A finer gift I could ne'er hope for."

Padraig nudged him with a sharp elbow, his limbs too loose to claim sobriety. "Now you."

Osborne let out a bark of laughter. "Aye, up you get, cap'n."

The call was taken up all over the deck, a rumble beginning in the planks as they stamped their feet. Maggie stamped along, impressed by his crew's fervor. Stokes's singing must be a rare treat.

When the rumble became a roar, Stokes got to his feet and held up his hands. "Lads, I hear you, and I will be pleased to give you a tune if O'Flaherty will deign to lend me his fiddle. But as we all ken how unlikely *that* would be…"

The men laughed, turning as one to find O'Flaherty frowning. Maggie watched them in awe. It had never occurred to her that the captain might play an instrument. O'Flaherty reluctantly rose from his seat, raising his fiddle up in offering, and they cheered.

"I'll not play alone, though," Stokes said as they passed the fiddle and bow across the deck toward him. "Davies? Scurlock?"

Music on a festival day was an inevitability, so the musicians among the crew shot up, instruments already in hand. The band assembled in an open area near the stairs: Engberg on his hurdy-gurdy and Inwood on his bones, plus Scurlock on the tambourine and Mullins on the pennywhistle. Davies stood on the first step, bringing him almost to Stokes's height.

The captain settled the fiddle under his chin and gave the bow a few test pulls against the strings. "Fisher's?"

The ability of seasoned musicians to perform together without rehearsal had always struck Maggie as miraculous. Engberg found a pleasing drone, and Davies and Mullins joined the captain on the melody, weaving descants and ornaments over and through the familiar tune.

The first dancer was Cadogan, balding and middle-aged, but as graceful now as he always was when he climbed the mainmast. He tapped and stomped his feet in the hornpipe's lively rhythm to his mates' clapping. His friend, Finch, jumped in on the second repeat, and soon six or eight of them were bounding about the deck, shoving furniture out of the way to create an impromptu dance floor. Maggie clapped along.

With a loud "hup," Stokes signaled to the musicians that he neared the end. He gestured with his bow to wind them down to the finish, and they lingered on the final note, Scurlock shaking his tambourine. Stokes ended with a flourish, his bow rising into the air like a feather in an updraft.

The crew erupted, and Maggie applauded until her hands stung. The captain bowed, pompous as a court minstrel, and handed the fiddle back to O'Flaherty. Davies started another dance tune.

The captain tried to wend his way back through the maze of tables, but thanks to the dancers' enthusiasm, there was no longer a path. His gaze landed on the empty chairs near Maggie and he wandered over, throwing himself into the seat beside her.

Up close, she could see the sweat on his brow and how his chest heaved from the effort of playing at such a devilish speed. His eyes were alight with a sort of exuberance she hadn't seen before.

"Well played, captain!"

He sighed. "It has been a long while since I played. I am always surprised how easily my body remembers what to do."

"Why should it surprise you? After your display this morning, methinks you regard your body too highly to doubt its abilities." She heard the words only after she had said them, lulled into complacency by the generous festival rations of beer.

Stokes stared at her, then broke into a genuine smile. "Ten lashes for insubordination—as soon as I recover from the shock."

The ship's boy skipped past, weaving around the tables.

"Burney!"

The boy halted mid-step and stood at attention in front of Stokes.

"Your captain's fists are empty," Stokes told him. "Be so good as to remedy this."

As he puzzled through the captain's code, Burney stood frozen until Stokes formed his hand around an invisible mug and pretended to quaff it. The boy's face lit up. "Aye, sir!" he lisped, moving at full tilt toward the beer keg.

Maggie snickered to herself, but it must have been loud enough for Stokes to hear. "I hardly recognize you when you smile," he said. "Where is the meek little baronet's widow I met in Bristol?"

She raised one eyebrow in her best imitation of him. "You met no such person. Had I been meek, I would not be sitting here now." They were bold words, a lie fortified by drink. She wanted to say she had left that woman in Bristol, but every day, she went to battle with her. If she convinced the captain she was brave, would it become true?

Burney returned with a mug full to the brim, balanced so he wouldn't spill a drop. Stokes thanked him, and he grew an inch taller before dashing away.

"Where did you learn to play the fiddle like that?" she asked.

"Here, at sea. My father's mate would play after supper. To pass the time, he taught me."

"Was this your father's ship?"

"He was the master of a merchant vessel, *Phoebus*. His dream was to explore uncharted seas, but he had to settle for importing spices."

Thus the *Merrow*'s innocent alias. "An apt name for a ship chasing a dream," she said. "Yet Phoebus failed to capture Daphne in the end."

"Aye, but he gave her good chase, did he not?"

"How easily men forget Daphne had no wish to be chased."

As soon as she said it, she regretted it. Stokes didn't want her opinion, and she was tired of rehashing this same argument, especially when it forced her to think of Robert.

She did, however, appreciate the beautiful irony: Robert had cornered her into an act of desperation of which Daphne would be proud.

The captain inclined his head. "I cry your pardon. I forgot to whom I was speaking. You are, after all, the authority on unscrupulous suitors."

Why was it so funny to hear Robert's grievous sins distilled into one polite word? It shouldn't be possible; the story was too ridiculous. It read like a Greek myth or one of Shakespeare's comedies. The only way her tale could be more outlandish was if she had, in fact, transformed into a laurel tree, or into an ass like Bottom.

No, she was more likely to play Titania and fall in love with the ass.

"Captain," a voice said.

There he stood, hair free from its binding and tangling in the breeze. He had drawn himself up to his full height, making him tower over them. He looked only at the captain, his expression bored. "Some of the lads are wonderin' who will be lucky enough to dance with Mistress Margaret," Matthew said.

She had heard her Christian name in his mouth dozens of times, but even after so short a stint aboard the *Merrow*, it sounded wrong. A garment that had shrunk.

"You believe it wise to allow this charming lady to trip it with you ne'er-do-wells? At least one will perish from pleasure."

"Worth the risk, I vow," Matthew replied. His gaze flicked to her. "'Tis a festival day, after all."

She glanced between them. The captain raised his eyebrows and shrugged, as close to a blessing as she would get.

"By your leave, captain," she said, standing.

"So given, Daphne."

Matthew offered his hand, the familiar feeling of his fingers distracting her so she didn't catch Stokes's remark until she was too far away to argue.

A chorus of cheerful shouts greeted her as they joined the revelers.

"Well met, Maggie!"

"Not too good to dance with the likes of us?"

"That's cheating, Kent! Why do I have to dance with *this* ugly bastard?"

Davies raised his voice over them all. "What'll it be, then?"

"Let the lady choose!"

Maggie balked at the responsibility. "I hardly know! Shall it be a Gathering Peascods?"

She made a ring with Cadogan, Finch, and two other couples as the musicians began the tune. Sometime during the chorus, she realized she had never danced with Matthew. The Donwells hosted Midsummer and Michaelmas feasts every year, and she had danced with every farmer and farmer's son in Gloucester except for the Kents, religious zealots who disdained frivolity.

That was something she had never understood. Dancing was an innocent diversion, a chance to socialize and shake off the day's worries. There was nothing unholy about it.

But then she touched his hand. They linked arms, and his body radiated heat. Was that his pulse she felt in the crook of his elbow? The ale she had imbibed brought all the blood and nerves to the surface of her skin. Her bodice was too tight. Shallow breathing made her dizzy. Or was it from spinning around?

After the final steps, the musicians improvised on the ending chord while the dancers bowed to their partners again. Matthew hoisted her up out of her curtsy. His thumb brushed across her knuckles, first one way, then the other. Not an accident. She shivered.

"You dance well," she said lamely.

Another brush of his thumb. "I'd a fine partner."

She pulled her hand out of his grip, conscious of how many eyes were on them. Lloyd appeared at her side, requesting the next dance.

It was when she was catching her breath in a chair on the periphery that Driscoll's friend, Leigh, approached her with his usual limping gait.

"I need a lamp wick."

She furrowed her brow. "I have none."

"Osborne says you're the only one what can find aught in the hold. Says you moved it all about."

"Lamp wicks are in a box on the second shelf from the top."

"Aye, I looked through all the boxes. There's no wicks."

Sighing, she got to her aching feet and led Leigh down to the cargo hold. She strode across the uneven planks, dented and scuffed from heavy crates and barrels. A candle flickered on a storeroom shelf.

Her footsteps faltered as she realized Leigh was no longer behind her.

A hand reached out from behind a stack of crates.

"Zounds!"

She glared at the owner of the hand. Matthew's teeth and eyes flashed in the flickering light.

Her heartbeat showed no sign of slowing, not with him so close. "Did you send Leigh?"

"'Tis a good story, Margaret. And he's keeping watch."

"The captain—"

"Hang the captain. He need not know."

"Then do not tempt fate! If Leigh knows we meet this way, someone else will find out."

"'Tis only one time."

She looked up at him, at a loss. She didn't have the heart to turn away and leave him standing there in the storeroom, even though she knew she should. A part of her—an ancient part—longed to feel her hand in his again.

"You are… beautiful."

At his words, her breath went shallow, imperceptible gasps to keep her alive without breaking the spell.

His heavy-lidded eyes flitted over her face. "I used to love to look at you. Whenever we sat on that hill, and the sun fell down on your face, I would ask God if I was worthy even to be near you."

She shouldn't let him say such things. He had no right to speak of love.

But when she spoke, her voice came out as a child-like whisper. "Did He answer?"

"If you are here, 'tis because He has given me another chance. I'll not let it slip away."

Another chance. That meant he regretted squandering the first one. It had to. Could she make him say the words? Make him tell her why he left?

He wrapped his arm around her. His embrace felt so natural, so familiar. This near, the scent of his skin evoked flashes of memory: the two of them sitting side by side, knees touching, watching barges float up and down the Severn. The little bunch of marigolds he gifted her for her birthday. The sunlight through the leaves the first time he kissed her.

It felt so good to be held. She melted into the angle of his arm and tilted her head up. The yellow candlelight revealed half his face, but his deep-set eyes remained in shadow, dark and dangerous.

A mad thought darted through her consciousness, slicing the rational thoughts to shreds: she wanted to kiss him again.

No one but Leigh knew Matthew was here with her. They could steal this moment and let the memory of it carry them until it was safe to repeat it.

He lowered his face and rested his forehead against hers, their noses brushing together.

"Oy!" came the whispered shout from the other end of the hold. Maggie sprang away from Matthew and whipped her head toward the stairs. Leigh hurried toward them, his light, uneven footfalls echoed by a second set on the deck above. Matthew was on the stern side of the hold in a flash, disappearing around a stack of barrels.

She snatched a lamp wick from the box on the second shelf and held it out to Leigh with shaking fingers just as Pratt hit the bottom step of the stairs.

It was late into middle watch when the revelers stumbled to their beds with their lamps, dispersing like a swarm of will-o'-the-wisps. The ship faded, becoming part of the darkness, just another object bobbing in the waves.

But Maggie's mind pulsed with light and color as she lay awake on the navigation room floor. She could feel the phantom of his hand in hers, of his warm, rough thumb skimming over the back of her fingers. It made her shiver to remember his eyes, his heat, his murmured words, simmering with passion.

How dare her stomach flutter and her heart pound for this handsome stranger when her mind knew him to be false? They had schemed together, made plans for their life together, and at the crucial moment, he had left her behind. There was no future in that, not if he remained silent. If he explained, she might forgive, and only then could she entertain thoughts of something more. She was a fool to let impulse win out over intellect.

But this was the farthest she had ever strayed, and those hands, that voice, even the smell of him was an echo of home, calling her back.

10

THE *MERROW* MADE for Boston, a town on the east coast Maggie had never heard of. Osborne said they were going there to pick up a job, though it seemed odd the crew would seek employment rather than plunder. The only assignment she was aware of Stokes accepting was the one that led to her presence on board.

Matthew's watch had shore leave first. He, Driscoll, and their usual gang fidgeted at the rail as their mates secured the gangplank. Maggie observed them from a distance, an itchy feeling of restlessness making her bounce on the balls of her feet. She hadn't touched solid ground for more than a fortnight.

Luke looked back at her while Stokes, Padraig, and Osborne descended to the dock. "Coming?"

No one had advised her to stay aboard this time. Her chest tightened in anticipation until Driscoll snorted. "Why's she got leave?" he said. "She's not earned it as we 'ave."

"She does her share," Luke argued.

"Not as I've seen, but then, mayhap I've been asleep. You're the sort what does most of 'er labor in the night, are yeh not?" His grin bared yellow teeth.

Leigh's and Coulthurst's laughter echoed harshly in her ears over the rush of adrenaline, and she stared at him, furious. Matthew gave him a half-hearted shove toward the gangplank, and soon the offenders were gone.

Luke nudged her with his shoulder. "Come on," he muttered. "He's not worth heedin'."

Her roiling anger disagreed, but she followed him down the gangplank, refusing to let Driscoll take her first shore leave away from her.

Their ship was one of about a dozen in the harbor that day. Sailors loaded and unloaded cargo, repaired split boards, patched torn sails. They all followed Maggie with their eyes as she stumbled by on her wobbly sea legs. She ignored them with as imperious a posture as she could, knowing exactly what they were thinking.

Matthew fell back in the formation until he was close enough he could whisper to her without the lads hearing. "I wish they wouldn't look at you so. They would turn away sooner if they could see you were spoken for." His knuckles brushed the back of her hand.

She pulled away before he could lace their fingers together, unimpressed with how he had handled Driscoll a moment ago. "But as I am *not* spoken for..." she said, glaring.

"What we do on shore is no one's business."

Her eyes flicked to Driscoll, then to Stokes at the front of the pack. They were both too far away to hear, but too close for comfort. "I mean not to test the captain's law."

"Law," he scoffed. "The captain is an arrogant ass. His laws are whims, nothing more."

"His whim saved me from an unhappy future. I will not provoke him, and you must do the same—for my sake, if not for your own."

He gave the heavy sigh of a long-suffering husband. "Very well. I'll be as careful as I can, though it be torture to stay away from you."

He lengthened his stride until he was no longer beside her. She stared at him, wondering how he could make her blood boil with exasperation one minute, and with something quite different the next.

They came to a building with a leaping rabbit painted on the sign over the door. Stokes didn't slow his stride, instead calling over his shoulder, "Try not to get thrown out before we finish our business."

Driscoll barreled through the doorway and the others streamed in behind him. Maggie waited a moment before realizing Stokes had paused to speak with her. Osborne and Padraig fidgeted in the background.

"You can find your way back to the *Merrow*?" Stokes asked.

She turned around to look the way they had come. The ship was still in sight; she could even make out the painted gold and green designs on the mast. "I am grateful for your concern."

He sniffed, which was as much of a laugh as he was willing to give her. "I am glad to know you have your bearings. But those lads," he said, tossing his head toward the tavern, "have not a single working compass between them, especially after a few rounds. I pray they remember whose crew they belong to."

"Is that a riddle?"

"Nay. 'Tis a warning."

"Captain," Padraig said. Stokes touched the brim of his hat with one finger, then whirled away to lead Padraig and Osborne up the street.

She huffed, bemused, and entered the Seely Hare. The group had commandeered a long table and had already waved over the barmaid. For an hour, they caroused as if they would never drink again, fighting for the honor of buying the next round—except for their mate Whip, who they ridiculed for his stinginess, and Driscoll, who suggested Leigh buy the next one.

Their rowdiness increased, a steady crescendo. The younger ones looked up to the older, taking their cues from how quickly Matthew tossed back his beer and how saucily Driscoll spoke to the barmaid. Their loud laughter embarrassed her, and the comments they made about the women in the room made her tense and irritable. She wished they could order a meal to soak up all the alcohol, but the Seely Hare was a tavern, not an ordinary, and she didn't think them likely to waste their coin on food, anyway.

When the officers returned from their business in town, Padraig and Osborne retired to a private table to do their own serious drinking, and Stokes joined Maggie at her end of the table. Matthew glanced sidelong at him and hunkered down over his mug.

The barmaid stalked over and slammed Stokes's first round in front of him. Noticing her foul mood, he grinned up at her. "Gramercy, mistress. That you have borne these lads' nonsense shows you are made of hard stuff."

She sniffed. "Friends of yours?"

"I will only own it if it will not lower your opinion of me." He leaned back in his seat, a casual arm crooked over the chair back. He wore his usual doublet unbuttoned to his navel, his shirt collar open to reveal the dark hair on his chest.

"I've not made an opinion as yet," the girl replied, humor reigniting behind her eyes.

"Then I must try harder to impress. What name is deserving of such a lovely creature as yourself?"

"Now, none of that, sir. I promised me mum I wouldn't fall in love with a sailor." She leaned her hip on the edge of the table, freezing Maggie out of the exchange—not that Maggie wanted anything to do with it. Stokes's flattery, however expert, made her roll her eyes. She pushed her empty mug toward the other empties in the middle of the table and stood.

The barmaid glanced over her shoulder at the movement. "Beg your pardon, mistress, is this one yours?"

"Nothing like!" she sputtered, her face turning red. To Stokes, she added, "I will be back to the ship before you have need of me."

"I'll walk you into town." Matthew shoved his chair back and clapped Driscoll on the shoulder in farewell.

She froze, wanting to protest, but not knowing how without drawing more of Stokes's attention. By some miracle, Luke insisted on going with. He and Hale rose from their seats while Whip downed the last dregs of his cup. The three boys would give the excursion an air of innocence. And maybe Stokes was too taken by the blonde in front of him to think much about it.

The captain frowned at her. "Any crew member yet on shore at six of the clock will be left behind."

Luke and the boys led the way, sometimes looking back to include Matthew and Maggie in their conversation. She was too busy scanning the storefronts and market tables to pay much attention. Sun, rain, and wind made a decent hat essential for a sailor, and Maggie was making do with the silly little hat she brought from Gloucester. She only hoped the expense wouldn't lighten her purse more than she could afford.

When the younger lads pulled over to study a table of gold chains and jeweled garters, Maggie smiled and shook her head as she continued on.

Matching her stride, Matthew said, "Do you not approve?"

"I only think 'tis frivolous. What use have sailors for jewels?"

"Show me a man aboard who's not spent all the coin in his purse on a filigree cloak pin or a half-dozen gold buttons. The captain may strut like a peacock, but we may not? Fie!"

She spotted a sign for a milliner and crossed the narrow road to the shop's front door, propped open to accept the fragrant summer breeze. She poked Matthew in the ribs. "I see no gold buttons upon that old doublet of yours."

"I spent my money foolishly enough when I first left home."

"And now?"

"Now, mayhap I'll spend it on you. What think you of this?" He plucked a red and yellow silk cap off its hook.

"Ridiculous." She tugged it out of his grasp and returned it to the wall. "I cannot afford it."

"Never mind the cost. What suits you?"

"Never mind the cost? You forget I have no income."

"But I have. What of this one?"

She placed her hand on his outstretched arm, urging him to stop. "You cannot buy me a hat. Everyone will know I did not pay for it myself."

"So? We are old friends. The lads and I oft buy trinkets for each other."

"Yet how easily friends may be confused for lovers."

He rolled his eyes. "This again."

"Yes, this again!" She darted a glance toward the back of the shop and lowered her voice. "This always! How can I make you understand? I do not take a single step without thirty men wondering where I am off to. If you think no one will notice you seeking me out, giving me gifts, meeting me after dark—"

"So let them notice! They speak of you when you're not about, you know—the things they would do if you chose one of them as your lover. But 'tis only because they may yet hope to be chosen. Choose, and they will relent."

He appeared sincere enough, but he couldn't believe his own words. After all, when he had assumed she was the captain's mistress, he had looked at her with nothing but contempt. If he truly thought her life would be easier if she bestowed her favor on one man over all the others, he was lying to himself.

His touch was tentative as he took her hand. She kept it limp, not wishing to encourage him, but unwilling to pull away. "Let them see it." He lifted their entwined fingers to his lips and kissed one knuckle, then another. "Let me be your choice. If there is no line between friends and lovers, as you say, why should we fear to cross it?"

His lips on her hand caused her mind to empty. Why was she resisting? Why did she care about anything other than the feel of his mouth on her skin?

No. The reason for her refusal was within reach, and she brought it back to the surface.

"I have nothing, Matthew. Nothing but the generosity of Captain Stokes. I have nowhere to go if that generosity dries up."

"You think I would leave you stranded on a pier?"

"Why should I doubt it? You stranded me before."

He let her hand drop. "Do not put your sister's blame on me. 'Twas she who forced us apart. I was a boy withal. Do you think I have not changed? Mayhap you think I *cannot* change!"

He could foist the blame on Elizabeth all he wanted, but it didn't alter the fact that he had left with no warning, no explanation, and no goodbye. "Prove to me that you can," she said. "I beg you."

If he was seeking pity or forgiveness, he would not find it until he deigned to acknowledge—to even hint at—his culpability. Did he not understand how she had suffered when he disappeared? How her crumbled hopes blew away on the same wind filling the *Merrow's* sails when it set forth from Bristol without her?

Matthew shook his head. "I knew it. I will never be good enough for the Honorable Margaret Donwell." He glared at her as he turned to leave. "Buy your own sodding hat."

Before she could call him back, he was already lost in the market lane.

11

TWO DOZEN UNMARKED bags crowded the hold.

Maggie discovered them when she did her tally of the *Merrow's* assets the morning after they left Boston. Neither the humble brown ledger nor the beautiful green tome of lies contained any mention of the new cargo, which someone had snuck aboard while she was arguing with Matthew in a milliner's shop.

Hermelin dozed atop the bags, round and white as a limestone pebble. She poked the makeshift bed, eliciting a yawn and a stretch from the indolent cat, and found the contents to be soft. Wool, most likely. Another bag squatted on the floor nearby, making a wider footprint than the bags of wool. She groped at it until she could identify it as some kind of grain. There was nothing improper about good English cargo. Why smuggle it aboard?

The overcast sky had given up holding the rain in, so she hurried to put her straw hat back on as she emerged from the dim hold. Her new head covering wasn't ideal protection from the weather, but it kept the drops off her face. It was also ugly and crudely made, but being that she had haggled with the seller and bought it with her own coin, it was her new favorite item of clothing.

None of the officers were on deck. Thinking she might find answers in the navigation room, she started up the stairs, wishing anyone other than Matthew was at the helm this morning.

Matthew's gaze flicked to hers before returning to the hazy horizon.

After their quarrel yesterday, they had little to say to each other. That is, Maggie was willing to speak to him, provided he spoke first. But Matthew must know where they were going, and curiosity overwhelmed pride.

She faced him, leaning her back against the sterncastle railing. "What is our heading?"

He kept his eyes forward. "Southeast."

"And our object?"

At length, he answered, "We're to intercept a Spanish cargo ship bound for the New World."

"I did not think the *Merrow* stalked her quarry in such a way. How do you know where it will be?"

He shook his head, flicking water droplets from the brim of his hat. "I've told you all I ken."

She lingered for a moment, wondering if she should say more. Bringing up their argument would only reignite it, she knew, but tiptoeing around on a ship this size was exhausting.

For the first time, he looked at her. "Did you sleep well?"

So that was to be his apology. "Well enough. And you?"

"My sleep is oft troubled of late."

"A shame, when you have so little opportunity. What is it keeps you awake?"

The brim of his hat tipped down, obscuring one eye. "Can you not guess?" he murmured.

The hairs on her arms stood on end as a peculiar tingling warmth ignited in her core. His eyes bore into hers as he leaned forward on the wheel. Maggie felt herself being lured toward him.

Hang him! A few mumbled words and a significant stare, and she was dough in his hands.

Boots on the boards below made the railing against her back shudder. She looked over her shoulder to find Stokes emerging onto the quarterdeck, his face turned up into the falling rain as if it confounded him.

It felt like providence for him to appear at the precise moment when she needed to escape Matthew's draw. She swept down the stairs, bidding Matthew "anon."

Stokes lurked in the officer's corridor to stay out of the rain, his fingers on the last few buttons of his doublet. "How may I be of service?" he said as he shrugged it off. The white shirt underneath was speckled with raindrops.

"You will not climb the ratlines in this weather, will you?"

"Only with your permission."

"But the wet ropes... Your hands..."

He held up his hands and appraised the calloused palms. "Methinks they are a trifle rough, but I have not had a complaint."

To preempt another sarcastic comment, she said what she had come down here to say. "I cannot find record of the cargo brought on in Boston."

"What cargo?"

She stared at him, confused. "What cargo? Why, a score of bags that were not there yesterden!"

"I assure you, we brought on no cargo."

"Certes, such a lack of cargo takes up a great deal of space in the hold. 'Tis out in the open where anyone may see it."

He grunted. "I gather Osborne failed to instruct you not to see it."

"May I not be privy to whatever scheme is underway?" she said. "If you intend for me to one day relieve him of the burden of the purser duties, should I not be in your confidence just as he is?"

"Osborne is my second mate. He has earned his place in my confidence."

She wanted to press him, to ask what she could do to earn the same right. Instead, she gambled and said nothing. As she hoped, Stokes began to fidget a few seconds into the silence. She waited, blinking, until he heaved a sigh.

"I will not tell you the name of our employer, nor the name of his client," he said, his voice clipped. "We are tasked with intercepting a ship as it leaves Spain. The cargo in our hold will be exchanged for whatever Spanish goods our employer has bargained for. When the exchange is finished, we return to Boston and wash our hands of the business."

"You find it distasteful?"

"Any interaction with the Spanish is distasteful. I would sooner plunder them than cooperate with them."

"Then they know we are coming. When you say intercept, you mean rendezvous."

"Aye."

"Why the air of secrecy? There is no violence, no theft..."

"Smuggling has its own risks. I am careful to avoid notice by both Spain and England, and I strive to protect the identities of those involved in the deal. If 'twere legal not to pay tariffs, they would not need us." He swung his doublet from the tips of his fingers like a pendulum. "The fewer members of my crew who know the details, the safer the deal and the safer my men."

It was not as much information as she had wished, but it was more than she deserved. Maggie was no one, and she had no right to demand his trust.

"Thank you," she said.

He almost smiled, for the first time since she had begun to hound him. "Thank me? For making you complicit?"

"For entrusting me with the safety of your crew."

He regarded her for a long moment. She struggled to hold his gaze, tempted every second to shy away from his unwavering attention. "Is there aught else?" he said. "I had hoped to complete my exercise before we encounter our... friends." His hold tightened on the doublet in his fist.

"Why do you do that?" she asked, waving at the doublet.

"What, pray?"

"Why dress in your cabin, only to undress out here?"

He fixed her with a wicked smile. "You require me to move about the ship half-dressed?"

Her face burned. "I require nothing!" Maggie did not often curse two men on the same day, but both Stokes and Matthew seemed hellbent on driving her mad. "I only meant it seems impractical."

He considered, lips pursed, before holding out his doublet to her. She took it as a reflex, only realizing what she had done once it was already in her hand. With a few practiced motions, Stokes tugged the hem of his shirt out of the waistband of his breeches and slipped it over his head.

It was impossible not to look at him. He stood there for a moment, posing, daring her to do just that.

"'Tis practical enough, methinks," he said, answering the question she had forgotten she'd asked. "If I leave my cabin already unclothed, I'm not like to get such a pretty blush." He smiled at her, then draped his shirt across her outstretched arm and bounded down the quarter deck stairs, the rain slicking his bare back.

Irksome devil. She glared down at the clothing in her arms. A cool wind sent drizzle under the brim of her hat to splatter against her hot cheeks, only proving what he had said: she was scarlet as a beet.

With a sinking feeling, Maggie cast her eyes toward the helm, only a few feet above her. From this low vantage, she could see the brim of Matthew's hat. There was no way he hadn't heard. She stomped down the corridor and flung Stokes's clothes into his cabin through the gap in the door, in no mood to add "laundress" to her list of unpaid duties.

Late in the afternoon, a ship emerged from the mist. It was big and sturdy, not beautiful, but well built and prepared to withstand the weeks of trans-Atlantic travel required to reach the

Spanish Main. As it approached, it raised a white flag with a barbed red cross. It was a question: which king owns your loyalty?

Captain Stokes ordered the raising of a plain yellow silk flag, one she hadn't seen before. It was apparently the answer the Spanish ship was looking for, because it altered its course to slide alongside the *Merrow*.

Aside from the officers and a few chosen sailors, the deck was deserted. Coulthurst dropped the last oilskin bag into the waiting pinnace. Driscoll and MacLoughlin hung on the pulley ropes, preparing to lower the pinnace into the water.

Maggie perched on the quarter deck stairs, looking through the railing like a naughty child peeping through the banister long after bedtime. She waited for Stokes to send her away, but his attention was on the approaching ship.

"The pinnace is loaded," Padraig said as he walked up to stand beside the captain.

"We await the *commandante*, then."

His posture was more rigid than usual, the only outward sign he was ill at ease. An eerie quiet blanketed the *Merrow*. Maggie pictured the men below, enjoying their banishment by smoking and gambling, or catching an extra hour of sleep. If questioned, they could say they had seen nothing.

The two ships kept their distance, close enough to shout at, but accessible to each other only by boat. Three men stood at the railing, dressed in dark clothing with black, broad-brimmed hats.

The man in the center raised his hand. "*Hola!*" His voice carried over the choppy water with more clarity than Maggie would have expected. "Blessings from Santa Eugenia!"

Stokes braced his hands on the railing and called back, "Greetings from Señor Amarillo."

"*Bien!*" The Spanish *commandante* said something to his mate, then turned forward again. "We send boat!"

"Aye," Stokes agreed. He gestured to his waiting men, who positioned the heavy pinnace and lowered it into the water. Stokes tilted his head toward Padraig. "You are armed?" Padraig nodded once. "Go to."

The three laborers and the first mate climbed down into the pinnace. Across the way, the Spanish boat already bobbed in the swells, a half-dozen oars making it crawl insect-like across the water's surface.

Maggie raised herself over the railing to watch their progress.

"*Miren!*" she heard the Spanish captain say. She glanced up to see him looking at her. "*Tienen una puta. Cree que está disponible?*" His lieutenants chuckled.

One leaned over the railing as if to see her better. "*Oye, señor!*" he yelled. "*Cuánto cuesta la hembra?*"

Stokes whipped his head around and spotted her by the stairs. "Leave the deck," he told her.

"What did he say?"

"*Now.*"

Her heartbeat quickened. She had yet to witness him lose his composure, but the menacing growl in his voice told her he was about to. Alarmed, she ducked around the corner into the galley.

The vantage through the tiny square windows in the galley was awful, even when she pulled a chair over to get a better look. The Spanish ship's bowsprit was visible, but the boats in the water were out of view.

Lloyd watched her from his seat at one of the tables, his face pale and drawn and a hunk of bread in front of him. A stomach ailment had kept him in bed most of the morning, but he seemed to be putting on a brave face. "How fares the deal?"

"Impossible to say. I only saw them launch the boats before I was banished."

"Banished?"

"One of the Spaniards said something the captain did not like. Did you know he spoke Spanish?"

He gave a laborious shrug. "I am not surprised. He's the sort of man who would prefer to meet his enemy on an even footing."

Maggie huffed with frustration and climbed down off the chair. It was no use; she would just have to wait until the business was complete. She returned the chair to its place and sat, propping her elbows on the table. "Go back to bed, Master Lloyd, if you feel so ill."

"I'm fine."

He didn't look fine. She sighed, knowing better than to argue. "Why does he hate the Spanish so?"

"More than a fortnight aboard and you've not heard the tale?" He leaned forward like a storyteller. "The late Master Stokes was killed when our young man was only a boy. Murdered by a Spaniard."

Maggie made the sign of the cross for the dead man. "How? Pirates?"

Lloyd shook his head. "They were returning from the Orient and sailed right into a skirmish—you remember, Essex's last expedition." He stopped himself and gave a weak chuckle. "Nay, you would not remember; you were but a child."

"My late husband sailed with Essex. Why did Master Stokes not stay away from the battle?"

"They were not given the chance. The boat was captured off the coast of Spain before they knew of it."

Maggie screwed up her face in disgust. "They captured an innocent merchant ship and killed only its master? For what purpose? If they suspected sabotage, they should have taken the whole crew prisoner."

"Aye, but they found no evidence of it. They were ready to let them go, in fact. 'Tis said Master Stokes angered the Spanish captain somehow. The man ran him through, then sailed away." He pantomimed the sword's thrust and the ship's retreat with two waves of one hand. "'Twas no act of war, but a murder in cold blood. And with young Stokes on board, to boot."

"But what reason did the captain have to kill an innocent man?"

"Behaving honorably is a choice, my dear. Some men are just… cruel."

And that cruelty had changed the course of a boy's life.

"What became of the elder Stokes's ship, I wonder?"

Lloyd stuck out his lower lip. "I cannot say as I have ever heard. The captain was yet a mite green when I came aboard. I would never have dreamed of prying. What I know is little more than fishwife gossip."

They fell silent, Maggie too distracted by the story and Lloyd too miserable for either to attempt further conversation. She wondered how young Stokes had reacted, whether his mother had been there to comfort him. How had he transformed from fatherless child to commander of an infamous pirate's ship?

Through the soles of her feet, Maggie felt the thuds and scrapes of activity on deck. She rose from the table and dragged her chair back toward the window. The Spanish ship wasn't where she expected it to be. She pressed her cheek against the glass to catch it disappearing into the mist.

She hopped down and turned to Lloyd. "Have you any need of me? I would like to help shift the cargo if the captain will allow it."

He waved her off and gave her a thin smile. "Go to. I will see you anon for dogwatch."

She had a feeling she would be cooking tonight.

A vertigo-inducing hole yawned over the dark depths of the hold, and MacLoughlin was dropping heavy-looking sacks into it.

She guessed someone caught them below, to prevent the bags from splitting open upon hitting the floor. As far as volume went, it was a much smaller amount of goods than Maggie expected. Only this in exchange for all that wool and grain? Wool was bulky, of course. Whatever was in these bags was small and costly.

Osborne oversaw the toiling sailors, a piece of paper clenched in his fist. She skirted the open hatch to ask him what she could do.

"Padraig checked it twice. 'Tis all accounted for." He examined the paper anyway, as if worried Padraig had missed something.

"Then we are bound for Boston again?"

"Aye, and most the crew'll get shore leave again in payment for sittin' on their arses."

She knew he couldn't help his surliness, but the more he grumbled, the more tempted she was to bait him. "Alack," she said, heaving a dramatic sigh, "if I had only known I could do no work and receive my regular pay, I would never have offered to help."

"Well, milady, as tha've been so awful helpful, I've a mind to double thy pay." He planted his fists on his hips, leaning in to share a secret. "By the by, whene'er a sailor shows me he's got a quick tongue, I set him to cleanin' the privy, for it shouldn't tek him long."

With that revolting threat hanging in the air, he flashed her a tight-lipped smile and stomped up the sterncastle stairs.

12

AFTER SUPPER, MAGGIE sat with the band, too tired from standing in for Lloyd to play much. The clouds hid the moon, but they no longer threatened rain. A cool breeze ruffled the wispy hairs at her nape.

The lads on watch—Matthew's mates—were at their posts, but with little to do other than keep the ship on her course, they chatted amongst themselves or sang along to the music. It was a comfortable, companionable atmosphere. Ever since Boston, she felt she had passed over some invisible threshold. The crew were all less wary of her, more friendly. It had taken almost a month for them to get used to her, and for her to get used to who she was becoming.

When the men made moves to light their pipes or find an out-of-the-way corner to sleep until middle watch, Maggie stood and stretched her back. A dice game had cropped up near the starboard guns. Someone was scaling the foremast ratlines. Matthew was at the helm.

She spotted Captain Stokes at the port railing, facing the sea. Lloyd's sad tale of the fatherless boy niggled at her, a painful sliver she couldn't remove. Before she had made the conscious choice, her feet were carrying her across the deck.

He sent her a sidelong glance, but neither spoke for a while. For her part, Maggie was content to gaze out over the black waves tipped with moonlight.

In the daytime, the ocean stretched from horizon to horizon wherever she looked, an unfathomable world of wonder and danger. But at night, when the black of the sea met the black of the sky, the world was small, contained, like the *Merrow* had slipped into an empty bottle. It should frighten her, the knowledge that anything could lurk out there beyond the limits of her human eyes. Instead, she chose to believe there was nothing. Beyond the railing, the sea dropped away and there was only black and stars. The ship was all that existed within this celestial sphere.

"Methinks you are falling in love."

His words chilled her blood. How did he know about Matthew? She wouldn't have called it 'falling in love,' but perhaps someone had seen them together in Boston and misinterpreted what was happening between them. "Sir?" she said.

"That look in your eyes a moment ago. You are falling in love with the sea."

Relief flooded her chest.

Stokes leaned his forearms on the rail and stared out at the water. "It is unlike anything else, is it not? The mountains and the valleys of the crashing waves. The silver stain of the moonlight. The bleeding heart of the sunrise. The vastness. The emptiness."

"I did not take you for a poet."

"I am no poet. I have sailed all my life—I have had many years to write my love letter. For some, sailing is employment. But ask Padraig, ask Pratt or Davies… The sea is our first love. We are spoiled for anything else."

His voice was soft, dreamy, nothing like the captain she thought she knew. She mirrored his posture, letting herself relax. The dew on the railing soaked through her sleeves.

"How did you learn to speak Spanish?"

Stokes chuckled, surprised at the abrupt change of subject. "I would like to tell you I am clever enough to have picked it up during my travels, but alas, I must be truthful. I hired a tutor."

An image of Stokes hunched over a quill and paper, a stern old Spaniard menacing him with a hazel switch, made her swallow a laugh. "A tutor?"

"The winters are long and I am not made to be idle."

"So you fill your time with learning? I can well imagine a scholar dreaming of being a pirate captain, but the reverse is less creditable."

"You do not believe me? Put me to the test."

"What did the Spaniards say of me this afternoon?"

He attempted a casual shrug. "'Tis not worth repeating."

"Yet it was worth banishing me belowdecks?"

"It was worth challenging the bastards. Not at the expense of my crew's safety and the success of our mission, however."

"It must have been some grave insult, then. I can well imagine what it was."

Whore. Neither of them spoke the word aloud, but it lingered in the air like a wisp of smoke.

"I despise such talk," Stokes said, sighing. "'Tis not the speech of a gentleman."

"A man may fashion himself a gentleman and act like a knave." It was just as Lloyd had said earlier that day: *Behaving honorably is a choice.*

Her mind went to Robert. What would she be doing now if Robert had not tossed her future onto that gaming table? Likely casting about for a new husband, someone to save her from becoming her aunt. Robert had given her myriad opportunities to put herself under his protection. He had been a relentless, fleet-footed madman with the endurance of a god. Naïve Maggie had assumed he would tire of the chase, that her polite demurs and abject refusals would make him stop.

Never, never, cried Apollo.

Yet, standing here on a mild summer night, enveloped by salt air and velvet dark, cradled in the *Merrow's* arms, she could not bring herself to feel pity for her sacrifice. She only wanted to enjoy this rare moment of peace.

He was right: she was falling in love.

Stokes stirred at her left. Twice now she had allowed herself to drift into a trance with him only inches away. She recalled a family trip to the seaside when she was a girl. The tide was out, and she spent hours watching the tiny silver fish trapped in the tide pools. She took off her shoes and stockings to wade in the shallow water. If she stood stone-still for as long as she could bear it, the fish would swim over and around her bare toes, as if she were nothing more than a pale hunk of driftwood. The moment she moved, they darted away.

"What thoughts have you so silent?"

His tone was gentle and low, as if he knew he had startled her the last time he broke their silence. She turned her head to find him watching her. In the darkness, she hardly recognized him. Shadows disfigured his face, and he sounded like a stranger. For some mad reason, she wanted him to smirk at her and make a glib comment, not ask her to share her cares with him.

"I was doing sums," she lied. "I was wondering what the cargo we brought from Boston was worth, and what sort of treasure we traded it for."

He rummaged in his purse and held up something small and black. "This sort of treasure."

In the dark, it looked so much like a dead beetle she recoiled. "What is that?"

"Cacao. From the Spanish Main."

She had heard of it, but she had never imagined something so valuable could be so unappealing. Intrigued, she dared to take it from him to get a closer look.

The thing was just as disappointing up close. It was the size of a plum pit, dark brown, with the texture and the smell of a dried bean. It weighed almost nothing. This was what a dozen bags of wool had purchased?

Stokes interpreted her scowl. "'Tis nothing to look at, but 'tis almost as dear as gold, pound for pound."

She shook her head, finding it hard to believe. Still, it was somewhat thrilling to know no one of her acquaintance back home had ever seen one of these, let alone held one in their hand.

She held it out to Stokes with reluctance. "Keep it," he said. "'Tis a bonus. On top of your regular pay." He flashed her the half-smile of a man too pleased with himself, then bowed and bid her goodnight.

Maggie remained at the rail, rolling the cacao bean between her fingers as she waited for the sound of his boots to stop at the door of his cabin.

It was probably a coincidence, but she couldn't help but think about her quip to Osborne earlier. Did Osborne tell him everything she said? Did others? It was a sobering reminder that if she slipped, he would know.

The last hour of the night watches was the quietest. Half the crew would be asleep, and the other half would struggle to remain vigilant until the eight bells relieved them of duty. Snores popped up all over the ship, proof that not everyone had succeeded.

A board creaked behind her, and Maggie slipped the cacao bean into her purse while she turned her head. In the dim lantern light spilling onto the main deck, Matthew approached, his steps light and deliberate. He put a finger to his lips and tilted his head over his left shoulder, gesturing to where the pinnace was lashed to the deck.

She looked around, scanning the rigging for good measure, but aside from a few dozing lads dotted around the ship, no one was about. She followed him to the far side of the pinnace. He pulled her down in the dark, narrow space between the boat and the starboard rail, and she sank onto her knees to be at his level.

Every part of her warned her this was a bad idea.

"You should not have left your post." She mouthed the words, but still she flinched at the volume of her voice.

"What were you and Stokes talking about?"

"Naught of importance. The cargo trade today." Something about the conversation seemed significant, but explaining that to Matthew would be foolish.

He rubbed his thumb over a metallic object in his hand. "Will you forgive me?"

"Forgive you for what?"

"You well ken. For losing my temper the other day in Boston."

Ah, yes: the least grievous of the sins for which she was awaiting an apology.

"You're right. We must be careful who sees us. But when you're within reach, I must touch you. I see you from afar, and my feet must carry me to you. I cannot bear to be so near and so distant." He held out the thing in his hand. "'Tis only a trifle, and undeservin' of such a beauty."

She took it from him and held it close to her face so she could make it out. It was a four-leaf flower molded in silver, about the size of a sovereign, with a blue gem in the center. It was soldered to the end of a pin about the length of her finger. If it was real silver and held a real stone, it would have cost him at least a month's wages.

But Matthew was a pirate, and she doubted any money had exchanged hands.

She enclosed the brooch in her fist to hide her trembling. His speech made every inch of her skin come alive, raising goose pimples and making her face flush. It was exactly the sort of thing Lysander would say to woo Hermia. Had he rehearsed it like an actor in a play? She didn't care.

A man who felt so deeply, who wanted her so desperately, must also feel guilt for wronging her in the past, mustn't he? He had eight years to push it from his mind, and only a few weeks to address it. She could wait a few weeks more. She thought she could wait months if he only kept looking at her with such worship.

"We must not linger." It was what she was supposed to say, and before tonight she would have believed it. But a seductive voice in the back of her mind had awakened from some deep slumber to assure her, *What harm would it do?*

She mustn't heed it. Stokes was watching. The entire crew was watching. If they weren't careful, she would lose the *Merrow*. She would lose the sea.

She looked into Matthew's dark eyes, and for a moment she thought he would relent, agree they had tarried too long, and send her off to bed.

Naïve Maggie.

His hand gripped the back of her neck, trapping her lips against his. He covered her mouth in fierce ownership, leaning over her, holding her against him. The familiar taste of him filled her senses. It was not a conscious choice to kiss him back—it was her body, her long-latent feelings for him, the memory of it. This was a dance she knew by heart, step for step. His lips were just as she remembered, the shape of his mouth imprinted in her mind. The smell of his skin brought images of the tree, the sunlight cascading through the summer leaves and landing in puddles all around them.

What she did not remember was his insistence, his appetite, his strength. There were new sensations within her own body as well. An unexpected, unbearable hunger grew in her core and spread to the bottoms of her feet, the tips of her fingers. She lifted herself up to meet him, rising on her knees until they were of an equal height.

He cupped her face between his hands, his rough thumbs scraping her cheeks. He slid his tongue against hers, sighed into her mouth, bit her lip. He was not gentle. There was no time.

A bell pealed across the sleeping sea.

Matthew and Maggie sprang apart. He didn't linger, didn't look at her, only climbed over her and returned to the helm, making no sound.

The bell tolled eight times to mark the beginning of middle watch. Maggie remained behind the pinnace while the sleeping sailors stirred, her skin hot and her lips swollen.

13

A BOUT OF still, sweltering weather chased away the storm clouds, making their progress slow and miserable. They sailed into Boston two days after encountering the Spanish ship. By then, the lads were surly and tense.

They also hadn't eaten well. Lloyd rose from his sickbed on the third day out from Boston to help Maggie with supper, but the bulk of the work still fell to her. She developed a new reverence for the cook's role on a ship this size.

Being launched from the frying pan into the fire distracted her from the memory of the kiss.

If she had the time, she would have analyzed each breath, each shiver, each heartbeat. She would have fretted and blamed and yearned and flagellated until the memory became pale and threadbare. She knew she would, because she had done it before. *Had she done it right? Did he enjoy kissing her? What did a handsome lad like Matthew Kent see in shy little Margie Donwell?*

This kiss was nothing like those. Those had been chaste, timid, a child's notion of a kiss. Now they were different people altogether. Pain, duty, discovery, and worry had hollowed them out and stuffed them back up, reshaping them into their present forms.

Those innocent children could not have guessed a simple kiss could be dark. Treacherous. Excruciating.

When she stumbled down the gangplank onto the Boston wharves, tripping into Mullins, the pennywhistle player, he caught her with a laugh and invited her to the Seely Hare. She thanked him and explained she was on her way to the church. "Scurlock's sermons leave something to be desired, and if there is a sacrament today, I should take it. The Lord knows I am fair drenched in sin."

They laughed together about the sorry state of her immortal soul, although he didn't know the half of it.

The thin strains of a choir streamed out the open doors of Boston's church, something like a goose with its squat body and its tall bell tower. Peeking inside, she gathered the priest was about halfway through the service. No one would go in or out for at least a half hour. She meandered around the building to the churchyard, feigning interest in the centuries-old architecture, until she found a shadowy corner where she could await Matthew.

Maggie should never have agreed to his risky, foolish request. It didn't matter that the captain's rule only extended the length of the gangway; anyone who saw them together on shore would scrutinize them at sea, waiting for them to slip. But his kiss addled her senses like a drug. A drug she would risk anything to taste again.

Matthew appeared a quarter hour later, peering around the corner of the church wall in search of her. She recognized the unstable gait of a sailor too long at sea, but he recovered his land legs much faster than she did.

He gathered her into his arms and kissed her until the hum of chattering parishioners spilled out the church doors. They struggled out of the undertow of their desire, giggling like children, and Matthew took her arm in search of another trysting place.

There was an inn one street over from the church called Friar's Folly. Matthew held the door open for her, and she ducked into the dim, low-ceilinged room. A layer of smoke drifted at head height, the result of a poorly drafting oven, but the floors were clean and there were open tables. Maggie was too hungry to be picky.

She envisioned them tucked behind an out-of-the-way table, chatting, holding hands, scooting their chairs close together until their thighs touched. She was about to gesture to a secluded corner, but Matthew had already walked up to the bar to find the landlord.

The old man had a curtain of shoulder-length gray hair, and both his nose and his ears were too large for his head. He stared at them, eyes narrowed in suspicion. "Aye?" he said in a wavering, high-pitched voice.

"God save you, gaffer," Matthew said, polite and cheerful. "We are passing through, and my goodly wife is fatigued from the journey. Have you a room to let for a while, that she may rest?"

Maggie stared at him. Dining in an ordinary was dangerous enough, but getting a room was madness. What if someone from the ship saw them descend together?

The landlord narrowed his beady eyes. "This is your wife?"

"She is the Elizabeth to my Zechariah." He put his arm around her and beamed down at her, an alarming display. She offered the old man a shaky smile to play along.

With a sniff, the landlord nodded. "Come." He tottered toward the winding staircase in the rear of the dining room and lifted his heavy feet to meet each steep step. Maggie followed him, feeling her patience ebb with each tread, and Matthew brought up the rear. When the old man turned the corner out of sight, Matthew reached up and caressed her backside through her skirts. She swatted his hand away.

The man brought them to the first room at the top of the stairs. There was a bed and a table, nothing posh, but as Maggie had noted downstairs, it all appeared well maintained. The blankets were clean enough, and the bed was even and plump from a recent stuffing. The tallow candles dotting the room were tall and new, and the soot stains behind them showed evidence of being scrubbed recently.

"Aught else?" the old man barked once Matthew and Maggie were out of the stairwell.

Matthew fished in his coin purse and placed a few pennies in the man's gnarled hand. "Dinner and some beer."

The room was silent for a breath while the old man frowned at the coins. Matthew added three more, and the wrinkled fist closed around them. The man turned to make the laborious trek back down the stairs.

"God bless you!" Matthew called after him.

"Ought we not to dine below?" Maggie whispered. "Suppose his knees give out the next time he comes up." She passed it off as a joke, all the while hoping he would take her up on it.

"If he has no one to fetch and carry for him, 'tis no man's fault but his own." Matthew closed the door. The clunk of the latch falling into place echoed in her chest.

"What was all that about Elizabeth and Zechariah?"

"Elizabeth, the cousin of Mary? She was barren—"

"I know the story."

"Boston is full of zealots," he explained. "Calvinists, most of them. I hoped it'd soften him. Seems I was right."

"He did not need softening. We could have eaten below. 'Twould have been less costly."

He came around the table and put his arm around her waist, drawing her against him. "I would have paid a king's ransom to be alone with you."

His kisses had lost their feverishness, now he had leisure to savor her. It surprised her how easily they fell into this routine. Their first kiss at the respective ages of fourteen and seventeen had been halting and awkward, although they had improved with frequent practice. This kiss was like a continuation, as if eight years hadn't changed everything.

A gradual shift in intention made his breathing ragged, his hands restless. He unbuttoned the collar of her shirt and trailed his fingertips across her collarbone, sliding the fingers of his other hand under her coif to tangle in her hair. He fisted his hand and tugged her head to the side, then bit the soft skin where her neck met her shoulder.

She made a sound of pain and surprise, but he kissed the spot, urging her to forgive him. He pushed aside the fabric of her shirt and kissed the curve of her breast above her bodice. She arched her back, and her intake of breath brought her skin up to meet him.

She felt the brush of his teeth right before the sharp burst of pain.

"'Sblood!" Maggie recoiled, touching her fingers to the sore spot. "Do you demand a pound of my flesh?"

"What?"

He would not have read the play she referenced, and he had never been impressed by her reading, anyway. "Nothing," she said.

Unperturbed, he trailed his hands down her hips and grasped her skirts, hiking them up one fistful at a time.

She shoved his arms away.

"What? What is wrong?" Matthew's face was full of surprise.

"You have no business under there."

"No business? That is the only business I plan to attend to today. More than once, if I can manage it."

He slid one hand up her thigh and around to her backside, while the other cupped the back of her head. He kissed her hard as he propelled her backwards. The back of her legs hit the bed, and she plopped down onto the mattress as he towered over her.

Some alchemy was at work in her stomach, and with a sickening twist, panic displaced pleasure. She ducked under his arm and dashed to the other side of the table.

Once she had put a piece of furniture between them, she could breathe again.

"I fear we do not see eye to eye." She redid the button at her collar and arranged the fabric so her skin, and the pink bite mark, no longer showed.

"What did you think we were doing?"

"Enjoying each other's company!"

"Then why did I get a room?"

"Aye, why did you?"

"Because you're nigh obsessed with that sodding rule! You'll scarce look at me because you're afeared Stokes'll think I fucked you!"

"And if you had your way, he would be right!"

"We are not on the ship. We may do whatever we please."

"Not so! Mayhap what we do in this room matters not, but our encounters aboard the *Merrow* do!"

"As I say! So why do you deny me?"

She stared, struggling to understand his logic. "Did you plan to bed me here, then ignore me when we returned to the ship?"

"Nay, Margaret." He injected his voice with the gentle, pleading tone one uses on stubborn children. "But have we any other choice? If we may not come together on the *Merrow,* our only chance is now."

"You knew me as a child. You knew I would not give myself to you before we were married."

"But now you have been married."

"That changes naught! Do you believe I have transformed into some wanton siren who lures men to my bed?"

"Yours are not the chaste kisses of a virgin."

Her blood froze in her veins. All the time she had been enjoying the taste and feel of him, the nearness of him, the memories it inspired, he had thought it a precursor to something more. He thought *she* had been seducing *him.*

Maggie sank down into a chair beside the table.

Good, chaste women did not kiss in churchyards. They did not follow men to whom they were not married up to a rented room, and they did not allow them to bite their naked flesh. Perhaps there was some truth to the notion that widows fall into inevitable lascivious behaviors. Perhaps the famous bloom of youth had, in fact, faded, and that was all it took to become wanton in a man's eyes.

He crossed to the table and knelt in front of her, covering her clasped hands with his palm. "'Tis like a madness, Margaret. You have taken control of me. I will await your command, though I wait in agony."

She looked down at his broad hand, seeing nothing through the haze of wretchedness. She didn't wish agony upon him, but what he asked of her was no trivial thing. What would it cost her to give in to his desire, to be used like her husband had used her? Could she transcend the pain, the indignity? And what would she gain? The little flip in her belly indicating desire, the pleasant sensation between her legs making her bold and reckless? Only *that* as payment?

These questions hounded her steps as she returned, alone, to the *Merrow*. Somewhere along the road, as the church bell tolled in its tall tower, she felt the familiar ache of loneliness, the longing to unburden herself and the painful reminder she had no one to tell. The same ache had accompanied her girlhood woes as well, woes too trivial for her family, too personal for the servants. She thought of the night of Robert's betrayal, how Captain Stokes had lifted her out of her despair. It was one of the few times in her life she felt heard.

Not that she could tell him *this*. The idea of losing the captain's trust, along with her new position and friends and freedom, made her throat tight.

Keeping the truth to herself wasn't a perfect plan. Others knew—Leigh, maybe even Driscoll. The captain was bound to uncover their treachery.

Unless she could convince him there was nothing there.

The officers ate at six o'clock, between first and second dogwatch. When Burney stepped up to the worktable to receive the tray of food, Maggie smiled at him with as much maternal warmth as she could summon. "I will take it up."

The heavy trenchers clattered on the tray as she climbed up to the quarterdeck. Propping the tray on her knee and stabilizing it against the wall, she freed her hand to knock on the captain's cabin door.

"Come."

The door swung open with a nudge of her hip. The image greeting her was of Stokes, Padraig, and Osborne sitting around the table and staring at her as if she had risen from the dead. She supposed she had little in common with the twelve-year-old boy who usually did this duty.

She swept into the room and served each man his trencher. They had already opened a bottle of something sweet and hoppy, a quality brew she was sure stayed hidden here, out of sight of the rabble.

"Maggie!" Stokes said, breaking the uneasy silence. "An unparalleled pleasure."

She removed the tray and stepped back, steeling herself for what she was about to say. Before she could begin, Stokes pushed back his chair and hopped up. "Sit, pray." He was already moving to a cabinet to retrieve a fourth goblet. He seemed flustered, unsure of what to do with her, and she felt guilty for surprising him.

"Nay, sir, I beg you, trouble yourself not. Only, an it please you..."

She faltered when Stokes placed the empty goblet on the table. He didn't fill it, but neither did he sit back down. Instead, he looked at Padraig and gestured with his head. Both mates rose to leave.

"Prithee, stay!" They froze, and she blushed. "I know what some of the crew say of me. It would not go well for me to be alone with the captain."

She half-hoped someone would deny it. *Nay, Maggie, not a soul on this brig thinks you are the captain's whore.* Padraig and Osborne looked at each other, and Stokes only watched her.

After a short hesitation, Stokes replied, "I cannot censure a man's private thoughts, but I can snuff out slander. You have as much right as any member of my crew to a private audience, if you wish it."

It *would* be easier without his lieutenants. Her indecision must have showed on her face, because Padraig stood and said, "I fancy a breath of air." Osborne followed him out, muttering about an item he left in his cabin.

When they were alone, Maggie felt her courage waning. "Forgive me for this intrusion, sir. I am loath to delay your supper," she began.

"Not at all, my lady. Pray, continue delaying my supper with your apologies for delaying my supper."

He said it with a straight face, but she recognized the teasing tone—and the hallmark use of "my lady," which he brought out whenever her behavior became too genteel for his taste.

She gave him a weak smile and went on. "A thought has been troubling me—a truth that is not meant to be hidden, but may appear so. I came here to assure myself that you know of my connection to Matthew and Luke Kent." Pausing, she gave him the opportunity to confirm or deny it. When he did neither, she blustered on. "Matthew and Luke were the sons of my father's tenant. We played together as children." She gripped her tray in both hands. "At one time, Matthew and I fancied ourselves in love. As much as two children can be."

Stokes waited her out, stoic and silent, his face grim. She thought of his warning when he had caught her with Matthew that first day, and of his coded message at Midsummer. *So given, Daphne.*

If he hadn't known already, he had clearly guessed.

"It ended badly. I had not seen him all this while. The more time we spend renewing our friendship, the more uneasy I become. I felt it would be safer if you knew our history."

"Safer," he repeated.

"I would not have you think I cannot be trusted to adhere to your rules of order."

He braced his hand on his chair back and looked down at his knuckles. "My rules of order prohibit actions, not feelings. As I said before, I cannot censure a man's private thoughts."

"I have no feelings for him, private or otherwise. I cannot speak for him, but—"

"Take care, Maggie, lest time make a liar of you." He raised his head, and his expression revealed no hint of emotion. "Have you any further truths to reveal, or may we at last enjoy our cold supper?"

She shook her head, her stomach in knots. This was supposed to relieve her anxiety, not augment it. Only a fool would mistake Stokes's flippant response for apathy. There was a cold edge to his words that convinced her he could see through her scheme. By trying to convince him of her trustworthiness, had she stupidly cast suspicion upon it?

Maybe if she kept her head down for a while, stayed away from Matthew, avoided his heated looks and his clever traps. But that meant weaning herself off him, and denying herself the intoxicating thrill of being held and kissed and desired by a man she once knew how to love.

14

MAGGIE CRAWLED OUT from under the navigation room table. Dressed only in her shift with her frizzy hair escaping from a hasty braid, she dragged the sleeping mat and blanket up toward her belly and rolled them into a tight bundle, then shoved it into a bit of empty shelf beside her extra clothing.

Her daily attire hung on a peg the ship's carpenter, Hargreve, had installed for her. She pulled on her grayish stockings and donned her grayish shirt. Both had been white when she left Bristol. The petticoat followed, then the overskirt. She had long since abandoned the cage-like farthingale that had given her skirts a fashionable bell shape, donating the willow switches inside to Hargreve.

Last came the bodice. It was made to be worn over stays, but tightening a back-lacing corset on her own was an exercise in futility, so she stopped putting them on within the first week. She kept the bodice laced for the sake of ease, and she had tied extra string to each end of the laces so she could pull them tight from the front.

Her coppery hair fell down to her waist when she combed it out, which she did now, using the bone comb she had kept from her former life. She wound it into a low knot and secured it with her comb and a few pins. Over her hair, she placed the yellowing muslin coif that hugged her skull and covered her ears, and she secured her straw hat to it with a hatpin. Then, stepping into her scuffed and tattered leather slippers, she emerged onto the deck.

Her mates were on watch. Of course, they weren't *her* mates—someone daily reminded her she wasn't a member of the crew. But she spent every other evening with Davies and Engberg and O'Flaherty, and in her estimation, it made her an honorary member of their watch group. There was Burney, swabbing the deck with a bucket of filthy water. Inwood was on the forecastle deck, banging a hammer. Gillies was at the helm, which meant there would be no covert flirting this morning.

On deck, Davies was shouting up at Engberg, who straddled the main yard, his blond head bent over the rigging.

"If we leave it too late, we'll have naught to offer them!"

"Nay, too soon! We have carols in our heads for months and months." Engberg leaned back, using his body weight to tighten a knot.

"How are we then to have the practicing of an entire show, yeh straw-headed nedget?"

Maggie wandered down to the main deck to join them. "A show?"

Davies crossed his arms. "Carols for Yuletide."

"Last *Jul* was best," Engberg said from above. "Nine parties, and we played taverns between. He is thinking we made a name of ourselves and he wants we should practice more."

Maggie squinted up at him. "Starting now? 'Tis only August."

He raised his hands to head height and shook them in exasperation. "I tell him! Too soon! I will not have same songs singing in my head day and night for..." His fingers tallied the time. "Four months!"

Davies waved him off. "'Tis no hardship for real professionals. Besides, now's when we've got the time. When the ship docks, we'll be too busy scrambling for work and lodging to meet up and play." He watched Engberg lower his chest to the yardarm, swing his leg over, and drop to the deck. Davies's only occupation seemed to be to catch Engberg if he fell.

"Fancy playing a few tunes with us this winter, Maggie?" he said. "The right patron would pay handsomely for a girl musician."

"Nay, she will go home."

They hadn't said a word about Matthew, which boded well. The relationship remained a secret so far, surviving on whispers and glances until shore leave brought them together for a few hours. None of the crew assumed she and Matthew would lodge together when the *Merrow* docked for the winter.

She didn't assume it either. Matthew had yet to ask her.

Not that she would do it, she reminded herself. Busybody neighbors would tear her to shreds when they learned she was living in sin. She would be an outcast in civilized society, little better than a prostitute. She would find another way to survive.

He could have asked, though.

"Ship off the port stern!"

At the lookout's shouted alert, Burney dashed up the steps to summon the captain, who sauntered out of his cabin to give the order to come about. The *Merrow* yawed at Gillies's hard turn of the wheel, the tight ropes creaking as they rubbed against her masts. The watch bell's furious clanging summoned the other half of the crew. Each knew his job: some grabbed weapons, some manned the guns.

Maggie's job was to stay out of the way until there was gold to count.

No one expected the plucky Spanish ship to put up such a fight.

The boom of the guns had Maggie cowering in a corner of the galley, certain a cannonball would tear through the wall at any moment. There were shouts from all corners of the ship, and she braced herself to hear screams of pain from the men she had grown to care for. With Gillies in full view at the helm, was Matthew safer on the main deck? Davies was a small target, but Engberg wasn't. She blanched, thinking of Stokes's yellow hat splattered with red.

The disturbing images didn't go away until long after the victory cheers had subsided. While Digby, the surgeon, patched up minor injuries, Osborne summoned her to appraise the Spanish ship's cargo, and she solemnly followed him to the other ship. Matthew was already there, helping Padraig determine the ship's seaworthiness, and she felt an overwhelming swell of relief to see him whole and unharmed.

This was her crew, whether her name appeared on the roster or not, and her eyes welled up at how fiercely proud she was to be one of them. For six weeks, she absorbed every lesson Osborne taught her, improving his inefficient processes and making everyone's jobs easier, and she did it all in gratitude to Stokes. She had to have proven herself to them by now.

They limped up the Thames at sunset with a few new holes in the hull and their prize tagging along behind them. She found the captain on the forecastle deck and stood beside him for a moment, choosing her words carefully.

"If only I could be more helpful to you in London," she told him.

Stokes turned and raised an eyebrow, immediately suspicious. "How?"

"Osborne takes on the burden of fencing everything himself. 'Tis admirable, but he will not accept my aid. Mayhap he does not find my work satisfactory." It felt wrong to play so coy with him, but she let the sentence dangle in the air anyway, waiting for him to take the bait.

"I assure you, everyone knows you are quite competent."

"I am glad of it. Yet how may I show him I will not fail him?"

"Why are you so ardent in your wish to be involved with the sale of the prize?"

Her stomach flipped. Coyness had been the wrong tactic. "I have been this ship's purser in all but name for weeks, but this part of the role is being kept from me and I do not know why."

"Because you are not a member of this crew." His words stung, and he must have seen it on her face because he gentled his tone. "I do not deny that you have proven your worth, but our business partners are our most vital asset, and their secrecy must not be compromised. My men have taken an oath to protect this ship, and they understand the consequences they face if they fail to do so. How do they know you will not leave the ship at the next port and deliver a mile-long list of crimes to the nearest bailiff?"

Maggie's mouth hung open. "I would never! How can you say I have proven my worth and label me a traitor within the same breath?"

"I do not label you anything."

"Then I will take the oath. What is needed? A Bible? A sword? Let it be brought."

"No. Bringing you aboard was my decision. It was not my most popular one, as you no doubt have noticed. I cannot sign a female sailor into the ship's roster mid-journey without the approval of a majority of the crew. If they had known of you when they joined up, mayhap it would be different, but—"

"Put it to a vote." The lads knew better than to talk back to him, but she had learned how to push that boundary, realizing that as long as he matched her quip for quip, she would escape unscathed.

His expression told her she was flirting with the edge of his patience. "I know these men. If some seem content with the current state of things, they would fall to pieces as soon as you received a share of their plunder." He pressed his lips together. "This matter is settled."

Maggie remained at the rail as he descended the forecastle steps. Even as the spires of the city came into view, when she should have been reveling in anticipation of her first London shore leave, she stared at the water below. Like a playwright, she concocted scenes and monologues, defending her position with impassioned shrieks, begging on bended knee. The Stokes character never relented.

They would dock for the two days Hargreve estimated to complete the repairs. Lloyd would ensure there was something to eat at mealtimes, but aside from those tasked with guarding the ship, the crew had leave. Maggie itched to set foot on solid ground. All she could think about was finding an out-of-the-way place to gripe about Stokes with Matthew. She puttered about while the lads dashed off to indulge their vices, wondering how long it would take the skeleton crew to return.

They lurched down the road at half-past ten, Padraig and MacLoughlin hanging off each other and singing tuneless snippets of songs in their own language while the others laughed and herded them toward the ship. Maggie stood at the rail as they trudged up the gangplank, taking in their sloppy state.

Engberg coaxed Padraig toward the officers' quarters while the others headed below, doubtless to drink some more. Matthew split off from the group when he spotted Maggie.

She settled her tailbone against the rail and fixed him with a level gaze, pretending not to be furious about how much time she had wasted waiting for him.

"How now, little lambkin?" He braced himself on the railing with one hand on either side of her, trapping her against his body. He dipped his head, and she smelled the beer on his breath.

If anyone was watching, it would be easy to blame the overfamiliar behavior on his drunken state. She just had to play coy and rebuff him like she should rebuff any man who took the same liberties. Pretending to rebuff him would not prove difficult, since she was in no mood to indulge him, anyway.

"You passed a pleasant evening, I see." She dodged his kiss and pushed out of the cage of his arms.

"Do not be a shrew. Have you eaten? Let us find an inn, wherever you desire."

She planted her feet when he put his hand on her back. "I cannot leave with you!"

He glanced around and regarded the sailors who were on guard duty. Up on the forecastle deck, Driscoll and Leigh were lounging with pipes in hand while Coulthurst snored beside them. "These are my lads! They'll not say a word. Besides, 'tis the captain you fear, and I see him not. Let us flee before he returns." She turned her face so his lips landed on the edge of her jaw. "I will take you to the finest ordinary in London. Or…" He brushed his nose against her cheek, his breath warm on her face. "We could skip dinner altogether."

His words sent a shiver up her spine, and she drew in a deep breath to calm her runaway heart. With her last ounce of rational thought, she braced her hands against his chest, hoping if someone happened upon them, she would remember to feign disgust and push him away.

But as he flicked his tongue against the sensitive skin of her neck, her mind narrowed to a single thought: she never wanted him to stop.

That was why she surprised herself by saying, "I cannot." It was a reflex, a habit; her tongue knew its duty when the rest of her body did not.

Matthew made a frustrated growl in the back of his throat, but he didn't let her go. "Why do you still deny me?"

"Because I am not your wife."

"Marry me, then, for God's sake."

She did push him away. The sudden kiss of cool night air was a balm to her burning skin. "You are a fool, Matthew Kent."

He stared at her, uncomprehending. "I cannot bed you because you're not my wife, but I cannot make you my wife either?"

"Ah, mayhap you are not a fool after all!"

"Why must women be so disagreeable?"

"Why must men be so obtuse?"

"God's death, Margaret, what do you want me to do?"

"Is it such a mystery? Nay, 'tis I am the problem. Certes, every girl dreams of marrying a man who only asked her so he could bed her. I am being a stubborn romantic."

"That is not why I asked you."

"Forgive my mistake, but you can see how I might have misinterpreted your intention."

"I timed it poorly. Must you punish me for it?"

Poor timing? She would laugh if she were not so near crying.

He did not remember how overjoyed she had been when a young Matthew had laid out his plan for taking her away. He did not know how that memory had been a lifeline in the darkest part of the night for eight years. He could not know she had reshaped that memory, replacing the innocent boy with the seductive man, replacing the hill and the tree with the deck and the mast. She had heard him say it hundreds of times in her mind, but never as callously as tonight.

Must she punish him? No. But by God, she wanted to.

"You may find a bit of supper yet in the galley." She couldn't bear to look at him as she brushed past and climbed the stairs to the navigation room. She dared to glance back as she opened the door, only to find him halfway down the gangplank. Off in search of a tavern, no doubt, to drown his sorrows in a mug of beer—or in something far warmer and softer.

Maggie undressed in the dark, rolled out her bed, and curled up under the canopy of the map table. She was amazed to find, even after all these years, Matthew could still make her cry herself to sleep.

She woke while it was full dark, feeling bleary and drained but not sleepy. No watch bell echoed, but she didn't need it to tell her it was very early. Both the ship and the sprawling metropolis enveloping it were quiet, and the creaking of the masts was the mating call of a mythical creature echoing out over the river.

For a few minutes she lay awake, listening for the thump of footsteps beneath her. Captain Stokes's nightly prowl began near enough to two o'clock and ended near enough to three that she didn't need the watch bell to sound the hours, but there was no movement on deck. He was probably on shore, snoring beside his lovely, costly bedfellow.

Had Matthew returned to the ship, or had he, too, found somewhere to rest his head?

Restless, Maggie got up and relieved herself using the bucket she kept in the room. It was not the foulness of the ship's privy that kept her away, nor was she squeamish at the thought of doing her business over a hole opening over the ocean. It was the four adjacent holes and the absence of a door that inspired her to find her own solution.

With no one about, she should be safe to dump the bucket and return to her room without being dressed. She layered her cloak over her shift and went out onto the sterncastle deck.

Someone was there.

Captain Stokes was as startled by her appearance as she was by his presence. He peered up at her from his position on the deck, long legs stretched in front of him, his back to the navigation room wall. For a confused moment, she stood there, frozen, her bucket dangling in her grip.

He nodded at her in greeting. She only stared. It was too strange to deal with first thing upon waking. Since he didn't seem about to explain what he was doing there, she skirted his outstretched legs and descended to the deck to finish her task.

He had not moved by the time she returned with the clean bucket. The trip there and back had given her curiosity the time it needed to wake up. "What do you do here?"

"'Tis closest to the stars," he answered, tilting his head back.

"Is not the poop deck closer still?"

He shrugged.

"How stands the hour?"

"Almost three."

She went back into the navigation room and returned the bucket to its corner, then perched on the edge of the map table.

Something in his clipped responses troubled her. She should leave it alone. What did it matter to her if he was stargazing on his own ship? Why should she care if he didn't deign to explain himself in a long soliloquy? He didn't want to talk, and she didn't want to know. Besides, perpetuating the myth of her lack of feelings for Matthew required her to avoid nighttime conversations with the captain.

No matter how much she enjoyed them.

Sighing, she went back outside and sat with the closed door at her back. She pulled her knees up and covered them with both edges of her cloak, folding herself up like fresh fish wrapped in paper. The sky yawned above them, dusted with the stars Stokes claimed to be viewing.

"Am I supposed to feel safer knowing you guard my sleep?" she said.

"You make it sound as though I make a habit of this."

"Do you?"

"I do not." He tilted his head from side to side to stretch his sore neck. "I heard a rumor. I am often awake this time of night, and if the rumor proved false, I would at least enjoy a few hours of quiet reflection."

She clenched the cloak in her fists. The rumor would, of course, involve her and Matthew, but how detailed did it get? Did he expect to catch Matthew sneaking into—or out of—her room?

He looked at her for the first time. His face was close enough she could make out the fine lines around his eyes. In the dim light of the lamp above, his eyes were green or gray or blue, not the brown she had assumed they were.

"I was told how Kent behaved toward you this evening." She felt the excuses hurtle up her throat like bile, but he continued before she could argue. "You may be old friends, but you know only the boy, whereas I know the man. I chanced to pass him in the street on his way to the Boar's Head. He was already drunk and cross, and 'tis well known that Kent's black moods can always get blacker. When I heard what had him so cross, I feared how bold he would become after another few drinks."

"I was in no danger," she insisted, although a thread of uneasiness wove its way into her explanation. "He only acted that way because he was in his cups, and I made him cross when I…" She couldn't tell him about the marriage proposal. "When I reminded him of your rule."

"Men may walk upright, but 'tis a fine line separates us from animals. My rules merely seek to prevent a bad situation from becoming worse. Special treatment creates inequality, inequality breeds jealousy, and jealousy leads to violence. So if celibacy makes a man miserable," he said with a wry smile, "then we must needs all be miserable together."

"Whatever you were told happened tonight, it appeared more damning than it was. Matthew and I are not lovers, I swear it."

The lie coated her tongue with its rancid oil, but there was no alternative. *We must needs all be miserable together,* she thought ruefully.

Stokes hesitated, then shifted his body so he could see her better. "Forsooth, I am no one to you. I am not so arrogant to demand that you heed my counsel—" He cut himself off and chuckled. "I find I am mortified to speak on this subject…"

She waited for him to collect his thoughts, or perhaps he was summoning his courage.

When he did, he said, "This is a quagmire of my own making. By allowing you aboard, I put every member of my crew in danger of falling in love with you, and though you be clever, I know not if you are wise enough to recognize them—us—for what we are. We are selfish men, Maggie, ever in pursuit of treasure. I urge you not to allow yourself to become a prize."

He looked down at his bent knee and scraped at a spot of dirt with his fingernail while she reeled from his speech. A rattling snore some yards away and the eternal lapping of the waves filled the long, empty moment.

She was touched, embarrassed, infuriated. How dare he presume to tell her who and how to love? How dare he do it with such compassionate eloquence? He made her want to divulge her secret, to seek his blessing, to assure him of her ability to make her own choice.

She watched him rub his finger over that spot on his knee, his lashes dark against the angle of his cheek, his lips crooked in concentration. Understanding bolted through her, aligning her confused reaction into a single realization. She liked him. She admired him, his morning charm and his wartime command and his midnight introspection.

And whenever he conferred with her, advised her, joked with her and teased her, he was telling her she was worthy of his respect.

She had long assumed she was no one to him, yet here he was, in the earliest hours of the morning, proving she mattered. And he claimed he was no one to her, yet here she was, in the blackest part of the night, insuring his trust with lies.

15

STOKES'S WORDS WEIGHED on her. Not because she strove to heed his advice, but because she was ashamed of how promptly she dismissed it. To her credit, she did sit Matthew down and tell him, once and for all, that he needed to cease the behaviors that were bound to rouse the crew's suspicion.

And he did. He stopped orchestrating clandestine meetings on the ship and never met her on shore leave unless they could sneak away unwitnessed. On board, they practiced a secret language of glances and codes. Every so often, he would slip her a piece of paper on which he wrote all the things he couldn't say aloud. They were crude love letters, poorly penned and awkwardly spelled, and he favored the explicit over the poetic. She read each one over and over under the cover of the navigation room table, flushing and trembling.

She adored him for giving credence to her fears of losing her place, for accepting she would not give him the thing he most wanted from her—the thing he rapturously described in his notes. And every boundary he agreed not to cross made her love him more. Elizabeth would scream if she learned the boy who had broken her sister's heart eight years ago had taken care to replace every piece, so only the cracks remained.

The *Merrow* captured four plump prize ships in September before the weather turned. October was cold and stormy, and the few prizes they encountered were hardly worth taking. A rumor began that the summer's voyage was reaching its end. Maggie did her work, played music with her friends, and tried to quell the rising anxiety. She knew she needed to make a plan, but the uncertainty that loomed was too powerful. And so, like a fool, she meekly waited.

The last week of October, Captain Stokes directed the *Merrow* around an outcropping of craggy English cliffs and up a wide river. Maggie had seen so many of these coastal towns now, and they all looked the same. The destination mattered less than the promise of a dry fireside, so until she spotted the inn with a bird painted on its hanging wooden sign, she had no idea they were sailing into Bristol.

She gripped the railing and stared at the Silver Starling, oblivious to the hubbub of the crew bringing the *Merrow* alongside the wharf. Would Robert be there now? Of course he would be. It was just the cruel sort of joke God would play. Was he wandering the streets, visiting tenants, waiting around corners for Maggie to discover him?

When she failed to pester Osborne about helping to fence the plunder, he bid her an uncomfortable farewell and watched her slink up to the poop deck with a worried expression. If anyone asked, she would have said she meant to stay out of the way up here. But by the intense manner with which she scanned the streets and gazed over the rooftops, it was clear she had chosen the highest part of the ship for its vantage.

"You're still as a gargoyle."

Matthew squinted up at her from three decks below. For the first time, she felt the setting sun warming her back, and she looked down to where her white hands gripped the rail. She loosened her fingers and flexed them, grimacing. How long had she stood here?

He climbed up to her, his agile body taking each short flight of steps two at a time. She scanned the area as she waited for him, but aside from a few familiar figures lounging on the dock, there was no one around. They would all be enjoying their brief shore leave. She felt a pang of envy, until she remembered nothing would entice her to step foot in this city.

Matthew leaned his forearms on the rail beside her and looked out over the glowing orange buildings. "'Tis strange every time I return. I always expect to see my father. He never came to Bristol, but I expect it all the same."

She licked her dry lips and nodded. "Every man on the street down there could be Robert."

"Did I tell you? I've not returned to Gloucester since I left. Not once. 'Tis a blessin' the *Merrow* has no friends there."

"Do you think of them? Your mother and father?"

"Not but rarely. Luke may've yet been young to be taken from his parents, but I turned away from them in spirit well before we left."

"What do you feel when you think of them?"

He did not speak of it often, but once, when he had been in a maudlin mood after a few mugs of ale, he described some of his childhood punishments. The boys had been lashed, burned, starved, all on top of the typical beatings rambunctious farm boys could expect from their fathers. Matthew protected Luke as much as he could, receiving more than his share of torment. Then, when he grew strong enough to fight back, his parents used Luke to keep him in line. All the while, they invoked the awesome wrath of God, praying that He would transform the hearts of their wicked offspring—or smite them.

When Matthew finally spoke, it was in a normal, unaffected voice, as if he answered this question every day. "Anger, most times. But aye, when the sea is calm and dawn is far off, and there is naught to do but remember... you'd not credit how near I am to shatterin' my fist against the mast." He nodded thoughtfully. "The day I meet my father again is the day he dies."

They were in full view of anyone who cared to look, but Maggie placed her palm on his hand and slid her fingers between his.

Robert's betrayal was a single event, not a years-long tradition, but she thought she could relate in some small way to that feeling of all-consuming rage Matthew described. She had been a rather normal child, but each misfortune, each test of her character, had been like nudging a pendulum. The more she endured, the further from center she swung. Anger might dissolve into despair, which could transform into howls of laughter. It began around the time she began spending her days with Matthew, as that was the dawning of her role as a future wife and mother. It worsened as she grew in wisdom and self-assurance but found herself trapped in too small a cage. It was bad when she married Sir John, worse when he made her a widow.

Then Robert had shoved the pendulum as far as it would go.

A few short months of having a purpose, learning new skills, and reinventing herself for new people had rendered a subtle change in her, however. She could calm herself better and laugh at herself sooner. She could sit, still and silent, and gaze at the stars without thinking of anything at all.

She had been managing fine until today.

"Let us talk of pleasanter things," Matthew said. "In a week, you'll be free of this ship full o' scoundrels."

"This is pleasanter? To be reminded I must needs start anew?"

"Anew, but not alone. I'll take care of findin' rooms for the winter. You've no need to worry."

"I…" She avoided his gaze by staring at their entwined hands. "I had not thought we were decided on the matter."

"What more is to be decided?"

"I have not agreed to live with you as your mistress. 'Twould be better if I found employment and rented rooms with a respectable landlady. I am certain I can—"

"If 'tis livin' in sin you fear, the answer is plain."

A shiver skittered up her spine. This was what she had prayed for, and yet, as she waited for the blow to land, a curious unease coiled in her belly.

"We've always been destined to take this path. Aye, we went astray, but we regained it just when we were meant to. Let us not make the same mistake again."

It wasn't an apology. She despaired of ever hearing him admit regret.

"I'm not wealthy or learned like the men you're accustomed to. I cannot woo you with rich gifts and poetry that speaks of your beauty. But I can promise to keep you and give you a comfortable home."

She watched his mouth as he spoke, which was as close as she could bring herself to meet his eyes. The sun cast half his face in yellow-gold light as it slipped below the horizon.

"And this also I can promise you: No man'll ever love you as fierce as I love you. I cannot bear the thought of you with another. Will you not have pity on me? Say you'll be my wife."

Pity, O Daphne.

Were women unique in their benevolence? Pity in itself was no evil. To feel for the most wretched of God's creation was to be human. But why did she have to make herself small to make a man comfortable, in the name of pity?

Maggie itched to move, to go anywhere but here, but she was rooted to the spot by the intensity of Matthew's gaze. What devil possessed her? What ill humor robbed her of her sense? She loved him, and she always expected to become his bride. This was the final act of the comedy, wherein the lovers paired up and vanquished the villain. This was the ending she deserved.

He waited. Her heartbeat whooshed, rhythmic and deafening. She swallowed the lump in her throat. There was only one answer.

* * *

She tapped on the door. "Come," came the immediate reply from within.

The corridor was empty, but she glanced backward anyway. Matthew was grabbing a bite with his mates in the galley, and Padraig and Osborne were off attending to their duties. Besides, he told her himself she had the right to request an audience.

She pushed the great room door open and let it drift closed behind her, careful not to let it latch. Captain Stokes stood before a ewer and basin, his face obscured by the towel he used to dry himself.

"Captain."

He lowered the towel. "Well met."

She watched his face for clues. It might have been the dreary October sky, but a cloud had seemed to be over him as he did his daily exercise. Following him to his cabin had made sense from a logistical standpoint, since he would be alone, but if the captain was in a stormy mood, this conversation was doomed.

He tossed the towel over a wooden rod on the wall and shrugged into his doublet. "I gather you are to be felicitated."

Gossip snaked through the crew with the speed of a trail of gunpowder, and Matthew, too smug to be cautious, had lit the fuse. It only took twelve hours for the captain to hear of her secret betrothal.

"You are not…? That is, we have not…?" She sighed and tried a third time. "We are not to be punished?"

"To what purpose? You would disembark in London next week, whether I punished you or not. Forsooth, marriage between crew members is not something I have dealt with before, so I thank you for bringing this issue to my attention. Kent will be dismissed if he repeats the offense."

"If he… marries again?"

"Aye. Although in such a case, he may have more to fear from God than from me. Bigamy, you know."

It was just like her first moments aboard. He saw her distress, and he set about distracting her with silly jokes. She was grateful. Grateful and furious. How could he tease her after she had wronged him?

Swallowing, she said, "You know a great many people in London, methinks."

Stokes gestured to a seat at the table and pulled out another chair for himself.

She perched on the edge of her chair and twisted her hands in her lap. "If you have found my work on the *Merrow* satisfactory, would you do me the great favor of giving me a reference? I know not what work I can do, but someone may be desperate enough to take me on, were you to vouch for me."

"If you allow it, I would be honored to ask around for open positions. Where shall I deliver news of my success? In what part of town do you and Kent plan to make your home?"

"Matthew and Luke are renting rooms in a place called Rotherhithe, I believe, but I have no… solid plans for my own lodging."

"Can he not provide for you while you establish yourself? I was led to believe my crew is paid uncommonly well for simple sailors."

"Methinks he will not be happy to learn I do not plan to live with him until we are married."

The captain examined her from across the table, saying nothing.

The silence made her face burn. "You must deem it strange I would protect my reputation even now."

"Your business is your own." He paused. "I wonder, however, at your hesitation to tell your betrothed your wishes."

She stared at the hands in her lap. "That is my own business as well."

Comforting sounds filled the void, creaks and bangs and the whoosh of the waves. She reminded herself to behave normally, to blink, to breathe, and as the perfumed air of the captain's cabin filled her lungs, her hands unclenched.

Stokes nodded for a few moments, his eyes unfocused. He breathed in through his nose and gave her a tight smile. "I will be pleased to offer my aid in seeking both work and lodging until… you no longer have need of it."

She was baffled to feel her eyes well with tears. "I have no right to ask for your help again, when I have not yet adequately repaid your first favor. I am so deep in your debt, I fear I may never claw my way out." She breathed out a timid laugh.

Stokes did not laugh with her. "This is not a transaction, Maggie. I am not tallying debts."

"Still, I do not expect to get something for nothing. Until I determine what to give in thanks for all the kindnesses you have shown me, I can offer only my gratitude."

"Indeed, that is the only payment I would accept."

She swallowed the tightness in her throat, refusing to cry in front of him again, especially when her tears were born from shame. It didn't make sense a ruthless pirate commander would treat her with such decency from the moment they met. Maybe it had nothing to do with her. Maybe she represented a wrong he needed to right. Maybe he mistook her for someone who deserved his benevolence. Whatever the reason, it struck her, then, how much she would miss it.

The night before, she and Matthew cuddled together in the shadows of the poop deck, planning their future in whispers. Matthew described his vision of her tending their home, raising their future children, waiting at the dock to greet him when he returned from a summer at sea. Eight years ago, she had shared that vision. But in the time since, she had known both the loneliness of playing the dutiful wife as well as the sense of purpose employment supplied. Part of her understood accepting Matthew's proposal meant her miraculous summer as a pirate was at an end. Now it was coming real, she couldn't bear the thought of being trapped in an empty home. Again.

When she expressed to him her foolish wish to seek employment, a hard gleam appeared in his eye she had never seen before. By the end of the conversation, she understood her error. Ever generous, he agreed to pretend it had never happened.

"There is one more boon I would ask of you," she said, ignoring the sudden chill. "Prithee, speak not to Matthew of my wish to find work. I will tell him when the time is right."

"And what time is that?"

The question irritated her. "When I have… When I have found the words."

She just needed time to discover the magical incantation to make him understand: the girl he thought he was marrying was someone who no longer existed. It would be a mistake to tether her just when she had learned to run.

Winter 1612/1613

So fared Apollo and the Maid: hope made Apollo swift,
And fear did make the Maiden fleet devising how to shift.

16

HOLDING HER CLOAK closed against the bitter wind, Maggie swung her oilskin bag over her shoulder. It bumped a sore spot on the back of her upper arm, reminding her she had vowed to forget it was there. The bruise would fade in a few more days.

As she stood in the street for a last look at the *Merrow*, a presence appeared at her side, blocking the wind and warming her with his residual heat. He offered her his arm, and she took it.

"I hope you have not tired of boat travel," Stokes said as they walked along the river, dodging busy sailors carrying heavy objects. "A ferryman will take us to Southwark. 'Tis cheaper than hiring a horse, and much easier on my delicate feet."

"That any part of you could be called delicate…"

"My pride, mayhap? You wound it whenever you remind me how much wittier you are than myself."

When they arrived at the nearest set of stairs leading down to the water's edge, he went ahead of her and offered her his hand. The early winter wind sprayed the brown water up to the top step, making the stone slick and treacherous. Stokes gave the ferryman their destination and dropped a few pennies into his hand, then helped Maggie into the boat. They sat side by side, facing the rower. He frowned at them, disinclined to chat with his passengers, so Stokes filled the silence by pointing out items of interest along the river.

Maggie followed his pointing fingers, but her eyes were drawn more often to the ships drifting alongside them, making their way toward the Pool. *That one needed new paint. That one was strangely rigged, probably from another part of the world. That one had more guns than the Merrow. That one was Spanish.*

After about a half hour, the ferryman maneuvered his rowboat alongside the Tooley Stairs, underneath the great London Bridge. A man waiting on the steps offered Maggie his hand, helping Stokes out as well before requesting the boatman's services for himself. Stokes supported her elbow as Maggie picked up her skirts to begin the careful climb.

Southwark was less populated than the opposite bank, the buildings less crowded together. Even the air smelled cleaner.

"And your friend is expecting me?" she asked.

He pointed them down a broad street. "Mistress Pylet is looking forward to having your help. The inn is prospering, but an assistant will alleviate some of the burden."

They turned down a side street, then another. The street narrowed and darkened as the two-story buildings blocked out the sunlight, their jutting upper floors giving them the appearance of a group of overeager listeners. A few people nodded at them as they passed, and the sounds of enterprise and entertainment drifted out of open windows and doors.

Tucked between a haberdasher's shop and a laundry, their destination was marked only by a painted sign. It showed a knife emerging from—or was it being inserted into?—a bejeweled scabbard.

It was a bit on the nose to name a brothel "Dagger and Sheath," but in Mistress Pylet's defense, it was the sort of apt name that would cause no confusion.

The dining room was much like that of any other ordinary, except the furniture was of high quality, and fresh rushes strewn with fragrant herbs covered the floor. At one table, two well-dressed gentlemen Stokes's age were being entertained by a lovely young woman with a heart-shaped face and a white-blonde braid. She wore no cap, and her shirt was parted to show the tops of her breasts and the deep cleft between them.

She chastised herself for the first thought that popped into her head, burned into her sensibilities by generations of shame-filled ancestors. They were not so different, after all. Not anymore.

Behind the bar, a cheerful publican in his forties was opening a dark glass bottle.

Stokes strode through the dining room, Maggie hurrying along behind him. "Well met, Young. Where may we find Mistress Pylet?"

"Captain! You are well met. Amelia is in her chamber. Have a drink while I fetch her for you." Young plucked two mugs from the shelf behind him. "I was just opening a bottle of Burns's."

They sat with their drinks while Young clomped up the stairs. Instead of being hidden in the back or tucked behind a wall, the stairs were in full view of the dining room, wide and well lit, caged on both sides by wooden railings. There would be no hiding when or with whom a patron ascended to the first floor.

Stokes lifted his mug in a toast. "To Maggie Bailey, the first daughter of a baron to set foot in a stew."

She chuckled and toasted back just as a voice echoed on the stairs, "'Tis indeed Will Stokes!"

A woman floated down to the dining room, her face lit by a delighted smile. She wore a plain gown in pale blue and left her glossy brown hair in loose waves about her shoulders. Her casual appearance only augmented her beauty—or perhaps it was the way she held herself, as if she ruled over the Dagger and Sheath.

When she reached the table, the woman gave Maggie a once-over and looked at the captain. "Is this she?"

Stokes had stood at the sound of the woman's voice, and the sight of them side by side, their beautiful faces turned toward each other, made Maggie's stomach flip. If this young woman was Amelia Pylet, Stokes had hidden an epic's worth of meaning in the word "friend."

"This is Mistress Margaret Bailey. Maggie, my good friend Ellen."

Ellen flopped down into the empty chair beside Maggie, positioning herself between her and Stokes, and propped her chin up with her elbow on the table as she examined Maggie. Her movements were graceful and full of life, like water burbling over rocks in a stream.

Not Amelia Pylet, then. Maggie tried to keep her expression neutral and pleasant, but she gave Stokes a pointed look, hoping for an explanation or a reprieve from the woman's stare.

Ellen interpreted Maggie's look as best she could. "You need not fear. Your bedchamber is next to Mistress Pylet's, and mine is at the other end of the corridor. You'll not hear a thing." She shot a sidelong glance at Stokes as her lips curled up in a provocative smile. "Unless the captain is overcome."

Maggie's education over the last few months had worn down the sharp edges of her shame, but Ellen's boldness still flustered her. She kept her eyes on the woman, not wanting to know what Stokes was thinking. "My bedchamber?"

"You are to apprentice Mistress Pylet, are you not?"

"Not—not apprentice, no," Maggie said, rushing to correct the misunderstanding. "I have no designs to become a woman of business. But I read and write and can do sums."

"She ran a ship of thirty men. I warrant she will have no trouble with a few girls." Stokes brought his goblet to his lips, but his hidden smile meant his speech was bait.

"Thirty men?" Ellen rolled her eyes. "'Tis a trifle, sirrah. Men are easy, like children. They need only food, sleep, and entertainment. All of which the Dagger and Sheath provides."

"You may save your proselytizing. You have in me a loyal disciple already."

It was one thing to understand the captain frequented brothels, but it was another to imagine him in this building, with this woman. Having witnessed his half-naked exercise regimen too many times to count, it disturbed Maggie how easily she could imagine it.

Movement on the stairs was a welcome distraction, and the middle-aged woman who came to stand beside the table gave Stokes a simpering smile. She wore a wine-colored skirt over a cylindrical farthingale, a cornflower blue jacket with pink flowers embroidered on the sleeves, and a starched collar to serve as the backdrop for her elegant grey coiffure. The rouge on her cheeks and lips were a stark contrast to her lead-whitened face.

She let Stokes kiss her hand before she deigned to notice his companion. "And you are Mistress Margaret. You are most welcome. The captain has told me of your skills with bookkeeping. I cannot say I approve of a woman sailor..." She narrowed her eyes as she scanned Maggie from top to bottom, perhaps searching for a crippling disease or a lost limb. "Nevertheless, I have no qualms about a woman secretary, and Captain Stokes assures me you are the best."

Maggie blushed at the excessive praise. "The captain is exceeding kind."

Ellen snorted, and Mistress Pylet shot a scathing look at her before fixing her face into a polite smile for Maggie's benefit. "Will you follow me?" She turned, her skirts swishing, and started back up the stairs.

Maggie stood and picked up her bag, but hesitated. This was the last time she would see Stokes. He had made good on his offer to help her find employment, and now they would go their separate ways.

She smiled at him. "My thanks, captain." Thanks weren't enough, but her throat was too constricted to say anything more.

The look he gave her was softer than his usual arrogant half-smile; it deepened the creases beside his eyes. "Mayhap you will allow me to call on you on Wednesday. To see how you fare." He reached out to give her arm a friendly squeeze.

She sucked in a sharp breath against the sudden pain, and he jerked his hand away. "Are you hurt?"

"Must have wrenched it in my sleep." Pasting on a bright smile, she bid him farewell.

Over his shoulder, she caught Ellen bringing Maggie's forgotten mug to her lips. The woman met Maggie's gaze and raised the cup at the last minute in a tiny toast. For a moment, Maggie felt a jealous ache; while she attended Mistress Pylet, Ellen would be with Stokes.

She admonished herself for being unreasonable. Ellen had more of a right to Stokes's attention than she did.

The first-floor corridor was dim, with only a few candles in sconces on the walls, but the result was a cozy, flickering glow that would hide any number of sins. A narrow opening led down to the servants' stairway, from which wafted the scent of baking bread and something savory bubbling on the hearth.

Doors lined the hall, all closed. As Maggie followed the madam toward her rooms, one door swung open and an older gentleman stepped out, straightening the sleeves of his jerkin. He bowed to the women as they passed. Behind him, she glimpsed a nude girl slipping a chemise over her head.

Through the window in the front wall, the weak light of the gloomy afternoon spilled onto a rug running the length of the corridor. It was worn down in the middle, but otherwise clean. The Dagger and Sheath boasted a modest sort of opulence, tidy and tasteful.

Mistress Pylet opened the door next to the window and showed Maggie inside. The sitting room was as tidy and tasteful as the rest, with a pretty little couch and two matching chairs, a low table, a desk, and a sideboard. Another door on the left wall would lead to the woman's sleeping quarters.

Maggie sat on the edge of her chair, both hands clutching her seabag. Mistress Pylet retrieved a large black book from her desk and took the seat opposite.

"Captain Stokes says you are familiar with keeping a ledger?"

"Aye, madam. I managed the ship's accounts and calculated the crew's shares. With the approval of the second mate, of course."

The woman opened the book to the most recent page and handed it to her. "Here you will see how our accounts are recorded. Each transaction is ascribed to whichever girl the patron requests—" She stopped and frowned. "You do understand what we do here?"

She must have noticed the shock on Maggie's face. "I do, madam. These numbers, though…" Did it really cost this much to hire a whore? It was no wonder Amelia Pylet needed a secretary; she must spend a majority of her day counting her treasure.

The madam sniffed, pleased. "We charge a minimum fee, but many of our wealthier patrons are exceeding generous."

"How much of the fee goes to the…?"

"The girls? A quarter."

Figuring the total owed each of Mistress Pylet's *girls* would be part of Maggie's duties, in addition to tracking the kitchen expenses and the bar revenue. In exchange, Maggie would earn three shillings a week.

It was not much—a pittance, in fact, considering the sort of profit the inn raked in—but she was overjoyed. The bulk of the coins in her purse she earned through blackmail. Her wedding dowry from her father was paid straight to her husband, and her widow's portion was so far out of reach it may as well not exist.

And now, Maggie Bailey would earn *three whole shillings*. Every *week*.

The interview complete, Mistress Pylet marched her back out into the corridor for a tour. Her bedchamber was next door, small but comfortable, not that she would balk at a private room with a bed after her summer in the navigation room. The other doors belonged to the six Dagger and Sheath girls. Maggie noted Ellen's room was, indeed, the first one at the top of the stairs, almost as far from Maggie's as it could be. She lightened her steps as they passed it; she was determined to be uncurious about whether the room was occupied, but it was difficult to hear over the creaking floorboards.

They descended the narrow servants' stairs and emerged in a cluttered pantry, which emptied them into the kitchen. Amelia introduced the cook, Vernon, a tall, sturdy woman who was far too overwhelmed to give Maggie much of her attention. She was in the middle of giving instructions to three young girls, the oldest around ten or twelve, the younger two no more than six. All were industriously mixing pie crust or chopping vegetables.

At the opposite end of the kitchen, a little boy stood on an overturned crate, his arms shoulder-deep in a washbasin. Beside him, an enormous cooking pot teetered on its side, and an even smaller boy stuck his tongue out as he scraped at the black crust caking the pot's walls.

At Duntsford Priory, children in the kitchen was a rarity, only occurring if a servant had nowhere else for the child to go. Surely this many little ones was more of a liability than a help.

"So many children!" she said.

Vernon had already returned to her work, so it was Amelia who answered, her sharp eyes following the children's movements. "A hazard of the job."

It dawned on her by degrees, taking so long to arrive she felt like a fool when it did. They were not random urchins; they belonged to the Dagger and Sheath. She studied the girls at the worktable, noting the colors of their hair under their caps, the shapes of their chins. Did one of them belong to the pretty girl with the blonde braid? Did one belong to Ellen?

Amelia brought her back into the dining room to introduce her to Young, the bartender. The blonde and both of her swains were gone, and where Ellen and the captain had sat, now there were only two empty mugs.

17

MAGGIE FELT EIGHT eyes on her as she hovered near the entrance to the Dagger on Wednesday. Stokes glanced over her shoulder to the four curious women at the back table. "You've not changed your mind?"

"Everyone has been exceeding kind," she said.

It was partially true. After four days at the Dagger, all but Ellen remained standoffish. It wasn't enough to make her give up, though.

"And your arm?" He nodded at her shoulder, and she blanched. He remembered that?

"Mending," she replied quickly, then changed the subject. "I thank you for your aid. Again."

"I am honored to be of service to you, my lady," He bowed his head, an ironic smile lifting one side of his mustache. She rolled her eyes at his teasing formality, as she always did.

This was the last time she would roll her eyes at him, she thought.

He held his hat to his chest. "And now I take my leave of you."

"God be with you, captain."

"Not 'adieu' yet. Only 'anon.'"

It was a nice sentiment. "Anon," she agreed.

With a final courtly bow, Stokes fitted his yellow hat over his dark curls and went out into the cold November evening.

Maggie kept her eyes on the floor rushes as she wandered toward the back table, not eager to resume the teasing that the Dagger girls began when they saw Stokes walk in the door.

Molly, whose cherubic, heart-shaped face wore a mean smirk, crossed her arms over her chest and looked around the table until she had everyone's attention. "So... he is *not* your lover?" she asked Maggie.

Mary and Denise sniggered. Maggie only sighed, weary of this tired topic.

"He does act like it." Molly arched her eyebrows. "You've only just arrived, and he's already paid you a visit."

"Mayhap he sought an excuse to look in on Ellen." Maggie turned to the dark-haired woman at her left. "He esteems you most."

Ellen shook her head. "By my troth, he has not come to me since the summer. To my dismay, I would add—he is a favorite of mine as well."

"Aye, we ken," drawled Denise, flipping her blonde braid over her shoulder. "You need not regale us with more stories of the handsome captain who always—"

"Shh!" Ellen fluttered her hands to quiet Denise, her face red with suppressed laughter. "Poor Maggie must not hear, I could not bear it!"

Though Maggie had promised herself she wouldn't think about Stokes's history with Ellen, it was a vow she had to renew again and again. She prevented her mind from completing Denise's sentence by focusing instead on Ellen's. "Since the summer? You forget Saturday last."

"Saturday last?"

"The day I arrived. You drank with him while I went above with Mistress Pylet."

"And when the wine was gone, he left. I could not tempt him to stay."

It was odd, the way practiced apathy tamped down the warmth threatening to spread through her limbs at Ellen's confession.

"'Tis clear his only interest is to see you, though heaven knows why," Molly said.

The fourth girl, Mary, whose sweet face and over-eager attempts at wittiness made her a pale copy of Molly, propped her chin on the heel of her hand. "If he's not your lover, methinks he soon will be."

"He knows I am not at liberty to be courted."

"Ah, that's right, you've a man already," Mary said. "Where is he, pray?"

"Aye, why have we not seen him?" Molly added.

As it always did, Maggie's fair skin betrayed her. "He is— I believe his lodgings are near the shipyards. 'Tis a long road to Southwark."

"My brother lives near Limehouse and I see him every Sunday," said Mary.

Denise chimed in, "My best patron comes all the way from Shoreditch."

"A lengthy trip would not deter an ardent lover," Molly said with her usual smug sneer.

Maggie bristled at the insinuation, more so because it might be true. "He only docked a few days ago. He is finding work, certes, and will visit when he can."

"Aye, give the lad a chance to get his feet under him," Ellen said.

As they spoke, another two gentlemen entered. Mary, Molly, and Denise looked up to assess the newcomers, but Ellen didn't spare them a second glance. Each girl had a free day in addition to Sundays, but even in her leisure time, Ellen wanted the bustle of the dining room and the attention of the salivating men who traipsed past her. Mistress Pylet had no objection to her hanging around, turning heads and piquing interests: when Ellen commanded a patron to try again tomorrow, it almost always resulted in a repeat visit.

Mary and Molly looked at Denise, who wrinkled her nose and shrugged. With the most senior girl, Frank, already occupied upstairs, and the youngest, Jane, already entertaining a patron in the dining room, Denise was next in the hierarchy. Either the new arrivals didn't interest her, or she was too comfortable where she was. As one, Mary and Molly rose and sauntered over to the newcomers just as Young arrived at the table to offer them drinks.

"You must not heed them," Ellen murmured to Maggie, her eyes fixed on Molly's back as the girl tossed her hair and perched on the edge of the men's table. "They are the unhappy sort who must make all around them unhappy also. Jealousy is a frequent visitor here."

Denise nodded. "We're none of us likely to find the sort of solid man like you've got."

Solid. Like Matthew's grip on her upper arm. Solid like the deck when she fell.

"How can you remain carefree when your work is so... difficult?" Maggie asked.

Ellen leaned forward and crossed her arms in front of her on the table. "We do try to appear so."

"Aye," said Denise, "most men prefer a gay woman to a dour one."

"Besides, frowning creates lines."

Another group of men entered, already roaring with laughter. This was the time of night when business began to pick up. The Dagger could expect to entertain patrons almost until sunrise, which was forcing Maggie to adopt a new routine. The nocturnal snoring and farting of sailors were replaced by the giggling and moaning that now lulled her to sleep.

"I'm off. Hope Frank's…" Denise glanced at Ellen and shrugged. "Well, we could use her." She pushed herself away from the table and plucked at the top of her bodice to ensure everything was on display before joining the rowdy group at their table.

Maggie looked around at them all, Mary and Molly with their duo of young lads, Denise with her passel of inebriates. Jane was disappearing upstairs with her patron. Amelia Pylet swept through the kitchen entrance and began her rounds of the room, ensuring everyone was having a good time.

Turning to Ellen, who surveyed the goings-on with amusement, Maggie said, "Only five women working at a time. Does that not create a bit of a backup? The inn gets rather busy after supper."

"None worth mentioning. Half the work's done out here, with some sitting on laps and some bawdy talk. Doesn't take long to finish 'em off upstairs, then on to the next."

She had her elbows on the table, not a very ladylike posture, but it enhanced her cleavage—she had admitted this secret to Maggie yesterday—and made her appear less intimidating. This last part Maggie could not agree with. Confidence radiated from her lovely form, no matter how hard she tried to make herself approachable.

"We do better than some," she went on, "where they only have one or two whores to satisfy their customers. And with Vernon in the kitchen, folk come from all over just for the food."

A shadow fell over the table: a young man, old enough to grow a mustache and beard, but young enough that he was blushing behind his patchy facial hair. His eyes were fixed on Ellen as if Maggie didn't exist.

"How now, my fine lad?" Ellen crooned, leaning farther forward.

The man's gaze dropped, and he pulled his eyes back up with effort. "Well met, Ellen. Do you remember me? I was here—"

"About a fortnight past. Aye, Master Edmond, I surely do remember you." Her smile turned coquettish. "What brings you back to our humble inn?"

The man's Adam's apple bobbed. "W-why, you do, I vow." He placed a hand on the table and leaned toward her in what he must have thought was a seductive pose. To Maggie's eye, he appeared more awkward and gangly this way.

Ellen frowned, a beautiful pout. "My sweet little fool, I have no company on Wednesdays! I am certain I told you."

His face crumpled with mortification. "Oh, well…" That bobbing Adam's apple again, up and down like a game of cup and ball. "I-is it Wednesday? How foolish of me."

"'Tis no matter. Your friends will stay for a drink, I hope, and if I cannot… *be of service* to you today, I am sure our bonny Denise can." Ellen's smile turned vulpine. "Mayhap you will find your way back here tomorrow. I am always well rested on Thursdays."

As she spoke, she trailed one fingertip across the back of the man's hand. A glassy-eyed look of wonder made his face slack, and he stammered out some unintelligible promises as he backed away. Maggie watched him return to his friends, one of whom held Denise in his lap and gazed up at her in adoration.

Ellen chuckled. "Men are so easy. Boys especially. The young ones are so sweet and bashful, I quite fall in love with them. Do you know, when I have a lad upstairs, I sometimes pretend I am a tutor, instructing him in the art of lovemaking."

Maggie smiled uncomfortably and looked down at the table, not sure how to respond. It would take a good deal longer than four days to get used to the sort of work Ellen did.

"Why do you blush like a virgin when you spent a summer on a ship full of randy sailors?"

Maggie shifted, feeling the blush drain away as her blood went cold. "Captain Stokes has a rule against fornication."

Ellen laughed, loud and sharp. "A ship full of randy sailors, and none are permitted to fuck? There must be a story there." She hooked her arm over the chair back, too interested in this new topic to worry about how she appeared to all the men who couldn't have her. "So if you couldn't fuck on the ship, where did you do it?"

"Why are you so certain I did?"

"Because you ended up betrothed to one of the sailors you spent the summer with."

"That does not mean I went to bed with him," Maggie mumbled, then attempted a carefree smile. "Mayhap I *am* a virgin."

"I trust your husband attended to that. God rest his soul," Ellen added, crossing herself.

How did Ellen know she was a widow? She narrowed her eyes. "The bottle of wine you shared with the captain loosened his lips, I see."

"Nonesuch. I was curious about you, and he answered. Besides, am I to believe Will Stokes, who's softer than lamb's wool, dropped you at a brothel knowing you were an innocent?"

"Softer than lamb's wool? Methinks he would die of shame if he heard you say so."

"He's not here; I'll say what I like."

This was a better topic than the one before. "Did he say aught else about me? That he is glad to be rid of me, no doubt."

"Mags, my love, a man who's rid of a woman does not visit her in the same sennight. I wager we'll see him again before ere long."

For a moment, Maggie let herself enjoy thinking she hadn't lost the ship and its captain forever. And then, as she always did, she donned the armor protecting her from things that couldn't be allowed to be true. "I see now why the ship so often docks in London," she said. "He is ever eager to see you."

If they were older friends, Ellen might have challenged her, but she only shrugged. "Now, tell me about your sailor lad. Where did you get up to mischief if not on the ship?"

If they were older friends, Maggie might have told her. That she had let Matthew lead her down a path she should have known better than to follow. That when she broke the captain's rule, she also broke a rule that had been imperative for her twenty-three years, until one day it wasn't.

That she deserved the five fingertip-shaped bruises on her upper arm, and she didn't deserve Stokes's visits.

Instead, she played the role of a girl she wasn't, blithe and worldly. She told Ellen about the secluded gardens, churchyard shadows, and smoke-filled inns where Matthew made her feel deliciously wicked. Ellen nodded and hummed at all the right times, coaxing more candor. Soon the disparate scenes became a chronology, progressing from the last weeks on the ship, to the marriage proposal in Bristol, to the audience with Stokes, ending with the last time she saw Matthew.

"Did he hurt you?"

This time, when the memory came, Maggie let it.

The scene unfolded behind her eyes. The actors broke their embrace and hastily straightened their garments, glancing about the hold to ensure no one had seen their furtive coupling. The woman's face was red with shame, the man's eyes heavy with satisfaction. She tugged at his sleeve before he left, and gave the speech she had so meticulously rehearsed, declaring her love and demanding her independence in one impassioned soliloquy. The man playing Matthew had grabbed the woman's arm, reciting his bone-chilling line on a growl: "So I'm to pay for this tumble? Had I known the cost, I'd've fucked a whore." He shook her with such force that she lost her balance. The woman looked up at him from the damp floor of the hold, weeping, apologizing, but he threw up his hands and left her alone among the last of the cargo—except for a white cat, who emerged from behind a crate and bumped his head against her knee as she gathered the strength to stand.

She had agreed to marry him. She had sealed her promise by being with him like a wife. She knew she would soon vow to honor and obey him. And still, she had failed to anticipate the fury her request would call forth.

"No more than I deserved," Maggie answered.

Ellen scoffed. "What sort of person deserves to be hurt?"

"I betrayed him. I do not wonder that he was angry. He forgot his strength, but after how sorely I disappointed him, any man may have done the same."

"That is neither fair nor true! I have met hundreds of men, and only a rare few turn violent. Such patrons are thrown out on their ears."

"Men who come here expect pleasure. Why should they become angry enough to hurt?"

"Any reason. No reason. Some men take pleasure from pain. I do not allow it, but other whores do."

Maggie thought of Matthew's sharp teeth and flicked the memory aside.

"Mama?"

A tiny voice chirped above Maggie's head. She turned in her seat to find one of the Dagger's little ones peering down at them through the banister, face as small and pale as a sprite.

Ellen's chair wobbled back on two legs as she sprang from it. "You must not be down here, my darling," she pleaded, casting a furtive glance toward the patrons assembled in the dining room. "Go back to bed."

When she had introduced her four-year-old daughter to Maggie, Ellen had called her "my perfect treasure, Katherine."

The child had hair almost as dark as her mother's, but there were highlights of lighter brown giving her a sun-kissed, burnished look, like someone who spent their days at sea. The analogy stopped there, however, for her skin was all white and pink and smooth, a blank canvas for enormous brown eyes. Those eyes were now red-rimmed and fixed on Ellen.

"Am I going to be an orphan?" came the little voice.

Ellen tutted. "Nay, my love. Has Ned been telling ghost stories again?"

"Francie said Moll must stop playing and go to sleep, and Moll said, 'I'll not listen to you because you're going to be an orphan,' and Ned said that's a ugly thing to say, and then he pulled Moll's hair, and Francie cried and said she didn't want to be an orphan, and I don't want to be an orphan either if norphans are ugly."

"Francie will not be an orphan and nor will you. Tell Moll I will come up in five minutes, and if she is not asleep, she'll get the switch."

Katherine sniffed. "Aye, mama." She stepped on the hem of her shift as she tried to stand, tripping and catching herself on the next step with the heels of her hands. She scampered up the rest of the steps and out of sight.

Ellen sighed and sat back down, her posture straighter than it had been before. "She knows better."

Maggie shook her head in wonder. "What a cruel thing for Moll to say. Yet Francie should not have taken it to heart—she seems such a steady lass."

"'Struth. She's only being foolish."

Ellen layered her hands on the table in front of her. It was a pretty, refined pose. It also hid the restless tapping of her thumb on the dark wood.

18

ALTHOUGH AMELIA REFERRED to them as "girls" and instructed Maggie to do so as well, it was not their preferred monicker. "Make no mistake," Ellen had declared a few days into Maggie's employment, "I am no little girl. I am a whore, and I have earned my title."

Ellen was their queen, though she was not the oldest and had not been there the longest. That title belonged to Frank, a willowy brunette of twenty-seven who spent most of her evenings closed up in her room with patrons Maggie often missed coming and going. Denise was next in the pecking order, followed by Molly and Mary, thick as thieves and so similar in looks and manners, it took her almost a week to tell them apart.

The youngest was Jane, sixteen and stubborn, intent on dethroning Ellen and establishing herself in her place. Unfortunately, the other whores had no patience for her childishness, which meant Jane could often be seen pouting.

Though Jane ignored her, and Mary and Molly teased her, Ellen and Denise decided Maggie was a lost lamb. And perhaps she was. By the third week of November, she still had not heard from Matthew, and it was beginning to look like she never would.

The bruises on her arm faded from purple to yellow, until one morning, they were gone. Seeing her healed skin brought on a strange melancholy, as if she might forget what she did to him as easily as her body forgot what he did to her. She deserved his silence. He had made his wishes clear, and she had ignored him. Worse, she had conspired against him with Stokes. If she loved him, she would have tried harder to find a compromise.

She could apologize. He and Luke were staying in a village called Rotherhithe, an hour's walk from the brothel. If she wanted, she could go to him to soothe his hurt feelings. Yet something prevented her. He might not forgive her, for one thing. Also, a deficient apology might prove worse than no apology at all, and she had no interest in acquiring a fresh set of bruises.

Then her courses came on, a reminder of what she had given him in exchange for a chance at happiness, and the relief was so great she wept. She had won the battle for her independence by losing his trust, and her tears proved which she valued more.

"Come, Mags, we're going to a bearbaiting."

Ellen clung to the doorframe of Mistress Pylet's sitting room, eyes bright with the promise of adventure. Her hair was pulled back in a simple tail under her lace-trimmed diadem cap, which framed her face like a halo. The neckline of her low-cut bodice showed through the gap where her cloak closed at her throat.

Maggie enjoyed being a hanger-on to the spectacle that was Ellen, but she looked down at Amelia's crowded ledger. "I cannot. Somehow the accounts are a disaster. Do you know how much Master Fowler charges us for the washing? If 'twere not so convenient, I would urge Pylet to look elsewhere."

Ellen pressed the backs of her fingers to her mouth and made an obnoxious yawning sound. "Suit yourself. We'll return before supper. If anyone calls for me—"

"Tell him you have been wild to see him again and assure him you will be back at any moment."

"Th'art an angel. Anon!"

The sound of the girls chattering in the dining room below diminished when they went out into the street, and she glimpsed them—Ellen, Mary, Molly, and Denise—through Mistress Pylet's window. The desk was positioned there to catch as much light as possible, and with how quickly the winter sky faded from dim to dark, Maggie would need to light a candle within the hour. She rubbed her eyes and returned to her task.

The numbers were not adding up. She couldn't understand it: all the incoming and outgoing money should be accounted for, but try as she might, she came up short. She slid the week's bills toward her and tried again.

The kitchen account was the culprit. Vernon's expenses were greater than the bills sent by the butcher and the greengrocer, by almost half a pound. She placed a mark next to the offending figures and closed the pen in the book to hold the page. It was too close to supper to trouble the kitchen staff and Amelia was off on an errand, so she wandered down to the dining room to wait.

Young nodded at her from behind the bar, where he unloaded a crate of bottles. The rustle of straw and the clink of glass was the only sound in the empty dining room as Maggie installed herself at Mistress Pylet's usual table in the corner—not presuming to sit in her seat, of course.

The stairs creaked as a patron descended. He looked around the room, his gaze passing over Maggie as if she wasn't there. He strode to the bar and said something to Young in a low voice.

"You'll be wanting Mistress Bailey," Young replied, lifting his chin in Maggie's direction.

For what? Her heartbeat quickened at the prospect of standing in for the madam. She hoped the man had a question she knew how to answer.

"I have the coin to settle my account today," the man said. "Where is the patroness?"

Maggie flipped open the ledger. "Mistress Pylet is out at present, but I will readily help you settle your account. Your name, sir?"

She located all the times the man's name appeared in Amelia's running list, and he paid her the total he owed. When their business was done, he gave her a respectful nod and went out into the street.

Jane, her honey brown hair loose down her back, crept down the stairs and peered around the dining room with narrowed eyes. She landed on Maggie and screwed up her nose.

"Gone, is 'e?" Hearing that deep-throated Northern brogue come out of such a delicate girl always came as a shock. She reminded Maggie of a much prettier Osborne.

"Aye, just this moment."

Her shoulders sagged in relief. "He's harmless, i'faith, but he will call me Isabel."

"If that is the worst thing he does…"

"Isabel's his daughter."

Maggie pressed her lips together and didn't reply.

"Reet, I'll be in me room." Jane whirled around and started up the steps.

The front door swung open, and a man in leather and brocade with a feathered hat sauntered in. Age was in the process of leeching the reddish blond from his mustache and beard, leaving white whiskers behind. Beneath, his face was pinched in what must be a perpetual scowl.

He saw Jane first. "What fortune," he crooned. "Await me in your chamber."

"Thy pardon, Sir Antony…" The tension had returned to Jane's shoulders. "I… I am indisposed todee."

"What nonesuch is this? You stand before me the image of good health. I will attend you once I have spoken to the madam." At this, he deigned to gaze around the room. Jane caught Maggie's eye and gave a covert shake of the head.

"You." Sir Antony fixed Maggie with a bored expression. "Where is the madam?"

Maggie slipped on her most honeyed voice, the one she used on Alinor when she longed for the old woman to shut up and leave her alone. "She is out, sir. I invite you to enjoy a cup of wine, or mayhap a light supper? I fear there are no rooms to let until Mistress Pylet reappears."

The man's face went red. "I do not sup here," he said, enunciating each word. "I do not drink here. I come here for one purpose, and I will not be denied."

"Of course not, sir. If you will only return in an hour or so—"

"Outrageous!" A droplet of spittle landed on the open ledger. "I have never known such insolence. I will not be turned away from so base a bawdy house as this one. My custom alone must count for half of this wench's income!"

He banged his fist on her table to punctuate his tantrum, and her heart thudded with a mix of fear and fury. She wanted nothing better than to gut the disagreeable pig with her vilest insults, but fear tied her tongue.

It had nothing to do with the lofty title of "Sir"—after all, she outranked him in another life. He was taller than her, stronger than her, and his ire made him unpredictable. She knew what a man's hands could do.

"I do cry your pardon…"

"Mistress Pylet would never dare refuse my custom! I have a mind to shut down this tawdry stew! Mayhap this bitch can change my mind." He turned to look at Jane, who grew pale under his wild-eyed glare.

Young stepped out from behind the bar, pushing up his sleeves, while Sir Antony moved toward Jane. At the same moment, the front door groaned open.

Maggie prayed it was Mistress Pylet, but she was already darting around the table, grunting as she slammed her thigh into the corner in her haste. "Sir Antony, I pray you, Jane is not to blame for this. While Mistress Pylet is absent, your quarrel must be with me. An it please you, I will suggest to the madam that your next entertainment be discounted…"

He whirled on her, his eyes hard and sharp, his posture erect and menacing. "I will not be ordered about by an impudent slut!"

She saw his arm fly up and back, and she cringed away from him, her own weak arm swinging up to deflect the blow. She had just enough time to wonder how much this would hurt.

The blow didn't come.

Captain Stokes was standing over them both, holding Sir Antony's trembling wrist in a relentless grip.

"Unhand me, sirrah!"

"Lower your fist." Stokes's voice was calm, but his face was forbidding.

The man thrashed, but a sharp, whispering *swish* made him freeze with an unmanly squeak. The point of Stokes's dagger dimpled the other man's doublet.

Stokes's mouth was at the man's ear. "Mayhap all this bruit has damaged your hearing. Shall I repeat myself?"

Slowly, Sir Antony extricated himself from around Stokes's imposing form, his eyes never leaving the dagger's silver point. When he was free, he tugged down the doublet that had ridden up over his round belly and glared at the captain. Stokes held the dagger in his left hand, his stance made more threatening by how casual it was.

Sir Antony shot Maggie a nasty look before storming out the door.

"Are you all right?" she asked the younger girl.

Jane smiled with tight lips. "Ta, Mags. 'E's a reet bastard. I'll not mourn 'im."

Both women returned their attention to Stokes. Jane put on her business smile. "Ta for comin' to me rescue so gallantly, sir. If 'tis company th'art after, I'm afeared there's none but meself." She leaned over the stairway railing in a way that displayed the bare skin above her neckline. Maggie felt a sharp twinge of embarrassment.

Luckily, Jane's sorcery proved ineffective on the captain. "I warrant you are more than enough, but that is not the purpose for my visit."

"Is there nowt I can do to change thy mind?" He gave her a pained smile, and she shrugged her narrow shoulders in resignation. "I'm Jane. Tha'll remember for the next time, I hope." The girl's gaze lingered on Stokes as she turned to mount the stairs.

Young slunk back to the bar, leaving Maggie and Stokes in the middle of the dining room. It was good to see a familiar face, better because of what had just happened. What *had* just happened? Were they meant to have a normal conversation now, when a moment ago she feared for her life?

"I am glad to see you," she said. "And not only because you prevented an unbecoming bruise."

"Is this my doing? Had I known you were in danger here, I would never have recommended you for this position."

"Nay, 'tis not your doing. Women may be menaced anywhere, I fear. In truth, before this afternoon, I would have told you I am quite happy here."

"Excellent well." He rapped a knuckle on the back of a nearby chair to fill the silence.

"Ellen will be back at any moment." *She has been wild to see you again.* This part of the rehearsed speech stuck in her throat. It was childish, but she didn't want to sell Ellen's wares to this particular patron.

The silence returned, now augmented by her awkward comment. She waited, feeling uncomfortable around this serious version of the captain. Where were the cheeky smirk and the rascally remarks?

"I bring an invitation," he said at last. "The Lord Chamberlain's Men are staging a new play at Blackfriars. 'Tis said to be diverting, but I am loath to go alone."

At the words "Lord Chamberlain's Men," her face lit up. She had yet to see one of Master Shakespeare's plays in person; the nearby Globe Theatre had closed for the winter by the time Maggie settled in London, and the girls could not be bothered to trek across town with her. "Aye, I have heard of it! How I long to see it. I am sorry to say, Ellen does not find the theater amusing, although I know she holds you in high regard."

There, the ghost of a smile. She didn't know what she said to provoke it, but she was happy to see it.

"I am at once flattered and horrified to learn you and Ellen speak of me."

She flushed. "Not but rarely, and only because you are the one acquaintance we have in common."

"And now I am wounded. Which is worse: to be spoken of, or never to be spoken of?" His lips turned up in their usual way, and it was like a heavy curtain between them parted. Here was the solid ground she had been missing.

"It must sting to know you are not an hourly topic of conversation…"

"Like an arrow to the breast."

"But you cannot expect to always be on a woman's mind if you appear but once a fortnight."

"No? Yet I take care to leave a lasting impression."

"That is charitable of you. We women are most forgetful creatures."

"Then you recommend I appear more frequently?"

"'Tis a subtle thing you hope to achieve. Show yourself too seldom, and you are in danger of being replaced. Too often, and she grows weary of the sight of you."

"These are wise words indeed. I bow to your expertise." He dipped his head in a mocking gesture of submission. "How must I proceed? Mayhap 'tis best I take myself away now, lest my return on Friday be too wearisome."

"'Tis worth considering, but as she has not yet seen you, you may be overzealous in your preparation."

"Who?"

Maggie furrowed her brow in confusion. "Ellen."

Stokes cocked his head and regarded her with a curious mix of amusement and bewilderment. "I fear this discussion has gotten away from me. Will you escort me to the theater or no?"

"Me?"

"I believed you to be somewhat of a disciple of this Shakespeare."

"I am! 'Tis a dear wish of mine to see his works performed on a stage."

"Then I hope 'tis not too great a hardship to accompany me to his *Winter's Tale*?"

Her heart swelled as she realized he was in earnest. "No hardship at all! I am wild to go. I thank you!"

"'Tis I who bid *you* thanks, for bestowing the honor of your august company."

She scowled at him and ignored his teasing. "You are certain there is no one you would rather take with you?"

"I am," he said.

It was only later, after she told Ellen all about the afternoon, that she realized with a sickening jolt how ironic her words had been. She had been teasing when she told Stokes men were so easily forgotten. Yet for a few minutes, and after only three weeks of silence, Matthew had slipped from her mind.

19

ELLEN LINGERED IN Maggie's bedchamber on Friday, her ostensible purpose being to offer beauty advice while Maggie dressed for her evening at the theater.

"A little rouge on the cheeks," she said. "The winter dark has made you pale."

Maggie glowered at the image of Ellen behind her in the mirror and ignored her advice, instead placing her new hat on her head and turning her face left and right to admire it. It had cost more than someone on her salary should have spent, but it was the first luxury she had bought with her own money. She chose it for its forest green color and the single brown- and white-striped pheasant feather tucked into the folded brim. That it was similar to Stokes's signature yellow hat was a coincidence.

Ellen had gushed over it when they saw it in the window the day before, but she had changed her tune since then. "I can lend you a hat that better frames your face. Here, let me arrange your hair in the new style."

Maggie swatted away Ellen's fluttering hands. "I have always worn it like this. If I take special care with it, he will believe I did it for him."

Ellen stilled her hands and laid them instead on Maggie's shoulders, giving her a brief squeeze. "Men adore believing such things. It would not hurt to let him."

"Would it not? I have no desire to make him believe what is not true." She reached up to smooth one eyebrow, then swiped an errant eyelash off her cheek. Her face was pale, she admitted, but not so lifeless as Ellen seemed to believe. The summer sun had provided her with a subtle glow and a galaxy of red freckles, and while they would be gone by spring, the hint of them remained.

She was eating and sleeping well, working hard and balancing it with companionship and entertainment. Her cheeks were round and her eyes were bright. She would never compare to Ellen, but in this light, she thought she looked rather pretty.

Not that it mattered how pretty she was tonight. Whatever beauty she might possess was meant for her future husband, whose three-week silence had allowed a potent dread to ferment in her stomach. Either their courtship was over, or his titanic fury required almost a month to subside. She thought she might give anything just to understand where they stood.

"Are you certain he is only a friend?" Ellen said.

"Of course. He has shown no sign that he desires more."

"And taking you to the theater does not signify?"

"He is too vain to be spotted alone at the theater. I am certain he invited me for his own purposes."

She chuckled. "That may well be true. Still, he could have found another willing woman to drape over his arm."

"He is so often at sea, I do not doubt his relationships on land are difficult to maintain. I was the convenient choice, certes."

"So many excuses! You will not allow that he likes you, for you do not give it a moment's thought!"

"If he liked me," she said, turning around on her stool, "why would he not say so? Men are not subtle. Matthew declared his feelings for me in words that could not be misunderstood."

"Forgive me, I had forgotten you were the expert on men, and I, a lowly student."

When Maggie descended the stairs to the Dagger's dining room at a quarter to seven with Ellen on her heels, Stokes was already there. He sat at a table with an older man in his mid-fifties, with graying brown hair that curled elegantly to his shoulders. His neat beard and mustache could have been modeled after the captain's—or perhaps it was the other way around.

The man had a goblet in front of him with an open bottle beside it, but he was ignoring his drink in favor of whatever story he was in the middle of recounting. The captain listened and gave polite nods at intervals. When he saw her, his expression was full of exaggerated relief, as if she had arrived expressly to rescue him.

His friend followed Stokes's gaze, and he quit his story mid-sentence to stand and bow. It was the most polite reception she had seen at the Dagger and Sheath, aside from Stokes's, and by the look on the man's face, she guessed it had something to do with Ellen.

"Bonsoir, mesdemoiselles," he said. Ellen brushed past Maggie to greet him, holding out her hand so he could kiss her fingers. "Will you introduce me to your beautiful friend?" Maggie caught his gaze dipping to examine her body, and it elicited the usual shiver of embarrassment. She was growing used to that assessing scan, like she was a new item on the brothel's menu. This man's glance, however, was more curious than hungry.

Stokes spoke before Ellen had a chance. "This is Maggie Bailey. I told you about the new purser—here she is."

Maggie flushed. "I believe a ship's purser is traditionally written into the manifest. And paid."

The Frenchman laughed and turned to Stokes. "I knew your Osborne was greedy for money. Now I see the order comes from you, no?"

"The captain was generous enough to shelter me. I was happy to work in exchange," she clarified, feeling guilty.

"Maggie is Mistress Pylet's secretary for the winter," Ellen added. "She is excellent with numbers."

"Très bien! I admire a woman who makes her own way. It is hard that we men hold the reins. Women are much the wiser sex, *hein?"*

Ellen took his arm. "Maggie and the captain are to Blackfriars to see the Lord Chamberlain's Men, and you are making them late, Jules."

He placed a hand over his heart. "My apologies! I detain you no more." He turned to Ellen. "Unless you would join Captain Moran and Mademoiselle Bailey? I will happily escort you to the theater."

The use of Stokes's alias surprised Maggie, but when she glanced at the captain, he was unfazed.

Ellen shook her head and smiled. "Another time. Will you come up?"

It always amazed Maggie how little effort was required when Ellen closed a deal. The other whores could often be found wandering the crowded dining room, simpering and giggling, sitting on laps and playing with hair, all to entice a man to go upstairs. Yet when Ellen beckoned, they followed.

This one was no different. He grabbed the wine bottle and grinned at her. *"Je te suis."*

The December air was cold, and light flurries of snow glinted in the glow of the lamps that lined the street. They exchanged a few pleasantries as they walked, but Stokes didn't look at her until they stood at the Tooley Stairs waiting for a boat.

"New hat."

Even knowing his smirk was more or less a permanent feature, she couldn't say for sure he wasn't mocking her—which was frustrating, because she happened to like this hat.

"The color suits you."

"Ellen helped me choose it."

"A woman of style, our Ellen."

Maggie was gripped by a sudden childish urge to poke at him. "She mentioned the other day that she has seen little of you."

"I regret that my absence should cause her pain." When he saw she had no patience for his arrogance, he rephrased his answer. "I have been busy of late. I mean not to offend her. And if I were truthful…" He turned to check for an incoming boat as his fingers came up to fidget with a button on his doublet. "I do not relish the idea of enjoying Ellen's company when one of my crew is under the same roof."

She knew it was a shortcut, a simple way to reference a complicated relationship, but she thrilled to hear him call her one of his crew. "Have you such qualms when you and your men are on leave together? I have seen you flirt with a dozen women in front of your crew."

"Aye, well, my dear mother urged me never to hide my light under a bushel basket."

"Pray, do not stray from your calling on my account."

"Flirting with women and bedding them are vastly different activities. One is often improved by spectators. The other is best done in private."

The dark hid her blush, and she modified her tone to further conceal her embarrassment. "If you like Ellen and she gives you pleasure, you should see her."

"'Tis most gracious."

He waved over an approaching boat, and she was relieved to end the conversation. Until the words were out of her mouth, she had not realized they were a lie. Stokes's bedroom activities should not interest her, nor even cross her mind. Why, then, was she so curious? Why could she envision Ellen's smooth honey voice saying, "Will you come up?" and Stokes's answering smirk? And why did it make her feel so wretched?

It was Ellen's fault. She planted a thought in Maggie's mind that should never have been there.

Outside Blackfriars theater, the queue was crowded and merry. The old monastery's caramel-colored timbers and white plaster glowed gold in the torchlight. A broadside nailed to a wooden sign declared "BLACK FRYERS THEATRE" and "THE WINTERS TALE" in large letters, with mentions of the principal actors and the playwright in a smaller hand beneath. The eager patrons huddled in their warmest clothes, but their cheeks were pink as much from anticipation as from the winter air.

At the entrance, Stokes requested admission to the pit and handed over three shillings without hesitation.

The pennies Maggie had gotten out of her purse in preparation bit into her palm as she clenched her fist. "So dear!" she hissed as they entered the floor level to find a seat on the benches. "I would have been equally happy in the gallery."

"Maggie Bailey, the great lover of William Shakespeare attending her first play by his hand, would prefer the gallery?"

He swept his arm in a gallant gesture and let her sidle down the row ahead of him. He doffed his hat as he settled in beside her.

She held out her fist, the pennies hot and damp, but he only looked at her in confusion. "For my seat," she explained. "'Tis only part, but I will repay the rest when next we meet."

He pushed her arm down until her fist rested in her lap. "Nay, my lady, I will not allow it. 'Tis my pleasure."

She looked sidelong at him. "You need not address me so."

"Will you deny me that pleasure as well?"

"What pleasure? Reminding me of my late husband?"

"Come, Maggie, if you wish to disarm me, you must try harder than that." He grinned at her. "If you would distance yourself from your husband's rank, I will oblige you. But may not a poor sailor enjoy being seen with a lovely young woman of stature?"

"Ah, 'tis clear now. You wear me as a jewel. Had you told me before, I would have striven to look more the part."

"By my troth, you do look it. No man who saw you would think you common." He plucked at the yellow brocade skirt of her borrowed gown. "Whose is this? Ellen's? It must be a gift from Bisset."

She smoothed her hand over the beautiful material. It was impractical for winter in England, but she loved the magical way it caught the candlelight. "She does enjoy dressing me like a doll. Is Bisset a clothier? I have not heard the name."

Stokes froze, his eyes widening a fraction in a look she would almost have called panic. He chuckled and shook his head. "You put me too at ease. I forgot myself." Seeing her confusion, he continued, "I distinctly remember refusing to name my business partners. But as you have met the man, I do not see how I can keep his identity a secret."

Ellen's patron, the Frenchman, had called him Captain Moran.

"The man at the Dagger? And you think this dress is a gift from him? Mayhap he recognized it. Is that why he stared at me?"

He smirked. "If you like."

She caught the implication and swatted his leg before steering him back to the subject. "So Monsieur Bisset is a cloth merchant?"

"I have said more than—"

"If you will not tell me, I need only ask Ellen."

He cast his eyes up to the stage, sighed, and looked back at her. "Aye, he is a cloth merchant. He does marvelous well for himself—in part because we help him to avoid a fortune in tariffs," he added out of the corner of his mouth.

Maggie thought about the Chinese silk that was in the hold of her first Spanish prize ship. "I remember Osborne speaking of him, I think, or another of your partners. Whoever it was seemed to enjoy painting himself as a victim of misfortune."

Stokes burst into laughter. "You have summed him up perfectly! He is a shrewd businessman, but he weaves stories that would melt a heart of stone. One time," he said in a storyteller's undertone, bringing his head close to Maggie's, "I had a hold full of Dutch wool, fiendishly popular all over Europe. Bisset spun me an absurd tale about the Earl of Suffolk's new Venetians... I cannot remember every detail, but he convinced me Dutch wool went out of favor while we were at sea." He rolled his eyes. "Of course, he offered to help me shift it at a loss to himself. Or so he claimed." His sigh was full of nostalgia.

Maggie cocked her head. "You sound as though you admire him."

"I was furious at the time, but aye, I suppose I do."

"Do you admire everyone who lies to you? How can you call him a respectable businessman if he behaves so?"

"I believe the word I used is 'shrewd.' Respectability is not a requirement in my line of work."

"But he manipulated you!"

"And if I had his talent for manipulating, I would use it to my advantage."

"Fie! You would not."

He jerked his head back as if she had swung at him.

Her outburst surprised her too, but she shrugged and mumbled, "You are too honest."

His expression didn't change. "Am I?"

"And too feeling. You confessed Robert's crime in, what, the second hour of my captivity? A few tears were all it took for you to ride to my rescue. You could not spin a falsehood any easier than I could spin straw into gold."

Even after all this time, it felt disingenuous to distill that dreadful morning into one flippant sentence. There was no question she had needed rescuing. How could she tease him about his honesty when it was the very reason she begged to stay aboard? He would never be a storyteller like Bisset, and for that, she was grateful.

The surprised expression on his face transformed itself as she spoke, and his eyes shifted, unfocused, beneath his furrowed brow. The silence made her itch, as did the knowledge she had finally gone too far. They had joked with each other a dozen times before with no hard feelings on either side, but for the first time, she had rendered him speechless.

She opened her mouth to take it back, but the words wouldn't come.

A moment later, the play began.

Aside from the bear, which was clearly a man on all fours covered in a bearskin, the moving performances had Maggie fighting back tears by the time the wronged queen was restored to life. The hundreds of candles lighting the theater shrank to dangerous stubs, and a heavy haze of tobacco smoke hung in the air, adding to the magic.

By the shouts from the gallery and the animated faces of the wealthy patrons seated on the stage, the audience enjoyed it as much as she had. They applauded as each company member took his bow, including Master Shakespeare. She craned her neck to see him, finally able to put a face to the name on the handful of precious quartos she had left on a shelf at Duntsford Priory.

The theater-goers filed out, chattering and laughing and reliving their favorite moments from the evening's spectacle. She walked with Stokes down the dark street, buoyed along by the throng of people.

"Finding a boat will take an age." He eyed the already long queue at the Blackfriars Stairs.

"I do not mind the walk."

She regretted it at once. Moment after moment, footstep after footstep, passed in awkward silence. A half-hour of this hell stretched ahead of them if she couldn't think of something to say. The captain didn't seem inclined to rescue her this time.

What she had said to him before the play was fat-tongued nonsense. Of course accusing a pirate captain of such a weakness as honesty would rankle him.

She wished she could assure him she meant what she said, while apologizing for the way she said it, but his posture was closed off. He looked ahead, glanced at the ground, darted his eyes side to side to search the dark alcoves for hidden cutpurses. He looked everywhere but at her. This silent Stokes was like the serious Stokes who had held back Sir Antony's fist. She didn't know how to interact with either.

"I thought the man who played the king gave an admirable performance." She watched out of the corner of her eye for his reaction.

"Certes."

"And Hermione. My heart nigh broke for her."

"A most compelling actor." His voice was flat, void of emotion. He wanted her to stop talking.

So she tried harder. "'Twas a bit heavy-handed, though, was it not? Hermione was accused of adultery, lost her child, *died*, and when she was miraculously restored, she forgave her husband's betrayal at once. I should have liked a more realistic story, methinks."

Stokes still didn't look at her, but she swore something about his posture shifted. "Hermione should not have forgiven Leontes, then?"

"He did nothing to deserve her forgiveness."

"He was remorseful."

"As well he should be. For ruining her like that, guilt should be the least of his punishments."

"You would have Leontes get his comeuppance, then. You would have Hermione take her revenge."

"Nay, I do not require Hermione to deliver justice, only to receive it. After what she endured by Leontes's hand, it should not be her responsibility to punish him as well."

"But is her forgiveness not, in a way, its own punishment? How could Leontes forget what he had done to her, with her a living reminder? Her goodness would always mock him for having hurt so good a woman."

"You assume his remorse is both painful and lasting. Can a man who treats the woman he loves with such contempt ever truly feel the consequences of his actions?"

He looked sideways at her, his expression unclear in the low light of the infrequent lamps. "Such a mistake should haunt a man for the rest of his life."

They were approaching a renewed feeling of easiness, and the topic was even shifting itself toward what she wanted to talk to him about. As she struggled to begin the conversation, London Bridge came into view. Increasing numbers of late-night revelers joined them, and they were forced to devote most of their concentration to keeping a straight path.

The Thames rushed below, wide and black, but one would never know it. London Bridge was less a bridge than a high street, with dark shop windows lining each side of the wide thoroughfare and residences rising two or three more stories above them. The street was not as busy as it was during the day, but carts and horses still trundled past on late-night business.

Foot traffic was dense in both directions. The Globe might be closed, but there was plenty of other entertainment to be had in Southwark, not least of which being the numerous illicit brothels. Maggie could expect to return to a crowded and rambunctious Dagger and Sheath, and she would have her work cut out for her in the morning with making sense of Amelia's scribbled notes.

When a glimpse of the river appeared between two buildings, Maggie drifted toward the short wall of the bridge's railing. Three weeks in London was not enough to tire of the sight of the Thames. Ships dotted the river's banks, their sails tucked away as they slumbered at their wharves. As always, the sight turned her thoughts to the sea.

She missed the briny scent of the air, the mustiness of the sodden planks, how tar and oil and hemp and gunpowder made up the *Merrow*'s unique perfume. She missed pink and orange sunrises, purple and red sunsets, and a flat, featureless horizon in every direction.

She missed the cozy lamplight after dark, the sailor's crude banter, O'Flaherty's lightning-quick bow and Davies's awful jokes. She missed black storm clouds, bracing winds, treacherous waves that felt so much like falling, so much like flying. She was in love with it.

But she didn't mourn its loss, as she should. Rather, a bright shard of hope made her impatient for an impossibility.

Stokes stopped beside her. For a moment, it was like they were on the ship again, gazing out at a star-studded horizon. Those moments of nighttime reflection were when she had felt closest to him. When he had felt realest.

"You once told me the crew would not condone the hiring of a female sailor mid-journey." She rested her hands on the wall. "You will forgive me if I read too deep into it, but does that not contain a suspicious number of caveats?"

"I do not grasp your meaning."

"Hiring a female sailor, for example," she said, turning to him. "When I was a guest of sorts, my presence was tolerated, but you drew the line at receiving shares. 'Twas not my sex that made me ineligible, but my status." He furrowed his brow. She pushed ahead. "Then you said *mid-journey*, as though the timing mattered. So I wondered if mayhap… a woman sailor could be hired *before* the journey."

He looked back out at the river, his gaze focused somewhere between the bridge and the twinkling lamps of Whitehall Palace. She scrutinized his face in search of some tic, some twitch that would betray what he was thinking.

His silence made her more nervous the longer it persisted, so she blustered on. "Surely you would not have used so many words if a simple 'no' would have sufficed."

He huffed out a laugh and glanced at her. "Would you have accepted a simple no?"

"No."

He turned to face her fully and smiled that familiar half-smile. It was almost enough to make her sigh with relief.

"'Tis your desire to toil among rude, unwashed criminals for six months out of the year? At least the criminals with whom you currently associate are easy to look at."

"Aye, but the Dagger and Sheath is regrettably landlocked."

"So 'tis the sea you want."

"I warrant you can relate to such a desire."

He looked down at the patch of bridge between them, no doubt determining how to gently let her down. The brim of his hat tipped up enough to reveal his eyes, glimmering with the reflection of the moon on the Thames. "I believe I *could* convince my crew to accept a woman as a mate, as long as she were a fixture from the beginning of the voyage." Joy filled her chest, but before she could respond, he held up a hand. "*But…* it would not change any of the *Merrow*'s rules of order. No man has yet tried to bring his wife aboard my ship. I may tell you now I would not allow it."

She felt like an imbecile for forgetting such an important detail. The captain was obsessed with equity, and there was nothing equitable about how Matthew had laid claim to her at the end of the summer.

"While we are on the subject…" His voice became light and impersonal. "I pray you will inform me when I am to congratulate you."

She found a chip in the stone wall and traced it with her fingernail, the only thing she could think to do to avoid meeting his eyes. The story was on the tip of her tongue.

"I will," she said, forcing her lips into a polite smile.

"What ho, captain!"

The shout came from behind her, and Stokes's head snapped up. He shot a quick glance at Maggie, then nodded at the newcomer over her shoulder.

She turned to find Meredith, the *Merrow*'s resident rope maker. He was flanked by three other men, all graying and balding. One man swayed, already deep in his cups.

"Maggie?" Merry came closer, squinting. "By my troth, 'tis Maggie indeed! How now, lass? What's brought you both out 'ere tonight?"

The men with him were impatient to move on, but Merry only looked more and more curious, as if he had stumbled upon some ancient, baffling text he was eager to decipher.

Maggie sorted through the weak explanations her frazzled mind could invent, but Stokes beat her to it.

"I happened upon her leaving Blackfriars, and as she had lost her friends, I offered to escort her home."

"Always the gentleman, is our captain!" Merry glanced back toward his friends and found they had wandered further across the bridge without him. "Best be off. I'll give Kent your love, then, shall I, Maggie?"

Before she could respond, he was touching the brim of his hat and shuffling away.

They watched him trot across the bridge, saying nothing until he had rounded the bend of Thames Street.

Stokes cleared his throat. "That will not become a problem for you, I hope?"

Yes, she thought. "Nay," she said.

And she created horror stories in her mind all the way back to the brothel, planning her defense for when Matthew arrived. It was possible, of course, that Merry would forget what he had seen, thinking it unremarkable Stokes might help a young woman home late at night. If he was as trusting of the too-honest captain as Maggie was, it might not occur to him Stokes had been lying.

But Meredith did not forget. Two days later, as she returned from mass, she met Matthew's languid form leaning against the plaster facade of the Dagger and Sheath.

20

"THE INN IS closed, I'm afraid." Frank's pointed nose and sharp features transformed her bored expression into something sinister. She didn't sound at all afraid. "Come back tomorrow."

"He's not a patron!" Maggie matched one of Frank's strides with two of her own. By the time she caught up with her, she was out of breath and her heart was pounding. That might also have had something to do with seeing Matthew here in her domain after so long.

Frank peered down her nose at him and grunted. By then, Ellen had arrived with Mary, each woman holding the hand of a little girl. The others gathered around, Amelia Pylet's stately pace bringing her up last. They assembled in front of the brothel, a pretty picture of a devout English family fresh from church.

Matthew looked around at them all, his eyes wary. On the ship, he was in his element, but now he found himself outnumbered by women—probably for the first time.

He doffed his knit cap and nodded while Maggie introduced him to her friends. When she got to Mistress Pylet, he bowed and looked away from the older woman's scowl.

If not for the children, who were hungry and restless after sitting through mass, they might have stood there all day in awkward silence. Denise's boy, Ralph, was the first to peel away, and young Moll raced after him, followed by their mothers. Ellen met her gaze as she disappeared through the doorway. Soon Maggie and Matthew were alone in the street.

She tucked her cold hands in the folds of her skirt. He looked up at her through his eyelashes, holding his knit cap in both hands like a timid boy. He was no different than when they had parted, his nut-brown hair loose about his cheeks, his shoulders broad from labor, his face tan and clean-shaven.

After the initial surprise of finding him here, she noticed a sort of thawing, a gradual shift from irritation to contrition. Why should he look different? It had only been three short weeks.

He swallowed. "How fare you?"

"Well."

He glanced at the brothel's dark windows, then up and down the street. There was no one around. There was also nowhere to go to escape the cold. He held out his arm. "Will you walk with me?"

It was quiet in Southwark, with most businesses closed and most families either still at mass or preparing their Sunday meals. In only a few minutes, they left the homes and storefronts behind and emerged into the countryside, where swaths of field stood empty save for the stubble of harvested crops.

They came upon a low stone wall, and Matthew invited her to join him on the makeshift seat. The farmhouses were spread out enough to ensure they would not disturb or be disturbed, but there was no shelter except for a few shrubs on the roadside. After three weeks in the crowded city, she felt exposed out here.

Birds chattering, then a distant cowbell, decorated the silence. The cold seeped through the layers of her cloak and skirts before one of them spoke.

"How is Luke?"

"Been learnin' rope making with a master down the docks. Same one what trained Merry."

Maybe she was paranoid, but lobbing Meredith's name at her felt like a test. If she didn't catch it, would he think she concealed something? "I saw him the other day. Meredith."

"He said."

So it had been a test. "He looks well," she went on, keeping her tone light. "As do you. Is there enough work to be had on the docks? Are you comfortable?"

"You will not tell me, then?"

"Tell you what?"

"About Stokes."

Her gut clenched. "Aye. I saw Stokes as well, though it matters not."

"It matters to me," he retorted.

She had missed him, and she had been feeling fondly towards him, but the new defensiveness in his tone rankled her. He had set her up, and now he would punish her for her honesty.

Then again, she should have told him before he asked. A good woman would never have been with another man in the first place.

She hid her guilt with bitterness. "Is that the only reason you came today? To scold me?"

"Of course not. You always do this! You always think the worst of me." He rolled his eyes to the gray winter sky. "Mayhap you are right to think the worst of me—mayhap I am cruel at my core."

Her need to soothe him, to reassure him, overshadowed the impulse to argue. That was how it worked: when he tore himself down, she built him back up, using her sweetest words and her gentlest touches. The results of her efforts usually pleased her: he would smile and kiss her, and she would gather strength for the next time.

"Nay, my dearest, forgive me." She laid her hand on his knee. "'Tis only that I have missed you. We have been apart for weeks. I worried you would never come again."

He touched the back of her hand with his fingertips, stroking from knuckles to wrist. The delicate, intimate feel of it ignited the familiar longing, and she knew she was done being angry at him. Whatever he asked of her, she would do.

"I stayed away too long. After that blow you gave me, I nursed my pain like a coward."

Hearing him blame her for his silence made her stomach drop. She had been nursing her own hurt feelings, never resolved to apologize, but now she learned he had waited for it, in vain, for three weeks. Why had she not gone to him?

"I ken that you've become accustomed to workin', and I ken that it may not be easy to change... but why did you go behind my back?"

She didn't have a ready answer. The one she wanted to give, the one that came first to mind, would never have worked: *I wasn't ready to give it all up, not even for you.*

He laced their fingers and squeezed. "I want to take care of you. I want to provide for you. You'll not let me."

"Why may we not provide for each other?" She hated the whine in her voice. "Would we not be doubly comfortable? Doubly happy?"

"What sort of man would I be if I could not keep my wife clothed and fed by the sweat of my own brow? You're a lady, Margaret. You deserve leisure. White skin and soft hands." He trapped her hand between his warm palms.

"If we marry, I will not be a lady—I will be a sailor's wife. Shall I lounge in my simple lodging pretending to be a queen while the other wives gossip about me?"

"And what if they do? 'Twill only be for a time. Soon you'll be runnin' 'round after our children and you'll have no time to heed the gossip."

She pictured them, her sons and daughters. In her mind, they dashed across a busy market square, laughing, darting behind stalls and carts and knees to hide from her. She summoned their faces, but they had none; their hair had no color nor texture, and their voices held no tone when they called her *mama*. To think of them made her shiver.

He leaned toward her down-turned face and kissed her, gentle, repentant. She was glad for the distraction. She lifted her chin and kissed him back, a flutter beginning in her stomach.

"Be mine, Margaret. Let us finish what we started."

Perhaps he was her destiny. Their meeting again after so much had gone wrong could not be mere coincidence. God had taken her husband, but He had provided another. This one, she could love.

She had been a dutiful wife to Sir John, but for Matthew, she would be better. Though she would be lonely while he was at sea, his absence would make their time together more precious. She would miss him too much to quarrel or nag, and he would never find fault with her. It could be a good life.

Better than a foolish runaway could ever hope to have.

She stole through the back door around dusk, which fell heavy and early. The Dagger's kitchen was empty, the coals in the hearth warm, but dark. It was long past suppertime, so she foraged for something to eat and brought her cold meal out into the dining room.

It was a common gathering place on frosty Sunday nights. The women could share candlelight and tend only one fire, and everyone kept an eye on the children. The littlest ones were playing some make-believe game under a table. Francie and Ned sat near their mother, Frank, helping her with some mending, and Amelia dozed with a book nearby. Across the room, Mary, Molly, and Jane giggled with their heads close together. Ellen and Denise threw dice, a pile of pennies littering the table between them.

Maggie dropped into the seat beside Ellen.

"Had a nice visit?" Ellen's tone was innocent, but her arched eyebrow was not.

Maggie shrugged and skewered a piece of cold goose with her knife.

Denise won the next three rounds while Maggie ate and watched. Ellen finally conceded, in too shrill a voice to be sportsmanlike. She shoved the coins toward the victor, and Denise scraped them off the table into her palm before joining the group of chattering magpies on the other side of the room.

Ellen crossed her arms and glared at Maggie. "Will you not tell me?"

"There is little to tell. We spoke. And reconciled."

"Who apologized first?"

"It hardly matters." She felt queasy. The cold leftovers must not be agreeing with her empty stomach. "And we are to be married."

"Much happiness to you both! When is the blessed day?"

"Very soon. He would have the banns read next week. Only…" Maggie looked over at Mistress Pylet, asleep, and Frank, intent on her task. With no one to hear, why could she still not tell Ellen the truth? "I promised Pylet I would stay the winter."

"A spring wedding is better than a winter one."

"But we cannot delay so long." Her response came too fast. She needed to calm herself, to behave normally. "He wants to establish our home before he leaves for the summer."

"Then what will you do?"

What indeed. When she told him of her commitment to the Dagger and Sheath, he surprised her by nodding as if he understood. She expected him to demand she quit her position, but he held his tongue.

There were other ways to force her hand.

"There was not time enough to discuss all the details."

"Oh, aye? And would that be because you spent all your time on *other* details?"

Ellen's expression was comical, dark eyebrows bouncing up and down. It would have elicited at least an eye roll under normal circumstances, but Maggie kept her gaze fixed on the food she couldn't finish. She scraped the tip of her knife across the trencher in a crosshatch pattern.

Ellen's fingers closed around her wrist. "What has happened?"

Saying it out loud would only make it real, but what choice did she have? Ellen was the only person in the world she could come to for something as awful as this. She breathed out the words, forcing Ellen to lean in to hear her. "I may be with child."

The grip on her wrist pulsed, a reassuring squeeze, and Maggie made herself tell the story. There would be no distancing herself from it, not while it was so near, not while she could still feel the cold stone wall under her and Matthew's hot breath on her face.

At first, it was as if his kisses had brought her back to life. He devoured her as their joint desire increased. She struggled to remain present, worrying a farmer or a pedant would wander by. There was nothing illegal about kissing in public, but she had never been the sort to do so.

He caught her hand and pulled it down to his lap. "This is what you do to me."

She yanked her hand away. *This* was not something she should be doing in full view of anyone happening by.

"Shy?" He chuckled. "Are you not a pirate?"

"Are pirates never sent to the pillory for lewd behavior?"

He looked around them, spotting a structure a dozen yards across the field: a goat shed, already occupied by a handful of sheep.

The air inside was humid and rank with filth and lanolin, despite being open to the winter breeze on one side. He pushed her against the rough wall and kissed her hard as he fumbled with the front of his breeches.

She couldn't understand how this was to work. There was nowhere to lie down, not that she would have agreed to soil her clothes in the muck. He was undeterred. His mouth went to her chest as he hauled up her skirts, handful by handful. He bit her above her collarbone. She made eye contact with a sheep.

Matthew lifted her leg to his hip and pushed inside her. His face was tight with concentration as he thrust.

She closed her eyes and remembered the bashful, fumbling boy who dared to kiss her, who tentatively parted her lips with his tongue, who boldly tangled his hand in her unbound hair. She summoned the desire that had once oozed through her veins like warm honey, the innocent hunger that made her kiss him back, thinking this was the epitome of wickedness before she knew how wicked someone could be.

And it began, the ache, the burn, the hum. She gasped at the strange way pain mixed with pleasure, at the commingling of memory with immediacy. Wanton women fucked in goat sheds, but not for free. She wanted pleasure. She demanded it. Hooking her leg around his hip, she moved in tandem, blindly seeking to harness the molten sweetness that filled her with each thrust.

He drove her hard into the wall, pinning her there with the full force of his body. He shuddered, then relaxed.

The thought flitted through her mind that it wasn't fair. Something had been about to happen, and she had lost hold of it without knowing what she had been trying to grasp.

As he kissed her neck, panting and damp with sweat, another thought replaced the first with terrifying clarity: choosing desire didn't absolve her of consequences. This was a path that ended in a cage.

Now, she looked up at Ellen, but her friend's face showed no hint of surprise or pity or disgust. Each time she had felt foolish speaking like this, Maggie remembered that it was Ellen, not Alinor, not Elizabeth. Ellen would not judge her. Ellen would know what to do.

And she did. "Come."

Maggie's hand shook as she let Ellen haul her out of the chair and lead her upstairs.

Ellen's bedchamber was untidy, with gowns spilling out of the wardrobe and shoes littering the floor. The table where she prepared her face and hair was a mess of cosmetics, pins, and jewels. Her bed was unmade, not that anyone expected her to make it a dozen times each day.

As soon as the door latch clanked into place, Ellen lit a lamp and crossed to the table beside the bed. She retrieved a bottle and a cup and held them out to Maggie.

"There is always a bottle of this rolling about the place. I make one up every full moon and take it for a few days until my courses come on. It will make you bleed, and a babe cannot grow in an empty womb."

Maggie stared at it. "It will kill the child?"

"Oh, love—seeds need time to grow. But if a child is growing… aye, you'd be like to kill it." Ellen unstoppered the bottle and poured a careful measure into the cup. It was dark and thick, smelling of wine and pungent herbs. "You need not take it now. Certes, you need not take it at all. Put it by your bed and think on it. Then drink it or toss it into the street. No one need know but you."

The thought of taking the cup from that outstretched hand made her wretched. A child was a blessing—that's what every woman in Maggie's life had told her. A child was the consequence of what she had done today, which was why sex belonged between a husband and wife. She could not be allowed to escape it.

No one need know but you. It didn't matter. Maggie could torture herself better than anyone else could.

Ellen placed the cup and bottle on her cosmetics table. "Did he force you?"

"Nay. I went with him. But I did not think to ask him to pull away before he…" She grimaced.

Dragging the chair from the vanity toward the bed, Ellen sat on the mattress. "Men tend to lose interest in talking when their pricks are wet."

Maggie huffed out a half-laugh as she took the chair. "I confess, I became mute as well. Nothing could have made me tell him to stop. It felt… unbearable, but *good*. Like…" She cast around for a metaphor. "Like dough rising?"

Ellen laughed. "Aye, very like! Only better."

"Like a bubble about to burst."

"Like taking out your hairpins and loosening your stays."

They were both laughing now, Ellen with her legs tucked under her on the bed, Maggie leaning back in her chair. The low lamplight gave the room a cozy glow. For a moment she was transported back to Duntsford Priory on a winter night, Elizabeth and Maggie huddled under the covers, laughing until tears streamed down their young faces. The joke was long forgotten, but what remained was the feeling of being part of something, of being half of a pair. It was a rare happy memory of her sister. Such memories never failed to make her sad.

She shook off her melancholy. "I did not know it could be pleasant. I only wish something came of it."

Ellen's brows furrowed in bewilderment. "Like what?"

"An ending— Something. It was over so quick…"

"Oh, poor Mags!" Ellen's face was red from trying to hold in her laughter. "Something does come of it! Have you really never spun yourself off?"

Maggie's eyes went wide. "Have I what?"

Ellen stared at her as if Maggie had just revealed herself to be a Spanish princess in disguise. She leapt from the bed and went to a cabinet, where it seemed she tended a miniature tavern. She selected one of the half-dozen bottles and brought it back to the bed, pulling the cork as she did. "'Tis only cider," she clarified, seeing the look on Maggie's face. "Methinks you will want a drop before I begin the lesson."

21

EVERGREEN GARLANDS FESTOONED the ceiling beams, arcing from one iron nail to the next with the bobbing rhythm of a sonnet. Dripping candelabras domineered the feasting board, and the clean carcass of a roast pig sat pink and white and ghastly in its greasy pewter tray, its fat head still encircled by a wreath of waxy bay leaves. The rest of the table hid beneath fruit pits, pie crusts, the cold dregs of a wassail in its bowl, and three dozen gravy-smeared trenchers.

The revelers responsible for the detritus laughed and sang snippets of carols, smoked pipes, shouted down the table to friends, and whispered into the ears of blushing neighbors. Ellen flirted with Jules Bisset, and across from them, Captain Stokes smiled at the pretty, sandy-haired woman who sat beside him, one of the girls Pylet had hired to balance the guest list.

For the dozenth time, Maggie peered down at the watch she wore pinned to her bodice. She pushed back from the table and crossed to the front corner of the dining room.

Davies and Engberg were wrapping up a tune as she approached. Davies grinned up at her. "Have a request, Maggie, my love?"

"A dance, methinks. They have had enough time for the meal to settle."

"What'll it be?"

"Something merry. A Rufty Tufty?"

"Right." He nodded at Engberg, who nodded back. "Fetch the lucky lad, and we'll to it."

As she returned to the other side of the room, she glanced at the windows, too fogged to see out. Her thumb rubbed the face of the watch as it ticked closer to Matthew's arrival. He wasn't invited, but he had insisted on coming. It was sweet of him, she reminded herself. She was only nervous about having to explain his presence to Pylet. That was all. Their tryst in the goat shed didn't signify.

Maggie tapped Ellen on the shoulder. "If you would lead the first dance, the musicians are prepared."

Ellen beamed up at her, then turned back to Bisset. "I'll not go alone," she told him, and to the table at large she added, "Up, you lot! Come and trip it!"

Maggie backed up to make room for Ellen to stand, and as she did, she met Stokes's eye. She blinked, and he had already looked away, turning to ask his conversation partner to dance.

Another ingredient of her anxiety was the notion of being trapped in a room with Stokes and Matthew after how things had ended on the ship. It didn't help that Stokes appeared to be avoiding her since Blackfriars. A merry evening, indeed.

"Mistress?"

When she turned her head, a man was offering his hand for the dance. Matthew could arrive any moment, but she couldn't refuse without saddling the Dagger girls with a reputation for being stingy. With a smile, she let him lead her to the dance floor, but she gave more attention to the door than her steps.

As they began the second set, the door opened, sending a breath of winter air to cool the dancers. Maggie went through the motions while Matthew wandered inside and glanced around. Young hurried from the bar to greet him, and the men exchanged a word or two before turning as one to search the dance floor. When Matthew spotted her, she raised her hand in a wave of acknowledgement, for Young's sake as much as for Matthew's. Young gave Matthew a look and another short speech before going back to work.

Matthew waited by the door, arms folded, watching her. As soon as she rose from her final curtsy, she went to him, muttering her thanks to her dance partner as she passed.

"You've forgot me, eh?" Matthew said, leaning in to kiss her cheek. His words sent a whiff of whatever he had been drinking past her nose, and her gut tightened. Him being drunk wasn't going to make this evening any easier.

She laughed and rolled her eyes, linking arms with him. "Come, you need not haunt the door."

As she led him toward the back of the dining room, out of the way, he craned his neck to inspect the group beginning the next dance. "Who was that, then?" He jutted out his chin at her former dance partner.

"One of Denise's, methinks. I took pity on him, for she was spoken for." The low amount of effort these tiny lies required was gratifying. She only needed to set the rules—say nothing to make Matthew angry—and they simply tumbled out of her mouth. Being his wife might not be as strenuous as she feared.

His arm went rigid in hers. He propelled her forward until they were partially hidden by a wooden support post.

His back to the dancers, he leaned forward and hissed, "What's the captain doing here?"

She glanced over his shoulder. The men all had their backs to the room, but there was Stokes's green and black doublet, his hair curling over the stiff collar of his shirt. Matthew had arrived while everyone was choosing new partners, so it was possible Stokes hadn't spotted him yet.

The captain turned his head, as if casually casting his eyes around the room, and looked directly at her.

"He is a… a friend of Mistress Pylet," she stammered, heart pounding.

Why did Matthew have to come? It was uncomfortable enough attending the feast as part guest, part servant, explaining endlessly to the patrons that she was not one of the Dagger's whores and repeating herself with each emptied cup. Then there was Stokes lurking in the background, chivalrous but aloof, reminding her she had broken something that night at Blackfriars. Now Matthew promised further torture.

She took a breath, calming herself. He was here because he loved her, missed her, needed her. That was worthy of shoving her selfishness aside for a few hours.

Fidgeting, Matthew glanced over his shoulder at the dancers and surveyed the few guests remaining at the long dining table. "These are your new friends, then? Rather a grand lot, are they not?"

"The madam prides herself on her high standards."

"I pray your standards are unchanged after such rich livin'. There'll be no roast boars when we wed."

"I well know," she said, bristling. "This is my employment, not my pastime."

"I do not dance with the foreman down the wharves."

"You would if the shipbuilder told you to."

"You do whatever she tells you, eh?" He leaned a shoulder against the pillar and gave her a sardonic look she had no trouble interpreting. Seeing her indignation, he scoffed. "You work at a bawdy house, Margaret. How am I to know which duties are yours?"

Five minutes he had been there, and already they were arguing. "Peace, Matthew. Let us enjoy the fete. Will you dance?"

"Not with the likes of them."

"What, then? There may yet be some food laid by if you are hungry. Or mayhap you would sit with me and listen to the music? Come, let us find a comfortable seat."

As she began to turn, he caught her arm. "Is there no other diversion to be had?" His fingertips drifted up her sleeve and followed the square neckline of her bodice. No one took notice of them, as far as she could tell, but she unconsciously flicked her gaze to where Ellen and Stokes and the others were dancing.

Pulling his hand away from her chest, she entwined her fingers with his. "Am I not diversion enough?"

"You are just the diversion I had in mind."

When he gave her that look, it was supposed to fill her stomach with butterflies. But the timing was wrong, the setting like something out of a nightmare, and instead of melting under the heat of his gaze, she shrank away.

"Margaret…" His tone was plaintive, airy, as he leaned toward her. He touched her waist, and she was in the dim, musky goat shed again.

"Not now, my love," she said. "They can see."

"Then let us go where they cannot see."

"Only patrons may go up."

He grinned and moved his hand to his purse. "I have coin."

As he played out his joke—fishing around for a shilling, holding it up in triumph—Maggie only stared. It was clear from his delighted expression that, to him, this was the pinnacle of humor, but she felt no urge to laugh.

"Whore" was such a convenient word, practical in any situation involving a willful woman. If she sold her body for coin, she was a whore by definition, but if she gave it away for free, she was still a whore. She was a whore if she remained unmarried, if she smiled too freely, if she bruised a man's ego. It was the surest insult to reduce a woman to the value she gave a man, so powerful that women measured themselves against it and mothers warned their daughters to avoid it.

And Matthew was happy to imply Maggie was a whore who hadn't been paid yet.

His face fell when he noticed she wasn't smiling. "Why do you scowl so? 'Twas but a jest."

Maggie bit her tongue. "I will see if Young will give you aught to drink."

In the back of the building, removed from the revels, the bar was quiet. It gave her a moment to breathe, to let her heart rate slow. While she soaked up the calm, a green brocade gown wafting the scent of rosewater flounced up to the bar. Ellen hooked her arm through Maggie's. "All's well?"

Maggie shrugged, not bothering to lie to her.

Ellen looked back at Matthew. "He does seem a mite dour. Ill? Or just ill-tempered?"

"Mayhap another drink will improve his humor."

"Another?" Ellen narrowed her eyes. "Nay, 'tis not the way of things. Drink makes a black mood blacker." She tugged Maggie away from the bar. "Let us see what I can do."

With her usual grace, Ellen skipped toward the pillar where Matthew was awkwardly leaning. Maggie had no choice but to follow, as long as Ellen retained the grip on her arm.

"What ho, Master Kent!" Ellen sang. "A merry Yuletide to you, friend!"

Matthew straightened and touched his forelock. "Aye, mistress, and to you." The corner of his mouth turned up as Ellen's magic took effect.

"'Tis a long way to come on a cold night, but the reward is worthy, I vow. Does not our Maggie look well?"

"Margaret always looks well."

"I came to beg a dance with her, but then I saw you were come. Now, which of you will partner me?" She flashed him her dimpled smile.

Maggie knew what Ellen was doing, knew she meant well, but it still elicited a spark of envy. What if Matthew couldn't tell friendliness from flirtation? Ellen was a professional, and Maggie was no match for her. Besides, managing Matthew's changeable moods was her responsibility; she didn't need rescue from it.

Luckily, he shook his head. "I'm not much one for dancing, and not with such fine folk, anyhow."

"Then we will find another pastime! A game of dice?" Seeing Maggie scrunch her nose, Ellen corrected herself. "Nay, Mags does not play dice. Cards, then. Let us play Triumph."

"Triumph cannot be played with three," Maggie said.

"Then we will find a fourth! One who may lend a deck of cards," Ellen added, laughing.

Maggie dreaded navigating such an awkward situation, adjusting her behavior to Matthew's expectations while matching Ellen's carefree demeanor, and the thought of adding a fourth person to their party made her queasy. If she were quick, she could choose one of the many strangers, someone whose opinion was meaningless to her.

Ellen was faster. "Jules!"

Monsieur Bisset's head snapped up at the sound of her voice, and he sent her an indulgent smile from across the room. While he hurried over to them, she explained in her carrying voice what she wanted.

The Frenchman's face drew itself into a melodramatic pout, as if disappointing Ellen was an unforgivable betrayal. "*Triomphe*? Alas, I have no cards!"

Behind him, Stokes's familiar voice offered, "I have." He detached himself from the group of dancers and drifted toward them.

Maggie's heart sank.

"Our savior!" Ellen said, her voice too bright. "Will you lend them to us? Jules, say you will be our fourth."

Bisset held up his hands while Stokes opened the purse at his waist. "No, no, *ma belle*, the captain must play. I am relieved, in faith, for I never play unless I must."

Maggie looked between them all, noting Bisset's relief, Matthew's discomfort, and the way Ellen's lips thinned when she smiled at Stokes.

"But you are so fond of dancing, Will," Ellen said. "We'll not tear you away from it."

"I am most fond of good company, and my weakness for games of chance is no secret." His eyes flicked to Maggie before he raised an eyebrow at Matthew. "We must needs take care to watch our tongues, lest we offend these ladies with our rough sailor's ways."

It seemed to Maggie like a polite acknowledgement of the men's connection, perhaps meant to show Stokes's intention to blur the line between their ranks for one night. By the hard set of Matthew's brow, though, she knew he didn't take it the same way.

She rushed to head off Matthew's response. "As for me, games of chance oft sour even the best company. Mayhap you wish to find a better pair—"

"We'll play," Matthew said.

Ellen bustled them all to the end of the feast table, and while the women stacked the dirty trenchers to clear a space, Matthew found an open bottle of ale and filled a nearby goblet. As an afterthought, he offered the bottle to Stokes, who poured a little into his own cup.

"Who will keep score?" Stokes said, setting the empty bottle back on the table.

"Maggie will do it."

"She has no paper," Matthew said.

Ellen held out her hand, palm up, to accept Stokes's deck of cards. "She has no need. We played Maw for two hours yesternight and she tallied every point inside her head."

Matthew snorted. "And you trusted her?"

"You were content to have her tally your wages for a summer," Stokes said.

"What do we play for?" Ellen went on, settling into her seat and shuffling the cards.

"Let us play for the joy of it," Maggie said. "'Tis a festival day. Must we invite envy and greed?"

"'Tis no proper game without real silver on the table," Matthew argued. "I've not come empty-handed."

"I fear I have." Maggie affected a light tone. "If we set the stakes too high, I shall be a pauper by the second trick."

"I'll pay Margaret's stake. She'll be holdin' my purse strings before ere long, anyway."

Maggie brushed some crumbs from the table.

With her usual grace, Ellen dealt the cards. "Mags is right. No jealousy among friends, not on a festival day. Why do we not play for something else? Something that cannot be bought." She assessed her hand of cards, then drummed her fingertips on the table. "I wager... a secret."

The others stared down at their own hands, wondering how to match her wager.

Stokes reordered his cards and spread them into a fan. "A boon," he said.

Matthew offered up a juggling trick. Maggie had little worth sharing, and Ellen had dealt her a poor hand, so she shrugged and wagered, "A recitation."

As they played, Maggie and Matthew against Ellen and Stokes, Ellen kept the mood light with witty observations, and Stokes responded every once in a while with his own. Everyone ignored how quickly Matthew downed his cup of ale, then another, while he silently focused on the game.

Despite her rotten hand, Maggie managed to pull off enough tricks to win, and Matthew leaned back in his chair with a smug smile while Ellen tossed down her cards.

"Well played," Ellen sighed. "Will you collect your winnings now, or shall I wager a greater secret for the next hand?"

"Sounds to me like a clever scheme to keep from paying," Stokes said.

Matthew crossed his arms over his chest. "I'll have my winnings now."

Ellen placed her forearms on the table and leaned forward. "I've a patron who calls his prick 'Maximus.'"

They all snorted with laughter, caught off guard by Ellen's unabashed lewdness. Stokes put a hand to his chest and adopted a tone of mock alarm. "I told you that in confidence!"

Ellen laughed. "I'd not dream of telling any of *your* secrets. What of yours, Matthew? Has it got a name?"

Maggie understood herself to be in the only room in England where such a subject could be discussed, with the only woman in the world who could get away with it, but still she thought she would burn to ash from embarrassment. To make matters worse, Matthew smirked and nodded at Maggie. "What do you call it?"

"Matthew!" Would it be childish to hide under the table?

"Do not forget to collect the rest of your winnings," Stokes broke in. "I must give you both a boon."

"I want an extra hour of shore leave," Matthew said, "whenever the *Merrow* docks in London."

"Ellen had only to tell one pitiful secret, yet I must give you untold hours of leisure?"

"One hour, then, at your will."

Stokes sighed. "Done. And what will you do with your hour of leave?"

"I'll bed my wife. But only when it pleases you, sir."

Matthew finished his drink, and the thunk of the goblet as his graceless fist returned to the table was the only sound in the strained silence.

Ellen was the first to recover. "If only all women had such attentive husbands!" She gathered up the cards and gave them a few hasty shuffles, as if the sound could keep the awkwardness at bay. "Another?"

"Deal," Matthew said.

Maggie heard them without heeding them, too busy instructing her lungs and heart to do their duties, too concerned about the sudden surge of heat in the too-small room. This was nothing new, this burning mortification, not where Matthew was concerned. Everything he did embarrassed her. Clearly she was oversensitive, unused to hearing lewd speech, too well bred to forgive rough manners.

But to witness him embarrass the captain—embarrass *Ellen*, even—proved more than she could bear. In time, she would grow accustomed to him; a day would come when he no longer surprised her. She had to survive until that day.

Ellen began to deal, but Stokes laid his palm on the table to block her. "Pray, seek out a player to replace me. Our rich repast does not agree with me." He pushed his chair back and stood, nodding solemnly to Ellen and Maggie before walking away.

They played a few hands of Post and Pair, but Maggie struggled to keep track of her opponents' bluffs. Out of the corner of her eye, she caught Ellen sending her encouraging looks. Matthew teased her for each game she lost, and something bitter and viscous simmered in her belly, impervious to her applications of cool reason.

She could make an excuse like Stokes did, or tell them plainly she no longer wished to play, or look Matthew in the eye and demand better from him. But she didn't.

It was Amelia Pylet who rescued her. The madam appeared beside Maggie's chair and looked pointedly up and down the table. "Why have these things not been cleared?" she asked Maggie in a low voice. "The maids should have seen to this an hour ago!"

"I know not, madam. I have not seen the kitchen staff since supper."

"Ask Vernon the reason for the delay."

Grateful for the reprieve, Maggie shot an apologetic smile to Matthew and hastened to the back.

The kitchen was far too empty for an occasion like this one. Vernon, twelve-year-old Francie, and a temporary scullery maid were each huddled over a portion of the worktable, slicing and carving various cold meats and cheeses. The other two permanent kitchen maids, Rose and Bess, were missing.

"Mistress Pylet wishes the trenchers cleared," Maggie said. "Where is everyone?"

Vernon grunted. "Rose and Bess've gone, the devil knows where. If Pylet wants 'er cold repast before 'er guests leave, she must enjoy 'er dirty trenchers a while longer."

Maggie sighed at the thought of the work ahead of her: dismissing the two flighty kitchen girls (assuming they could be found), hiring new ones, and explaining it all to Pylet. "Very well." She unbuttoned the cuffs of her sleeves. "Lend me an apron."

Vernon nodded at a hook on the wall, and Maggie tied the cleanest one around her waist before rolling up her sleeves. "Before you go," Vernon said, "dump this pail out back." She nudged the bucket on the floor next to her foot, overflowing with fat trimmings and turnip greens.

The handle was greasy, but it wasn't hard to keep a tight grip on it with how tense her muscles were. Would this night never end? At least she had a task now, something to keep her busy. Something to keep her out of Matthew's reach while she calmed down.

The winter air was heavenly on her flushed skin, and she took in a bracing breath. A dim torch beside the kitchen door was the only light in the alley. She stepped over the threshold, then jumped when she saw a shadowed figure leaning against the wall.

It was only Stokes, arms folded, one foot braced against the wall, eyes wide with surprise.

On the *Merrow*, she would have had some witticism for him, something about how the Dagger was fortunate to have a privy *inside* the building, or how he must need the stars to navigate back to the party. He would have smirked and shot another one back. Tonight, though, she could scarce look at him.

He glanced down at the bucket. "Ah. You have not come in search of me, then."

"Why would I?"

"Why indeed."

She interpreted his look as best she could. "I do not intend to apologize for what he said."

"I expect no apology."

"He only meant to shock."

"It takes more than a bawdy remark to shock me."

They were accomplishing nothing, talking like this. If he had nothing to say, why should she linger? She strode to the trash heap and emptied the pail over it, then headed toward the door.

"What boon would you have asked, if Kent had not been so brazen to speak for you?"

His voice stopped her, and she turned. "Brazen?" She hugged herself against the cold. "He will be my husband. His word is my word."

He snorted, pushing off the wall. "You will adopt *that* man's words as your own? Words that you believe require apology? Words that made you dour and dismal from the first he opened his mouth?"

"I am not *dismal*! Do not think me unhappy because I do not flirt and giggle like Ellen and the others."

"I do not *think* you unhappy. I know it."

She laughed without humor. "And how is that?"

"To begin, I opened my eyes."

His sarcasm rankled her, and she dug her fingers into the flesh of her upper arms since she could not, in good conscience, strangle him. She shouldn't argue, especially since he only spoke the truth, but she hated that he saw so much she thought she could hide. His concern embarrassed her, and she was tired of being embarrassed.

"You are mistaken. I am content to marry him. He loves me."

"Does he? Can he? The man is a knave, a thief, a tosspot—"

"And your helmsman," she retorted.

"If your requirements for a husband resemble my requirements for a pirate, one of us is bound to be disappointed."

"You do not know him as I do."

"I have sailed with him for nigh on ten years, and I have been his commander for half that time. Forgive me, but methinks 'tis *you* who know him not."

She rolled her eyes. Yes, there was a sizable gap in their mutual history, but the boy she knew peeked out from the man Matthew had become, and it had to count for something. Why else would she stay with him? If a stranger treated her as Matthew did, she would run. Captain Stokes would never understand.

His eyes flashed in the torchlight. "If you are resolved, God knows my counsel is fruitless. By all means, let a small-minded man whittle you down until you suit his needs—"

"Why are you being so cruel?" She stared at him, bewildered. "What can it matter to you what I do? You are neither my father nor my husband, nor even my captain. Who are you to scorn my choices?"

He stared back, pursing his lips. "You are right. This is not my place. As you know, I suffer from a deplorable surplus of feeling."

His disdainful tone made her shiver more than the December breeze. She knew her gaffe would come back to haunt her one day; it was only fitting that it chose a night when she was already as wretched as she could be.

"I will stay here a while longer," he said. "Methinks we must not enter together."

As she put her hand on the door, he sighed. "I only wish you merry, however sorely I have bungled the telling of it. Pray, forgive me."

Whenever Matthew offered an apology, she forgave him, if only to keep the peace for a time. But there was nothing requiring her to take pity on Stokes. She imagined how satisfying it might be to flash him one of the rude gestures so prevalent on the *Merrow* and storm back into the kitchen.

The thought soured immediately. If she forgave Matthew for every apology that was much too little and came far too late, it would make her a hypocrite to withhold forgiveness from someone who actually meant it. And she wouldn't be so foolish as to drive away one of her only friends.

"'Tis forgiven." She let a tight smile flicker over her face to underscore her words. "If we must quarrel, let it be on a worthier subject."

Ellen was still entertaining Matthew at the end of the feast table, a card game splayed out between them.

Maggie hefted the stack of trenchers they had moved out of the way earlier. Ellen furrowed her brow. "That is Bess's to do!"

"Bess and Rose are not to be found." Maggie sent Matthew an apologetic grimace. "I fear I must neglect you for a time. There is no one to clear up."

She heard Matthew sputter a few sounds of protest as she turned with the heavy trenchers and headed back to the kitchen.

"Margaret!" He had followed, and now he shuffled alongside her, trying to get her attention. "You are no servant!"

"I am a servant. I am Mistress Pylet's secretary."

"You're not a scullery maid."

"It appears I am now."

They entered the kitchen, Matthew hindering her by insisting on staying at her side. The two women at the worktable gave each other a look, and young Francie stared, a forgotten knife drooping in her grip.

"You're a lady, not a tavern wench."

"Keep your voice down."

"When I agreed to let you work—"

She let the trenchers slide into the full washbasin from too high, and the dirty water splashed her apron. "Ah, so you have at last agreed I may work? I am glad of it. Now prithee, let me work."

When she turned to go back for more dishes, Matthew remained at her heels. "I came all this way to see you. If you loved me, your first duty would be to me."

Maggie stopped abruptly, causing Matthew to stumble into her. They needed to have this argument somewhere, but Pylet was in the dining room and Stokes was in the alley.

It seemed the kitchen staff was about to enjoy a spectacle.

"I am glad to help where I am needed, for it proves to my employer that I may be relied upon. If you loved *me*, you would not endanger my employment. I am not made to be idle, and this work gives me purpose. Do not seek to take from me that which I prize. Not when it causes you so little harm."

"'Little harm'? What of humiliation? I've said you'll not work, and you defied me. I'll not be cuckolded by your fancy. A wife's duty is to her husband, to honor and obey him, and the first day the banns are read is the last day you lift a finger to serve any man but me."

The bitter thing that had been brewing inside her all evening boiled over, sending scalding acid through her veins, bubbling up her throat in the form of words she knew she would regret.

"I am not your wife, not yet. Do not..." She cast about for a word and snatched at the closest one to hand. "Do not whittle me down until I fit into your pocket alongside all your other possessions. If you want *me*, you may have me whole, or not at all. If 'tis only a wife you require, find another who would better suit."

The blow struck without warning.

Later, she would return to that moment and try to envision the look on his face (serene or wild?), the arc of his arm (across his body with the right, or an inward sweep with the left?), the orientation of his hand (palm or knuckles?).

All she could remember was the surprise, then the pain, then the hubbub that broke out in the kitchen when Vernon descended on Matthew with a wooden spoon, shouting, "Out, out, you vermin, get out!"

22

WHEN HE VISITED her on Christmas, he touched her tender cheek and vowed never to lose his temper again.

Every Sunday afternoon after, he trekked from Rotherhithe to Southwark to see her. He brought her gifts, took her to bearbaitings and plays, told her how he missed her.

Every Sunday evening, as he walked her home from wherever they had been, he pulled her into an alley and kissed her. He was so in love with her, he said. He could not bear to be parted from her. He needed her to take him in her arms, or he would perish. The incident with the goat shed, Ellen's tonic, and the nail-biting week before her courses resumed soured her to the idea. Then a memory of her bruised arm or her pink cheek would flash in front of his eager face, and she didn't think she could refuse.

The night of the goat shed, Ellen had tutored her about pleasure: ways to give pleasure to a man, ways to find her own. In the alley one Sunday, she knelt down and tried one. He enjoyed it. She didn't have to lift her skirts. An amenable solution had been found.

Every Sunday morning, she reminded herself to have courage. There was no need to endure a lifetime of this. She heard Stokes's sarcastic voice in her head: *By all means, let a small-minded man whittle you down…* There was so little left of her.

Every Monday morning, she looked in the mirror to make sure she was still there.

By contrast, her life at the Dagger was merry and productive. Aside from the weekly shortage in Vernon's kitchen budget, everything was attaining equilibrium. Pylet relied on her, the whores liked her, and Ellen was better than a sister.

Matthew wanted to take this from her. Why wasn't that enough to make her leave him?

One Wednesday evening in late January, she sat with Ellen in the Dagger's dining room, an open bottle of cider between them, as the crowd of patrons grew in size and boisterousness. Vernon would usually leave when a reasonable hour for supper had come and gone, but tonight, a gaggle of young lords sailed into the inn and dangled a heavy bag in front of Amelia Pylet's face, and suddenly, the kitchen hours had changed.

From their table near the back, Maggie and Ellen could hear Vernon's sharp, high tones and Amelia's low ones. They exchanged a look.

"I'll not be sold to one of those fops, no matter how rich he claims to be," Ellen said. "I never mind telling them to come back tomorrow, but Pylet cannot turn down a fool with a purse."

"The one in the green jerkin is not so bad," said Maggie. "Not even him? Not even for… a pound?"

Ellen wrinkled her nose and shook her head, glancing up as Molly descended from above with a satisfied patron. "The commandment says to remember the Sabbath day and keep it holy."

"I believe that refers to Sunday."

Molly plopped down at their table, hair a little mussed, but otherwise looking pert and put-together. She reached for Ellen's cider mug and tossed back its contents.

"Sunday is the day of our Lord," Ellen continued, "and Wednesday is the day of our lady."

Molly screwed up her nose and returned Ellen's mug. "I never heard that. That's papist talk withal."

"Not *Mary*." Ellen poured herself more cider. "*Me*. I am a lady, and Wednesday is my day of rest."

Maggie snorted. "Methinks the Archbishop may take umbrage to that."

The cider was strong and sweet. Ellen splurged on her days off, and this second bottle made everything soft around the edges. It also made those young lords rakish and charming, rather than spoiled and loud.

She lowered her mug, but the table came up to meet it sooner than she had expected. She giggled and smirked at Ellen. "Say true: you would not forget your Sabbath just a little if that lad in the green tossed you a unite?"

"He's tossing about unites, is he?" Molly craned her neck to see which one she meant.

Ellen laughed. "Of course he's not. And nay, I would not, not for a purse of shiny, new-minted unites. Pylet can order Vernon around all she wants, but she will find me a stone wall." She took a swig of her cider and smirked back at Maggie. "If you fancy him so, why do not *you* take him up?"

Molly laughed as Maggie choked on her mouthful of cider. She covered her mouth and coughed, eyes stinging and throat burning.

"He'll not want you now," Molly said. "Your face is red as an apple."

None of them noticed Amelia Pylet emerging from the kitchen until she descended on them, fresh from her victory over Vernon. "You have seen the band of young gentlemen who are new arrived." She frowned in disapproval at the giggling, choking women before turning to Molly. "I trust you are refreshed enough to attend them?"

"Aye, ma'am."

"Bring them supper once it is prepared. Vernon assures me 'twill be no time at all."

The madam swept away with the grace of a duchess, and the three women looked at each other, all sharing variations of the same exasperated grimace.

"She will have her way, eh?" Ellen said.

"'Tis clear now why Vernon skims a bit of cream off the top of the jar," Maggie agreed.

She was surprised to look up into two serious faces.

"What's your meaning?" Molly said.

Maggie's blood went cold. She shouldn't have said anything—she had no plans to reveal Vernon's crime, to Amelia or anyone. The drink was making her sluggish. "None. Nothing! I only—"

"You only meant to call Vernon a thief, did you?"

"Hush, Molly," Ellen said.

"Nay, in sooth!" It would not do to earn Molly's wrath. She had a habit of making those she disapproved of miserable. But Maggie couldn't put the secret back in its box. "It must have been an error in my sums—"

"Aye, 'tis easily believed." Molly's eyes were cruel. "For all your fancy talk of numbers, methinks you're naught but an empty-headed nobleman's daughter pretending to be somethin' she's not."

"Molly, leave her be."

The girl pushed her chair back and stalked off into the dining room, returning to her carefree, seductive manner as she approached the table of newcomers.

Maggie turned to Ellen and gave her a helpless look. "'Twas only a jest," she said, hearing the whine in her voice. "I noticed a few coins missing from Vernon's account. I care not if she takes it. What a hypocrite it should make me if I did, when my friends are all criminals."

Ellen interrupted Maggie's meandering apology. "You have not told Pylet?" When Maggie shook her head, she laid her hand over Maggie's arm and squeezed. "You must promise me you never will." This was the most serious Maggie had ever seen her. "I pray you, Maggie. I will never ask anything of you again, only swear it."

"Why? What is this great secret? Why is Molly protecting Vernon?"

"She is not protecting Vernon," Ellen whispered, glancing to where Amelia was mingling with the patrons. "If you love me—if you love all of us—swear to me you'll not tell Pylet."

Maggie drew in a laborious breath and let it out in a single huff. "Very well."

Ellen patted her arm. "God bless you."

When Friday and Saturday trundled along at their usual pace, with no one acting odd and both Vernon and Maggie still employed, she was prepared to chalk everyone's behavior up to bad humors.

These days of the week were known to be busy and profitable, and Maggie outdid herself keeping the ledger up to date and tidy. It was some of her best work. She even doctored the laundry bill to absorb two of the shillings she knew would be missing from Vernon's budget, as a curtesy. If nothing else, it might help convince Amelia to seek out a less expensive launderer.

Then, as she dressed for Sunday morning mass, Amelia Pylet burst into her bedchamber without bothering to knock.

The madam wore the subdued morning attire she saved for church. It was all wrong on her, the colors drab, the cut conservative, the hoops too narrow and the bumroll too small. Her handsome face, usually made up with white powder and red rouge, was alarmingly natural.

The two parallel lines beside her mouth were deep as she frowned at Maggie. "You will not be attending mass this morning."

Maggie pretended her mind wasn't racing with calamitous scenarios. "Very well, madam. May I know why?"

"I know what you are doing, and I will not stand for it." Amelia lifted her chin. "You are dismissed."

The floor collapsed under Maggie's feet.

"While we are at mass, you will pack up your things and leave this house. I thought it better to conclude this business quietly, as a gesture of goodwill for the excellent work you have done."

Maggie regained her center of gravity, but a combination of the early hour and the absolute madness of the words she was hearing made her slow to comprehend. "My work is excellent, but I am dismissed?" A laugh bubbled up—it was the only response to what must be a joke—but Amelia's face was too serious. She swallowed it. "For what reason? Of what crime am I accused?"

"'Tis not a matter of crime, but of ethics. I do not disapprove of your profession, but I will not allow you to steal my patrons. When Captain Stokes convinced me to take you in, I placed my trust in you—"

"Steal your patrons? I am a secretary, not a whore!"

"I have known a number of whores who could read and write. 'Tis a clever disguise, but not an impenetrable one."

She wanted to laugh again. Was she going mad? "I am not a whore!"

"You lured away Captain Stokes and Sir Antony Brudenell. If there are others, I have not discovered them, but these are insult enough."

"*Stokes*?" She did laugh then, at the absurdity of it. "Stokes is Ellen's patron! What reason does *she* give for his absence? Even better, why do you not ask the man himself? I've seen neither hide nor hair of him since Christmas."

"This is not as quiet as I had hoped. Will you not save us both the embarrassment?"

Maggie's blood was boiling, her energy manic, her mind buzzing as she linked further defenses. She had been an accessory to piracy, smuggling, pandering, even Vernon's embezzlement. The list of things she *had* done was long. She would not suffer punishment for something she had not done.

If Amelia wanted her to leave quietly, she would go out like thunder.

"I am not embarrassed," she said. "I have done nothing to make you distrust me. You say yourself my work is excellent!"

"Aye, and I will regret losing your skills as a secretary—"

"Who is the other?"

"What?"

"The other patron you accuse me of stealing. Captain Stokes, and who?"

"Sir Antony Brudenell, as you well know."

It was no effort to keep her face blank of recognition: Maggie had no idea who Antony Brudenell was.

Amelia furrowed her brow, for the first time looking uncertain. "The girls understood that Sir Antony no longer comes because of you."

Almost before she finished speaking, Maggie knew who had told her. Sir Antony was Jane's patron, the rude one who would have hit her if Stokes hadn't arrived at that moment. Yes, Sir Antony avoided the Dagger now because of Maggie, but who could have reasoned that he stormed out of the Dagger and into her bed?

"That is true. I refused Sir Antony's custom on behalf of Jane, who was unwell, and I fear my refusal drove him away. But that is all! What does Ellen say? She will speak for me."

"You have no accomplices among my girls."

As she stared at Amelia, the fight drained out of her. Even Ellen? How could she? Molly was behind it, of course, and she had turned Jane and the others against her. How could they frame her for this ridiculous crime?

"I am falsely accused." Maggie's voice sounded small and pitiful to her ears. "Do not dismiss me, I beseech you."

Relief washed across Amelia's stern features when she realized Maggie's resistance was waning. "I pray you will be gone before we return from mass." She stepped forward and held out three shillings, Maggie's weekly salary. They clinked together as they fell into Maggie's outstretched hand. Amelia closed the door behind her.

Maggie stood frozen beside her wardrobe, staring at nothing, her thoughts a chaotic jumble. Stokes a patron, and her closest friend a Judas, even after—

Vernon.

Maggie had dashed the four steps to the door and put her hand on the latch before she remembered herself. It wouldn't make any difference. She was outnumbered and outmaneuvered. Any attack she made now would be a dying animal's last swipe of the claws. Who would believe her?

They wouldn't need to believe her: she had the evidence in writing, months of it, every missing penny she had helped Vernon conceal. This unasked-for secret would cause her to lose her livelihood, her home, her friends. Who was Vernon to her, that she should sacrifice so much?

Then she thought of Ellen. *She is not protecting Vernon*, she had said. Whoever they were protecting was worth sacrificing Maggie for.

It wasn't fair. None of this was her fault. None of it had anything to do with her, except she knew a tiny part of a larger secret. Did no one care what happened to her?

What *would* happen to her?

The door creaked, and Maggie jumped at the sound. Ellen tiptoed into the room and bit her lip.

"Did you hear?" Maggie said.

"Everyone heard. 'Tis not fair nor just, to throw you into the street, after all you've done…"

She grabbed Maggie's hand and shoved a pouch into her palm. Inside was a meager handful of coins, mostly pennies and groats.

"A portion of your thirty silver pieces, is it?"

"That is not fair, neither," Ellen retorted. "You've a right to be cross, but I did not sell you out."

"Is there aught else? I need to pack up my things." Her tone came out as cold as she intended. She loved Ellen, but someone else needed to share this pain.

Ellen hugged herself. "You will be all right. You have somewhere to go, you have a little coin… You will be all right."

Maggie didn't answer while she blustered around the room, dragging things off shelves and out of trunks. Only the sound of the door latch alerted her Ellen had left.

Maggie swore under her breath, every foul word and creative oath she could think of, as she shoved her things into her seabag. There wasn't much—a few knickknacks, her sonnets, her extra underclothes. The habit she was wearing was one of Ellen's old gowns, and the petty thief in her decided to take it with. Her green hat would go on her head, and her cloak would go around her shoulders. Then she would be gone.

And there was only one place she could go.

23

A LIGHT, INCESSANT drizzle turned the streets to slime. Maggie kept one hand at her shoulder to secure the strap of her seabag, and the other held the hems of her skirt and cloak out of the mud. Both hands were wet and frozen. Her hat was a cold, soggy weight on her head, and the shoulders of her cloak were no better.

Of course it would rain.

She had not yet seen Matthew's lodgings, but she knew how to find them: follow the Thames east out of Southwark until the parish of Rotherhithe coalesced from the countryside. He had spoken often enough of the boardinghouse's proximity to the Swan Inn, wherever that was, and someone there would be able to show her the way.

Lamplight oozed onto the muddy road from a squat building with a hitching rail in front, one miserable beast sneezing and stamping in the rain. With her sleeve, Maggie swiped water out of her eyes and peered up at the facade. This could be the Swan, but with the way the artist had rendered the bird on the wooden sign above, it could just as easily be the Goose.

In the warm haven of the dining room, she flexed her fingers and looked about for the innkeeper. One man, probably the owner of the horse outside, broke his fast at a corner table, a spoon in one fist and a pint of beer in the other.

The innkeeper clomped down the stairs and slid behind the bar. His shoulders were sharp, his hands knobby, a grotesque doll made of sticks. He gave Maggie a distrustful glare.

"God ye good morrow," she said with as pleasant a country air as she could manage. "Where may I find Master Walsch's lodging house?"

"Walsch's? On what business? Whoring's unlawful, y'ken."

It would require more energy than she possessed to puff up with indignation, so she sighed and gave him a level look. "That is not my business. Will you not direct me?"

He considered her, his withered lips a closed sphincter, but relented, sending her back out into the rain to the building three doors down on the left.

Walsch's was solid and not much to look at. No decorative architectural elements, no window boxes for spring flowers, just plaster walls and dark wood beams. It was a simple boarding house, full of day-laboring bachelors who were likely sleeping off the drink of the night before.

After the welcome she received at the Swan, an uneasy feeling had burbled up in her stomach. She didn't belong here. Was there nowhere else? No one else to turn to for help? Stokes's name leapt to the front of her mind, but it was a thought she couldn't bear to entertain.

Maggie pounded on the door, and it opened after a brief delay. A tall, olive-skinned young man in the entryway stared wide-eyed at her, scanning her from top to bottom. "God-a-mercy, mistress! Come." He opened the door further, graciously giving her room to step out of the rain.

She dropped her skirts and flexed her stiff fingers.

The man looked at her with more concern and kindness than she expected from someone who lived here. "Who may I call for you?"

"Is Matthew Kent within? Or Luke?"

"They're like to be above. 'Tis lie-abeds we are on Sundays."

He closed the door behind her, shutting out both the rain and the scant light from the overcast sky. The entryway plunged into darkness. "Will you sit?" the man's voice said. "I'll fetch 'em for you."

As her eyes adjusted, she could see he was gesturing toward a bench set against one wall of the dark-paneled hallway. She thanked him and dropped her seabag on the floor with a wet thud. He was halfway up the stairs before he stopped and called, "Your name, mistress?"

"Maggie—Margaret."

Before he reached the top step, a door upstairs creaked open. The man said, "Visitor," and another voice replied, "Aye, gramercy, Joshua." The two men descended together, and Joshua nodded at her before splitting off to enter another room at the end of the hall.

Luke looked older than the last time she had seen him. Could three months make such a difference? He took in her bedraggled state, concern transforming his face. "I heard your voice. What is't? Some calamity?"

She peeled off her hat and tried to smooth her wet hair. "Is your brother above?"

Luke balanced on the balls of his feet, ready to spring into action. "He's asleep, but I'll wake him."

He put his foot on the bottom step, but she waved at him to stay. The grueling trip had been long, but not long enough to unravel the knot of apprehension in her stomach. Maybe if she rehearsed her speech on Luke first, she would feel braver when she saw Matthew. "Do not trouble him yet. Is there a place we may sit and talk? With a fire, mayhap?"

He led her into the same room Joshua had entered. A few rectangular tables took up most of it, and a large stone hearth occupied the far wall. The tables were dirty with bits of food and spilled drink left over from supper. The man called Joshua sat in a chair by the fire.

Seeing she would have an audience, Maggie slowed her steps. Luke noted her discomfort. "'Tis either here or above."

Joshua looked up as Luke scraped another chair up to the hearth. He was mending a stained, threadbare shirt with the dexterous, knobby fingers of a sailor.

"Joshua Noon," Luke said, "this is Maggie."

Maggie unclasped her cloak. "Well met, Master Noon."

The man looked at Luke. "Matthew's, um...?"

"Aye." Luke busied himself finding Maggie a chair and looked at neither of them.

"A family matter? I will go." Joshua stuck his needle into the fabric and gathered his things.

After he had vacated his chair, Maggie hung her cloak on it and angled it toward the fire. In this weather, she would be lucky if it dried before tomorrow. How cramped was their bedchamber? Would there be room to hang her wet things? She felt a pang of guilt for the imposition, knowing Luke would suffer the most from it.

"Your friend seemed to know of me."

Luke poked the logs in the hearth and added another. The delicious warmth of the fire washed over her shivering frame, and she stretched out her hands in welcome. "I'm like to have spoke of you and Matthew," he said. "We talk while we work."

She was sure there was more to that story, but she let it go. "Making rope? Are you content with that trade?"

"Makes me more useful on the *Merrow*." He leaned forward, elbows on his knees. "Why've you come? Matthew planned to call on you."

"He may save himself the trip. I am dismissed from the Dagger and Sheath."

"Dismissed? What did you do?"

"One of the whores conspired to have me sacked." She explained as well as she could. It felt good to speak it aloud, and to have Luke nod along. She would miss having someone like Ellen to talk to.

"I am certain I can find other work," she concluded, "even without Mistress Pylet's good word, but I had room and board there, and now…"

"You'll stay with us!" Luke stated it like a foregone conclusion, not an invitation nor, thank God, a sarcastic grumble. "'Tis a modest chamber, but snug. You can look for a new position in the morning."

Her chest expanded with love and relief. No young man would be pleased to cram into a single room with his brother and sister-in-law, but at least he didn't seem unwilling or out of sorts about it.

"Matthew has come round, then?" she said. "He was not best pleased the first time I shared news of my employment."

Luke's face fell. "Ah, not as such…" He smoothed his palms over the knees of his breeches, looking every bit the boy he was. "But he must, aye? Walsch will be cross when he learns you're here, and 'tis only a month now until we may return to the ship. Where will you go then?"

"Wherever Matthew wants me. I can hardly put off marrying him now." She hoped her tone conveyed humor. Luke's awkward smile showed how amusing he found it.

The fire crackled in the hearth. Somewhere in the house, a door opened and closed, and a pair of voices rose and fell in casual conversation.

"What of you?" she said, her voice loud in the empty room. "I had not thought what you would do when we wed. I would welcome you to stay with us as long as you wish."

"Worry not on my account. I've a summer to think on it."

Of course. She did not like to think about the six or seven months of loneliness stretching ahead of her. As soon as Matthew settled his new wife somewhere, he would kiss her goodbye and disappear to sea, with no plans to return to London unless Captain Stokes commanded it.

"And you'll not come back to the *Merrow*?" he asked.

"How can I? The captain does not allow husbands and wives."

"But you were good! We were always paid on time. Just do as you did last summer and weep in front of Stokes."

It wasn't a joke she found funny, but it was one she heard often on the ship. "I had ceased weeping by the time I asked to stay aboard," she said, voice low and sharp with sarcasm.

"Well, what harm would it do, anyway? You do not wish to stay here alone all summer, do you?"

She didn't answer, instead listening to the snap of logs and the increased sounds of movement above. The boarders were rousing themselves at last. She wondered how they justified not attending mass with the rest of the country. Being bachelors, they lacked a wife or mother to remind them to do what they should.

That would be her job now.

"I should not like to be found like this." She gestured to her damp clothing and rain-slicked hair. "Is Matthew like to have risen?"

"I'll show you the way." He picked up her seabag while she gathered her hat and cloak. They were now hot and damp instead of cold and damp, which was at least some improvement.

Luke opened the third door at the top of the stairs and said, "Surprise for you."

The room wasn't much bigger than the one she had left behind at the Dagger. It was spartan, too, as she had expected a sailor's rented room to be: a bed with a trunk at its foot, a cluttered table with two chairs, a wardrobe with one door ajar, a hearth, a window.

And Matthew, shirtless, his face pink from shaving and his eyes red from sleep.

He tossed the cloth he had been using to wipe his face on the bed. If she had expected him to be pleased or even surprised to see her, she was about to be disappointed. "Margaret? Why've you come?" His voice was gruff with disuse. "How stands the hour?"

"Not yet ten of the clock."

"I'll be below." Luke dropped her bag on the floor and closed the door behind him.

"You did not tell me you were coming." Matthew cleared his throat and raked his hair away from his face with the fingers of both hands. He must have had a late night if he was this sluggish.

"I did not know I would. You are not pleased to see me, then?"

He dragged in a deep breath and blinked rapidly, trying hard to rouse himself. "Aye, marry, I am always pleased to see you." He crossed to her, bare feet silent on the wood floor, and gave her a perfunctory kiss. He noticed how damp she still was, and it prompted him to glance at the sky beyond the window. "You walked here in that?"

There could be no more stalling—she had to tell him. While she debated how to begin, she draped her cloak over the back of a chair and set her hat on the seat, freeing her hands. That felt too exposed, though, so she busied herself straightening, smoothing, layering, and tucking the folds of the cloak while she told Matthew the story.

Practicing it on Luke had made it feel like someone else's life, a story she could tell without emotion. When she got to the end, the part where she packed her things and found her way here, he spoke. "Little fool, you would not wait for me? I could have escorted you here."

"Where, pray? Where was I to have waited? I was cast out of the house."

"No neighbor? No ordinary? Instead, you walked clear across town in the rain and mud! You could have been molested, robbed…" He ticked off each misfortune on the fingers of one hand. "You're like to fall ill now as well, and I am no nursemaid."

The callousness of his response was so unexpected, she wondered if she had done something wrong. Had she misrepresented her plight? Where was his indignation, his sense of injustice?

"Should I not have come to you? Mayhap you would prefer I seek lodging elsewhere?"

He rolled his eyes. "Peace, Margaret, be not cruel. I'm right glad you've come to me." He put his arms around her and kissed her forehead. "How I have wished to have you here with me! Southwark is a world away. Now we may at last begin our lives together."

She laid her cheek on his shoulder, glad for his warmth, and breathed in the familiar smell of him, letting out her frustration and disappointment on a sigh.

He smoothed his hands over her back in comforting circles. "You must see now how ill that position suited you. I only wish you had heeded me."

Matthew's remark would have riled her if she had been in a different mood, but she had spent all her energy battling Amelia. She would concede this time.

In fact, it gave her a sort of perverse relief to know however much the circumstances of her life changed, Matthew never would.

24

"I PUBLISH THE Banns of Marriage between Matthew Kent and Margaret Donwell. If any of you know cause or just impediment why these two persons should not be joined together in holy matrimony, ye are to declare it. This is the first time of asking."

The old priest droned the banns over the heads of fifty St. Mary's parishioners, making Maggie shiver when he announced her real name. It was foolish, as there was no connection between this tiny church in Rotherhithe and her family in Gloucester, but she knew the paranoia would accompany her to mass all three Sundays until the ordeal was over.

The first week at the boardinghouse had gone quickly, if only because she had intentionally forgotten every awkward interaction. It was obvious from the beginning she was unwelcome: Walsch only boarded single men, mostly laborers on the wet docks or the timber wharves. Matthew somehow convinced him to let her stay through the month. Still, seven days into this arrangement, Walsch made it clear he was impatient to be rid of them all. So Maggie hid in their room and tried to earn her keep.

Household management was a skill Maggie had learned and practiced since she was old enough to pronounce the word "husband," but it had almost nothing in common with the household labor she was now expected to do. She was charged with laundering, cleaning, and fetching water from the well behind the house. She removed dust and ash from the flat surfaces, wiped tallow candle soot from the walls, swept and scrubbed the floor, and polished the leaded windowpanes. Her muscles ached, and her dry, cracked hands stung whenever she gripped the broom handle.

These were tasks that fell to her servants back home, and she would never again take such help for granted. Nor could she keep from dreaming of replacing her broom with a pen and puzzling out a sum.

The second week of February was cold, and a sharp wind gusted through the gaps of the doors of St. Mary's. The priest intoned the lesson for the day. It was from the same Gospel as the last several services; she knew because she was now the most devout member of the parish, attending matins and evensong daily. While the lads labored, she slipped out of the house and found whatever diversion she could, sometimes walking as far as the east edge of Southwark after matins and then wending her way back alongside the frozen river.

As it was Sunday, though, Matthew was with her. He showed no emotion as the priest read from the Gospel of Mark. There had once been a Mark Kent, the brother between Matthew and Luke, but she couldn't remember how she knew. Maybe Luke had told her once, in passing.

"'But from the beginning of the creation God made them male and female,'" the priest recited. "'For this cause shall a man leave his father and mother, and cleave to his wife…'"

The old man's face was pale, the skin loose, the jowls trembling. She guessed from the tight fit of his skullcap he was bald under it.

"'And they twain shall be one flesh: so then they are no more twain, but one flesh.'"

He made a revolting slurping sound to recapture the extra saliva the word *flesh* had produced. She shivered in her seat and heard Matthew sigh.

"'What therefore God hath joined together, let not man put asunder.'"

The pew was hard under her sitting bones. How she missed her childhood in Gloucester, where a comfortable section of benches were reserved in honor of the Donwell family, padded with woven cushions and appointed its own copy of the Book of Common Prayer. Such a luxury would never be hers again.

They stood to sing and knelt to pray. Before the Eucharist, the priest published the banns for the second time. She had known it was coming, but it gave her an odd jolt. When the moment to object was past, the feeling of queasiness remained.

On Thursday, Maggie and Matthew hurried down the main street, chins tucked against the wind. "Only six days," Matthew was saying. "You're certain you do not wish to send word to your father?"

She mumbled something in the affirmative.

The frozen ground was uneven with wheel ruts and hoofprints. They moved down the road with a combination of care and haste, anxious to arrive as quickly as possible without twisting an ankle.

"You'll like this one better than the others. 'Tis in the heart of Southwark, so you'll not want for entertainment. The landlord's a good man, I'm told. Old Draper at the Swan gave me the direction."

Their search for accommodations had taken them all over, from Rotherhithe to Southwark and across the river to Whitechapel. Matthew's choices prioritized frugality over comfort and safety. She didn't have high hopes for this one.

But time was running out. Their lease at Walsch's extended only to the end of the month. She could not afford to delay much longer.

She stared at the bolt of muslin that needed to become new shirts for her and Matthew. It was a pauper's trousseau compared to the one she had prepared for her marriage to Sir John.

It shone white against the soot-stained wall of Matthew's room, out of place and mocking. How did one solicit the aid of a crafty little elf to transform it overnight into a neat stack of perfect garments? She would pay the price. Yet no matter how many times she wished it, it remained a bolt of cloth.

Matthew shook her awake on the last Sunday. A stalwart candle flame flickered on the table, holding the dark at bay. "We shall be late," he said. "Why are you yet abed?"

The collar of her chemise was wet with sweat, and the painful throbbing in her head made her dizzy. The same words had been running through her mind all night without reprieve, twisting and expanding and reshaping, but always intelligible: *This is the third time of asking.* She swallowed her nausea and changed into a dry shirt.

She attended the preacher's words with only vague interest. Her body felt itchy, incorporeal.

He spoke of Lot's wife, who turned back to view the burning city. Too stupid to follow instructions, too willful to keep her eyes on the path ahead.

The Gospel lesson taught of the angel who came to Elizabeth, who delivered her from her disgraceful barrenness. *She is the Elizabeth to my Zachariah,* Matthew had told the old man in Boston.

The words flowed over her, rising and falling. None of them were real. This was a fever dream, and she only had to endure it.

She couldn't recall later whether he had read the banns or not.

"Why do you scowl so?"

Was she scowling? Her thoughts had been more inward than outward. If only Luke were here to distract her, to force her to fix her behavior, but he was downstairs supping with his friends. There was no one to pretend for. Just Matthew.

"Is it not to your liking?" He pointed with the handle of his knife to the plate of food she had forgotten to eat. She shook her head and rotated the trencher as if another angle would make the food more appetizing. "Are you ill?"

"Nay, I am well." It was only by the grace of God the roiling bile in her stomach had yet to force its way up her throat.

He peered at her through narrowed eyes. "Feverish?"

"No."

"Yet you have been in a state for days. What ails you?"

"Naught ails me." She practiced hiding her feelings from him enough she was sure she could fool him even in her weakened state. She rolled her shoulders back and set to eating.

When he set down his knife, some tension in her back released. She preferred when he didn't have a knife in his hand.

What a thought to have about her future husband.

"Is it… a woman's ailment?" She shook her head. "Are you with child?" His posture straightened as his eyes brightened.

His excitement irritated her. When she thought about falling pregnant, all she ever felt was all-consuming terror. "Of course I am not."

"Then what? You're a bride three days from her wedding day, yet you're pale as a corpse laid out for burial. What madness has taken you?"

It made her want to laugh, this poetic comparison, but not because it was laughable. Was that madness? Finding amusement in unamusing things? Then maybe she was mad.

No, she *knew* she was mad. She knew it weeks ago, when the feeling of dread had first taken root. When she understood what she felt for Matthew was potent and binding, but it wasn't love.

Not the love she wanted, anyway, the sort the poets wrote about. She had no right to demand a legendary hero for her bridegroom, but legends were heightened, augmented, polished versions of human experience—stories, yes, but stories rooted in truth. So why could she not have the unremarkable, unpolished version of a love story?

Eight years ago, it had felt like one. Their love had been innocent and good, and she carried that love with her all this time. When he reappeared, the noble knight back from the crusades, she had been overjoyed at the chance to love him again. Too overjoyed to consider the man who returned might not be the boy who had gone away. And the woman present at their reunion was not the girl he had left behind.

Why did she tether herself to this cruel man? Why did she allow herself to be claimed as his prize when he had done nothing to deserve her?

Captain Stokes knew why. He knew the night in the alley when he scolded her for her foolishness. He knew it before she did.

She was a coward.

It wasn't right to stay. It would cause her pain. But she couldn't stop the events in motion. The banns were published, the date was set, and she would let the story unfold unhindered. Not because Matthew's strength frightened her. No, the flaw was inside of her, a belief she mourned, but couldn't dislodge: worthlessness. Her happiness wasn't worth all the trouble she would cause if she left.

She had let it get this far, and she deserved the consequences.

"I am well," she told him. "Pray do not trouble over me."

"You must think me a blessed fool! Are you angry with me?"

"Nay, Matthew."

"Then why cannot you look at me?"

She shrugged, keeping her eyes on the table, but he wouldn't relent.

"Look at me, Margaret. What is this about? Money? Are you still thinking about that bawdy house?"

She shook her head.

"You are still on about working for a wage, are you?"

No, she knew better than to hope for that.

He paused, a new idea forming. "Is there another man?"

She recoiled, just as disgusted by the thought as him. "Do not dare think it!"

"Who? Stokes?"

"Stokes? Fie!" She almost wished it *was* him. Perhaps another dose or two of the captain's sarcasm would have strengthened her spine.

"One of the men in this house, then? I always wonder what you find to do here all day."

"What do I do?" She waved her hands at the clean walls, the tidy wardrobe, the glittering window. "What do I do? I wash and sweep until there is not a speck of dirt remaining, and when that is done, I wander the streets until you return, because you will allow me no other occupation. I do not seek work, I do not speak to men, I do nothing except what you ask of me, and each lonely day *kills* me."

"So I have made your life a misery, have I?"

"You have made me a sweet little wife whose only purpose is to serve her husband, but that is not what I am." Her voice wobbled, and she tensed, remembering the last time she had tried to tell him the same thing.

"This is the life we planned years ago. You begged me for it! What can have changed?"

"*I* have changed!" She thumped her chest with the flat of her hand, her voice breaking. "I have survived a husband. I have lived on a brigantine and kept accounts for a brothel. I have seen more of England in a summer than most see in a lifetime. I am not the child you abandoned all those years ago."

"This is my fault, is it? My punishment for not marrying you then? The blame must also lie with your bitch of a sister."

A humorless laugh burst out of her throat, loud and shrill. "Aye, Elizabeth is fierce, but 'twas *you* who left me on that hill. You took your revenge on Elizabeth and sacrificed me as you took it. Have you never wondered what it was like for me to sit there for hours, certain any moment I would see your head cresting the hill? Mayhap you did not know how long I waited, how long I hoped. I made excuse after excuse for you, for *eight years*, and not once have you admitted feeling any regret for leaving me behind. So tell me, Matthew: why should I choose you now when you did not choose me then?"

His eyes were unfocused, seeing something hovering over the table between them, and muscles rippled along his jaw as he clenched and unclenched his teeth.

She looked at his fist, tight and white-knuckled. Any moment it would fly through the air and connect with her face. If she apologized, admitted she was unwell, that she hadn't meant it, maybe she could still save herself.

But she didn't want to apologize. She had done nothing wrong.

Matthew sighed and let his chin drop to his chest. "You have asked this of me before." He looked up at her, and she expected anger, sadness, some expression to bring life to his eyes, but his face was blank. "Very well. I am sorry, Margaret. I promised to take you away from Gloucester and make you my wife, but I broke my promise. I regret it more than I can say."

She prepared to fight back tears while the weight of these long-awaited words settled around her. A moment passed in silence, and she continued to wait.

No change came over her, no feeling of relief or swell of compassion. He admitted the one thing she had been sure he would never admit, and yet… she felt nothing.

"I understand now why you feel you cannot trust me. I will do better. I did not deserve you eight years ago, but I will endeavor to deserve you now." He reached across the table. Her fingers tensed as his hand closed over hers. "Say you will forgive me. Let us have a fresh start."

Maggie took a deep breath and let it out, feeling her muscles tense as if bracing against a fifty-foot wave. This was going to hurt.

"No."

He threw up his hands, making her flinch. "For what other sins must I make amends? What may I do to earn your trust?"

"I do not know! I only know I am unhappy. I have been for weeks. I do not want this." The words that seemed unspeakable yesterday gushed from the crack in the dam. Her eyes filled with tears, half from sorrow, half from relief. "I am sorry, Matthew. I tried to be content. I tried for so long that now… I fear there is nothing you can do to change my decision."

She was right—it hurt. It was a heavy stone in the center of her chest, making it hard to swallow, impossible to breathe.

That was only the emotional pain. Any second, Matthew would let loose on her, grab her hair and throw her to the ground and pummel her for what she had done to him. She wasn't convinced she didn't deserve it. To feign normality for weeks, to accept his hospitality, to let him believe she would still go to the altar with him… How cruel she had been. If he lost his temper, she could understand it, even if she had to be his victim.

So when he walked out the door without even looking at her, the elaborate scaffolding holding her together fell apart, and she shattered with it.

25

"MISTRESS DONWELL!" THE landlord's sharp voice rang in the corridor, a startling violation of the silent house.

With the boarders at their work, Maggie had leisure to sit at the table or curl up on the bed and feel sorry for herself, as she had done for four days. On Tuesday she was still reeling, but on Wednesday she dragged herself out of doors in search of employment. Today she dressed, but that was as far as she got. Tomorrow, she would be homeless.

She unraveled herself from her spiraling thoughts and sat up. The room spun. Had she eaten today?

"Mistress!"

With a sigh, she left the room and found Master Walsch glaring up at her from the bottom of the stairs.

"Visitor," he said. He pointed an accusing finger at her and added, "'E's not to come up."

She descended the steps out of duty, too tired to realize she could refuse. Somewhere in her desultory thoughts, she wondered about her mysterious visitor. It didn't matter; Matthew was the only person she couldn't bear to see.

With one exception, apparently.

Captain Stokes looked up at her from the entryway, his yellow hat in his hand. With a warning look, Walsch disappeared down the hallway.

Maggie cleared her throat. "Good morrow, captain."

"My presence is unwelcome, I see." He glanced up and down her figure with an alarmed expression. What about her appearance troubled him? Her rumpled clothing, her too-narrow waist, the circles under her eyes? She hadn't looked in a glass recently enough to guess.

"Luke is at his work, and Matthew is… not here. Have you a message for them?"

"Is it so unfathomable the message may be for you?" He held the brim of his hat in both hands and rotated it, the brown-speckled feather swirling and flapping. "I have a boon to ask of you."

She led him down the corridor to the great hall and sat at the cleanest-looking table, not bothering to light a fire. He went to lay his hat down on the greasy surface, thought better of it, and settled it on his lap as he took his seat.

"How did you find me?" she said.

"Ellen thought you might be with Kent, and Meredith gave me the direction." His expression hardened. "She told me how you were dismissed."

This was what she had wanted from Matthew: anger on her behalf. But that was weeks ago, an eon ago. She hardly thought of it now.

"What is this boon?"

He leaned back in his seat, a storyteller winding up. "Yesterden, I received word from Osborne. He is to be a father, he tells me."

"I am happy for him. I did not know he was married."

"He was not, but he says he published the banns the day he learned the woman was with child. She wants him to give up sailing. He is apprenticing a blacksmith or a carpenter or the like. An *apprentice*, at his age." Stokes shook his head.

"'Tis brave of him to start anew." *Is the woman worth the sacrifice?* Maggie kept that question to herself.

He leaned forward, resting his forearms on the table's edge and clasping his hands in front of him. "So I come to you."

Her heart skipped. It was impossible that he was about to make her an officer on his ship. It would be too perfect, too divine. She had done nothing to deserve such a gift.

"I pay the crew *per diem* while they ready the *Merrow* to sail, but I shall be overseeing repairs, hiring new crew—I cannot be all places at once. I prithee, will you help?"

Yes. Whatever he needed, she would do it. Her chest constricted as she struggled to hide her delight.

"I will not inconvenience you for long. A shilling a day for your trouble, and only until I have found Osborne's replacement."

The warmth inside her fizzled out.

"I am sorry to ask you. I think it may stir up trouble with Kent. Methinks I know what your answer must be."

"Why are you here, if you claim to know my answer?" Her steely tone was tempered by grief and sharpened on the mention of Matthew's name.

"Supposing you were at liberty to come to my aid, I would not waste my time looking elsewhere," he said. "Osborne gave me little enough notice."

The sentiment was not romantic, but his words acted on her like an incantation. Of course she would come to his aid. How could she forget the favors he had done for her? Here was her chance to rescue him as he had rescued her, Matthew be damned.

It was unfair of him to put an expiration on a thing she wanted so fiercely, but she had born it in November, and she could bear it again.

Then again, why must she bear it?

"I will do it." She spoke without considering the consequences, without giving him time to deny. "I will be your purser. Mark my name in the ledger, give me an officer's berth, and promise me five shares. I know the job better than anyone, and what I do not know, I will learn. Why waste time hiring someone to do a job I am prepared to do? Take me."

"Maggie…"

This was stupid, to put a vice around him when he was offering her a way out of her doldrums, however temporary. She couldn't stop herself. "There is yet time for your present crew to become accustomed to the idea. To any new crew, I will already be a fixture. Was that not your objection, the approval of your crew?"

"What of Matthew Kent?"

She shrugged, feigning indifference with all her might. "His approval is no longer my concern. He left this house four days ago. I have heard nothing since."

"Left?"

"We quarreled."

The set of his mouth was stern, his brows lowered, but there was an alertness to his unblinking gaze. His eyes were a rather pretty hazel, she could now see. "Meredith told me you were to be married yesterden."

"Meredith could not have known," she said.

He stared and stared at her, his scrutiny too keen to endure. She looked away.

"Then you are not Kent's wife."

She shook her head. "We are finished, Matthew and I."

Stokes leaned back in his chair and crossed his legs, propping his ankle on the opposite knee. The felt hat in his lap tipped, but he caught it by the brim and dangled it at his side in one fist. She couldn't tell from her vantage if it dragged on the dusty floor. It was impossible to picture him in a dirty hat.

He cleared his throat. "That must have been difficult for you."

For a second time, one compassionate word had her holding back tears. His concern was for her, a nobody, not for the man he had sailed with for nearly a decade. Ellen was right: he was far too soft.

Perhaps, then, he could be molded.

"What say you, captain?"

He sighed. "I am gratified you love the *Merrow* as much as I, but I cannot demand this of my crew. 'Tis too great a change."

"Wherefore? I spent half a summer aboard. A whole summer would be no different."

"My crew faces shipwreck and bodily harm every day, not to mention the threat of hanging."

"And yet we both disembarked unscathed in November."

Again that sigh. This time, it took a moment for him to speak. "Who quarreled with whom?"

"What does it matter?"

"If you are to be in close quarters only days after your falling out, I must needs know which of you will be pining for the other."

Maggie's fists were hidden under the table, and she clenched them hard to disperse a little of her glee. He was using the wrong tense if he meant to deny her. "It will not affect my work, if that is your fear. I cannot be impartial to any man if my primary purpose is to see each receives his fair share."

Stokes tapped his fingers on the table in quick succession. "Nine shillings per week, guaranteed for a fortnight, even if I hire a purser tomorrow."

He was trying to bribe her into backing down. Why? Because of Matthew? It would be awkward, but she was the only one who needed to worry about it. "Take me on for the summer, and if my work is unsatisfactory, set me ashore again."

His fingers tapped. "One pound sterling, paid today, and another the Thursday after next."

She needed to take his offer. It would allow her to leave this cursed house, reunite with her friends, step aboard the *Merrow*, and pretend all was well. Two pounds would tide her over until she found employment elsewhere. She would be a fool to refuse.

But accepting meant giving up her last chance to go to sea. He had given her a glimmer of hope, so she snatched at it. "You need a purser, captain. Here I am."

He looked up at her from beneath his lashes, pleading. "You will not do this for me? You will force my hand?"

That was precisely what she was doing, and it was low of her. Was she throwing away any cordiality that might have once existed between them? Would she make him regret having taken a chance on her? Was the *Merrow* worth all that?

Like the coward she was, she remained silent.

He rose from his seat. "Greenland Dock, eight of the clock." Jamming his hat on his head, he added, "And may God have mercy on us both."

As he left, her eyes caught on his hat. She had not noticed when he came in, but the smooth felt brim was crumpled and creased in the back, as if it had been crushed in a hot, tight fist.

26

FOR AN OUT-of-the-way town she had never heard of, Penzance had a busy port. The sailors swarming the docks varied in color from pale pink to earthy brown, and the bits of overheard conversation put Maggie in mind of exotic marketplaces and vast deserts. By the number of awestruck looks she amassed, they found her just as strange to look at.

Stokes and Padraig flanked her, her own personal guard. She was about to meet their Cornwall contact, a man who could move almost any sort of goods. Which was fortunate, because their last prize saddled them with a frustrating variety of textiles, spices, tools, and even a religious relic (from the Spanish inscription, she guessed it was supposed to be St. Paul's belt).

She had recorded the man's alias in her inconspicuous little ledger, the same size and shape of her beloved book of Shakespeare sonnets. The ledger also contained notes about the other half-dozen merchants and fences she had met in the five weeks since the *Merrow* set sail on the first of April. The full list of all their English friends would fill an entire book, and that didn't include the ones in Scotland and Wales. How Stokes kept track of them all was anyone's guess.

The trio crossed the square, where the colorful ribbons of a maypole fluttered in the sea breeze, left over from the May Day celebration that must have thronged the green a few days ago. At her right, Stokes gave a low chuckle.

"Tell me not that you disapprove of maypole dancing," she said.

"Pardon? Oh, nothing like." He jerked his head to the line of shops on the south side of the square. "Abernethy's. The site of a memorable occasion three or four years past."

Padraig sniffed. "Best forgot, I'd say. Makes me shiver to think o' all that blood."

"Yet you must admit, you've never had a better shave."

Maggie gawked between them, waiting to be enlightened.

"A minor skirmish and a tiny scrape," said Stokes. "Abernethy is the best barber-surgeon in Cornwall."

"Lucky we were near," Padraig added, "or you woulda lost your arm."

With a snicker, Maggie peered past Stokes at the storefronts, searching for the barber-surgeon's trademark striped pole. "A close shave in more ways than one, then?" Stokes was kind enough to laugh at her joke, but Padraig was silent, as she expected. The last time they had been friendly with each other was the night of her abduction last summer.

She reached behind her and dragged her long, golden-red braid through her hand. "Mayhap I will pay Master Abernethy a visit. This mess is become too much trouble."

"And lose your best feature?" Padraig said. "Why, there'd be no reason to keep you 'round."

"My hair is my best feature? I always thought my nose was rather nice. Aside from the freckles."

"Makes you look a true Irish lass, it does."

"That is the only reason you tolerate me, of course."

He shrugged. "Makes it easier to feign that I do."

Padraig's tone was light, but she knew better than to consider it a playful joke. His displeasure at learning of her promotion had been the most obvious out of all the crew; only Driscoll's disgust was more pronounced. She and the first mate had reached a tenuous truce in the last few weeks, thanks to how competent she was in her work. He could complain about her as a woman, but she vowed never to give him reason to complain about her as a purser.

"What say you, captain? Her hair or her nose?"

Maggie cringed, wondering what sin she had committed today to make Padraig want to humiliate her.

Stokes glanced at Padraig, looking right past the nose in question. "I do not employ sailors for their good looks. How would you have gotten the job?"

"There must be somethin' you like about her."

"Aside from her neat hand and her skill with numbers, you mean?"

"Aye, the lass's *skills* were ne'er in doubt."

Her face flushed with indignation and embarrassment. "Be hanged, Padraig MacCraith!"

"Enough! Here is the Lark and Rook." Stokes's stormy expression sent a chill down her back as they pulled up in front of their destination. "'Tis not the sort of place for children. Must I leave you both outside?"

Padraig stared straight ahead, his mouth a thin line. "Nay, sir." Maggie echoed him in her smallest voice, not that she deserved the captain's gibe; Padraig's rudeness was appalling. She had heard it all before, last summer, and some of the crew still whispered about her behind cupped hands, but she had not expected such blatant animosity from a fellow officer. Their truce was more tenuous than she thought.

The Lark and Rook was the sort of tavern Maggie would never have set foot in twelve months ago. It was dim and dirty, smelling of pipe smoke and an eye-watering mélange of human secretions. She was wearing the only shoes she had, so she picked her way across the floor as Stokes led them toward a table in a dark corner. The few unwashed, half-drunk patrons watched them from beneath heavy brows.

Their contact arrived a quarter of an hour later and the negotiations began. Maggie's skills improved with each sale. She had even begun attempting subtle manipulations when she thought she had a good read on her negotiation partner. Unfortunately, this man had been at it much longer than she had. Short of lying to him, which would create far more trouble than it was worth, there was little she could do to move him. They agreed on a price and a collection time, then shook on it.

"Not every deal will be a wild success," Stokes said as they trooped back down the docks.

"I did what I could."

"'Twas not *all* you could do, I vow," Padraig said. "He's a man, after all."

Maggie clenched her fists as blood roared in her ears. Twice in one afternoon? She stopped short and glared at him. "I fear I missed an important tutorial, then. Did Osborne fuck every buyer, or only the comely ones?"

Padraig prepared a retort, but Stokes put an arm across his chest to separate him from Maggie. "Take a walk, MacCraith," he said, voice low. Padraig's usually pale face was red, and he glared at her before stalking back the way they had come.

She watched him go, her outrage fading to bewilderment. "Have I done something to offend him?"

"I cannot credit it."

She crossed her arms, hugging her waist. "'Tis getting worse, you know… Nay, you would not know. The lads are careful to hold their tongues around you."

He was silent. What would she have him say, anyway? That he was sorry he hired her and it was time for them to part ways? She needed to keep this drama to herself.

She breezed into a new subject. "Davies and Engberg expect me at the Lion for supper. They would no doubt welcome your company."

"I have some things to attend to. Pray, sup with your friends."

Ah, yes, she thought. Another reminder that there were friends, there were enemies, and then there was Captain Stokes.

She found her way to the Lion alone and spotted Engberg's hair, a beacon in the dim light of the ordinary. As she wove between the crowded tables, a careless glance snagged on Matthew. He was crammed at a table alongside Driscoll, Leigh, and Coulthurst. Driscoll was in the middle of a tall tale of his courage and cunning, no doubt.

She locked eyes with her former lover and felt the familiar crawling dread he would at last break his silence. Their interactions were tense, but civil, so she didn't think he was responsible for the rumors. It didn't require much intelligence to notice two people who had left the ship intent on marriage had returned no longer speaking to one another.

Each man had a theory as to the reason. Those who liked her were, for the most part, sympathetic. Those who didn't had come up with less flattering assumptions.

Davies was sitting with a view to the door, and he patted the empty place at the table with a smile. He and Engberg were joined by Gillies and a new crewman, a career sailor named Arthur.

"Look who's decided to grace us with 'er presence," Davies said as she sat down. "How'd you fare, then?"

Gillies raised his hand to flag down the barmaid. "What's your drink?"

"Same as you. As for the deal, 'tis done, and that is all I may tell you."

Arthur swallowed a gulp of beer and thunked his drink on the table, his big, red hand dwarfing the mug. "A secret deal, eh?"

"Nay, she means it did not go well," Davies said.

She glowered at him. "I said no such thing."

"If it went well, we'd know all about it."

Engberg nodded his agreement.

She looked around at the men. "I am not such a braggart, am I?"

Gillies hid behind his beer and Engberg looked a little embarrassed, but Davies shrugged. "Th'art a pirate, and no mistake. Show me a man here who does not dream of glory."

She had to acknowledge the truth of it. Davies neither hid nor apologized for his musical talents, and he adored having an audience. Driscoll, holding court at the far table, was another sort of performer. And Maggie did often tell her friends of her successful negotiations, especially as she gained confidence and independence.

Today's failure was a disappointment not only because she wanted the *Merrow* to prosper, but because she wanted to be its hero.

The barmaid set down a mug in front of Maggie, and before the woman turned away, Maggie ordered another round for the lads. If she couldn't be the hero of the *Merrow*, she could at least be the hero of this table for a quarter of an hour.

27

THEY TOOK THEIR next prize a week later in the stretch of sea between England and Belgium, and Stokes set a course for London. This would never be unwelcome news; it was the crew's favorite port, with its wealth of diversions.

Maggie suspected it was Stokes's favorite as well. If they docked more than a day, he would disappear to his London residence, which he leased year round. It seemed a frivolous expense, but she knew better than anyone he could afford it. As accustomed as she was to seeing him on the deck of the ship, she caught glimpses of the courtier imprisoned within.

They drifted around the curve of the southern coast in the darkness of middle watch. Maggie couldn't sleep. Tomorrow she would meet their London business partners—four of them—without the support of Padraig or Stokes. Every step of the transaction would be her responsibility, and it was a complicated operation she only understood in theory. It made her nervous to be released from Stokes's apron strings at a moment where she faced a higher-than-normal likelihood of failure.

Her cabin was stifling, but she resisted going out on deck. She had heard Stokes skulk past her room at his usual time, around two, and he had yet to return to his cabin. If she went outside, she would find him there, gazing into the blackness.

Last summer, she had enjoyed standing beside him in companionable silence. This summer, the silence had changed. He steered conversations away from anything more philosophical or sentimental than the weather, and he often excused himself from her presence as soon as he could come up with a reason. She was quick to catch on, at least, and now she avoided him as doggedly as he avoided her.

But it was terrible being trapped in her cabin, with a whole ship above and below to prowl in the night. How long would she live in fear of bumping into him? Bumping into Matthew wasn't as uncomfortable. At least she knew why *he* wasn't speaking to her.

At six bells, she swung her legs out of bed and dressed.

As she emerged onto the quarterdeck, the black void of Stokes's figure was barely visible against the charcoal sky. He was on the forecastle deck, as far from her as he could be; no one would believe she had come upon him by accident. She glanced up and behind her, but the top of the helmsman's head belonged to Keith, not Matthew. Thank Christ for small blessings.

Stokes didn't so much as turn his head as she climbed up to the bow to take the place beside him.

"Suppose I had been an assassin," she said.

"Your step is the lightest of my crew."

"My upbringing, I suppose. All those dance lessons." She supported herself on the railing by her forearms, leaning forward to feel the salty mist from far below.

How long could they go without speaking? Evidently, she was about to find out. An uneasy minute passed with only the crashing waves to break up the silence.

"I am eager to see London again," she said, when she couldn't stand it any longer. "'Tis the nearest place to being my home."

"What of Gloucester?"

"I fear Gloucester is lost to me." He didn't press her, and she didn't want to talk about her family. "Where are your people from?"

"I was raised in London."

Silence curled around them again.

"Have you any advice for me? For the morrow?"

He shot her a brief glance, his eyes catching the milky moonlight. "You hardly need it. Least of all from me."

"Who better to advise than the captain?"

"Osborne is the better peddler."

"'Tis a long journey to Yorkshire to ask him."

It pleased her to see him smile. "Very well." He gripped the railing and stared down at his knuckles. "I advise you to keep a clear head and let not your judgment be clouded."

She had hoped for a more tailor-made sentiment, but she took it. "I will do my best."

He turned to look at her. "Are you worried about tomorrow?"

"I do not relish the thought of making myself a fool."

"I have known a good many fools. You are not of their number."

It was a very different sentiment from the one he expressed at Christmas. If he thought so well of her, why did he remain distant? Apologizing after all this time would require courage and ingenuity to bring it up—not that she could decide which apology to start with.

Instead, she stood beside him and let her eyes drift across the star-studded canvas into which they floated, thinking how little she deserved the gift of his regard. She had lied to him, insulted him, coerced him. She had let her embarrassing Matthew drama play out on the stage of his ship. To behave so terribly to so good a man was proof of her status as the queen of fools.

In the dark, it was just possible to make out the shape of his profile, his short beard coming to a point at the tip of his chin, his mustache curving over his lip, his nose not quite straight as it led up to his brooding brow. Black curls whipped about his forehead and ears. He was handsome, gallant but rakish, that potent combination of valorous knight and dastardly villain. After seeing him every day, his good looks seldom registered anymore.

He caught her staring, and her stomach dropped.

"What fault do you find in me?" He raised an eyebrow.

"None!" At his smirk, she blushed. "Rather, I was not—"

"If you have finished your examination, I will take my leave." He pushed away from the rail and touched a finger to his forehead, in lieu of tipping his hat.

She nodded, her inner monologue peppered with oaths as she berated herself.

This had been just as ill-conceived an idea as she had known it would be. He had been cordial, but she was no closer to breaking through the awkwardness. Catching her staring only set her back. She kept her eyes trained on the ocean ahead while she listened to Stokes's footfalls on the stairs and across the deck. When she determined she was safe from him, she started back toward her berth.

At the bottom of the forecastle stairs, a shadow separated itself from the darkness beside the overturned pinnace.

"How now, Maggie?" came the rough voice.

Her heart thumped at the surprise, but she took a breath and peered at the sailor. A square face, light hair, sturdy frame, a little shorter than her. She groaned inwardly. "How now, Driscoll?"

The man stepped toward her, his light footsteps incongruous with his stocky build. "Had a nice chat with the captain?"

"'Tis no concern of yours." Her skin prickled with gooseflesh.

"In fact, I am a bit concerned. 'Tis only that some of the lads've wondered…"

"Is this the same foolishness that began last summer? You may spare me. I know well what you have wondered, and you are mistaken."

"Am I? For you did seem marvelous comfortable up there together."

"I owe you no explanation and I need not defend myself to you."

Before she could brush past him, he muttered, "You're not liked, you ken." She paused mid-step, long enough for Driscoll to add, "I can help."

"How?"

"I've a bit of clout with the lads. They look up to me, as it were." His smile was an ugly expression on that flat little face. "I'd be right pleased to tell 'em they've got it wrong. That you're not fuckin' the captain."

She needed to leave, to go to her cabin and close the door and never find herself alone with Driscoll again. She knew what he was about to say. But she didn't move.

"And mayhap, as thanks…" He leaned in so she could smell the sour stench of him. "You'd transfer your affections to me."

"That will never happen."

"Nay? Pity." This close, she could make out his stubble, even in the dark. "I've heard what that pretty mouth can do."

"How dare you speak this way to an officer?" Her whispered voice was too brittle to hold any real menace, and he heard it for the empty threat it was.

"Lucky I don't count you an officer."

"I wonder that you are so bold. If you believe the captain is my lover, why would I not go to him and tell him what you have said?"

Driscoll snickered. "Never said *I* thought you were fuckin' him. 'Tis plain you're not. Don't doubt he'd go for it, though. I wager we'd all like a turn."

Mortified, furious, speechless, Maggie did what she should have done in the first place and turned her back on Driscoll. She felt him watching her all the way across the deck and up the quarterdeck stairs.

28

MAGGIE DROPPED DOWN into the ferryboat, the *Merrow*'s hull rising like a colossus beside her, glistening with river water. Hale steadied her, and she sat beside Burney. Behind her was fifteen-year-old Peter, new to the ship and eager to prove himself. This was her little crew of runners. The first element of her mission that could go wrong.

The ferryman maneuvered them across the Thames. It was a nimble craft, changing direction with ease to dodge the huge shipping vessels jostling for first entry to the Pool. They bumped into the Tower Stairs and climbed to street level.

She turned to the lads and gave them as good an impression of Osborne as she could muster. "You know your instructions?" They all nodded. "Go to," she said, and they scattered.

The last few vessels they had waylaid had been well stocked with goods, but the ships themselves were not worth the trouble of taking. It was a blessing she wouldn't have to fight the frenzy at the Pool and bribe the customs officers. Also, it freed her to meet one of their business partners while the lads summoned the other three, and she had chosen one special.

Jules Bisset's clothier shop was a sizable building with glass windows and a new-looking door. Inside, stacked bolts of cloth lined the walls, sorted by color and type in a recurring rainbow. A table near the front held samples of ribbon, cord, lace, and buttons. In the back corner, a curtain concealed the inside of a changing stall. A memory of being fitted for her presentation gown flitted through her mind.

The other corner held a desk, piled with papers and parcels, and behind the desk sat Jules Bisset.

"Bienvenue!" he sang, skirting the desk to hurry toward her. He wore the same rich, fashionable garments that were the hallmark of his style, and his gray hair was pulled back into a tail. He began to make her a handsome bow, then started when he recognized her. "Ah! Mademoiselle…"

"Maggie Bailey, sir. I am come on behalf of our mutual friend, Captain Moran."

"You have been at sea! I wondered why I do not see you at the inn. Come, *s'il vous pla"t.*" He ushered her further into the shop. "The captain is well?"

"Excellent well."

"Bon, and how may I help Captain Moran?"

"'Tis quite the reverse. The captain has an opportunity for you."

Bisset's face was friendly, but his eyes studied her, looking for some trick. "And he has sent you? Not Monsieur Osborne?"

"Master Osborne took leave of the *Merrow,* and his purser duties fell to me."

"Ah, yes? His pay falls to you also, I hope." His eyes twinkled. She had almost forgotten about her sarcastic retort when they first met.

"We are just arrived in London, hoping to… meet with old friends."

The man leaned in close and lowered his voice. "Silk? From China?"

"Twelve bolts."

Bisset fluttered his hands as he dashed to the door and latched it. He waved her over to his desk and went to sit behind it, then seemed to change his mind and offered the chair to her. He reminded her of a bird, flitting here and there, always moving, always watching.

She sat and told him what the *Merrow* had in its hold. He took notes as she spoke, jotting figures in the margin of his ledger.

When she was done, he looked at her with forlorn eyes. "So much!" he whined. "I would indeed love to help the *capitaine,* but so much cloth will be too dear. Business is not so good, all the beautiful lords and ladies have gone into the country. *Pauvre Bisset,* I say to myself. *C'est un temps très difficile, vous comprenez.*"

She got the impression he was slipping into his native tongue on purpose to inspire pity. He looked despondent, his brow heavy, the lines beside his mouth deep as canals.

Poor Bisset, indeed. If times were as difficult as he claimed, his healthy belly paunch would have been the first to go.

Maggie gave him her warmest smile. *"Oui, monsieur, je comprends.* Forgive me for troubling you. I will return to the ship. Mayhap the captain knows another clothier or draper in town..." She put her hands on her knees as if to rise from her seat.

"Attendez!" His hand shot out to stay her. "I have some demand for silk, and 'tis not easy to come by." He ran his finger along the list of items he had scribbled down, and he gave her a number.

As she expected, it was far too low. "Very well, I wager 'tis a fair price for the silk brocade. When do you wish to collect it?"

"The brocade? What of the velvet?"

"I had not thought you wanted it! What is your price for the velvet?"

There was an irritated slant to his brow now he was catching on. He sighed and named another number. "For all of it," he clarified.

She countered with a figure one and a half times what she knew the fabric was worth. He balked and shot back another number.

They continued in this way for a few minutes, each conceding as little as they could. Eventually, he gave her that sad look again. *"Ma chère,* I am an old man doing what I can to stay afloat. You will not help me just a little?"

"I understand completely, monsieur. My share of this prize will scarce buy food for my six dear babes, and they all need new shoes as well. And of course, being a woman, my share is so much smaller than my shipmates'..."

It was a gamble to lay it on so thick, but she was emboldened by irritation. No wonder Osborne had always given in—the man was a walking, French-speaking headache.

Bisset's eyes glimmered. "Tell me what price you hope I will pay."

His English was so precise now, she knew it had been an act from the beginning. He was ready to negotiate.

She made another gamble and told him the bottom-line figure she had calculated. "'Tis more than fair," she said. "You would pay half again as much if you purchased from a local merchant, and certainly twice if you fetched it yourself. You will find it of excellent quality, and if it does not meet your high standards, I will be most willing to renegotiate."

He stared down at his ledger, gray brows knitted together. "How did you land on this sum?"

"I asked around in Cornwall." This gamble made her more nervous, but if it won him over, it would be worth it. She slipped a little book from her purse, found her messy arithmetic, and showed it to him.

He leaned over her and nodded, muttering to himself in a mix of English and French. "*Très bien. Alors*, this figure is too high." He pointed to the number she had estimated for the bolts of twill. "'Tis not much in favor today, not at this time of year. *Là*, this…" He underlined the word "velvet" with his fingernail. "This I can sell. Methinks you have valued it too low for London."

His honesty surprised her. He didn't seem the type to relinquish the upper hand, and her chest expanded at the realization she may have impressed the infamous Jules Bisset.

"*Hélas*," he was saying, a friendly grin on his face, "you cannot raise your asking price now. *Bon*. I accept. But I will not gloat, for next time you will be ready for me, *hein*?" He winked at her.

She couldn't help but smile. She could see now why Stokes envied Bisset. He was not hard or cruel, only maddening.

"Do you prepare so for each negotiation?" he asked.

Bisset was a special case, but still Maggie never went into a sale without knowing what she wanted out of it. "Captain Moran has been good to me. I have no wish to bring shame upon him or his ship."

He nodded, looking her up and down. "Loyalty, intelligence, and courage. Pray, do not let the captain forget what a treasure he has, *mademoiselle*."

It was more compliment than she could handle, and her instincts demanded she lower herself somehow to balance it. "*Madame*," she said. "I am a widow."

"Your pardon. So one must add 'wisdom' to your list of assets, *hein*?"

Maggie let her triumph hurry her steps east to Cheapside. There she would find a disreputable underground tavern, where she would have the pleasure of repeating the afternoon's ordeal three more times. The instructions the boys had delivered gave each contact a specific meeting time so no two overlapped. It meant she would sit in the filthy, nameless tavern for over three hours, waiting for each man to arrive.

The four o'clock and five o'clock transactions went well, perhaps because she was still channeling the unflappable expert negotiator persona she had donned for Bisset. Soon, she would be at leisure for a few hours and free to return to the ship for a spot of supper. Her stomach rumbled its approval.

It had to be nearing six o'clock when the door opened, and Maggie looked up, hoping to see her last client. The silhouette of

Captain Stokes swung the creaky door closed. He spotted her craning around the support pillar she had been hiding behind and picked his way toward her.

"Not checking up on me, are you?" In fact, she hoped he was. She was bursting to tell someone about her afternoon.

"Can a man not buy a drink in this town?"

"How stands the hour?"

"Almost six of the clock."

She leaned around the pillar in the other direction, as if the buyer might have slipped in while Stokes distracted her. "One more," she said, sighing.

He put his hand on the back of the empty chair across from her. She wondered if he would sit, but he only shifted his weight and remained standing. "How have you fared today? Better than you feared, I hope."

"Methinks the lads will be pleased with their payout."

"And Bisset, your most formidable adversary?"

Gleefulness flooded her chest, and it caught in her throat as she tamped it down. It wasn't boasting if she was only answering a question. "He agreed to my asking price."

Stokes's eyes widened. "Marry come up!"

"Faith, he did." His look of utter disbelief made her drop her modest facade in favor of the smug smile she had been concealing.

He fumbled about for an explanation. "Was he… ill?"

"He appeared in fine health."

"I am all astonishment."

"'Twas no small feat. I admit, I am as surprised as you."

"What promises did you make him?"

That joking tone of his had never bothered her before, but some distrustful part of her recalled Padraig's cruel jab in Penzance. Her smug smile faded. "None it would shame me to make."

"Shame you?" He glanced around as he slid into the chair beside hers, then leaned in conspiratorially. "We are pirates. We do not know shame, only treasure."

"And in pursuit of this treasure, you wish me to…?" She shrugged and waved a hand, hoping he would supply the end of the sentence so she didn't have to. Strange. She had thought her innocence long worn away.

"I *advise* you," he corrected, "to use the weapons in your arsenal. A man may use menace, but a woman has charm. You need not make any false promises, nor promise aught you do not wish to give. Only consider your sex may be a boon."

She was already shaking her head by the middle of his speech, and now she rushed to cut him off. "I could not. What a fool I would seem! Ellen is the seductress, not I."

"To my eye, there is only one thing sets you and Ellen apart."

"Allure?"

"Practice." With an incredulous look, she prepared to list the other traits she could only aspire to, but he leaned back and continued. "Such a thing is not like to work on Bisset, though, speaking of Ellen."

"What? He seemed so attentive to her each time I saw them together."

"That is precisely my meaning. The man is sore in love. He speaks of removing her from the Dagger and making her his mistress. Your seduction would be wasted on him, certes."

She watched him for signs of discomfort, but he appeared untroubled. "I am glad to know such news causes you no grief."

"Grief?"

"I wondered if you might be envious."

A look of understanding washed over his features. "Marry, I know not what planted that thought in your mind, but permit me to pluck it out. I am not in love with Ellen."

She blushed to remember the times she had prodded him about their mutual friend, and the embarrassing miscommunication that nearly lost her an invitation to *The Winter's Tale*. This piece of information lifted a weight she hadn't known she carried—simple relief to be in on the secret, no doubt.

"Have you eaten?"

She shook her head and lifted her half-full mug, the same one she had ordered two hours ago. "Unless you count this."

He took it from her, sniffed it, and grimaced. "I do not. Will you sup with me?"

This easiness was such a stark contrast from last night's awkwardness it put Maggie off balance. Why would he seek out further opportunities to spend time with her after how she had embarrassed herself last night?

Recovering as quickly as she could, she said, "I know not when I will be finished with Master Spicer."

"Then I will await you at the King's Arms in Holbourn. You may recount which… method of attack had the greatest success."

"Forsooth, I do not always find success with the *usual* method."

He shrugged his shoulders and rose from his seat. "Mayhap 'tis a signal to try another. If you require practice, I am at your service."

Practice… flirting? She readily admitted she would not find a better tutor. Did this mean they were friends again, despite her many foibles? The thought filled her with warmth.

Then practicality breezed in. Her Driscoll secret bubbled up whenever she was near him, and as she was resolved not to tell him, it wouldn't be wise to meet him for supper. Driscoll was as volatile as one of his guns; there was no saying what he would do if she tattled. If Stokes took her side, which he would, such favoritism would only confirm the rumor Maggie was so desperate to quell.

It wasn't fair. In these last ten minutes, her heart had felt lighter than it had for months. She should seek out these sporadic splashes of sunshine, not hide from them, but concern for her own wellbeing made her prefer the haven of shadow.

The tavern door swung open, and the newcomer spotted Stokes at once. The men grasped arms in greeting. This must be Spicer.

"May I present my new purser, Maggie Bailey?" Stokes said. "I leave you in her capable hands, for I have business in Holbourn." He nodded his farewell and turned to go.

Supping with him would bring her a step closer to rekindling their friendship. She had no desire to hurt his feelings by refusing. Maybe he had advice on how to deal with Driscoll, or would solve the problem himself. Moreover, she wanted to go.

"Enjoy your supper, captain," she called after him, shrinking from the light.

29

MIDSUMMER STALKED CLOSER, and the days were glorious and balmy. The odd storm tossed the *Merrow* about, but when the sky was sunny and blue, the waves sparkling, the air warm and salt-scented, it was like a fairytale.

Maggie, though, was living a different sort of story. She spent most days skulking furtively about, nervous and irritable. She could count on Davies and Engberg, but that left a score of others who openly disapproved of her presence. They did subtle things: standing in her way, looking over her head, pretending they hadn't heard her and forcing her to repeat herself. Innocent things, drops of water on a stone, but destructive nonetheless. There was also Driscoll, stirring up mischief in dark corners of the ship, his threats like black clouds on the horizon. Stokes had been right: now she had a share of their plunder, the novelty of her feminine charm had worn off.

To compound things, she couldn't pass through this season without thinking of Matthew, the Matthew she had loved as a girl. Echoes of his impassioned speech about running away together. The interminable creep of shadows as dawn turned to midday and still he didn't come. These thoughts would bring her to the more recent past, to the Matthew she had rejected, and she wondered if she had ever loved that Matthew at all. Maybe their affair was only a way for her to right the wrong of the past, to puzzle out the mystery. Clearly it hadn't worked. Now he was one more buried trap on the ship she used to love, poised to spring at the next false step.

But, she reasoned, if she didn't talk to anyone, nothing could happen to her.

It wasn't difficult to stay busy. They ran a quick smuggling operation out of Boston after leaving London, captured and offloaded two more prizes, and were now on their way to Dover with another batch of stolen goods in the hold.

Pen in hand, Maggie inventoried it with her usual care, down to the last drop of Madeira (of which there were many drops—seven casks full). She drifted to the other side of the hold and counted the minutiae lining the shelves: rolls of twine, pewter mugs, candles. She marked down what needed restocking, then rubbed her forehead with the back of her hand, another headache brewing.

Her quill was dull and her arm was tired of holding the book, even though it was the smaller of the two. She looked around and found the task exhausted. There was nothing for it: she would have to find something else to do.

After sharpening her quill in her cabin, she opened her orderly ledger and gazed fondly at it for a while. Then she tucked it back in its usual spot, beside her worn copy of Shakespeare sonnets. It was risky keeping the real ledger in her room, out in the open, but the conspicuous decoy ledger was much more likely to draw the attention of any crotchety customs officials, not that she had ever encountered any. It seemed no one would ever see her fine work.

It was nearing the end of forenoon watch, according to the bells. She poked around her cabin, hoping she had stashed some food away, but her stores were empty. Again she would have to go out, a quick dash down the stairs before ducking into the galley.

But there would be no dashing or ducking, because Stokes and Padraig were at the railing, staring at the enormous ship sailing toward them.

It was beautiful, shining and new. Blue and red paint gleamed on the rail and the hull, and a matching flag, too small to make out from this distance, waved at the top of the mizzenmast. The *Merrow* had no contracts underway, no clandestine meetings planned. Any ship they met was either to be avoided or pillaged. This one matched the *Merrow* in size and firepower, and it clearly had no intention of being avoided.

Stokes cursed under his breath

"What flag is that?" she asked.

He kept his eyes on the incoming vessel. "The sodding English."

She looked again. A change in the wind stretched the flag out so she could see the red and white cross over the blue and white background, King James's banner for a united England and

Scotland. The ship belonged to their own navy. Did they know what the *Merrow* had been doing in these waters?

Stokes shook himself out of his paralysis and barked orders. "All hands! Run up the English flag! Pratt—" The bosun appeared at Stokes's elbow. "I want your best on deck and your worst out of sight. Gillies, see that the charts reflect a voyage from Porto to Bristol. Padraig, find some men to help Maggie secure the hold."

They all hurried to their tasks, hearing the undercurrent of unease in Stokes's gruff commands. Her insides roiling, Maggie took a step toward the stairs to the lower decks, but Stokes grasped her elbow.

"I cannot hide you," he said. "You are best able to answer any questions they will have about our cargo."

"I am ready." She made to pull away so she could get to work.

"They will ask other questions." His tone was more adamant now, more worried. "About how you came to be on this brig. What answers will you give?"

Maggie hesitated. He was right: a woman on a merchant ship was a curiosity. The role she intended to play when such a time came was plausible and innocuous, but awkward. She wished they had discussed this before, when the mood wasn't so tense.

"They will not be surprised to find the captain travels with his wife," she said.

He drooped as he exhaled, though she couldn't tell whether it was a sigh of relief or defeat. Looking down at the deck, he gave a nod, as if to himself, then looked up at her and nodded again. "Aye. Can you do it? Play at being Mistress Stokes?"

"I will try." The idea of it was making her heart race. It was not so different from singing for the crew, she told herself, except singing for the crew was less likely to see them all hanged.

"Speak only when you must, and do not stray far from the truth. You will become mired in falsehoods."

"Aye, sir."

"Will."

She nodded and tried it on. "Will." This was her only line, and she would not disappoint him.

His hand still encircled the bend in her arm, and she felt his thumb brush a small arc over her sleeve, one way and then the other. With a small, reassuring smile, he released her.

She dashed up the steps to the navigation room and tore the green decoy ledger from the shelf, nearly bashing Gillies in the head as he hurried to stage the table as if they were navigating home from Portugal. The real ledger would be safe in her cabin, tucked beside her Shakespeare sonnets.

Her cabin. A jolt of panic struck her. The captain and his wife would share a cabin, wouldn't they? She saw Padraig directing Luke and Hale down to the hold to hide their stolen cargo. They needed to know what was in the decoy ledger, and she couldn't be two places at once. With a grunt of frustration, she swung down the stairs to the hold.

By some miracle, Lloyd was coming up as she was going down.

"Thank Christ," she breathed. "I need a married man. Prithee, go to my cabin and move everything you can to the captain's quarters. Lay it about as if a woman lives there. Stack my books—all of them—on a shelf, with the Shakespeare sonnets on top."

To his credit, he took the steady stream of odd instructions in stride. They brushed past each other without another word.

In the hold, Padraig, Luke, and Davies were prying away the false floorboards and pieces of wall that would hide whatever loot should not be found on board. She flipped open the ledger and turned to the most recent inventory she had fabricated. Hale stood nearby with a small barrel in his arms.

"Leave that," she said, then pointed to a set of wooden crates full of items they had pilfered from the last ship's captain and said, "Hide those." As the boys shoved them into the dark cavities, she set Davies to work on another trunk and the princely casks of Madeira.

"Leave one cask," she said, thinking fast. "Put it in front of that crate of silk."

As the men dropped the last floorboard into place, a dull thud came from the starboard hull. "'Twill be the English longboat," Padraig said. "Quick, lads, to your positions."

The men dashed up the steps and Maggie trailed behind, attempting to appear serene while ignoring the frantic pounding of her heart. She lingered in the shadows and watched the scene on deck.

Stokes stood in the center of the ship, the yellow hat affixed to his head. Padraig slid into place beside him. Pratt was nearby, and behind him stood a straight line of able seamen at attention, arranged in order of seniority. Matthew had pulled his hair back, and Burney had his chest puffed out as if his end of the line was the place of honor. They appeared calm and professional, nothing like the rabble of misfits Maggie herself had expected to meet when she heard the *Merrow* was a pirate ship.

Two sailors, apparently the vanguard, climbed over the gunwale and eyed the crew. After them came two sharply dressed lieutenants. The commander was last, tall and narrow, with a red, weather-beaten face and a windswept gray wig under his black felted hat. His elegant red and black jacket, tailored to accommodate a fashionable belly paunch, fastened with brass buttons all the way to his chin, where a little ruffle of white collar peeked out. He wore matching breeches and white hose, and his shining black leather shoes slapped the boards as he stalked toward Stokes.

"Captain Sir Nicholas Seger of His Majesty's ship *Vigilant*," the commander barked. "Are you the master of this brigantine?"

Stokes doffed his hat with his usual aplomb and made Sir Nicholas a sophisticated bow. "Captain William Stokes, sir. We are honored to welcome you aboard. May I ask the reason for your visit?"

Sir Nicholas narrowed his eyes and scanned the deck, as if expecting to find illicit activities being performed in the open. "The Crown has a right to inspect any vessel sailing in British waters."

"Do we pass muster, sir?"

"There are reports," Sir Nicholas went on, ignoring Stokes, "of pirates marauding the North Sea and the Channel. What is the name of this ship?"

"*Phoebus*, sir. I would question reports of her being spotted in the North Sea, as we have spent the summer running between Portugal and Bristol."

"You will not object to an inspection."

Stokes set his hat back on his head and gave the commander a thin smile. "I will not object to any measures that will speed the both of us on our way."

He showed no trace of anxiety, but beneath his facade, he must be as nervous as she was. Perhaps he would have had a promising career on the stage.

Sir Nicholas nodded to his lieutenants, who split up to search the ship, each trailing an armed seaman. One went up the stairs toward the navigation room, the other down the hall toward the officer's cabins. Maggie prayed Lloyd had done what she asked.

"I shall need to see the ship's log," Nicholas said.

Stokes turned his head and locked eyes with Maggie. Her breath hitched. Sir Nicholas followed his gaze, a look of displeasure passing over his face as she stepped into the sunlight. She handed Stokes the book.

"Gramercy, my love," he said. To the awestruck commander, he added, "Sir Nicholas, this is my wife, Margaret Stokes."

She gave a deep curtsy, trying to picture how someone like Anne Brown of the Silver Starling would have curtsied to Sir John Sherman, but her show of deference only annoyed him. "The sea is no place for a woman! Madam, who is tending your children?"

His face grew purple under his sunburn. She hadn't expected Sir Nicholas's views to be so misogynist. Other captains brought their whole families with them on their travels—Stokes himself had been raised at sea. "We have not yet been blessed with children," she said.

"Nor would we receive such a blessing if we remained on opposite sides of the Channel," Stokes added.

Maggie bit her tongue almost hard enough to draw blood, either to keep from laughing or shrieking, some hysterical outburst. Under less serious circumstances, Stokes's quick wit would impress her, but now she begged him to hold his tongue.

The commander's face arranged itself in a dour frown as he held out his hand for the ledger. The crew watched him flip through the neat pages.

"Your purser has a good hand and a commendable orderliness." He closed the book and handed it back to Stokes.

"My wife keeps the accounts. She agreed to the task when I lost my purser last autumn, and I would be a fool to replace her."

More flowery speech when he should have said nothing. The old man's disapproval of her was obvious to Maggie, but Stokes seemed oblivious. She took hold of his arm and squeezed once, hard.

A cloud passed over the commander's face, but before he could express his feelings on the subject, one of his lieutenants appeared at his side.

"Sir," the young man said, handing him a small, leather-bound book. "We found this in the captain's great room."

Maggie's blood became ice.

She had doomed them all. She should have hidden the real ledger, thrown it in with the smuggled goods, but there had been no time. It appeared so innocuous among her other books. How was she to know this lieutenant would search every item in the captain's berth?

She pictured the march to the gallows, felt the rough scratch of the noose around her neck. Would her bones break from the fall, or would she dangle, choking, until the darkness closed in?

Sir Nicholas opened the book and flicked through it, scanning each page's contents with such leisure, Maggie was sure her pounding heart would give out from exhaustion.

He landed on a page he seemed to find interesting and lifted the book a little higher. "'My love is as a fever, longing still for that which longer nurseth the disease.'"

Maggie almost swooned. Stokes's solid form was the only thing keeping her upright as she clung to him, her knuckles white on his arm. He brought his other arm across his body and covered the backs of her fingers with his warm, steady hand, and she let out a breath as her shoulders relaxed.

"One of my favorites," Sir Nicholas said, turning a few more pages before closing the book and examining its plain, worn cover. "Master Shakespeare is a genius with words. I take delight in seeing the Lord Chamberlain's Men whenever I am in London. I am pleased to find a fellow poetry lover on this ship." He handed Stokes the book with a smile.

Play along, she prayed. Sir Nicholas's jovial mood would not last if Stokes told him who the sonnets belonged to.

"Aye, his plays are some of the best I have seen," Stokes said. "We saw his *Winter's Tale* at Christmas."

"How did you like Blackfriars?"

"Right well, sir."

"I like it not, but 'tis far more convenient than the Curtain. And the Globe, of course, is an ideal venue."

"I have not been there. 'Tis clear you are a greater lover of the theater than I, Sir Nicholas."

The other lieutenant returned from the navigation room. "Nothing of note, sir."

Nicholas's dour expression was gone. He bounced on his heels and said, "We had better inspect your hold, captain, if you would lead the way."

Stokes shook off Maggie's grip and passed her the ledger and the sonnets. He glanced at her, his expression neutral except for the conspiratorial eyebrow raise.

In the hold, the lieutenants poked through the boxes and barrels. Sir Nicholas directed a few miscellaneous thoughts at Stokes, returning to the subject of the theater. Had he seen *Titus Andronicus*? Which players did he prefer, the Chamberlain's or the Admiral's? Had he gotten the chance to see a play at the Rose before it was torn down?

Maggie half-listened to his ramblings, too intent on the lieutenants' search. She prayed she hadn't missed anything. She prayed they would stay away from the loose boards in the wall.

"Is that Madeira?"

Somewhere along the line, Sir Nicholas halted his questioning long enough to notice the prominent cask of fortified wine in front of him.

Maggie met Stokes's gaze. This would be a risky maneuver.

"A gift from my husband," she said. "Its price was so reasonable, he could not resist. Do you enjoy Madeira, sir?"

He was still in a positive enough mood he didn't seem bothered by her address. "As often as I can get it!"

Maggie looked at Padraig. "Master MacCraith, would you be so good as to bring the Madeira up and help Sir Nicholas's men secure it in the longboat?"

Padraig's eyes flicked to Stokes, who nodded. Sir Nicholas was too busy pretending to demure to notice. "Nay, mistress, I would not deprive you of such a gift."

"You and your men are surely in need of refreshment after your work today."

He immediately lost interest in thinking of polite ways to refuse. Padraig brought the cask above, and the boarding party followed soon after, their inspection complete.

"Keep a sharp eye out," Sir Nicholas warned as he prepared to return to his ship. "There are some who forget we are no longer at war."

"God be with you, Sir Nicholas," said Stokes.

Matthew aimed the *Merrow* north toward Bristol while Stokes, Maggie, and Padraig watched the *Vigilant* drift east. The crew went about their tasks and regular watches resumed, but the three of them neither moved nor spoke until the English ship was a speck on the horizon.

Padraig broke the silence first. "Nearly soiled my breeches."

Maggie didn't know whether to laugh or cry. She turned to Stokes. "The cost of the Madeira can come from my wages."

He snorted. "I should add a cask of Madeira to your wages for daring to bribe a naval officer."

"Aye. The lass is a pirate." Padraig clapped a bewildered Maggie on the shoulder and bounded up the stairs.

Stokes removed his hat and scrubbed his face with his free hand. "God's blood, Maggie, I thought we were dead."

"Have you never suffered an inspection before?"

"Aye, we have, and the terror is the same every time." He gave her a pale imitation of his smile. "Having you aboard was an interesting variation. I'd never have guessed Sir Nicholas was such a despiser of women."

"You are partly to blame. I commend your acting prowess, but methinks you did not take into account most husbands disdain their wives."

"Was that your experience?"

It was the first time he had ever asked about her marriage. She couldn't tell if he wanted a serious answer or a flippant one, so she gave him both.

"If you were to take a few inches off Sir Nicholas's height and add them to his middle, you would be looking at the image of my late husband. The same gruff manner, the same infuriating self-importance. And yes, the same disdainfulness. We did our duties to each other, but we were not friends."

"That was my mistake, was it? Speaking of you and to you with a shameful amount of civility?"

The return of his usual wit made her smile. "Aye. If we are ever to repeat this charade, you must endeavor to dislike me."

He chuckled, pointing at her with the hat in his hand. "If we are ever to repeat this charade, you must endeavor to be dislikable."

30

O'FLAHERTY'S FIDDLE SCREAMED above the waves' rhythmic crashing. The band matched his fervor, bringing forth raucous, unrefined noise resembling well-known melodies. The lads were too jolly on festival rations of ale to notice.

The Midsummer drinking started early, with the dancing following after. Soon the sloppy shout-singing of sentimental songs would begin, and at the rate they were going, the majority of the crew would drop into unconsciousness before midnight.

Maggie adored it.

She was one of them now, for better or worse. She had earned the right to eat and drink alongside them, and she was free to celebrate with as much abandon as they did. Her fingers fluttered over her instrument with the confidence of a musician who had already downed a few mugs of beer. She laughed at Davies's awful jokes and hooked arms with Engberg as they wandered, giggling, toward Lloyd's banquet table. Matthew and Driscoll respected the invisible line dividing the deck, and they stayed on one side with their supporters while Maggie enjoyed the company of hers. The wind and the waves were mere nuisance, and they feted the solstice recklessly.

A rapid volley of clanks pulled everyone's attention toward Captain Stokes, who stood on the first step of the quarter deck stairs and banged his mug on the railing. The sun behind him dipped below the horizon, providing an orange and pink backdrop for the speech he was poised to give.

When they quieted, Stokes gestured to the sunset behind him. "Thus ends the longest day of the year!" The crew stomped and shouted as if they had achieved something tremendous, and the captain had to wait for them to wind down before he continued.

"This is not the celebration you are accustomed to on land. There are no bonfires, no garlands, no maypole—"

"What's that, then?" Meredith interjected, pointing to the nearest mast, which earned him a round of mixed chuckles and groans.

Stokes went on. "Yet I count myself fortunate to celebrate on this fine brig with you fine men. And woman." His eyes lighted on Maggie, then shifted. "And Davies."

Davies sputtered in mock anger while the men nearest him clapped him on the back. When the laughter subsided, the captain said, "This life we choose is full of uncertainty. Were we not all reminded of it three days ago when we were boarded?"

The men around Maggie booed and grumbled at the mention of the naval ship, drowning out his words. He held his hand aloft to quiet them. "Aye, 'twas a perilous thing. It caused me to remember our time here is but brief. To put pleasure aside in the belief there will be time enough on the morrow, or in the new year, is folly. We are men of action. We do not sit idly by and await opportunities for fortune or glory, or fine food and finer company. Nay, we seize them!"

Shouts of "Aye!" and "Huzzah!" rose from the gathered sailors. Maggie raised her own mug and let out a whoop before tipping her head back and downing the rest of her beer.

"So eat, dance, sing… and drink!" Stokes toasted his crew, then put his cup to his lips. He tilted it bit by bit, his Adam's apple bobbing as he drank. Someone started a low vocalization, and one by one they joined in, rising in pitch and volume with each gulp before erupting into madness when Stokes brandished the now-empty mug.

His voice was barely audible over the revelry, but Maggie watched his lips form the words, "This may be our last chance!"

They were all on their feet, hollering, laughing, the air vibrating with the manic energy of two dozen people vowing to live every moment. Maggie let her eyes drift over the deck, scanning each toothy smile, each pair of red cheeks, each head thrown back in laughter. Davies, Matthew, Burney, Driscoll, Luke, Padraig. She let a wall come down inside her, relieved to feel safe for one night. She knew the feeling wouldn't last, and tomorrow she would return to her routine of working up the courage to do something, change something, to make the *Merrow* home again.

But tonight she would revel.

O'Flaherty dragged his bow over the fiddle strings, fingers flying as a jig came to life. Inwood encouraged the reckless tempo with his bones, Scurlock's drum beat pulsed in Maggie's chest, and Davies and Mullins swung into the melody while Engberg laid down a drone. By the time Maggie realized she should be playing along, the men had chosen their dance partners and she was too moved by the music to imagine sullying it with her own contribution. She laid down Davies's flute—her flute now, since he bought himself a new one with his Yuletide earnings—and clapped along.

"Up you get, Bailey."

She turned her head and found an open palm held out in front of her. Her eyes followed the line of his arm to his face, his lips beneath his mustache gently curved.

The charming way the corners of Stokes's eyes cinched together, even when the expression on his lips couldn't be called a true smile, was how she could always tell when he was teasing her. She hadn't given it much thought before, but now she was certain she looked for those laugh lines every time they spoke, to confirm he was smiling.

He dropped his offered hand. "I see you find me lacking."

Her stomach gave a queasy flip, and she rushed to shake off her distraction. "Gramercy, but I am not dancing. I have turned down every lad who asked."

"And true to form, I took it as a challenge." He glanced at the drunken dancers. "There's the second set. Think you'll make your choice in time for the final bow?"

She wrinkled her nose at him in good-natured irritation. "I have said I am not dancing. What makes you believe you will succeed where others have failed?"

"My good looks and shapely legs."

She laughed. "I am sore tempted."

"Come. A bonny lass should dance on Midsummer. 'Tis writ in the Bible, methinks."

"Aye, St. Paul's letter to the Corinthians."

This time, he laughed. "'Tis nearly the final set. Dance with me."

"Do you command it?"

His smile faded. "Of course not."

"Then I thank you for your kind offer, but I decline."

She had vowed to only play and drink, because it wouldn't be worth the fallout if she danced with one man and not another. What would Driscoll do if she refused him? What if Matthew extended an olive branch she couldn't bear to accept? She hadn't, however, expected Stokes to ask her, and the resulting regret was a surprise, too.

She readied herself to apologize, to minimize the damage she had done to the captain's ego, but he only nodded. "Mayhap that is the wise choice. I was like to confound you with my dancing prowess. I should hate to embarrass you."

"Embarrass me? Do not forget, sir, I studied under a very expensive dance master for much of my childhood. I warrant I am your match, at the least."

He gestured to the dancers. "Prove it."

"You first. No doubt one of the lads will stand up with you."

"I do not make a habit of dancing with my crew."

"You asked me."

Stokes pressed his lips together, then reached over and plucked her empty mug from the table. "If I cannot dance, I may at least make myself useful." Without giving her time to argue, he turned in the direction of the keg.

She watched him weave between the tables, perplexed. She had assumed he asked her because he was in the mood to dance. It flustered her to think he wanted to dance *with her*. What was she supposed to do now? Should she remind him she was unworthy of such a compliment, or just pretend the exchange had never happened?

Stokes returned and plunked a full mug of foamy beer in front of her before dropping into the chair beside her. His movements were just shy of controlled, only barely graceless. As he drank from his own mug, she remembered the things he had said were fueled by drink, and therefore not worth heeding.

"I enjoyed your speech," she said. "'Twas both grim and inspiring."

"Just as I intended, then."

"You were rather shaken by Sir Nicholas's inspection, I suppose."

"You were not?"

"I was shaken, but methinks I trusted we would survive."

"You have more trust than I. Which of us is the fool?"

"'Tis I, certes. I have not your experience to know I am a fool."

"I have no experience swinging from the gallows, yet I know how easily I may find myself there. I could be hanged tomorrow."

"Nay! You could not be hanged so early as tomorrow. You must suffer through a trial first. 'Twould be the day after tomorrow, at the earliest."

She liked this easiness, this return to the bonhomie she had been mourning since the winter. That night at Blackfriars had wounded it, and her reunion with Matthew had atrophied it. When she forced him to hire her—there was no denying that's what she had done—she thought she had killed their friendship for good. That he was sitting beside her, letting her joke with him after all she had done… She didn't deserve it.

Stokes was looking at her with a fond little smile. The look stirred something in her belly. Rather lower, actually.

She had stared at him with just such a look and been teased for it, so she took advantage of this chance for some turnabout. "What fault do you find in me?"

He didn't start or stammer as she had done when he asked her the same question. Instead, the wrinkles beside his eyes deepened. He raised his mug to his lips and looked away.

Mullins's whistle carried over the chatter with the opening strain of "Heart's Ease," a simple dance she learned as a child. A mix of nostalgia, beer, and that look on Stokes's face had her thunking her mug on the table and reaching out her hand. "Up you get, captain."

He didn't argue, only took her hand and allowed her to lead him to the dancers, who had already formed squares and were well into the first set. They were all evenly matched, each group made up of two pairs, leaving Stokes and Maggie at the bottom alone.

"How do you propose we accomplish this on our own?" he asked.

"'Twill require some ingenuity. Have you the courage?"

In response, he bowed to her in time to the music.

It didn't require as much ingenuity as she feared. Whenever they were to turn to their side partners, they repeated the same steps with each other. As a result, she became too familiar with the warm press of his hands and with the masculine scent of him, leather and salt and the unique perfume of his skin beneath it all. They had both pushed up their sleeves against the heat of the evening, and their forearms slid against each other as they hooked arms to turn, the taut ropes of his muscles flexing against her skin.

A troubling thought surfaced, so startling she almost missed a step: entwined like this, the distance from her lips to his was insignificant. No distance at all.

She batted the thought away as soon as it came, but that curious voice would not be silenced. Were his lips rough or soft? Would his mustache get in the way?

The blame lay with the beer and her own loneliness. The captain was lovely to look at, as well as honorable, clever, amusing, and just a little wicked, but she couldn't *desire* him. He was her captain, her mentor, her savior. They were as ill-suited now as they would have been if Maggie retained her former life, even with their fortunes and stations thus reversed. She couldn't have him. So she couldn't want him.

He smiled at her, and she recited the words to herself again.

The dancers bowed as the musicians brought the song to a close, and Maggie's beer-weakened knees attempted a curtsy. At the same time, the deck tilted in the wrong direction. She windmilled her arms, and Stokes reached out with cat-like quickness, righting her with a firm grip on her upper arm and steadying her with his other hand.

It was not an embrace, but Maggie's fevered imagination made more of it than it was. She willed her traitorous fingers to remain still when all they wanted was to trace the laugh lines on Stokes's face.

She smiled with false bravado and made herself shrug out of his grip. "We must make way for the next dance." He trailed her as she strode back to her table, and she glanced at the men she passed, Keith and Meredith and Hargreve. What cruel thoughts were swirling in their minds?

"Will you have another?" Stokes said.

"In faith, I should not have had this one," she muttered. Seeing the shadow that crossed his face, she brightened her tone. "Your festival rations are too generous, and I am poor company when I am in my cups."

"I do not agree. The more you drink, the more charming I appear."

She hadn't been willing to call it flirting, but this confirmed it. With no willing barmaid to hand, he landed on Maggie as the next target on which to practice his skill. And like every target before her, he felled her with only a few well-aimed attacks.

I cannot have him.

"Methinks I have endured enough teasing for one night."

The words tumbled out before she could consider their effect, but it was instantaneous. Stokes froze, the coquettish smile still on his face, and then his expression relaxed into polite neutrality. "Forgive me."

There was nothing to forgive. Her peevishness wasn't meant for him: it was she who heard the friendly banter and interpreted it as something more. She allowed herself to entertain the lovely, ludicrous thoughts.

He glanced around the deck, and when his gaze returned to hers, he was the steely commander, the cool aristocrat. "The hour grows late. I bid you good night."

She mumbled something, a coward's reply, and watched him weave through the clustered tables, down the contents of his mug, and drop the empty cup in the waiting washbasin. He took the quarter deck steps by twos and ducked into the darkness of the officers' quarters.

Maggie slouched in her chair and wallowed. Would they never be friends, thanks to her uncanny ability to bungle every sensitive moment? It occurred to her to blame Matthew, the first man to set her heart racing. Perhaps falling in love with him eight years ago opened the door for future suffering.

Or was Ellen to blame? She put the thought in Maggie's mind that a woman could search for and seize her own pleasure. In practice, Maggie was as likely as a dormouse to stalk her prey. And Captain Will Stokes could never be the object of her hunt.

She was drunk, but not drunk enough to forget about the two dozen witnesses to her flirtatious behavior. Dancing with Stokes only confirmed the rumors Driscoll threatened her about, and with this new ammunition, it was only a matter of time before he struck.

But if they saw her continue celebrating after the captain had turned in for the night, it might lessen the significance. She could dance with one or two more lads, make some bawdy jokes, prove she had no favorites, and with luck, they would forget all about it by forenoon watch.

She picked up her mug. If she was going to do this, she needed another drink.

The keg was beside the quarter deck stairs. She traced the path Stokes had taken, patting Davies on the shoulder and mussing Burney's hair as she passed them. Luke was busy filling his mug, and Hale waited a step behind, swaying like a willow branch. At least she wasn't that far gone.

Hale belched and dropped his mug on the deck with a clatter. The dregs of beer in the bottom splashed all the way to the hem of Maggie's skirts. He gazed down at the mug, his chin tucking into his neck as he tried to focus on it. Maggie chuckled and stooped to pick it up, bracing her knee on the ground when she discovered she was less steady than she thought.

As soon as her fingers touched the fallen mug, someone kicked the back of her shoe. A shock of liquid splashed over her neck and head. She looked to the side in time to see Leigh grappling with the sauced Hale for balance, taking both of them down to the deck with a painful thud.

Maggie struggled to her feet, stepping on her skirts three times before she could stand, all the while cringing as the beer trailed down her jaw and neck and trickled into her shirt.

Luke guffawed at the two drunks on the floor, then looked at Maggie's sodden state and laughed harder.

The lads on the ground groaned and stirred. Leigh rolled onto his back and rubbed his elbow. Hale looked around in a daze, unhurt and unbothered.

"'Taint good enough trippin' over your own feet, so you have to trip over Maggie's?" Luke held out a hand to help Leigh up.

Maggie pulled her sleeve down over her fingers and wiped the warm beer from her skin.

"All right?" Luke asked her.

It wouldn't do to show her embarrassment, so she rolled her eyes at Leigh. "I'd not thought you so in danger of falling for me."

Leigh frowned and avoided her eyes. "Didn't see you."

She flapped the wet collar of her shirt and peeled off her coif. It hung limp and dripping from her fingers. Someone behind her called out, "Is there aught more you'll be taking off?"

A chorus of laughs covered up the oath she flung back at them.

Leigh helped Hale to his feet and waited his turn to fill his mug, and the business seemed forgotten. Irritated, Maggie stomped up to her cabin to wash up. Her bodice was unsullied, and she could live with a wet collar, but having her head uncovered was too similar to the scenes at the Dagger and Sheath. As drunk as they were, she wasn't sure the lads could distinguish between a ship and a brothel.

She untangled her wet, sticky hair from its braid and poured a little water over the worst of it. While her hair dried, she rinsed the coif and reached for the hook where she stored her spare one.

It wasn't there. She searched the folds of her cloak and shook out her other apron, but it didn't appear. Lloyd had moved all her things to Stokes's cabin a few days ago. Could she have missed it when she moved them back?

Visiting Stokes's great room was, of course, counter to her goal of dispelling the rumors, but maybe the lads were too far gone to notice where she'd disappeared to. It would only take a moment.

There was no one in the officers' corridor, and a glance down toward the deck showed everyone reveling. She tapped on Stokes's door, feeling abnormally jittery.

He was still dressed. A candle burned on the table behind him, beside a pewter goblet and a dark glass bottle. His expression was stern as his gaze trailed over her unbound hair. He flicked his eyes to the corridor behind her before stepping aside to allow her entry.

She turned at the sound of the door latch scraping into place.

He didn't ask why she was there, only watched her like a buck surveying a huntsman. He leaned against the door, his hands behind his back.

"Forgive me for disturbing you," she said.

"How may I be of service?"

They were all politeness, all civility. Why did the camaraderie and the jests seem so out of reach, especially now they were alone with no one to pretend for?

"The day we encountered the *Vigilant*... I suggested we masquerade as husband and wife..."

"Aye."

"So I asked Lloyd to move my things in here..."

"I remember as if 'twere only days ago."

She blushed. There was the teasing tone she wanted, but it made her feel as foolish and awkward as ever. "Have you seen my coif?"

He took in a breath and held it before repeating, "Your coif?"

"My second one. Leigh spilled his beer, and I was obliged to change caps, but I cannot find it."

His lips twitched. "He spilled beer on your head?"

"'Tis difficult to explain. I do not doubt the lads will leap at the chance to describe my ignominy on the morrow."

While she spoke, she repeated her new mantra to herself. *Do not touch him. You cannot have him.* He leaned against the door, his posture casual but his eyes wary. Two strides would have her standing nose to nose with him. No distance at all.

"Have you seen it?" she said. "I cannot go back out there with my head uncovered."

"Must you?"

His words were soft, his voice low. Drunk, she was having trouble distinguishing truth from fantasy; if she heard any seduction in his tone, it must be in her mind. "'Tis the surest way I can think to dispel the rumors," she said.

"Rumors?"

"You know. That I gained my position in an unorthodox manner… That you are flouting your own decree against mixing aboard the ship." Alcohol and nervousness loosened her tongue. "One of the crew has told me he intends to expose this lie as if 'twere the truth. I merely wish to continue on as I have been, proving my innocence however I can."

"Who is it threatens you?"

"'Tis well in hand," she lied. "I meant not to trouble you with it." He opened his mouth to argue, but she cut him off. "Now it appears I have followed you to your cabin, so I must needs find my cap and return to the festivities."

Stokes hesitated, then spread his arms in an invitation to search.

The coif was on a shelf, just above eye level, folded in half. She applauded Lloyd's thoroughness, hiding it up there when time had been so scarce. Maggie waved it at him and moved toward the closed door. "Gramercy. Good rest, sir."

He perched on the edge of the table. "You are returning to that den of vipers, are you?"

"'Tis nothing. You must not trouble over me."

"'Tis my ship. I shall trouble over whatever and whomever I please."

"Then I urge you to choose something of greater value to trouble over." She turned her face away, hoping the yellow lamplight would blur the redness of her cheeks, and grasped the latch with her trembling hand.

"Will you—!"

The tightness in his voice made her stomach drop. She turned, eyes wide, and pressed her back against the door, devastated to think she had angered him.

He gripped the table edge on either side of his hips, his head thrown back as he took in a steadying breath. With his neck exposed, she could make out the shadowy movement of his Adam's apple as he swallowed and sighed. When his eyes met hers again, the dark warning in them sent a jolt through her. "'Tis not yours to determine what I value."

The few seconds they stared at each other lasted a century. The latch was warm and slippery under her fingers, but the urge to flee had vanished.

He valued her. The idea of it was a bubble of joy that swelled in her chest, so excruciating she felt her ribs would crack. It lifted her off the deck, past the topsail, into the glittering night. It swept her up, up, and all the while, she begged herself to come down, knowing how much pain the fall would bring.

She could not have him. She shouldn't even want him, or any man, after what she had endured with Matthew. The girl who dashed toward love cared nothing for the woman who would suffer the consequences, and the gallant captain wouldn't always be there to rescue her.

The thought inspired a feeling, no more than a shapeless impression, of an *always* with the man who now filled her vision. The man whose long, vulnerable neck demanded to be traced from the edge of his beard to the vee of his collar. The man whose lips could not only be made for smirking.

Pushing himself away from the table, Stokes took three deliberate steps toward her and stopped just within her sphere, close enough her instincts told her to move aside. Why did her feet refuse to comply? She fisted her hands in her skirts, panicked, praying he couldn't see the outline of her heart as it drummed out *kiss me, kiss me, kiss me.*

Her heart's song ended with the sharp rasp of the latch.

Stokes eased the door open, careful not to bump into her despite how close she stood to it. A clear dismissal.

Without a word, Maggie edged past him and into the dark corridor.

She was a lonely, dithering, drunken fool. That was the only explanation for the fanciful nonsense bedeviling her all evening. She was grasping at ghosts, desperate for a connection. Why could she not have chosen jolly Davies or sweet Engberg instead, someone whose rejection wouldn't raze her to rubble?

The idea of rejoining the festivities exhausted her, but she mustered the remains of her tattered willpower and went back to her cabin to braid her hair.

When she opened her door, the room was hidden behind Driscoll's square shoulders.

Her body told her she was in danger even as her mind grappled with the image before her. All she knew was the question of what he was doing in her quarters could be answered with the frantic imperative, *Get him out.*

"Well." The single candle cast half his face in shadow and painted the other half in grotesque relief. "By Cock, you *are* fuckin' 'im."

Get him out.

"I'm impressed. I'd not thought you had it in you. But you did *have it in you*, did you not, you li'l tart? More'n a few times, I wager."

Get him out.

"Seems I've been sellin' meself short. Methinks the cost of me silence has gone up."

Get. Him. Out.

She found her voice at last. "I was with the captain for only a few minutes. How long have you been lurking here like a coward?"

"Long enough. And a few minutes is all the time it takes."

"Aye, in your experience, the act takes, what, one minute? Two? Mayhap as many as five, if one counts the time it takes you to get it up."

Quicker than her eyes could track, he pinned both her wrists in one of his broad hands and covered her mouth with the other. She cried out at the suddenness of his violence, but the shout only echoed inside her head and died in his palm.

He pushed her against the wall and leaned in, crushing her body with his so she could only squirm in vain. "I've killed men twice your size and I've had whores half as willin'," he breathed into her ear. "I could take you and it'd be over before you could scream. And if you squealed to anyone, you'd find yourself at the bottom o' the sea. 'Tis a dangerous place, a ship is. Any number o' ways to tip overboard."

She tried to bang her elbows into the wall to cause a commotion, but the grip holding her wrists was unrelenting. Instead, she kicked the wall with one foot. Driscoll stomped down on her other foot with such force she screamed. Tears spilled onto his hand.

Maybe it had been enough. Maybe someone would hear that pathetic thump and come running. There would be no getting out of this on her own.

"But there's one more thing I want you to know." He leaned away from her enough to look her in the eye. She was too scared of further pain and too mesmerized by his cruel gaze to fight him. She stood rigid, pinned between him and the wall.

"You're not worth it," he said. "I've a good thing here, and the captain don't tolerate fuckin' on his boat. I wager he'd not take kindly to me meddlin' with things what are his, neither. So you can cease your weepin'. I've no use for a dried-up, lyin' slut."

He removed his hand from her mouth. The air was clammy on her damp skin, and tears evaporated from her cheeks.

He gave her an eerie, toothy grin. "You're safe so long as you get off at the next port. And you will, one way or another."

At last, he released her wrists, and the blood rushed painfully into her fingers. He stepped away from her. Before he left, he tugged one side of his shirt out of his breeches. Then he hurried from her cabin and clomped down the quarter deck stairs, in full view of the crew.

She could have screamed. She could have followed him. She could have ignored the hubbub he was causing on deck and gone straight to the captain. Instead, she did what she always did when faced with a hurdle that appeared insurmountable.

Nothing.

31

CAPTAIN STOKES STOOD with his legs braced apart on the floor of her cabin, his arms crossed over his chest. Maggie considered this his commander's stance, in stark contrast to the relaxed swagger and casual lean of the sophisticated gentleman pirate.

For her part, she sat on the edge of her bed, her shoulders hunched, her eyes cast down, in stark contrast to anything resembling a woman of integrity.

"He is demanding you leave the *Merrow*, and if you will not, he insists on a trial."

"I will leave."

"I cannot help you if you will not defend yourself!"

"I have no wish to defend myself. I will not remain here with him. He threatened my life."

"Then he will be put off."

"For what crime?" She looked up at him. "Lying is punished by a fine, not by dismissal."

"Threats of violence are another matter. I may deliver any punishment I deem fitting."

She swallowed past the tightness in her throat, hating that wonderful willingness to fight for her when she didn't deserve it. "'Tis of no use. He has his story and I have mine. No one may be assured of the truth of either."

"I am assured of it! I know you did not compel him to come to your cabin, and I know you did not use your superior position to make him submit to you. If I know it, the crew knows it."

"But his supporters—"

"Hang his supporters. The man is a known liar and a bully. Forsooth, I would believe him more readily if he put it about that you *did* take him to bed, for I do not know him to routinely abstain from sleeping with a beautiful woman."

She stared up at him. "This is my defense, is it? He must be lying because no man would refuse to bed me? Well, then, I am better off leaving!"

"Your defense is that you were with me. Why should you invite a man to your quarters when you were in mine?"

"Nay, I will not confirm every man's suspicion and diminish your honor in the same stroke. Let them think I was alone."

He dropped his arms to swing limp at his sides. "Why will you not fight this?"

Which reason would she give? Both were true, but one was harder to speak aloud.

She didn't think she could tell him this was the way she was. She was built to be acted upon, to be commanded and positioned and dismissed. To be pursued, to be captured, to be ensnared by her own desperation. Why struggle if the outcome be fated?

But he didn't believe in fate, and he was too kindhearted to admit her worthlessness. So she gave him the other reason, the one that placed the blame on shoulders that weren't hers.

"Let us accept the truth at last," she said. "I may struggle to carve a place for myself here, but a hole dug in the sand will not endure a changing tide. I was never fit to join your crew. When I was a novelty, such unsuitableness could be forgiven, but now I am a fixture, and the crew has passed their verdict. I have deluded myself that if only I could prove my worthiness, I would be accepted. But I am selfish. And foolish. Your crew does not deserve to suffer a plague such as I."

He opened his mouth as if to refute, but she pressed on. She laid everything before him, the anxious thoughts that kept her up nights, the hurtful rumors that had her creeping about the ship by day, the angry silence she endured from Matthew and everyone loyal to him. She painted a picture for him of how the crew saw her: a siren, a harlot, a witch whose black magic had cursed their easy lives. Perhaps she embellished things to drive the point home—anything to conceal her own failings as long as possible.

The only information she held back was the strange feeling that came over her last night when she danced with him. Sobriety had changed nothing; she could not shake it even now, even as he stood in her cabin begging her to be better than she was. He was good and just and beautiful, and she could not have him.

When she finished, he fixed his gaze on the arms crossed over his chest, a frown creasing his brow. His shoulders rose and fell as he breathed. "I do not accept it."

Whatever thimble-sized reserve of strength she had when he stepped into her cabin ten minutes ago was long spent. "I do not know why you have closed your eyes to it, but—"

"Not that. I do not accept your resignation."

"That is of little import when my choice is already made."

He cast his eyes to the ceiling and huffed. "What am I to do? No man could hope to perform the purser duties as competently as you have."

"Any man who can add two and two together would be a better fit for the role. 'Tis not my competence that makes me an object of derision."

"Then stay! Do your work, prove to them your worthiness—"

"For what reward? To be hated and slandered? To be miserable? This life is not worth the heartache, no matter how much I—" Her heart jumped into her throat, choking her. She looked down at her hands clenched in her skirts. "Love the sea."

She felt his gaze on her, a burning sun singeing her cheeks. In the long, shame-filled moment, the ship creaked, a wave gave a muffled roar, and her heart clanged like the clapper of the watch bell.

"This is your choice? To resign your position?"

"Aye, captain."

"You choose to leave the *Merrow* without a purser in the midst of a seven-month voyage?"

Tears welled up in her eyes. Why must he twist the knife? It had been torture enough plunging it into her own breast.

His posture softened. "Very well. I accept, if you are so resolved. I pray you will be so good as to continue performing your duties until you leave the ship."

She nodded, facing the wall opposite the door so he wouldn't see the tear slipping down her cheek. "I will," she said, her voice thick.

"What did you say?"

She swiped the tear from her face and turned back to him. "I said, 'I will.'"

"Ah. For a moment, I thought you said my name." He touched his forehead in farewell and left her to her thoughts.

* * *

They kept the chalk cliffs to port as they rounded the coast of Kent early the next morning. They would be in London by late afternoon, unless the gathering storm clouds had anything to say about it.

By the blue-gray light of dawn, Maggie packed and tidied and prepared her faithful ledger for whoever would wield it next. Strangely, her book of Shakespeare sonnets wasn't on the table in her cabin, where she had returned it after Sir Nicholas's inspection. It grieved her to lose it after all this time, but she wasn't about to go looking for it after the business with the coif.

She couldn't bear to face the crew, even those she considered friends, until the tolling of afternoon watch set her stomach growling. Davies, Engberg, and Arthur were kind not to mention the spectacle that had been unfolding since Driscoll fled her quarters on Midsummer night.

After luncheon, she would tie up loose ends. A final inventory of the hold, a last perusal of the false ledger, and whatever other minor details she could put in order to make Will's—that is, the captain's—job easier.

It was pointless to try on his Christian name as often as she did. It was akin to drawing a strand of perfect pearls out of its silk bag, polishing them, and returning them to whence they came because there would never be occasion to wear them.

Maggie knew Matthew would be at the helm when she climbed up to the navigation room, so she deliberately averted her eyes as she passed him. The sound of his voice stopped her.

"Where will you go?"

Feeling Matthew's heavy gaze on her back, she halted with her hand on the door. She was reminded of all the times they had talked and schemed up here with their faces turned away from each other, as if anyone had been fooled.

It didn't matter if she was seen speaking to him now. They were almost nothing to each other, and soon they would be even less.

"I do not know," she said, turning to face him. What had inspired his question? Guilt? Concern? Morbid curiosity?

He pushed his hair away from his face. Why didn't he pull it back into a tail with all this wind? He always had been vain.

"May I offer a suggestion?"

"If you must."

"Marry me."

He caught her arm before she could turn away. "I care not what happened," he said, his words fast and breathless. "I care not if the rumors are true—any of them. Driscoll, Stokes… I forgive it all. I want you for my wife, for better or worse. You need not make your way alone."

How gracious, she thought. How broad-minded of him to forgive her for outrageous acts she would never commit. Why had she not left yet? Why did she listen to this lunacy?

It was because they both knew she had nowhere to go once the ship docked in London. She and Matthew were not suited, but the icy vice of desperation didn't care about that.

"I must needs return to my work."

"Margaret—"

"Why do you call me that?"

His brow wrinkled. "'Tis your name."

She looked at him without really seeing him. Rather, she saw him as though he were a stranger, his face unfamiliar, his form a random assemblage of limbs. Handsome, but lacking something fundamental. What she had felt for him may never have been about *him* at all. In any case, it was gone.

She turned away and entered the navigation room.

Safe behind the door, she let her shoulders slump and closed her eyes. Her chest felt heavy, stuffed full of lead. She took in as much Matthew-free air as she could and let it out again on a sigh.

Her erstwhile bedchamber was the same as always, except Gillies was more fastidious than Osborne. There was only one chart on the table, where Osborne would have layered several, too eager about charting the next course to clear up after the last one.

A small leather book sat atop the chart, its strap untied and trailing like an estuary over the map. How had her sonnets wound up here? The damp and the salt had warped the pages and stained the cover. It resisted her when she curved it back on itself, and she skimmed her thumb along the edge of each page as it sprang back to its preferred shapeless shape.

Something fluttered to the table: a scrap of dirty canvas, cut from an old sail. She couldn't remember using it to mark a page, nor what page it might have been marking.

She retied the thong and tucked the book in her belt for safekeeping.

The watch bell's incessant clanging called all hands on deck. Maggie poked her head out of her room but heard no commotion or shouts, just shuffling feet. A meeting, most likely.

With a sinking feeling, she prayed it had nothing to do with her. Stokes knew she wished to disembark without a fuss.

The lads assembled with their customary haste, shrugging to each other and craning their necks to find whatever ship or landmass required their attention. Maggie spotted Davies and raised her eyebrows, but he knew as much as she did.

The captain appeared on the quarterdeck and trotted down to the bottommost step, where he had stood to make his inspiring Midsummer speech. He marked the occasion with his yellow hat, its brim peeling away from his face with the force of the wind.

He scanned their faces one by one, searching. His eyes didn't stop as he passed over her, causing her to sigh in relief. A moment later, his voice boomed out over their heads. "Simon Driscoll!"

Oh, no.

She hoped the man had committed some new, unrelated crime. This was beginning to look like a trial, and she wanted no part in it.

Driscoll raised his hand from the back of the crowd. "Here." The men who stood between him and the captain shuffled to either side, as if words and glares lobbed across the deck could maim.

Stokes allowed the tension to fester, gangrenous with patches of confused mumbling. The men looked between him and Driscoll until at last he spoke. "Master Driscoll, for making threats against the life of a superior officer, I relieve you of your position on this brigantine." The murmurs and grumbles increased, but Stokes spoke over them. "You will disembark at London and never again seek employment aboard the *Merrow*."

"Is this a joke?" Driscoll's face reddened.

"Nay, sirrah, it is not."

"I've not threatened no one! Who accuses me?"

"On Midsummer night, you threatened to rape Maggie Bailey and murder her if she spoke of it."

More murmurs shimmered through the crowd.

"I never did! That hussy's lyin' to save her own hide!"

"Save? She has agreed to leave the ship, which would have been her punishment were she found guilty of the crime you accused her of. What purpose in lying?"

"'Tain't just! I want a trial!"

Stokes spread his arms. "Here it be. This is my final judgment. I could throw in a flogging, if you like."

"This be no trial! What grounds? What evidence?"

"You are a liar and a knave and I never liked you overmuch." He was enjoying this; she could see it in the tilt of his lips and the confidence of his posture. "As for evidence, if any man will speak in your defense, I will hear him."

Driscoll sputtered, his face purple. He goggled at his mates, waiting for them to trip over each other in their haste to defend him. With a thud, he smacked the center of Leigh's chest with the back of his hand. "Tell 'im 'tain't just!"

Leigh swallowed. "'Tain't just, captain."

Driscoll made a strangled sound of frustration in the back of his throat and cast about for another supporter. The number seemed smaller than it had before. "Kent!" He pointed a finger at Matthew, who stood several feet from him, his head down. "Tell him. Tell him I never did it."

Matthew met Driscoll's glare for only a moment before returning his gaze to the deck.

Driscoll stared, frozen, too astonished to react. He tightened his fists, and the rage returned twofold. "Kent, you sodding sack of horseshit, you swore!" Driscoll stalked toward him, and someone nearby put out an arm in a halfhearted attempt to prevent fists from being thrown. It didn't come to that, for Driscoll wanted an explanation, not a fight. "You swore this would work, you bleedin' liar!"

He turned full on to Stokes and declared, "'Twas Kent what planned it. I'll not go to the gallows for this fuckin' coward!"

Maggie was cold, a standing corpse. The wind buffeted the side of her face, the deck tilted beneath her practiced feet, but she didn't feel any of it. Driscoll's words were the nonsensical throes of a drowning man, but even without knowing what he meant, her body believed it. She believed Matthew had done something terrible.

Driscoll could not be stopped now. "I was only to scare her and force her off the ship so he could ride in on his white horse and scoop her up, like. He swore she'd marry him were she desperate enough. Now I did my part, and he's standin' there like a damned mute!"

How could it be? Maggie's life had been mundane, her sins few compared to some, but she had been sentenced to be betrayed over and over again. There was no justice in it.

"Why?" Stokes said. "Why do something so cruel to the woman you wished to marry?"

"Money," Driscoll snorted, answering for Matthew. "She's rich, innit? Widow of a bloody baron, got sacks of money goin' to seed.

Told him it was a waste of time, as she's said she'd not have him, but he'd not heed me." He turned to Matthew, who was watching him, stricken. "And now she never will, yeh great noddy. Seems you'll not retire after all."

Driscoll's recital calmed him; he had grown used to the idea he was beyond salvation, and now he could enjoy the chaos of bringing Matthew down with him.

Maggie felt nothing. She watched the scene unfold from the gallery, heard the grumblings of the groundlings, listened to the players' speeches about some other woman, some other fool. Stokes's posture was broad and powerful, the stance of a celebrated orator. He had been well cast, she thought. The mask Driscoll wore was hideous and comical. And that was not Matthew, but a man in a Matthew-skin.

Her mind drifted as she turned to watch the white cliffs slide past, interminable. Stokes's voice came from the top of that cliff, but she made out most of the words even over the wind. "What say you, Kent?"

Silence. The player had forgotten his lines.

She returned her gaze to the stage, and Matthew, the real Matthew, met her eyes. He didn't speak. He had nothing to say.

This morning, he asked her to marry him again. It had felt spontaneous, serendipitous. It didn't seem possible it was a performance. She almost told them that: Driscoll had to be lying, because Matthew wasn't clever enough. She couldn't face that he had deceived her day in and day out for months.

"Aye. I set Driscoll to frightenin' her." Matthew's admission made gooseflesh on Maggie's arms. "But I did not do it for money. I love her."

"Come off it!" The new voice rose above their heads, and as one they turned to see Luke Kent throwing up his hands in exasperation. "For once in your fuckin' life, will you not show an ounce of honor?"

"Shut your fat hole," Matthew growled.

"She's a decent lass, and you've done nothin' but treat her ill since the day you met. Was it not enough to break her heart all those years ago? You've had to do it again?"

Matthew lunged for his brother, but Mullins and Meredith held him back.

Luke raised his chin to address the crew. "He's done it before, you ken. He tried to marry her when we were young, but it'd never go off, so he lured her out of the house and stole what he could, and off we ran." Luke found Maggie and pleaded with her with his eyes. "I was a boy, and he was my brother. I'm not proud I went along. For all it matters not, I'm sorry for my part in it."

She thought Matthew had been lying when he told her Elizabeth was to blame, but only because she hadn't been listening. Elizabeth insisted their father would never bless their marriage, and what would Matthew gain from marrying a disowned daughter? His aim had only ever been to become a Donwell, and failing that, he took his revenge on the family by emptying the girls' jewelry box and breaking Maggie's heart.

When she reappeared in his life, the widow of a wealthy man, he got a second chance. He called it fate, and she was doomed to it.

Poor Matthew. To go to all this trouble, oblivious her dower was gone.

Poor Matthew? No. *Damn Matthew.* Everything she had endured was for nothing.

Matthew escaped from his captors and went after his brother. She thought she saw someone get in the way, thought she heard Stokes barking commands and the crew shouting curses. The wind was cold on her burning skin, and above it all were the waves pounding inside her head.

Her feet carried her across the damp planks, through the tumult.

Then her palm was pink and stinging. The shouting quieted. Matthew's cheek was red. And next she was at the rail, looking out over the churning sea.

32

WHEN SENSATIONS RETURNED, she listed them. The solid railing beneath both hands, one palm sore. A wrenched shoulder. A rawness in her throat, from a scream, perhaps.

Behind her, the sounds of men at work. No more shouting and scuffling. The waves crashed beneath her now, not inside her. In fact, there was nothing inside her. She was a shell made of shards.

Light pressure on the small of her back. A knife? No, a hand. She knew it was him without turning her head.

"Come," Stokes said.

She pushed away from the rail and preceded him up the quarterdeck stairs. He nudged her forward towards his open cabin door, and when they were within, he latched it.

He said nothing, and she was mute.

She leaned on one of his chairs, its back taking the place of the rail she had been gripping. She didn't know what she would do if she were left to drift, unanchored. Maybe she would career away. Maybe she would sink.

"What thoughts have you so silent?"

Something wild inside her roared, and she breathed until it slunk back down. "Cannot you guess?" she said, her voice flat.

"I would rather have it from you."

The chair had sharper edges than the rail, and it dug into the meat of her palms.

"Lying, deceitful, cowardly, sodding—" The words died as her throat closed around them. She ground her teeth. "Fucking *knave*! He played me again and again. He plucked all my strings in just the right order. A master!" She laughed.

In a sudden swell of anger, she toppled the chair, relishing the satisfying thud and clatter as it settled on the floor.

"And I sang for him! I went along every time. He told me he was true when I knew him to be false, and I trusted *him* rather than *me*? What manner of fool am I? What manner of coward, to meekly nod and smile and never call him out?" She began pacing at some point, but now she halted in her tracks. "No, I *did* call him out. I did, and he always had an answer, so I thought it must be me, *I* was the one who could not be trusted, *I* was the betrayer who let a man love me and then cast him aside. *I* was the cruel one."

Stokes said nothing.

"You knew this whole time. You knew he was a Judas! How could you not tell me?"

"I did tell you." His eyes flashed. "More than once, in fact."

She was too hurt, too disgusted with herself to admit it was true. "You let me be drawn into his web—you watched it happen!"

"Let you?" He let out a bark of laughter. "*Let you*? No, Maggie. You cannot demand to be the mistress of your own fate at one moment and become a helpless waif the next. If you wish to make your own choices, the consequences of those choices are no one's fault but your own. *That* is the cost of the freedom you so ardently desire."

He had never shouted at her before. She had seen his exasperation when something didn't go according to plan, or the dangerous growl when he coiled to strike, but never had his emotions bubbled over like this. He stared at her, eyes narrowed, cheeks ruddy, mouth set in a firm line.

Until this moment, rage had sustained her. Even as Luke told his story, even as Matthew met her gaze and didn't deny its truth, even as she stood at the rail and burned with the injustice of it all… Even then, all she felt was rage. It honed her thoughts, held the fragile splinters together, so all she could do was hate what Matthew had done.

At Stokes's words, she broke.

He turned his face away as the tears spilled down her cheeks. She tried to take a breath, but it caught in her throat. Soon she was sobbing, unable to swallow the low moans of despair, the shuddering gasps.

Fie upon him, she thought, but it was Stokes she meant, not Matthew. She had cursed Matthew a dozen times and would curse him a thousand more, but Matthew had only lied to her. She was familiar with liars; everyone was a liar to some degree. Stokes had spoken pure truth, and it knocked the wind out of her.

Fie upon him for not consoling her and telling her it wasn't her fault, that she couldn't have known. Fie upon him for not concealing his disgust of her. Fie upon him for seeing straight through her and exposing her for the coward she was.

When Stokes put his arms around her, she flinched at the surprise, then melted against him as he gathered her tightly into his embrace. She wept into the fine fabric of his doublet, smooth against her cheek, too lost in her misery to care that he saw her cry.

Her nose pressed against the pulse at his neck, and she counted it, beat after beat, as she breathed in the warm fragrance of his skin, the same sweet perfume she had noted her first day aboard. Another breath, and her shoulders ceased shaking. Another, and her throat relaxed. In time, her heartbeat matched his. They breathed together, chests meeting and receding like waves on the shore.

Her face was sticky with drying tears, and she dabbed at them with the cuffs of her sleeves. What was she to say now? How was she to recover from such an explosive, childish display?

"Methinks you do not hold the lads so gently when they weep."

His voice rumbled against her cheek. "They do not like it known."

She leaned away from him with some reluctance. Just as she had anchored herself on the rail and the chair, she anchored herself on him. Awkwardly, she rubbed the wet spot on his shoulder as if she could clear it, and out of the corner of her eye, she caught his smile.

With heavy limbs, she reached down to right the fallen chair and sank into it, exhausted in body and mind.

"This is the second time I have been reduced to rubble by a man's lies, and you have been present on both occasions." Her voice was low and rough from crying, and she cleared her throat out of embarrassment.

Stokes busied himself with a bottle and two goblets. He set one in front of her and sat in the chair opposite.

"Is it I who am cursed, or you?" she added.

"A weak man believes in curses or fate or the will of God. A strong man exerts his own will."

"And what of a woman?"

He poured her a glug of wine. "I have no experience as a woman, but I imagine there is not so great a difference. Are you not as responsible for your choices as a man?"

"When we are allowed choices." She traced her finger around the base of her goblet. "My father set my future for me. 'Tis the reason I became entangled with Matthew at the first: I dreaded following the path put before me. I only wish I had been wise enough to see the path I chose was covered in brambles."

"We are easily fooled in our youth. Besides, Kent hid who he was from you. How could you have known?"

"Was he always so cold? Did he change over time, or was he cruel from the first?"

"Men choose this life for many reasons. For some, 'tis desperation, but if a man cannot stomach it, why stay? Why make it his career? Matthew Kent was a pirate before he joined my crew. That is why he is still here, and why his actions, despicable though they were, do not surprise me."

"So every man on this ship is cruel and deceitful?"

"Aye." He drank from his goblet, and she watched for a sign he was teasing her. She hadn't expected him to agree to such a ridiculous statement.

"Davies?" she said. "Burney?"

"Any man who will make it his life's work to steal from innocent merchants and thumb his nose at the king's laws must, at the very least, be cruel and deceitful. No honest man is out here causing harm, wreaking havoc, and lying to naval officers when questioned." He leaned back in his chair. "We are all either twisted by nature or broken by circumstance, and this is the life that appeals to our lust for revenge or rebellion or danger. Or, indeed, cruelty. So yes, every soul aboard is a pirate. Including yourself. I have seen you squeeze a ha'penny out of a man who swore he could go no higher. I have seen you charm the breeches off a navy captain. And God knows you were glad to put my balls in a vice when I said I would not hire you on this summer. When you know what you want, you know how to get it."

The way he spun the stories made her sound savvier and more ruthless than she was. As if she had known, even a little, what she was doing. True, she had felt the rush of satisfaction when a sale went her way, but that wasn't piracy. The seedy taverns provided the danger; the rest was just business.

"We make port in an hour or two. What is your will?"

"My will?"

His eyes flicked up to hers. She heard it too, the way her voice caught on the simple word.

"Driscoll proved your innocence. You've no need to resign your position."

"And Matthew?"

He hesitated. "Do you believe he commissioned Driscoll to harm you? Such a conspiracy is grounds for dismissal."

"Methinks he did not know what sort of mischief Driscoll would make."

"Can you be sure? Mayhap his instructions were clear, and Driscoll was glad enough to follow them."

"It rings false. I cannot believe it of him."

"Try." He had one forearm braced on the table as he leaned forward. "Tell me he paid Driscoll to hurt you. Tell me he threatened you."

She did want to punish Matthew, to take from him what he took from her, but not if Stokes would suffer the fallout. He had already conducted one sham trial today; if he dismissed Matthew on false charges, the crew could mutiny.

"I will not ask you to sully your good name," she said. "Punish him if he has trespassed, but do not bend the rules for me."

"Will you not seek justice? As it stands, he will only pay a fine. That is no fit revenge."

Choosing not to ruin Matthew's life might be the right thing to do, but that didn't mean she liked it.

"Without a purser to do the sum, take care you do not mistake the amount he owes." She glanced up to catch his reaction.

The corner of his mustache twitched. "I have not the head for sums. 'Tis thirty shillings to a pound, is't not?"

"Forty." Charging Matthew double was more than enough.

His expression was amused, his smile a little wicked. The same fondness from last night softened the lines in the corners of his eyes, drawing her in, poising her at a precipice.

Before she fell, she looked away.

"Where will you go?" he asked. "Home?"

She knew at once the answer was no. Running back to that stifling cage of memories made her physically recoil. It was nonsensical: home had stability, a roof and a bed, hot meals, shoes with no holes.

It also had Robert, and the fierce disappointment of her family. Would they deign to see her? Would they listen to the tale before casting her out to fend for herself? Better to plan to fend for herself from the beginning.

She gave a slow, laborious shrug as she sighed, bone-weary. "I will find work," she said, with more confidence than she felt.

"What of Green? He has spoken well of you."

She screwed up her nose at the thought of working for or with the *Merrow*'s armaments dealer acquaintance in London. "I have not the stomach to deal in war."

"There might be some work you could do at the Customs House. I will speak to Taylor when we dock—"

"I cannot accept another kindness. I have naught to offer in return."

His posture shifted. "I require naught."

"How can you have attained your position without collecting debts?"

"I do collect debts."

"Not from me."

"For you owe me none."

"Nonesuch," she said with a weak laugh. "Your pity saved my life, and that is a debt I may never repay."

He snorted. "You were in no real danger from Robert Sherman."

"Not Robert. I speak of when you came to me in Rotherhithe."

The humor in his eyes vanished, the smile replaced by a grimace. "Maggie, that was not—"

"I had no plan to yield, but you could have walked away. Your need was not so great. But you pitied me. 'Twas writ on your face when you saw me on the stairs."

If he hadn't dropped his gaze to his lap—if he had kept assaulting her with that heartbreaking look of regret—she could not have continued.

"I am glad of it," she murmured. "I would have… well, I do not know *what* would have become of me. But when all about me was darkness, you brought me a lamp. You saved a life I deemed not worth saving, and I will not squander it. Should our paths ever cross again, I hope I will at last have something to give you in thanks for all you have done."

He was silent, his eyes cast down the length of the legs stretched out in front of him, ankles crossed. By his silence, there was nothing left to say.

She rose from her seat, her body aching, her eyelids heavy. Whatever courage she had summoned to speak so openly to him was spent. He noticed her moving after a moment's delay, and he stood as well, ever the gentleman.

Knowing this was goodbye, she held out her hand. Perhaps he would shake it as a fellow officer; perhaps he would bow over her knuckles like a nobleman. All Maggie cared about was touching him one last time.

He took her hand and raised it a few inches, then seemed to think better of it. He covered the back of her hand with his other one. "We bid each other farewell, then."

"Aye."

"London is not so big a town." He released her.

She flexed her fingers at her side and forced herself to meet his eyes. "We are bound to meet again."

Liars, the pair of them.

Autumn 1613

But when she saw her breath was gone and strength began to fail,
The color faded in her cheeks, and beginning for to quail,
Her hair was turned into leaves, her arms in boughs did grow,
Her feet that were ere while so swift, now rooted were as slow.
Her crown became the top, and thus of that she erst had been,
Remained nothing in the world, but beauty fresh and green.

33

MAGGIE TRIED TO take Stokes's advice not to put stock in fate, but when she asked Jules Bisset whether he knew of any need for seamstresses, he told her his secretary had just been poached by a nobleman and he needed her to start tomorrow. Also, a newly widowed customer of his had rooms to let near Bartholomew Close across town. And this gown was never collected by its commissioner, so consider it an advance and throw that tattered abomination on the fire, *s'il vous plait*.

She feared the magic would blink out and she would find herself beside a cold hearth like the Little Ash Girl if she questioned her good fortune. So she didn't.

Two weeks into her employment, she sat behind the simple wood desk in Bisset's office, one of two rooms making up the living suite above the shop. Bisset had since purchased better-appointed bachelor quarters in a more fashionable part of the city, so he rented the bedchamber out to his new shopkeeper, Horton, and Maggie used the anteroom for her work. By the waning evening light, she reviewed the day's accounts, every line receiving the same meticulous examination. She rubbed her eyes.

Bisset popped his head around the door frame. "Close up when you leave, *hein*?"

"Why cannot Horton?"

"I gave him the night off."

"But—!" She sighed. "That is his purpose, to carry out your work when you cannot!"

"And your purpose is to manage my *journal*," he said, referring to his daily schedule with the French pronunciation. "Yet you have not asked what engagement I dash off to this night." He waggled his gray eyebrows.

"Where do you dash off to, monsieur?"

"To sup with my dear friend Ellen."

"I did not think that the sort of engagement you wish me to record in your diary."

He waved away her cynicism. "Do you have a message for her? You are friends, no?"

Maggie gave him a neutral smile. "Prithee tell her I wish her good health."

Truthfully, she hadn't thought much about Ellen since they parted ways. Ellen wasn't responsible for her dismissal from the brothel, but it felt like a betrayal. Would it have been so hard to stand up for her, at least a little?

"You had a… *on dit, 'brouille'?*" At her blank look, he waved his fingers in the air, hoping to pluck the correct English phrase from the ether. "A fight? You are no more friends?"

"Nay, I fear we are not. Mistress Pylet dismissed me. Did you know?"

He frowned. "For what reason?"

"Mayhap Ellen knows. Forsooth, I do not."

"*Bon*, I will find out for you."

"Nay, sir, you need not—"

But he was halfway down the stairs, bidding her *bonsoir*. If there was some plot in which to meddle, meddle he would. She only wished he would leave her out of it.

Ellen came by the shop the following afternoon. Maggie chanced to spot her from the office window. Her dress and hat were fashionable and ostentatious, her bodice cut low. A passerby nearly collided with a cart, unable to tear his eyes from her. The same, then.

Maggie stepped into the back of the shop in time to hear Ellen ask Horton for her. "Well met," she said.

Ellen swiveled to face her. "Mags!" She rushed forward and took both of Maggie's hands in hers. "How now? Jules told me I would find you here. What providence! How I have missed you! You look well."

Her warm manner was so unexpected, Maggie felt herself thawing toward her against her will. She had thought their relationship over, the bridge burned, but Ellen didn't seem to agree.

"Come, let us find a drink and a quiet corner to talk." She turned toward the door, holding Maggie's hands.

"Are you at leisure to do so?"

Ellen laughed. "'Tis Wednesday, the day of our lady!" She gestured to her smiling visage and dipped a mock curtsy. Her playfulness was catching, and though Maggie had some work still to do, she allowed herself to be swept down the road to a respectable ordinary.

"I am sorry for how things ended," Ellen said once the polite inquiries had been satisfied. She poured them each another goblet of cider and set the empty bottle on the table between them. "Mistress Pylet treated you ill. We all did."

"Aye."

Ellen was right to look chagrined. "'Twas Molly's doing. You frightened her when you told her about Vernon skimming off the top. She took it upon herself to right matters."

"But why? Can I know the great secret now?"

Ellen gave a drawn-out sigh and cast her eyes down. "Aye, for now it matters not. Frank is dead."

The most senior of the Dagger's whores, the mother of Francie and Ned, and the person at the brothel Maggie knew the least about. She put on an expression of shock and dismay to hide her shameful apathy.

"We all started pitching in as soon as she knew she would not get better," Ellen went on. "A few shillings here and there when we could spare them. Then we started to take on her patrons to give her time to rest. We hid it from Pylet as long as we could, so Frank could keep her position for as long as possible. And then she could not hide it any longer."

That was why Maggie knew nothing about Frank. She would watch the other girls at work in the dining room all night, but Frank never came down. It had been odd, but not intriguing enough to occupy more than a morsel of Maggie's thoughts. Yet the whole time Maggie worked there, Frank had been dying.

"Mistress Pylet would not truly throw a dying woman out of her house, would she?" she asked. "What provisions did she make for Francie and Ned?"

"None! 'Tis why we had been hoarding our coin and stealing from the Dagger. We knew Pylet cared not what happened to the children." She reached out to touch Maggie's arm. "I am sorry Molly sacrificed you, but I pray you can see now why she did."

Poor Frank, and her poor little ones. Maggie had to be disposed of before an errant word brought the whole thing crashing down. And Mistress Pylet, the shrewd businesswoman, a person Maggie had looked up to! Did all the Dagger girls have such generosity to look forward to when age and infirmity rendered them dispensable?

"Where are they now?"

"The children? Francie washes at Master Fowler's laundry, thank the Lord, but there is nothing for Ned as yet. He is not like to be taken on as an apprentice anywhere decent. We should all like better for him than to labor, but if he must, he must. Though he is yet too small to be much help to anyone."

"Ned is a clever chap, is he not? I do not doubt he could run messages. Bisset is forever arranging meetings and shipments."

Ellen's eyes brightened. "Of course! How could I have been so daft? He will be darling in a little blue suit, with Jules's coat of arms on his sleeve… I will make it so!"

They wiled away the rest of the afternoon, sharing stories about their lives, gossiping about shared acquaintances. Half the names Ellen dropped were unfamiliar, but Maggie pretended well and laughed and gasped whenever a story warranted it.

She told Ellen what had happened between her and Matthew and gave a brief, unemotional synopsis of what had caused her to settle in London. The details were too fresh in her mind, and she tried not to dwell on them.

"And how is our Will? Handsome as ever, I warrant."

"You know, I once thought him in love with you."

Her laugh was loud and musical, infectious enough to turn heads. "A wondrous thought, to be loved by him! I do treasure our friendship, and I have missed his visits to me, but, well, what use am I to him when he has you?"

Maggie could feel the blotches of pink spreading across her cheeks. "He does not have me! Why should you think it? I was betrothed to Matthew all winter, and Stokes was my employer all summer."

"What matter? 'Tis not a crime."

"On the *Merrow*, 'tis indeed a crime. No liaisons between crew members."

"Sooth, I forgot. But now you are no longer of his crew, you may liaise as often as you wish, may you not?"

In theory, she was correct, but there were more hurdles than that to overcome. First, Stokes didn't know where to find Maggie even if he wished to, and she would not blame him if he washed his hands of her after the trouble she had caused him. Second, the *Merrow* only docked in London when it was convenient, so she couldn't say when she *would* see him again.

Third, and most notable, Maggie knew better than to "liaise," with her feelings as disorienting and bothersome as they were. She didn't doubt he would agree to a roll in the clover, like any man, but she knew she would never recover from it. The refrain to every verse was *I cannot have him*; having him was not impossible, but it would prove intolerable.

She put on her bravest face to lie to Ellen. "I suppose you are right, but it makes no difference to me. Besides, I doubt he feels more for me than any bachelor might."

Ellen leaned in, unable to resist some hint of romantic intrigue. "And if he did?"

Maggie looked sidelong at Ellen and pressed her lips together to hide her smile. "He is bonny, is he not?"

They giggled like children, Ellen squeezing Maggie's hand.

When they had both recovered enough to speak, Ellen sat up straight. "Now we're talking of bachelors, I've a bit of gossip for you. If you wondered why you haven't seen Jules today, 'tis for the simple reason that… *I've only just left him*." Her eyes twinkled with merriment as she awaited Maggie's reaction.

Dutifully, Maggie's eyebrows shot up. "He engaged you for the whole night? And all morning, too?" She knew about Jules and Ellen already, of course, but Ellen seemed to want a dash of theatricality, and Maggie didn't mind obliging her. "What of the 'day of our lady'?"

"For Jules, I make an exception. He gave me these, as well." Ellen turned her head so that her pearl ear bobs danced in the light. "He wishes to keep me."

Maggie cooed over the pearls and expressed her well-wishes, making Ellen beam.

"We will be free of the Dagger at last! Kate does not deserve to grow up in that horrible place. He is most sweet with her, you know. I wonder betimes if she may be his daughter, for all it matters not."

"Does it not?"

"She was born without a father, and naught may change that. Mayhap one day Jules will look upon her as his own, and give her the rights a father gives his child, but I care little for that as long as he looks upon her with affection. To show her men are not cruel by nature."

"But if he never acknowledges her, who will provide her dowry?"

"I will, if she requires one. I may hire her a tutor, put a little money aside for her future… Were I Jules's wife, I would be

bound to his will, but as his mistress, my money will be my own.
'Tis the best life I can give her."

"What of respectability?"

The moment the words left her mouth, she knew she should not have spoken them.

Ellen's face flushed. "Hang respectability! Who is her mother? I destroyed her every chance for a decent life when I first lifted my skirts for coin. But now I may do this for her. And for myself." Ellen took a sip of her cider, a clear sign she was done with the conversation.

Maggie felt wretched. Who was she to judge Ellen? Neither of them had achieved the life their parents had dreamed of for them, and here Ellen was trying to give Katherine the best chance at future happiness. She was to be commended, not censured.

Maggie, too, was chasing a life better than the one she left, and unlike Ellen, she *had* the blessings of financial support and a good name—both of which she threw away the day she boarded the *Merrow*. Why did they remain her metric for success?

"Pray pardon," she said. "You are right. Bisset is a good man, and I am happy for you."

Ellen was sliding her finger along the rim of her goblet, a pout on her pink lips. "Gramercy."

They sat together for a moment, and Maggie wondered what else she should say to prove her contrition.

"We will get to see much more of each other, I vow," Ellen said, perking up.

And just like that, they were friends again.

34

BY MID AUGUST, she seldom thought of him anymore. The poets claimed distance sharpens devotion, but she was sure it was only proximity that had set her heart to pounding. Maggie kept her mind occupied by plans and figures for Bisset's new warehouse, relegating Will Stokes to a fond memory.

Her rooms at Routledge House were simple and comfortable, and now she had the space and the salary, she began collecting small luxuries. A little hat, a pretty brooch, an ivory comb, a book of verse. They were new treasures for her new life, and she hoarded them like a magpie.

Her treasures from the *Merrow* remained at the bottom of her seabag, which was shoved in the back of her wardrobe. She had tried to unpack it once, but the smell of it set her to trembling. Over time, she forgot about it.

This morning, in a search for her nicest pair of slippers, she found it. She expected the sight of it to put her off, but she felt neutral, even serene. Why was she holding on to these things, which were surely ruined from the salt air they had been sealed up with? Most of it was destined for the trash heap.

The scent hit her as it had before, brine and canvas, sour from remaining undisturbed for eight weeks. She had used her spare clothing to protect her prized baubles, and now she unwrapped each bundle, casting the dirty, frayed linen aside. Davies's flute. Matthew's silver pin. Stokes's tiny black cacao bean.

Her sonnets.

The leather thong was stiff and tacky, reluctant to allow her access. When she finally untied it, she bent the book back and let the pages whir by. The smell of the old paper and the feel of the book in her palms brought back the memory of her last day on the ship, in the navigation room, after Matthew's last-ditch proposal. A bookmark had fallen out. It hadn't bothered her before, but it did now. She had never seen that scrap of canvas, and she was sure she hadn't left her book on the navigation room table. Someone took it from her room. Someone marked a page. Someone left it for her to find.

She knew who she wanted the culprit to be. It was just the sort of aristocratic courtship ritual that would delight him, after all: slipping curated couplets and notes of affection into the possession of one's beloved. His mistake was in the execution. She would never know who her mystery suitor was, or what sentiment he wanted Shakespeare to express for him. She could only imagine.

So she did, for a long time.

She met Bisset at his shop at her usual hour, despite her unforeseen trip into reverie. He was in an excellent mood, as he had been for the better part of a fortnight. Business had never been better, and Maggie now juggled his diary, his distributors, and making sure his employees received their pay. Today he set her to work projecting sales figures, grinning the grin of a man who saw himself sitting on a pile of gold.

In the afternoon, he sent her to assess the progress the builders were making on the new warehouse. The property was cheap because the neighborhood was rough, so she brought Abraham, Bisset's hired muscle, to provide the required menace. They completed the mission without encountering any problems, and she gave him a favorable report when they returned to Throgmorton Street.

"*Bon*," he said. "A missive came while you were away. A young supplier wants to do business. Will you meet him and hear what he has to say, to decide if it is worth my time?"

"Where will I find him?"

Bisset leaned down to examine the note he had scribbled on his desk. "The Bell Inn. Cheapside."

"When does he expect me?" She narrowed her eyes at him. "*Does* he expect me?"

It would be just like Bisset to forget to mention his secretary was a woman. She had surprised two potential business partners this way, and one of them had taken his business elsewhere because of her.

He put on his charming salesman face, but she didn't need to hear his pitch. She shot him a look of disapproval and repeated her question about the meeting time.

"Three of the clock," he said.

"And who shall I ask for?"

Bisset waved his hand. "I forget it. Ask for the man who is looking for Bisset."

"Can you remember nothing? An initial? What if I meet the wrong man and buy twenty sheep instead of twenty bolts of wool?"

"You must speak very clearly, then, *n'est-ce pas?*"

At half past two, she set out for Cheapside. The Bell was a clean sort of place, the windows open to admit a breeze and push out foul smells. She cast about for the sort of man who might sell cloth.

All thoughts fled when she met the wide-eyed gaze of Will Stokes.

Had her girlish fancies this morning manifested him? Her first instinct was to feel guilty, as if she had pulled him away from some important task so he could feature in this chance encounter.

He stood as she approached and smiled, not his pirate's smirk, but an expression of genuine pleasure. She held out her hand for a shake while he moved close to embrace her, and they fumbled, awkward and laughing.

"What do you do here?" he said, voice full of wonder, then stopped himself. "Forgive me, that is no fit greeting. You look remarkably well."

"Well enough that you remark upon it? Then I must have looked remarkably ill when last we laid eyes."

"I have not seen you so attired since our jaunt to the theater." His eyes scanned her wardrobe from fashionable hat to impractical slippers, and she shivered as if she could feel the path of his gaze. "You are doing well for yourself."

"I have found good work as secretary to Jules Bisset."

He frowned in grim amusement. Realization dawned on her at the same moment.

"You are the new assistant I am to meet," he said.

"And you are his prospective supplier! I do believe we have been positioned like pieces on a game board."

Bisset would answer for this when she returned to Throgmorton Street.

He pulled a chair out for her. "Have you another meeting after this?" she asked him as he settled himself opposite.

"I have, at half-past."

"How may we speak on both business and pleasure in so short a time? Let us have business first."

Playing the hard-nosed negotiator with Stokes was too reminiscent of her disturbing performance in Rotherhithe, but since Bisset now paid her wages, she had little choice. In the end, she gave him as fair a deal as she could and despised every unpleasant moment.

A pretty young barmaid dropped off two mugs of ale as they finished the negotiation, and Stokes thanked her briskly as he took a sip. His reserve amused her; surely the barmaid deserved at least a roguish smile, if not a flattering remark.

"I enjoyed that not," she said, lowering her mug with a shake of her head. "Bisset must manage all future dealings with the *Merrow*, for I want no part of it."

"Oh?"

"I do not relish standing opposite you on the battlefield. Bisset may fight you if he wishes. I would be your ally."

Smiling, he lifted his mug in a toast. "Well spake. To our allegiance."

"Now to the business of pleasure? Tell me of your adventures. There have been many, certes, these two months gone."

"Two months?" He blew air past his closed lips, struck by how much time had passed. "I have never stayed away from Town so long."

"Why did you stay away?"

He shifted in his seat and shrugged. "We took a job."

She waited for him to say more, but he let his vague response hang in the air. "This job," she prompted, "is it completed?"

"Nay. We must set sail again ere nightfall."

"So soon?"

She hoped he didn't hear the high-pitched dismay in her voice, but by his amused half-smile, it was clear he did.

"In faith, I had not thought to complete my dealings in so short a time, but I would not be reasoned with—so Padraig would tell you. There was an account I was eager to settle, and fate has smiled upon me."

"Tut. A weak man believes in fate."

He chuckled and shook his head. "And a fool speaks in proverbs."

"What more is required for this mission of yours?"

"I know not. I meet with Green anon, and then I shall know more."

"You cannot say, then, when you will return." She tightened her fingers around her mug, irritated at herself for being too obvious.

"I cannot. A fortnight hence, mayhap longer. I *can* say I have no wish to stay away. London is full of diversions."

When she met his gaze, a shiver ran up the base of her spine. She recognized it for what it was and took a breath to dispel the feeling. In the early days with Matthew, those frissons of delight propelled her toward disaster. This inconvenient infatuation with Will Stokes needed to remain hypothetical.

"What diversions do you hope to enjoy when you are at last at leisure?" she asked, smiling as innocently as she could.

"Methinks a visit to the Globe would be merry."

Her eyes widened. "You did not hear! 'Tis gone, burned to the ground."

"You jest!"

"Rather a cruel jest, is't not?"

"Very well, is there aught else for us to do in Town these days?"

"I may only guess what sort of amusements Padraig would enjoy—"

"Aye, my lady," he said, stopping her with a wave of his hand, "you demure very prettily. Pray tell me what amusement *you* would enjoy."

She frowned, pretending her heart wasn't fluttering like a hummingbird. "I do not demure. Why should you spend precious shore leave with someone you are well rid of?"

"In sooth, Maggie, I am a common sea captain. You must needs speak plain to so simple a man as I." He leaned back in his chair, his eyes bright with amusement. "Do you insult yourself on purpose to deter me, or am I to argue with you for your gratification?"

If he could tease her like this, he must not have guessed the truth: that she was overjoyed to think he wanted to spend his leave with her, and at the same time terrified she had misunderstood him. Nothing would induce her to reveal her feelings until she was certain he reciprocated.

"You wish me to speak plainly?" she said. "Prithee, lead the way. How may I convince you of my unworthiness?"

He watched his own mug as he rotated it, the base scraping the table with each turn. For a moment, he was silent, and then a distracted smile bloomed on his face.

"I chanced upon an intriguing verse some weeks ago, on the subject of worth." He tilted his head as if searching for the words. "'Some glory in their birth, some in their skill, some in... riches, garments, hounds—'" He shook his head. "I have not the memory for rhyme."

She knew at once which sonnet he meant, hazarding a guess it had once been marked in her book by a scrap of old canvas. But she kept silent, waiting.

With an unhurried air, he leaned forward, resting his forearms on the table. He clasped his hands together, his thumbs sliding against each other as he fidgeted. She stared, fascinated by the dark hair on his knuckles, following his veins until they disappeared beneath the cuffs of his sleeves. Such strong hands, but so restless. She wanted to reach out and calm them, but she kept hers clenched together under the table.

"It seems to me," he went on, watching his hands as intently as she was, "a thing's worth is set by he who treasures it. I am ever astounded by the fools who find no value in the things..." He swallowed. "The things I treasure."

As he spoke, he unlaced his fingers and slowly tilted his right hand, exposing part of his calloused palm. His fingers twitched, then gently unfurled.

It was an offering.

Maggie's breathing was shallow, her pulse the only thing she could hear aside from his bewitching voice. Before she lost courage, she brought her left hand out from under the table and let it rest casually an inch from his. She could extend a finger and touch him. It was no distance at all.

He chuckled. "Listen to me, prattling nonesuch when I am meant to be answering your question." Their eyes met. "Waste your breath if it gives you pleasure. You will not convince me."

You cannot have him, a voice inside her said.

Why not? another voice answered.

Her index finger extended of its own power and brushed over his.

Behind her, the door opening caught his attention. He pulled his hand back just as a touch on her shoulder made her jump.

She looked up into the smiling face of Padraig MacCraith. He leaned down to kiss her cheek, and she marshaled her senses enough to return the embrace, half out of her chair. Her clumsy limbs didn't belong to her, and her mind was too foggy to understand his uncharacteristic greeting.

"Look who I've found." Padraig gestured to Green, the *Merrow*'s weaponry contact, who had entered the inn behind him.

Stokes shot her a resigned smile, the same look she sent him, and stood. "Well met," he said to Green. Then to Padraig, "You will keep Maggie company, will you not?"

"Aye, captain." Stokes motioned Green to a vacant table on the other side of the dining room while Padraig dropped into Stokes's vacated seat.

"You look well," he said.

"And you. How now?"

"Grand."

She peered at him, wondering how she could punish him for what he had just interrupted. "Not ill? Drunk? 'Twas the warmest greeting I have ever seen you give. When last we met, you liked me not."

He flexed his shoulders and stretched his neck, uncomfortable. "I did always like you, but I like you more now you're off me ship."

She laughed in surprise at his honesty. "I had not known I was a thorn in your paw. I am sorry I gave you grief."

"'Twas a fine ship we had before you, but the captain threw a bonny lass onto the deck and the lads dove like gulls. Seemed they'd never cease their squawkin'." He winked at her. "'Tis a mite quieter now."

"I can well imagine."

He waved over the barmaid. "And to tell the truth, we lads feel a wee bit responsible for how you left us. I'm right glad to see you're no worse for it."

"The captain says you took on a job that kept you from Town."

"Aye. The King's navy is patrolling the Channel—well, you remember Cap'n Seger of the *Vigilant*. We've had to lay low awhile. A countryman of mine in Dublin had a task for us, somethin' we could do 'til Seger turned his back."

"Smuggling?" she asked, her voice low.

"This 'n' that."

She glanced across the room to where Stokes and Green sat, their heads close together. "I am surprised Ireland has anything to sell a man like Green."

"Green's not buyin'."

His tone was troubling. If Green was *selling* weapons to the *Merrow*'s Irish employer, did Padraig know what they would be used for? Menacing Spain was one thing, but fomenting rebellion was treason.

"And you are bound again for Ireland anon?"

"Tonight. We had word the *Vigilant* was dealin' with a spot of trouble off the coast o' Spain. We must needs slip back through while she's lookin' the other way. I told Will 'twas an errand not worth the risk, but…"

She liked the way his Christian name dropped from Padraig's lips, as if Maggie was finally in on the secret of his true identity. "He must have felt Green was the only one who could help him complete his task."

"Nah, we've friends enough in the west. He's here lookin' for you."

Maggie's eyebrows shot up, and he went on. "We've had cargo burnin' a hole in the hull for weeks, but he'd not sell it 'til we could make it safe to London. Hoped to meet as many of our friends as he could, methinks, to ask 'em if any knew what had become o' you."

She was the account he needed to settle. Glancing again at the far table, adoring the lines of Stokes's statuesque profile, she chuckled uncomfortably. "A foolhardy errand indeed. I am no longer his responsibility."

"You know Will. He's St. George born again. I told him you were a cunnin' lass who needed no rescuin', and I was right. Look at you—dressed in finery and bonny as ever."

Drunk with joy and entertained by this over-complimentary Padraig, she let herself laugh, really laugh, for the first time in as long as she could remember. She pressed her hands to her stomach as if to alleviate the pressure against her stays and smiled so widely she could barely see Padraig over her cheeks. It felt almost as good as knowing Will Stokes was here expressly to see *her*.

"You two have come round to each other, I see."

Clearing her throat, she grinned up at Will, who stood over the table with his yellow hat in his hand. "Be on your guard, captain. Your mate is showing signs of lunacy. He says I am bonny *and cunning*."

Padraig threw up his hands in mock outrage, but Will blocked his repartee by gesturing at him with his hat. "I am loath to put an end to this reunion, but Green invites us to his warehouse. Go to. I will follow."

Raising his eyebrows, Padraig planted his hands on the table's edge and pushed himself up out of his chair. Passing behind Will, he patted Maggie's shoulder and leaned in for another quick press of the cheek before following Green into the street.

Will winced. "I knew not my time would be so short."

"No matter. I am needed in Throgmorton Street," she lied. He gestured for her to lead the way, and she went out into the golden light of the afternoon. A cart rolled by, and across the way, a shopkeeper stood in his doorway smoking a pipe. The air was fragrant and warm, the road damp from a summer shower.

She knew Green's warehouse was near the river, and she was bound north and east. This was where they would part ways. It should be easier this time, knowing she would see him again, but something constricted her lungs and squeezed her heart. She studied his face as he smiled at her, taking in the familiar beard, lips, nose, and eyes as if she had never seen him before.

"I will expect Bisset's men at six of the clock?" he said.

"Sooner, I hope. I will send them to you at once."

"You did not always have designs to be a woman of business, but it suits you."

"Things change."

"Thank the Lord for that."

She squared her shoulders and put on a bright smile. "We have said farewell so often, I am become most adept at it."

"One day we shall say it for the last time, but 'tis not this day, methinks."

Heart pounding, she offered him her hand. "Safe journey, captain."

He took a step toward her and lifted her hand, his mustache prickling her skin as he brushed his lips over her knuckles. "Will," he said, the name warm on her fingers.

Her breath caught in her throat. "Will."

Smirking, he squeezed her hand and dropped it to perform one of his regal bows. Then, returning his hat to his head, he set off to meet Padraig. When the city swallowed him up, she reluctantly turned in the direction of Throgmorton Street. If she hadn't been wearing her nicest shoes, there would have been nothing keeping her from skipping all the way back to the shop.

35

"VISITOR ASKING FOR you, mistress." Horton's voice echoed up the narrow stairwell to Bisset's office.

She propped her pen on its stand and bounded down to the shop, grinning like a fool. Visitors were rare, and Ellen would have just pushed her way upstairs. It had to be him. In case her guess was wrong, she schooled her features into one of her amiable saleswoman smiles before passing through the doorway onto the shop floor.

His hair was long enough to tuck behind his ears, but otherwise, he was the same Will she farewelled in front of the Bell Inn four weeks ago. She forced her feet to keep a measured pace, even though every part of her body told her to leap into his arms.

He kissed her cheek, tickling her with his beard, and stepped back a safe distance for the usual conversational niceties. As she asked about his voyage and answered questions about her health, she kept her eyes fixed on him, memorizing him anew. How she had missed him.

The familiar voice had ceased telling her she couldn't have him. Now, a timid echo replaced it: *Will he have me?*

Will dropped his hat on the desk where Horton completed transactions, obscuring the tidy order slips and bills of sale. "I have a business proposition for you."

"I have said I will not do this." She held up her hands to prevent him from continuing. "Bisset is down the docks. You may either seek him there or speak to him when he returns."

"This only you may accomplish for me."

His tone took on a hint of mystery she couldn't resist. He glanced behind him to see where the shopkeeper had gone. Horton was near the front, smoothing and refolding bits of cloth.

Deeming it a safe enough distance, Will lowered his voice. "I have secured an invitation to a celebration at Hattecliff House on the twenty-fourth of October, in honor of the birth of Edward Treningham's heir."

"Lord Treningham? How have you managed such a miracle?"

"Treningham's steward is a right dunce at cards."

She fixed him with a disapproving look. At least he was luckier at cards than at dice. "How much was this invitation worth?"

"May one put a price on supping and drinking with knights and barons? As you are so practiced at the activity, I beg you to accompany me."

She wanted to tell him, from experience, that it wasn't worth as much as he thought, but he was so eager to go—and he wanted her with him. "Have you somehow acquired two invitations?"

"We gave so convincing a performance for the commander of the *Vigilant*, I have no doubt we can reprise it for a few bored noblemen and their wives. The man assured me the list now reads 'Captain Sir William Stokes and Margaret, Lady Stokes.'"

To hide the delicious thrill his words inspired, she dipped a sarcastic curtsy. "I congratulate you on your unexpected rise to knighthood!"

He shrugged as if it meant nothing, but his face betrayed his pleasure. "Infiltrating such an event requires a title, and this seemed the one least like to cause suspicion. 'Tis a fall in stature for you, however."

"I must take care to leave off my jewels."

"So you will come?"

Such a public appearance wasn't wise, but how dangerous was it, really? She had been missing long enough no one would be thinking of her. She knew few high-born people in London, and none who would recognize her.

Besides, the risk was the reason she would say yes. Bickering with Bisset was the only peril she enjoyed in this sedate life.

"I would need a new gown..."

"Order whatever you wish—garments, shoes, jewels. Have the bills sent to my man of business. Here..." He rifled around on the desk under his hat for a blank slip of paper and jotted down the direction. "If you require further payment for your trouble, name it."

"Do you know the cost of a new gown? I dare not ask for yet more, lest I leave you a pauper."

"I assure you, my lady, you will not." He gave her his haughty smirk. If he could do that at Treningham's party, he would be well suited to mingle with the baron's wealthy guests.

The shop door opened. Will held out the paper and said, "If you've a customer, I will take my leave."

The woman who had entered wore the fashionable attire of a wealthy woman, the brim of a smart hat angled across her face. A lady's maid trailed her, carrying a parcel. They looked around at the colorful walls, the lady pointing to something and turning her head to make a remark to her companion. Horton approached the lady and bowed, capturing her attention before she noticed the others in the shop.

Maggie's hand went out of its own accord and gripped Will's arm. She didn't know what she needed of him: to conceal her, to catch her, or to stay beside her until she could think again. Her blood had turned cold, her mind gone blank.

Will edged toward her and whispered, "What is't?"

"My sister."

There was nothing to consider, no decision to make. Speaking to Elizabeth or even alerting her to Maggie's presence was unthinkable.

She turned on her heel and escaped up the back stairs.

As one of thousands of nobodies in this sprawling town, she should be living an anonymous existence. The realization any member of her family could appear at her doorstep at any moment caused her world to tilt. She would never be safe, would she? Not until she was the last one alive.

It was a melodramatic thought. A reunion with Elizabeth would be difficult and almost certainly painful, but neither of them would suffer mortal wounds. Yet she wasn't ready to face it, even after all this time. The further she traveled from the life she had before, the more treacherous the return journey.

As she paced in front of the window, keeping a close eye on the street below, she wondered what had become of Will. No one had exited through the front, and she could hear Horton's and Elizabeth's voices below. Maybe he had escaped into the alley.

She felt a sudden wave of irritation that Elizabeth had cut short a rare opportunity to spend time with Will. Four long weeks she had waited for the *Merrow* to return to London. How long would he stay docked this time? When would he return? Was this the only chance she had to see him before Treningham's celebration in a few weeks? It had not been enough. It never was.

The prospect of infiltrating an elite gathering had been exciting only moments ago, but now the threat of danger had increased. Would Elizabeth attend? What other relics from her ancient past would she unearth there? Will did not know what he asked of her by requesting her aid. For him, it would be a party. For her, it would be a seance.

Almost an hour after she fled upstairs, Elizabeth and her maid appeared in the street below, moving west. A few moments later, Will left also, his yellow hat a beacon her eyes could follow to the end of the street.

Horton's familiar footfalls sounded in the stairwell. He popped his graying head into the office and waved a folded slip of paper at her. "From the gentleman you were speaking with earlier."

It was the direction Will had scribbled, with the date "24 October" looping beneath it. At the bottom, in a messier scrawl, he had written:

household liverie
delivery fortnight - departing Towne
Bell Chepeside half 4
W S

While she had been cowering above, Will had spied on the conversation below. If Elizabeth was expecting her new livery to be completed before she returned to her husband's country seat, Maggie only had to keep her wits about her for two more weeks. There would be no chance of running into her at Treningham's party.

She looked at her watch. Almost two o'clock. Her ledger was open on the desk, and she distracted herself with sums and figures until a quarter to four, checking the time so frequently it seemed to slow. If she arrived at the Bell Inn early, she risked interrupting a meeting. Will hadn't said anything, but from his unshorn hair and his long absence from town, she assumed he was still working with Padraig's Irish contact. She wanted nothing to do with whatever operation he had entangled himself in.

She closed the ledger and hastened down the stairs to let Horton know she was leaving for the day. The shopkeeper was at the desk, composing a bill of sale.

In front of him, staring in wonder at Maggie, was Elizabeth.

It wasn't fair.

Maggie made a choice. "Well met, Lady Chichester."

"Margie?" Elizabeth's normally pale face was ashen, her lips parted.

Horton looked up from his desk, then swiveled his head between the two women, curious.

"Maggie. Maggie Bailey, madam." She said it with the inflection of a polite prompt, as if she didn't want to embarrass the woman for having forgotten her name. Her eyes, though, were cold. Elizabeth needed to understand her name was not all that had changed. She needed to understand her sister was lost.

Elizabeth looked dazed, but she was collecting herself. "Of course. Well met, Mistress… Bailey."

Maggie asked for it, but the sound of her new name from Elizabeth's lips was like an arrow to the lung. She hid her sharp intake of breath by clearing her throat. "Monsieur Bisset will be overjoyed you have chosen to give him your patronage. Our cloth is the finest in London. I pray it meets your approval."

"Lady Chichester made her selection earlier this afternoon," Horton said. "She has come again to purchase more."

"New garments for my sons," said Elizabeth.

Sons. The child she was carrying last spring had been a boy.

Tears filled Maggie's eyes, but a deep breath and a few blinks dispelled them long enough to say, "Excellent well, madam. I leave you in the care of Master Horton. Adieu."

Elizabeth's face was blank now. She had always had better mastery over her emotions than Maggie. The only betraying detail was the movement of her throat as she swallowed whatever she had been about to say. "God be with you."

Maggie curtsied and breezed out of the shop. The tears came as she rushed down the street toward Cheapside, but she swiped them away. She hated the choice she had made. Regret stuck in her throat, no matter how many times she tried to swallow it. Regret her nephews would never know her; regret her words must have been as painful to Elizabeth as hers had been to Maggie.

Elizabeth could be cold, but Maggie couldn't remember her being cruel. What Maggie had done… it was cruel. Her sister hadn't deserved it.

And all to prevent a drawn-out reunion. All to avoid taking responsibility for what she had done. All to meet Will at the Bell Inn at half-past four.

36

WILL FIDDLED WITH the folds of his oversized ruff, tilting his head back and peering down his nose. His beard fanned out over the starched folds like a peacock's plumage in precisely the wrong orientation. Maggie couldn't help but snort with laughter at his ridiculous posture.

"What? Is it coming undone?" he said, panic-stricken.

Maggie took hold of the nearest wrist, pausing him mid-fluff. "It will if you keep playing with it. The starch only lasts so long."

He lowered his hands to his sides, giving the bottom of his doublet a tug as he did. Expensive orange silk peaked through slashes in the supple leather, bold and masculine, while dainty lace edged the cuffs of his shirt sleeves. Midnight blue ribbon striped his gray Venetian breeches, drawing the eye down to the orange stockings that enhanced the shape of his muscular calves. Only his leather slippers were plain, but no one would be looking at his feet. It was strange to see him without the yellow felt hat; this one had a tall crown pleated with black silk, encircled by a gold ribbon and a stiff, narrow brim.

He had paid just as much for her ensemble, even though Bisset had let him have the fabric at cost, but hers was nowhere near as ostentatious. Her skirts were trimmed with yellow ribbon down the front to echo the flowers embroidered on her cream bodice, and a red jacket kept the October chill at bay. She replaced her customary coif with an understated lace diadem cap, since it allowed the warm colors of the gown to set off the red of her hair, according to Ellen. The conservative design assured the gown would serve her for a year or more, since she would only play a knight's wife for one night.

That was a promise she had made to herself as she dressed this evening. Who knew if Will would develop a taste for infiltrating elite gatherings, but unless something changed, she wouldn't indulge him again. She couldn't bear to.

Following her disastrous run-in with Elizabeth in September, they passed a few happy hours at the Bell Inn, chatting as friends—and only as friends. She sensed a deliberate distancing, none of the flirtation or the vulnerability he had shown when they reunited in August. She matched his reserve, reasoning that if he liked her, he would tell her. He didn't tell her, and that was the last she saw of him until now.

Four more weeks of agony forced Maggie to admit to herself that she was in love with him.

But tonight, she would end the torment. If he didn't confess his feelings first, she would.

God, she hoped he would.

Will's gaze flickered over the crowd of partygoers awaiting entry. She had never seen him so ill at ease, and it was adorable. "Nervous?" she said.

"Never." He produced his right hand, palm up, and she placed her hand in his warmer one, giving him a reassuring squeeze.

The hall was already crowded by the time they had inched all the way to the entrance, a sea of colorful hat plumes fluttering like so many tropical birds. Over their heads, greenery and ribbons festooned the doorways and windows, gilded by the cheerful glow of dozens of lit candles. Anyone who felt they had the social standing to push ahead to the front had already done so, which left Will and Maggie among a small group of nobodies at the back. No one would hear them announced.

An austere gentleman wearing a heavy chain of office stood just inside the entrance to the hall. It was the marshal's responsibility to announce each family unit as it arrived, but the servant beside him, fidgeting behind a tall desk littered with parchment, was the one who fed him the proper names and titles.

"Lord Treningham's steward," Will whispered in her ear. The first trial was about to begin.

When they stepped up to the entrance, the steward met Will's gaze and nodded, then pointed with a bony finger to a line on the sheet of paper. The marshal looked down, then raised his head and bellowed in a hoarse voice, "Captain Sir William Stokes and Margaret, Lady Stokes."

They sailed into the vast assembly hall, part ballroom, part dining room. A hundred or more people milled about, talking and laughing and admiring each other's attire. Sugar sculptures and colorful cakes weighed down a long banquet table along one wall, and at an adjoining table, a pair of liveried servants filled dozens of goblets from pitchers. Music was coming from somewhere, but in the crush, Maggie couldn't pinpoint the musicians' hiding spot.

From Will's stiff posture and darting eyes, it was clear even the finest gathering at the Dagger and Sheath paled in comparison to this. His hand in hers was moist, his grip tight.

She leaned in. "Some wine, mayhap? Something to do with your hands?"

He steered them through the crowd toward the refreshment table and took two goblets, handing her one. A press of his hand at the small of her back propelled them to a safe viewing location at the edge of the assembly. The way he touched her reminded her of the *Vigilant's* surprise inspection, but then they only needed to con one man. Now they needed to con every person in the room.

"Do you see anyone you know?" he asked, his eyes roving the crowded hall.

"Not a soul. That is, I think I recognize one or two people, but no one I may count among my acquaintance." Lifting her wine goblet as if to drink, she extended a surreptitious finger to point at a man in the crowd. "I believe that is Lord Edward Folsham, the Earl of Hereford."

"Hereford, you say?" A woman peeked around Will's shoulder, her full eyebrows raised in interest. The doughy softness of her jowls and the shadows under her eyes placed her well into her thirties, if not older, but her fashionable gown and elaborate hairstyle were those of a young woman on display. She smoothed her hairline with steady fingers. "I suppose it would be impossible to be introduced to him…"

Bewildered, Maggie shook her head. "I am unknown to His Grace. I only recognized him because he once visited my father."

"Did he visit with his late wife? I have heard she was a rare beauty."

Maggie shrugged, smiling as pleasantly as she could despite the woman's prying.

The woman frowned. "Your father must be a man of consequence to host an earl. Who is he, pray?"

"I am not much in favor with my father. Methinks he would not like his name linked with mine."

"My doing, I fear," Will broke in, dazzling the woman with his smile. "His lordship was not best pleased when I stole his daughter away."

Maggie raised an incredulous eyebrow at him, hoping the woman would assume "stole" was a romantic euphemism rather than a confession.

"An elopement?"

"Nothing like that," Maggie said, just as Will replied, "Exactly so."

She shot him a warning glance, but he just pulled her an inch closer to him with an arm around her waist.

"My wife does not want it known how low she stooped to marry a poor sea captain," he said. "To which I say, she is so clearly my superior in grace, beauty, and accomplishments, there is no sense in trying to hide it."

She suppressed the urge to roll her eyes. Would he never learn to rein in his false praise?

Something ugly flashed across the woman's face, but a bright smile replaced it. "If only all were so fortunate to find love in marriage." She inclined her head in a polite bow and wandered the edge of the crowd, her gaze locked hawk-like on the Earl of Hereford.

Will's shoulders shook, and she looked up to find him holding in laughter. She elbowed him in the side. "Be not cruel."

"Do not tell me she is not a ridiculous creature!"

"Mayhap, but she is to be pitied withal." Will's raised eyebrow didn't surprise her, so she leaned close to explain. "On the hunt for a husband, I vow. From her speech about love, I gather she was not fortunate in her first marriage, which is pitiable, however common. And if Hereford's wife was a beauty, mayhap she fears she cannot tempt him, but you see she is determined to try." His arm around her suddenly felt boastful. She twisted, letting his fingers skim her back before they fell away. "Had I gone to France with Lady Crane, I would have been circling the halls in just such a way."

"I was not aware you regretted forgoing that trip."

"Why should you think I regret it?"

"Methinks you are not likely to have an earl for your second husband. Unless you wish me to secure an introduction to Hereford?"

"And then what? Play out a false divorce to free me from this false marriage?"

"Too common. Methinks I would rather make you a false widow with false news of a shipwreck."

"Too slow! You would condemn me to a twelvemonth of false mourning. I have endured all the mourning I can bear."

"It would be more diverting this time, for I could haunt you whenever it pleased you."

She snickered. "'Twould make the winter pass swiftly, but all the long summer I would sit alone awaiting your apparition."

He looked away, taking a sip from his goblet.

A new tune started up at the other end of the hall, flutes and viols carried along by the mournful beating of a drum. It lacked the liveliness of a group of drunk sailors, but she recognized the melody from the first few notes.

Their eyes met at the same moment.

"Heart's Ease," he said.

The humid midsummer air and Will's strong forearms flooded her memory. She looked down at his proffered hand, remembered how his calloused palm felt in hers. If she danced with him again, she would be irretrievably lost.

But spring was an age away.

They abandoned their wine and joined the dancers, arriving in time to make the opening honor. It was a more stately version of the Heart's Ease they had danced together on the ship, but her heartbeat could not maintain a similar calm. Every time they came together, she grinned. Every time his side partner took him away from her, she mourned. When they hooked arms, she leaned into him so they touched from shoulder to elbow, made brazen by the role she played. No one knew them, so no one knew he wasn't hers.

As the musicians played the last chord, they bowed, the men bending one knee and pointing the other toe, the women sinking to the ground like a meadow of colorful toadstools.

Will helped her to her feet, and she let him lift her hand to kiss her knuckles. At the last moment, he shifted his grip, rotated her wrist, and touched his lips to the flesh of her palm. Her breath hitched at the shock. He held her there for an excruciating moment, and she stiffened her fingers, afraid to let them brush his cheek.

When at last he lowered her hand and led her back into the crowd, she couldn't register the movement of her feet, the proximity of the other revelers, or the announcement of the next dance. Her palm tingled as if he had singed her skin.

This was proof, wasn't it? Or was Will simply a flirt who kissed women's palms every day he wasn't at sea? Was she making more of it than it was?

She wouldn't mind if there *was* more of it—at least a dozen more.

Cheeks flushing, she focused on putting one foot in front of the other. It made her reaction sluggish when someone almost collided with her.

She was primed to see Robert Sherman. For over a year, she expected to see him everywhere she turned. It explained why she recognized him before he recognized her.

His gaze was unfocused, not meeting her eye as he apologized for his clumsiness. She turned her face away and brushed past him, praying harder than she had ever prayed before that he would not make the connection.

"Margie?"

She turned with as much grace and hauteur as she could, even though every joint and muscle in her body demanded she flee. Oblivious, Will continued on. The void of his absence pressed on her, but some amount of pride yet aglow inside her prevented her from turning around to look for him, to make him wrap his arm around her and hold her upright as she did this impossible thing.

Robert had not changed much. His attire was as stylish as ever, and he had gained weight: two indications he had not yet spent all of his inheritance. Most gratifying was the slack-jawed expression on his boyish face. If he hadn't expected to see her, it might give her the advantage. Yet she was surprised to feel afraid, cornered like a small animal, despite spending all that first summer practicing the sorts of devastating things she would say if she ever saw him again.

"We thought you were…" Robert cringed away from her, and she realized he was seeing a ghost.

"Dead?" she said. "Not yet."

"I am pleased beyond words to see you looking so well."

"I care little how you feel." A surge of anger displaced her fear. In his twisted mind, her presence here, dressed in silk and brocade instead of pauper's rags, somehow vindicated him, as if everything had turned out for the best.

If he had played out this meeting over and over, as she had, this was not how he had envisioned it. He looked warily about until his gaze landed on something past her head. A shadow crossed his face. "I gather you are being taken care of," he drawled.

She looked over her shoulder into Will's stony face. The wave of relief steadied her for a moment, but then she sent up a prayer to any god that listened, begging them to keep Robert from recognizing Will as the man from the Silver Starling.

"My husband is most attentive," she said.

"May I offer my sincerest wishes for a fruitful and happy marriage. Your family will be most gratified to know you are safe. You have been missing so long..." He emphasized the word *missing* and glanced at Will, hoping to shock him.

"You need not trouble yourself with delivering news of my health," she said. "If my disappearance caused my family as much distress as you and Lady Crane showed upon my abduction last July, then I would think the knowledge that I am alive would only upset them."

The muscles in Robert's jaw flexed. "Are those... *events* common knowledge among your acquaintance?"

"I hold it as a general rule to keep no secrets from those I love."

"Tosh!" He lowered his voice and sneered at Will. "You knew your wife had been captured and ransomed by mercenaries, and you still married her?"

"Ransomed by *you*," she hissed, taking a step toward him. "How dare you imply I have a mark against my character when 'tis you are holding the pen!"

"Does the man have a tongue, or do you always speak for him?"

"As your quarrel is with her," Will said, "I have little to contribute."

Robert gave her a smug smile. "He admits he will not defend you!"

"From what?" Will's posture shifted as he brought his left arm behind his back, drawing Robert's eye to the dagger Will wore sheathed at his hip. "She survived capture by mercenaries. I warrant she will survive you."

Robert narrowed his eyes. "Have we met, sir?"

Their luck had held for so long, it seemed impossible it would come crashing down now. But if Robert identified him, Will would go to the gallows in the morning.

"I would be most astonished if you had," she said, thinking quickly. "The first question I ask each person I meet is whether they associate with villains and knaves. 'Tis why I have been fortunate enough to avoid you ere tonight."

Robert coughed and adopted a more contrite tone. "Whatever my mistakes, I have been out of my mind with worry since you disappeared."

"Since you sold me to pirates, you mean?"

"I know not what madness took me." He kept his voice low, still hoping to keep their conversation private. "I was a fool."

Madness. Foolishness. Neither was an excuse for the choice he made at that gaming table. She examined his face, as pitiful as it had been when she brought him into her room at the Silver Starling.

He continued babbling. "I am at your mercy. Prithee, you must forgive me."

"What right have you to ask me? I had thought any connection we once had was dissolved that day." She smoothed the embroidery at the front of her bodice with shaking hands, too close to losing her composure. "I have held up my end of our agreement and told no one of our mutual acquaintance what you did. I imagine you said nothing to my family. Pray, let us continue in this way and hope our paths do not cross again."

Robert wouldn't relent. "By my troth, Margie, I never wished—"

"That is *not* my name." Her raised voice attracted the attention of a few of the revelers who stood near them. Robert's eyes flickered across each curious face as he grimaced with embarrassment.

Will pressed a steadying hand to the small of her back. "Come away, my love. Let us find more worthy company."

She gave Robert a last look, memorizing the despair on his miserable face, before weaving through the crowd. In the entrance hall, the music and chatter were subdued enough she could hear herself think. Her heart slammed against her breastbone, shaking her whole body.

Will appeared at her side, but she couldn't look at him without falling apart. "Forgive me. I cannot stay here."

"There is nothing to forgive." He tried to position his face so she would meet his eyes, but she turned away even more. "Tell me what I may do."

She shook with adrenaline, so wound up, the let-down was bound to be dramatic. His concern was already causing her defenses to crumble, and she felt the telltale tightness in her throat signaling imminent weeping. "Think not of me. Prithee, stay and enjoy the night."

Before the tears could come, she moved away from him down the hallway. A surprised page opened the front door for her, and she let the gust of cold air shock her into numbness. With long strides, she began her determined trek through the dark streets of London, holding herself together through sheer force of will.

After only a few paces, she noticed the second set of footsteps echoing her own. She glanced behind her, and the sudden surge of emotion at the sight of him was too much. He had every right to stay, but he hadn't hesitated to follow her.

She had known he would. She had counted on it.

Maggie took in as much chilly autumn air as her lungs would allow, mopping up the tears until her cuffs were wet and her face was dry.

37

"YOU NEED NOT have left." Her voice ricocheted off the facades of the crowding buildings. "I know how much trouble you went to for this evening."

"There will be other evenings. I would rather see you safe home. The city is dangerous at night."

"I am grateful for your company, but I am sorry I dragged you from your fun."

He shrugged. "Methinks I am more at home in a dockside alehouse."

"Nonesuch. You are at home wherever you go, I vow, but you do look splendid in your finery. Even I was tempted to snatch your purse."

"Gramercy. I cannot think of a finer compliment."

She allowed the silence of the sleeping streets to settle over them. The way was treacherous with only a handful of lit lamps on each street, so she focused on avoiding puddles and filth while the wide pupils of Will's eyes probed the dark alleys and alcoves. Within a few minutes, they would be back in the familiar environs of Bartholomew Close.

The companionable silence was a healing balm, allowing her to let the events of the past few minutes slide away. These moments with Will were precious; thoughts of Robert had no place here. Instead, she pasted happier thoughts over them: his praise of her to the husband-hunter, his defensive stance when they faced Robert, the embers burning in his eyes as he kissed her palm. It was a masterful portrayal of a man in love.

But she knew he could slip on a persona as easily as he slipped off his doublet. How much of tonight had been a performance? She formed and reformed the question in her head, becoming emboldened with every step closer to home, closer to the moment she would have to say goodbye to him.

"You did not heed my advice," she said.

"Advice?"

"Again, you played too doting a husband. 'Twas more than any woman should expect."

"I am sorry you have such low standards for husbands. 'Tis just how I would hope to treat my own wife."

"You must have had a good model."

"Not to my knowledge. I was yet young when my father died, and my mother went soon after. The uncle and aunt who raised me were terrible to one another." He paused. "In a perverse way, they were excellent models."

"I gather your uncle did not often compliment his wife, or dance with her." *Or kiss her palm.*

"He did not. I am not much practiced in the ways of marriage, but 'tis my belief if a man is lucky enough to have a wife whom he treasures, he would be a fool if he did not daily remind her of it."

How could she remain his friend when his mere presence inflicted such unbearable happiness? Each brief shore leave had been an island of easy, joyful hours scattered across a bleak expanse of gray, busy weeks. It terrified her to think she had misinterpreted every cue, letting herself depend upon a fantasy. Her heart would break if he couldn't love her back.

But then she remembered his lips on her palm.

Gathering her courage, she pushed away from the safety of the shore.

"I commend your acting prowess. You played your part most convincingly."

"In my abundant experience as a smuggler and a counterfeit, I find the most convincing lies are based in truth."

Her heart sank as she recognized the buildings of her street. There was no more time to demur. "And what... *truth* served as the foundation of your counterfeit tonight?"

Stopping before the front door of Routledge House, she waited, hands shaking, stomach twisted. He faced her. The thought of looking into his eyes was unbearable, but not seeing his reaction would be worse.

The lamp over the door gilded his cheeks; its flame danced in his eyes. He shifted his feet, bringing him a few inches closer. No distance at all.

"You are too wise not to have guessed."

The low timbre of his voice seeped under her skin, flooding her, capsizing her. The descent was peaceful, a slow sinking into crystalline certainty, and when she sighed, it was the last breath of the woman she was before.

She ebbed toward him, and he met her there, hand drifting to her face to anchor her as he kissed her. His lips molded to hers, sweet and yielding, filling her senses with the fragrance she would always associate with midnight on the *Merrow*: the subtle spice of his beard oil, warmed by his skin. The street and the buildings dissolved, and it was just her and Will and the moon, three points of light in the blackness.

His mouth was soft, but his mustache was rough, and the two sensations only deepened the ache his nearness always caused. For too long she had itched to touch him, to kiss him, and now that she could, it wasn't enough. Somehow he knew, and he angled to bring them closer. His shuddering breath as he took her lower lip made her hot, tense, weak. It was better than she had imagined every time the benevolent dark summoned the memory of him to her lonely bedchamber. She needed to see him there, lit by her lamp, silhouetted against her door. She needed him to transform her fantasies into prophecies.

Kissing him once more, she brushed his nose with hers and drew back. His thumb grazed her cheek as he watched her, his breathing unsteady, his eyes shifting to take in every detail of her face.

"You must not go home in the dark." The words came out half whisper, as if part of her worried she would frighten the magic away. "I have a lamp to lend. Will you… come up?"

Ellen made it look so easy, but when Maggie said it, she shook with fear. She had been kidnapped, married a stranger, escaped an abuser, and bribed a naval officer. Why was *this* the most difficult thing she had ever done?

He glanced at the dark windows of the upper floor. "I doubt your landlady will approve."

She should care about that. Instead, she pushed open the door.

Mistress Routledge was doubtless asleep, her senses dulled by her nightly glass of sack, but still they stole up the back stairs and darted into Maggie's chamber like mischievous children. Maggie picked her way across the dark room to light a candle in the hearth's banked embers, and soon a dim orange glow gave the shadows shape.

The room was only in slight disarray from her rush to prepare for the evening. As she looked around at the familiar furniture, her courage began to fade. She had never done something so brazen. Will was right: Mistress Routledge and the other nosy old women on the street would be shocked by her behavior.

She brought the candle to the table in the center of the room. The flame shivered as she lit a hooded tin lamp with her trembling hand, its glow eliminating the deepest shadows. Without a word, she pushed the lamp across the table to Will.

He looked at it, then up at her. She met his gaze, willing him to stay, but too much of a coward to say the words.

He chuckled. "Maggie… I will go if you tell me, and I will stay if you ask me. Do not make me guess."

Every time he said her name, her heart beat faster—from the beginning, from the moment he dubbed her "Maggie" that dreadful night. It made her linger near him in the hopes he would say it again. It made her love her new identity, the person she became after she met him.

It made her bold.

She took his hand, lifted it, and pressed his palm against her lips. His fingers curled, a light touch on her cheek.

"Stay."

His eyes were dark in the dim light, but she saw the tenderness in his gaze as he examined her face. He took off his hat and tossed it on the table. "A moment." He brought his hands behind his head and fumbled with the strings and pins of his ruff. It came loose, along with a few of the pins, which shone dangerously in the lamplight. "I am not averse to the use of torture devices in the bedchamber, but there is a limit."

She giggled. "Is there aught else you will be taking off?"

He dropped the ruff in a heap on the table and raised an eyebrow. "Fickle woman. I recall you instructing me *not* to undress in your presence."

"The circumstances are a little changed, methinks." She looked away and added, "You were my captain then."

He caught her hands and bundled them together on his chest. His heartbeat quickened beneath her fingers. How could a heartbeat be erotic?

"When I was your captain, you were beneath me—beholden to me. That is finished. I pray you, let me be only Will." He lifted her hands and pressed them to his lips, breathing deeply. "I require nothing, and I expect nothing. If you no longer have need of me, I am gone. Whatever your command, I will obey."

She knew what it was to desire and be desired. Each man in her past had acted on their desire without restraint, and her enjoyment of it depended on a kiss or a caress, something to awaken the slumbering thing in her core that made her wanton.

Now here was Will, anxious and honorable, asking her to want him, and it took the air from her. She was being given a chance to enjoy this man, whose touch was fire, whose beauty was sunlight, whose words and glances stirred up feelings of longing more wonderful than any she had known before. This course was hers to choose.

Her fingers unpinned her lace diadem cap and tossed it atop his forgotten ruff. "Does this mean I can no longer be beneath you? Because I very much want to be."

His sigh of relief mixed with a low, sensual laugh. "That's my pirate wench." He wrapped her up in his arms, dipping his face toward hers. The sight of his signature half-smile set her blood aflame. "What else have you learned living among whores and thieves, I wonder?"

She kissed him long and slow, enjoying each new sensation: the scent of his skin, the scratch of his mustache, the taste of his lips. She combed her fingers through his beard, finding the sharp cliff of his jaw, the line where the soft skin of his neck began. She traced a path down his throat, along the edge of his doublet, up the side of his neck to explore the curve of his ear, the softness of his curls. She sought to memorize every inch of this new topography, each hill and valley.

He didn't rush her. The longer she kissed him, the closer he drew her against him, winding his arms around her waist and the small of her back. While she explored the tiny details of his face, he painted the shape of her body in broad strokes, his hands warm and strong as he smoothed them across her back, her shoulders, her waist and hips. She breathed him in, expanding into his arms, enjoying the luxurious feeling of being close to him with no agenda, no course, no limit.

She let the tip of her tongue slip against the seam of his lips, and he opened to her. He gripped her tighter as her arms went around his neck, and her body sizzled with energy, radiating out to the tips of her fingers. He moved his mouth to her cheek, her ear, her neck. She felt the gentle scrape of teeth and braced herself for pain, but he only kissed her there, leaving a trail of tingling scorch marks along her collar.

The room felt hot and close, though neither of them had built up the fire. Her breaths came faster, and she heard herself making sounds of pleasure as he tasted her skin. Craning her neck for more, her eyes landed on the bed. That was where her wicked mind urged her to take him, hoping he would sate this nebulous hunger inside her, but she felt a nervous twinge when she remembered how it had been with Matthew. Would there be pain? Would there be a child?

She gripped the silken locks of his hair between her fingers and tugged his face back to hers, eager to feel his lips again. He seemed content to kiss her forever; he had grazed and fondled her over the thick fabric of her gown, but he hadn't lifted her skirts or told her to lie back. Maybe she was moving too fast. Maybe she misunderstood what he wanted from her.

"Command me."

The words were a guttural whisper against her mouth, sending a pulse of desire between her legs. He entwined his fingers in her hair and slid his tongue over hers. She didn't answer with words, only arched against him and opened her mouth for more. A quiet groan rumbled in the back of his throat, and he gripped her tighter, angling her face so he could lick into her mouth, tongue decisive and thorough.

He stroked her bottom lip with a last flick of his tongue. His face hovered a hair's breadth from hers, teasing her, but he didn't kiss her again. "Tell me how I may serve you."

How *he* could serve *her*? Matthew had never asked such a question; she only knew how to serve herself. Her laugh came out too harsh. "How should I know?"

"Ah. I nearly forgot about your abysmal taste in lovers." He kissed the tip of her nose. "With one exception."

Hearing him refer to himself as her lover almost made up for the fact that he wasn't kissing her anymore. Instead, he spun her around and brushed her hair aside to press his lips to the back of her neck.

"If you do not know what you need," he murmured, "we must find it out."

He pulled out the ribbon securing her bodice and unlaced her stays, making her groan in satisfaction. He snaked his arms around her waist under the loose garments, closer to her skin than ever before.

"Is that all you require?" he said, nuzzling her nape.

She pulled her arms free of her sleeves and reached behind to unfasten her heavy skirts, dropping everything to the floor. Turning, she went to work on the buttons of his doublet. "Let us not stop there," she said, smirking at his slack-jawed expression.

When he stepped out of his breeches, they stood for a moment, staring at each other in nothing but shirt and hose. She liked him better this way, unadorned. His elegant finery fit him well, but it appeared to her like a suit of armor, shrouding his true form beneath ruffles and lace. She wanted the man from the ship. The sailor who hung from the ratlines. The poet who gazed out at the star-studded sea.

They had reached the point of no return. Maggie sat on the edge of her mattress, trembling with trepidation and desire, and reached for him. He took her hand and kissed the pad of her thumb, the heel of her palm, the inside of her wrist as he knelt on the floor in front of her. With both hands, he caressed her ankle and then her calf as he found the cuff of her stocking above her knee. His mouth followed it as he rolled it down, his mustache sweeping the tingling skin of her leg as he left a meandering trail of kisses all the way to her heel. He gave the same attention to her other leg, then trailed his lips back up and kissed the inside of her thigh. He kissed her again, finding a more sensitive piece of skin. Her head fell back as she lost herself in the tantalizing feeling of his mustache brushing her inner thigh.

"Tell me to touch you," he said, his breath a caress all on its own.

Swallowing, she nodded. "Touch me."

He pushed the hem of her chemise up her lap, and she watched his fingers follow the path his mouth had made along the inside of her leg until he reached her sex. Bracing his palm on her leg, he brushed her curls with his thumb, then dragged it down her wet folds. She drew in a sharp breath, shocked at so gentle a touch burning like fire.

He stroked her with one hand while he lifted her other leg to rest on his shoulder. "Tell me to taste you."

She furrowed her brow. "Taste me?"

His breath was hot between her legs before she realized what he planned to do. She tensed in abject mortification at the unexpected, electrifying feeling of his tongue. He had to stop this, but each time she opened her mouth to tell him, all that came out was a gasp. Her whole body shuddered as he licked and sucked. She turned to flotsam, oblivious to everything but the unholy feeling of his finger as he slipped it inside her, then brought a second to join it.

His fingers stroked her from inside while the tip of his tongue flicked over her clitoris, each movement winding an unbearable spring inside her abdomen. Her breath came in quick gasps until the tightness snapped in a burst of terrible pleasure.

She stifled the sob that threatened to escape her throat, instead emitting a pitiful, kitten-like squeak.

Will lifted his head, wiping his mouth and beard on his sleeve. His grin was wicked as he looked up at her. "Silence is a paltry reward for a man's labor. If you are at a loss for words next time, you might consider screaming my name."

Dazed, she watched him get to his feet and pull his shirt over his head. The only clothing he still wore were his orange stockings, secured by garters straining against the powerful muscles of his thighs. He sat beside her to remove them, and she stared, fascinated, at the erection emerging from a mass of black curls.

"How many have given that to you?" he said, dropping a stocking to the floor.

She looked up at him, eyes wide. "*That*? None!"

"None? How is it I am the first to make a woman as delectable as you die the little death?"

"Oh, *that*." She dared to brush her fingertips over his naked thigh, itching to know how he would feel in her hand. "Nay, that was not the first time. Ellen taught me about *la petite mort*."

His head snapped up, a stocking dangling in his grip. "You and Ellen…?"

She giggled, blushing at the absurd notion. "Nothing like! She instructed me, but I did it myself."

His eyelids drooped as he made a sound in the back of his throat. In the next moment, he had her on her back and was kissing her, hard, demanding. The new taste on his lips belonged to her, she realized, the thought a fleeting one in the torrent of need coursing through her.

His rough palms slid over her bare hips and across her stomach, fingertips grazing the bottoms of her breasts. He tugged at her chemise and she raised herself off the bed to help him pull it off.

Before he could distract her again, she closed her hand around him, and her sex pulsed to think of him filling her.

He sucked in a breath and looked at her with heavy-lidded eyes. A slow, lazy smirk spread across his face.

"Do not make some roguish remark, as I know you are about to do." She narrowed her eyes at him, tightening her grip as a warning.

He pushed her back down on the bed, resting one muscular forearm beside her head. "Then stop my mouth, Maggie."

His kisses were a spell, a potion, fascinating and inebriating. Every movement of his lips and tongue matched hers or anticipated hers, as if he could see into her mind. Drunk on him, she rubbed him against her wetness, desperate to give him the same pleasure he gave her.

Except his pleasure might have consequences for her.

"I do not want a child."

He looked down at her, curious. "Ever? Or tonight?"

"Tonight."

"Then this is a path we must not follow."

He was hard in her grip; he must want her. So how could he bear to stop? He should be offering alternatives, begging her to take him, assuring her that her concerns were foolish.

"You could pull away before…"

"There is still a risk." He traced her features, following the curve of her cheek, the line of her jaw. He lowered his head to nip at her earlobe. "Ellen's daughter was conceived in just such a way." Feeling her tense, he lifted his head and added, "Not by me."

She hadn't known it wasn't a guarantee. Feeling foolish, she released her hold on him, the air cooling around them.

With the tips of his fingers, as soft as a whisper, he outlined her lips. No one had ever looked at her like this, with curiosity and reverence and need. "Let us not stop on that account. I am certain you can find your pleasure at least once more before the dawn." His fingers trailed down her throat and rounded the curve of her breast.

"What of your pleasure?"

"You are my pleasure."

He kissed her, lips warm and soft and full. One kiss became another, and another, and she ached for him. He found her hand and entwined their fingers together, trapping her arm over her head before moving his mouth down to her breast. He placed a ring of kisses on her sensitive skin before drawing her tight nipple into his mouth and suckling her. She stroked his hair with her free hand and tried to pull her other out of his grip, but he kept it pinned.

She whimpered. What had she been thinking about? Why had they stopped a moment ago? It couldn't be important. When she felt his finger seeking her entrance, she forgot everything.

"Make love to me," she begged.

"What do you think I'm doing?" His tongue flicked her nipple as he moved his finger in a slow, firm rhythm.

She gasped and squirmed. "I need you inside me."

"Hmm." He raised his head to look her in the eye. "And what *I* need does not signify."

Instinct told her to shift her body, and the pressure of his finger shifted too, making her gasp at the newfound intensity of the pleasure.

"You do not wish to know what I need?"

How could he expect an answer from her while he fingered a relentless tune between her legs, playing her as recklessly as he played his fiddle? She licked her lips and captured one panting breath to murmur, "What do you need?"

His nimble fingers slid in and out of her while the heel of his palm provided the vibrato. Her nerves sang for him, a steady, incandescent crescendo.

"I need to see you come again."

She shook her head against the pillow of her loosened hair, unable to bear the torture but desperate for it. She closed her eyes against the white-hot light, and when it took her, she cried out a wordless moan. His fingers slowed as she ceased bucking beneath him.

His voice was light with amusement. "'Tis pronounced *Will*, but methinks you were closer that time."

When she opened her eyes, he was staring at her, a half smile on his lips. She attempted to smile back, but she couldn't be sure her muscles were obeying. "Does it feel like that for you?" she slurred.

"Good? Aye, that it does."

She watched, mesmerized, as he sucked the taste of her from his fingers, his cock twitching against her leg. Before tonight, he had been her kidnapper, her captain, her friend. This was a side of him she had never seen, and everything about it drove her mad with need. She wanted more. She wanted him undone.

He freed her hand and lounged on his side, his head propped on his fist. Rolling to face him, she let her gaze roam over the long lines of his body. His legs were shapely and dark with hair, and between his legs, his cock was long and hard and inviting. She reached for it, stroking the length of it, rubbing her thumb over the soft tip. Each new movement made him grunt or sigh or gasp. It felt powerful having such a strong man under her control.

"Can I do for you what you did for me?" She moved her grip along his shaft, slow, gentle, just as Ellen had once described it to her.

Will's hand closed around her wrist. "I assure you, you can."

"But you do not want it?"

"A word has not been invented to describe how I want it." He brought her hand to his face and kissed her knuckles. "But I vowed you would only know satisfaction."

"I remember no such vow."

"'Tis a vow I made to myself… many months ago."

If he wished to dissuade her from touching him, admitting a months-long infatuation was not the way to go about it. She stroked the fine hair of his chest. "After how thoroughly you have ravished me, 'tis only fair I do the same to you."

"What is your obsession with fairness?" She had meant to make him smile, but it seemed to have the opposite effect. "Why must it be 'this' for 'that,' and not a gift freely given?"

There was some truth to it, but tonight had nothing to do with that. How could he lay there, teasing her with the beautiful sensuousness of his naked body, and wonder at her motives? It wasn't gratitude that made her want him.

Pushing at his shoulder, she coaxed him onto his back. He looked up at her with exasperation. "I want only pleasure for you tonight," he muttered.

She brushed the backs of her fingers against his cock, and he hardened at her touch. "You are my pleasure."

The sight of him in her hand, the soft skin sliding like rich silk under her fingers, fascinated her. She moved her fist over him, attuned to his every flinch and breath as she learned what he liked. He pulled her down to kiss him, fisting a hand in her hair, his low moans vibrating against her lips. She trailed kisses down his neck and collarbone and made her way across his chest, flicking her tongue against his nipple, grazing her lips over his ribs, nuzzling the line of hair that led to the cock in her fist.

Poised above him, she hesitated. Ages ago, a lifetime ago, this had been a tool to render a cruel man harmless. She waited to feel disgust, either at herself or at the memory of Matthew, but it was eclipsed by the powerful lust that had transfigured her from the moment Will kissed her. She was the woman in the stories, the most wanton of widows, a creature of hedonistic pleasures. The feast before her made her mouth water.

He groaned when she took him in her mouth, swirling her tongue around the head to taste the salty tang of the moisture seeping from him. He shuddered, so she did it again, and again, making him arch his back and push further into her.

She thought of how he would soon tense beneath her, unable to speak, too overcome with the pleasure she gave him. She thought of the explosion of colors he would see behind his eyes when she brought him to completion. She thought of him twitching and limp, all because of her.

Yes, she was wicked.

She sucked him into her mouth, pressing her tongue flat against the bottom of his shaft, and she kept her fingers wrapped around the base to stroke him in time. He moaned and dug his fingers into her hair, urging her to move on him. She obliged, sliding over him again and again.

"Maggie," he said, voice tight, "I may come."

Good, she thought, and sucked him harder. His body was becoming tense, she could tell. She longed to touch him, kiss him, watch him as he found his release, but she was responsible for that release and she could not stop now.

"I cannot..." The breathy uncertainty in his voice was unbearably erotic. "'Sblood..." He was moving beneath her, hips thrusting as she brought him ever closer. Finally, he ground out, "Fie, Maggie!" and emptied himself into her mouth.

She stayed with him through the final shuddering and swallowed, then watched his eyes flutter open.

"Saint Peter, is that you? Surely this is heaven."

Stretching out on her side next to him, she smoothed a hand over his chest. "Methinks such acts are forbidden in heaven. It feels... depraved."

He chuckled, a low rumble she could feel under her palm. His heavy arm fell over her as he pulled her close, fitting her face into the hollow of his throat and kissing the top of her head. "Hell, then. I care not, as long as you are there."

38

SHE HANDED HIM a cup of pear cider, the only refreshment she had to hand. Entertaining men was not a typical use for her bedchamber, so she cast about for places to sit and things to eat, all while blushing at the less-than-pristine state of it. To his credit, Will made himself at home on his stool in front of the fire, and he accepted the perry as if it were a cup of Madeira.

He had held her for a few luxurious minutes, playing with her hair while they both allowed their breathing to return to normal. She whined when his warmth left her, but he only chuckled and pulled her wool blanket over her before throwing his shirt on and tending to the fire. There was a cheerful blaze in the hearth by the time she had collected herself enough to join him, wearing her usual night shift.

"I thank you for building up the fire," she said, cupping her perry in both hands and settling onto the folded blanket she had thrown on the floor.

"I am required to have a knack for it." He picked up the iron poker and prodded a log. "'Tis the family trade, after all."

She stared at him as the flames illuminated his smug smile. He looked pleased enough with himself that she was sure he had made some sort of joke, but…

Rolling her eyes, she groaned. "'Stokes.' Terrible."

He propped the poker beside the hearth. "We need no longer observe the polite formality of laughing at jests, I see."

"When you make one, I will laugh at it."

He slid off the stool to sit beside her on the floor, and she fit herself easily into his right side, letting her head rest on his shoulder. How comfortable this gentle contact was, and how necessary it had become in such a short time. She had sat with

Matthew like this on occasion, but their relationship was characterized by furtive couplings and stolen kisses. She couldn't even fathom sitting like this with Robert.

He sipped from his mug as they watched the fire, but hers rested on the floor, forgotten in her limp fingers.

After a moment, his gentle voice rumbled through her. "What thoughts have you so silent?"

She let out a breath. "I was thinking of Robert. You will wish to make a jest about thinking of other men while I sit beside you, but I beg you will not. I have not the stomach for it."

"You once accused me of being too feeling, yet now you fear I will laugh at your distress. Methinks you do not know me as well as you claim to."

She stiffened, mortified that he remembered her gaffe. Her instinct was to argue, but how could she? This very evening, hadn't she made excuses for each touch and kind word? Hadn't she half-expected him to stay behind at the party while she wandered home alone? She had constructed a facsimile Will Stokes out of her own insecurities, and she brought him out whenever it suited her.

"I have thought often of that night, of what I said." She rotated her mug on the stone hearth, needing something to look at that wasn't him. "I knew even then I hurt you somehow. I broke something between us."

"Hurt me? How could such praise hurt me?"

"In faith, I do not know. I have tried to make sense of it, but I cannot. We were rarely at ease together after that."

He had become still beside her. She looked up at him, their faces close enough that if he turned his head, she could kiss him. But he stared into the fire, his jaw tight.

"That was my doing." He leaned away from her and took a swig from his mug. She missed his warmth, despite the hot fire. "Your pronouncement of my eagerness to help you—to *rescue* you, I believe you said... I did not understand the truth of it until that moment."

"You regretted it?"

"Nay, forsooth..."

"What, then? What offense did I give?"

"None," he insisted. "You only revealed what I had been too blind to see. But you were betrothed—" He stopped himself with a shake of his head and looked down into his mug. "I have spent a year hiding my feelings from you. You'll forgive me if I have trouble speaking them now."

The twisting flames in the hearth were all she could bear to look at. Her throat felt tight, as if she were about to cry, but she didn't feel sad, exactly. She didn't know what to feel.

A *year*.

It was impossible not to return to the events of the summer and pore over each memory for proof of what he claimed. She found examples everywhere, diamonds scattered among the rocks. Every time he pulled strings for her, stood up for her, teased her, he told her how he felt. She had loved Matthew for a time, and it made her blind, not only to Will, but to the knowledge there might be another way to love and be loved. A better way.

Then, just when the scales fell from her eyes, she demanded Will make her a member of his crew, and it tied both their hands. It was no wonder he wanted to distance himself from her.

She had so many questions she wanted to ask him. When he approached her in Rotherhithe about helping with the purser duties, had it been an excuse to see her once more before they sailed? Was their Midsummer dance a lapse in judgment, or a resolution to enjoy what little opportunity for happiness their short lives allowed?

Could he ever forgive her for being such a fool?

Before she could ask any of them, he cleared his throat. "You said you were thinking about Robert."

Had she? It didn't seem important now. "I was only thinking I should have known better. It was always a possibility we would meet at such an event. I should not have taken the risk."

"I am sorry for my part in it, but 'twas too small a risk to heed. What are the odds a man from Bristol should appear at a private fete a hundred miles away?"

"It hardly matters. He has seen me, and he will tell my family."

"Why would he be in contact with your family?"

"Because my father is a peer, and I assume he will be grateful to Robert for delivering news of his prodigal daughter." She grunted and brought her cup to her lips. "Whether the news is welcome or not."

"Is your father so uncaring?"

"My father was likely as saddened by the news of my disappearance as he was relieved. 'Tis costly to feed and clothe a widowed aunt *and* a widowed daughter. I had few prospects before I was married, and almost none when my husband died. I would have remained a burden to my family for a long while."

"I do not understand. Your husband was a gentleman. Did he leave you nothing?"

She had trained herself not to think of it for weeks at a time, because it made her feel stupid and guilty to remember what she had done. "Not… exactly. I was entitled to my widow's third."

"Your widow's third?" He put down his mug. "You have a dower moldering away somewhere and you have not considered retrieving it?"

His posture had changed. He was alert, energized. He turned his body toward her and met her eyes for the first time since she had refused to laugh at his joke about the fire.

This was how Matthew must have behaved when he hatched his plan to marry her.

"Alas, I do not," she said, more brusquely than he deserved. "My father required me to give him the control of it until I married, and I departed for France a fortnight after I signed the missive. My family believes me dead, I vow, and thus my dower died with me."

"Yet here you are, hale and hearty. Go before your husband's solicitor and demand your due."

"I cannot!"

"Why not? Sherman knows you are alive, and surely he will resurrect you if you do not. No doubt he will do all in his power to ensure you cannot reclaim your fortune. You must strike first, before he can undermine you."

You, he said, not *we*. It was a subtle distinction, but it soothed the warning voice insisting Will was no better than Matthew. "Can he do such a thing? 'Tis a third of his father's property. He cannot hide it or dispose of it."

"He can and he will, if he is clever enough, or if he employs a competent solicitor. I have met the man only twice, but I would bet my life his favorite color is gold."

She considered. Every so often over the last year, when her purse was light and her troubles were heavy, she returned to the memory of standing before her father, pitiful and weak, caving to his will as she always had. That was the version of herself she despised the most.

"My father remains the steward of my affairs. Should I appear now, 'twould only benefit him."

Will pulled a face as if he found the idea ridiculous. "'Tis yours. Take it back."

She shook her head skeptically. "I will speak to Bisset's solicitor in the morning and see what advice he would give." Then she narrowed her eyes at him. "The discovery of my dower has pricked your interest."

"I am a pirate, Maggie. I have made a career out of preying on whoreson lords with more money than decency. The only difference between Robert Sherman and my usual quarry is the flag under which he sails."

"He is not your 'quarry' at all. 'Tis not piracy, 'tis… bookkeeping."

"All the better, for that is your area of expertise." He looked at her for a moment, cocking his head. "The means to purchase your independence has been within reach all this time. Why did you not seize it?"

His tone was gentle, his expression open, but she felt attacked. It was only because she knew how foolish she had been, and she hated admitting it. "Why should I have endeavored to open a door that I, myself, shut and locked? I had not the means to defend myself against my father. To return to him on my knees would mean returning to the sort of woman he required me to be." The thought of it was making her throat tight, so she took a steadying breath. "And giving up all I had gained. Davies, Ellen… You were all truer friends than any I had known before. How could I leave you behind and go back to a place where my worth was measurable in pounds sterling?"

He shifted so he was once more nestled at her side with his arm around her. Kissing her temple, he rested his cheek on the top of her head. "Methinks you have it rearward. With your dower, you can buy your freedom. Your family has no claim on it, and unless you allow it, they have no claim on you, either. Take your plunder and make your own way."

Maggie swiped at a tear that escaped unbidden from her eye. "But it is not mine. I have never had anything that is mine, until I began earning my own living. I do not…" Her voice broke, and she took a shuddering breath. "I do not want to be Sir John's widow for the rest of my life."

"That cannot be altered, but 'tis only one of the many things you are. And if this contract has attached to it a dower, there is no shame in accepting it. 'Tis not an identity. 'Tis bookkeeping."

She laughed despite the tears. He made it sound so reasonable, so doable. Why had she lived in fear of it?

"I am resolved," she said, her voice only shaking a little. She dried her face with the cuff of her sleeve before laying a hand on his knee. "But I am afraid your services as a pirate will not be needed. This is my plunder."

"'Twas I who put the idea in your head. What am I owed for my contribution?"

"Very well. Name your fee."

"Ten pounds."

She laughed. "Th'art mad! Two pounds. Even that is over-generous."

"Nine."

She felt his breath on the outer rim of her ear. He pulled her hair away from her neck and brushed his nose against the skin behind her ear.

"Two."

He chuckled low and soft, and she felt it rumble through her. "Seven."

His lips were warm on her neck, and she felt her skin flush. She reached up to play with his hair. "Two."

"Are you familiar with the concept of haggling?" The arm around her waist tightened, and his thumb brushed the curve of her breast.

She took in a sharp breath. "More than you, I vow."

He stroked a line from her ribs to her hip with the backs of his fingers, then retraced it in the other direction, his feather-light fingertips skipping on the loose fabric of her shift. His mouth still at her neck, he kissed her once, twice, three times, a constellation to navigate by. For the fourth, he parted his lips and flicked the tip of his tongue over her skin. Her body's reaction was immediate, her breaths coming shallow as she anticipated each new shiver.

"I admit," she said, mind hazy, "your way of haggling is much more diverting than mine."

Will tilted her face up to his with one finger under her chin, and she melted into him as his mouth claimed hers. This slow, decadent kiss was no less potent for being unhurried. In fact, the delicious slide of his tongue as he savored her put her in mind of the obscene way he had feasted on her earlier, and the ache between her legs returned, just as sharp as if he hadn't already spun her off twice. Could it happen a third time?

Overwhelmed, seeking relief, she took the kiss deeper, wishing she could consume him. He made a low sound of pleasure in the back of his throat and leaned into her, the hand that had been supporting him now free to slip under her shift and smooth over her bare leg. Then it was easy to overpower him and push him to the floor, straddle his hips, run her hands over the hard muscles of his chest, push his shirt aside and kiss his neck. Needing more, she suckled his skin, licked the hollow of his collarbone, obsessed with the salt and satin of him.

This was what had been missing with the others. It was this addiction, this consuming need, too sublime to comprehend, too powerful to resist. Would the fever break when this was over? Or was it a wasting disease, certain to leave her a pitiful husk when he went back to sea?

Reluctantly, she braced her hands on his chest and pushed herself up. He watched her, head tilted in a question, and she gazed down at his dark hazel eyes, his tousled curls, the way the firelight gilded his face like a heathen idol.

"When do you return to the ship?"

He smirked. "Finished with me already?"

She snaked a finger along the furred cleft of his chest. "Far from it."

"Good. 'Twould be a shameful waste if you did not use me a few more times before tossing me on the heap."

Her hand stilled, even though she was certain he was joking. Almost certain. "Is that what you want me to do?"

"With my whole heart," he said, his fingers digging into her thighs. "Use me, Maggie."

That wasn't what she meant. "What if I have not the heart to toss you on the heap?" She took in an unsteady breath and steeled her resolve. "What if I wish to keep you?"

He tucked his elbows back and used them to raise his head and shoulders off the floor. With his brows knitted together, his smile was bewildered. "Fie, Maggie, if you throw me out, I will break to pieces."

She clambered off him and sat at his side, trembling. The distance helped to clear her mind, to assure her whatever was said next would be fueled by sense, not desire. "When do you return to the ship?" she asked again.

He sat up and arranged the hem of his shirt to cover the tops of his thighs. "I have a short list of tasks to complete on the morrow, but the rest shall fall to Padraig and Hargreve. She will be ready for winter in less than a fortnight, God willing."

"Your voyage is done? So early?"

"Only a sennight or so. The timing of Treningham's invitation was awkward, but 'twas a gainful summer, and the lads were content to start spending their coin a few days earlier than usual."

She had been preparing to be bereft when he set sail again, but the thought of having him in town for the whole winter made her heart glow. "So I may keep you after all."

"If that is your will."

Smirking, she crawled to him, and he watched with wolfish eyes as she settled herself across his lap again, groaning when she ground against him. She stroked her fingers through his beard and gave it a teasing tug. "My Will?"

The corners of his eyes crinkled as he gazed up at her. With one fingertip, she traced the line under his eye that curved over his cheek, her favorite of his many laugh lines. He caught her hand and pressed his lips to the center of her palm. "That I am," he murmured.

When the sky lightened to gray and the fire in the hearth died down to embers, she watched from her window as he slipped through the front door of the house and slunk down the silent street.

She retrieved her blanket from where it lay in a tangled heap on the floor and took herself to bed, but not to sleep. Instead, she lay awake reliving every touch, every kiss, every word, every smile, her heart full to bursting with the joy of it.

39

MAGGIE WOULD HIRE a horse to bring her the hundred miles to Bristol. She packed enough essentials for a few nights at roadside inns, one night each in Bristol and Gloucester, and the tedious return journey. She also had a letter from Bisset's solicitor, whose advice had convinced her the trip would be worth her while.

Abraham, who had become more Maggie's personal guard than Bisset's, was willing to accompany her for the fee she offered him. She selected a sturdy mount for him and paid the stable keeper a few shillings to ensure both horses were saddled and waiting when she departed early the next morning. Her purse felt lighter already, and soon the costs of food, lodging, and stabling would empty it.

Then she sent young Ned, decked out in a tidy blue suit, to deliver a note to Will.

It took her the better part of an hour to decide the subject, and in the end she kept the message brief and informative. "I have met with Bisset's solicitor," she wrote, "and he assures me the law will support my suit in Bristol. I journey by hired horse on the morrow and will return to Town within a sennight. I would thank you for your wise advice if you vowed to remain humble, but as I know you will not, I only send this promissory missive to acknowledge my debt to you in the amount of two pounds sterling silver."

With shaking hands, she added, "It will grieve me to leave you," before folding and sealed it, sure another moment of reflection would have her scratching out the words. Last night was too wonderful to be anything but a dream.

Ned returned a few hours later with a reply in Will's florid hand.

"Your servant delights that his mistress shall not be grieved. Certes in your haste you have neglected to note the location of the livery stable from which you ride and your hour of leaving. You may therefore look for me outside your lodgings at dawn, that I may have the honor of escorting you hence. If such an hour be displeasing, mayhap you will rather I wait on you tonight, in which event I am pleased to devise sundry sport for our pastime. Your most humble servant, Wm. Stokes."

The poor message boy slumped, exhausted and dusty, into a chair by the fire. She couldn't very well send him back with another reply, even though Will deserved one for his cheek. It was for the best: the way the heat pooled in her core at the thought of Will's "sundry sport" made her certain she would invite him to stay the night. Mistress Routledge would throw her out if she did.

There would be plenty of time to chastise him on the journey.

"He's not much to look at, is he?" Will said the next morning as he loaded his things into the panniers flanking the horse's wide hipbones.

Maggie allowed the stable hand to help her onto her sidesaddle. From this height, it felt natural to give him an imperious glare. "Forgive me for not rearranging every plan of mine to accommodate your lofty standards."

He smirked up at her and got himself onto the horse with his usual grace. They trotted through London as the sky brightened and the city awoke.

"First to Bristol?"

"I have sent word to Master Chauncey, Sir John's steward, asking him to meet us Tuesday afternoon. We will stay the night at the Silver Starling, then continue on to Duntsford Priory."

"And you sent a note there as well?"

"I did." She screwed up her nose. "I expect 'twill be an awkward reunion."

"What will you tell them?"

"I... have not decided."

"What sort of man is Lord Donwell? Will he slaughter the fatted calf to celebrate your return?"

"He was never a tender man," she said, the words careful as she considered. "Mayhap he grows soft in his dotage. My absence is like to have had some effect as well. I worry his pride was sore wounded by my adventure, and that he will not forgive it."

"Then I am sorry for him."

They lapsed into silence while she envisioned the reunion at Duntsford Priory. The more she imagined it, the crueler the fantasies became, manifestations of her anxieties and her own unresolved feelings for the man who had raised her without seeming to like her.

Will's voice brought her out of her reverie. "What role may I play to best serve you? Silent bodyguard? Doting husband?"

"I might inspire some small amount of mercy if I may prove I have not been loose in the world and unmarried all this time. That is, if you can bear to continue the charade for a few more days."

"That will increase my fee."

"How—What fee?" she sputtered, laughing at the absurdity. "You insinuated yourself into my plans with nary a 'by your leave'!"

"You promised me two pounds."

"Very well. What additional fee do you require?"

Will squinted up at the morning sky, appearing to make a calculation. "Two… nay, that is too dear. Only one of your kisses."

A shiver ran through her, and the memory of his lips returned to her watering mouth. Her voice came out an unattractive squeak. "Three."

He sighed. "I cannot compete with such expert negotiation. Five, and no more."

"Done." She wanted to reach over and pay him at once, to draw him down off his horse and let his hands resume their exploration of her. The first traveler's rest felt a long way away.

The miles flew by with such an amiable travel partner. Once she landed on the approach she would take with her family, what sort of story they might deign to hear, she and Will put their heads together. With a generous helping of his flair for the dramatic, they workshopped the romantic epic of Maggie's adventure, anchoring each fantasy in a truth so she had some likelihood of being believed.

They rehearsed their parts and laughed at the absurdity of it, and when the story was as watertight as they could make it, they turned to other topics: stories about their childhoods, their thoughts on religion and politics, their opinions of the best taverns on the north side of the Thames. At noon and at suppertime, they chatted over their meals at identical, unremarkable roadside inns, tired and sore from the journey, but not out of things to say.

That night, the innkeeper showed them to a private bedchamber. It was an expense she hadn't planned for: if she had brought Abraham, they would have bedded up with other weary travelers to save coin. But Will insisted, slid a few shillings to the innkeeper, and looked at Maggie with an expression that made her stomach flip.

The room was too small. He would see every flaw, hear every snore. The marriage might be a sham, but the wedding night was real.

"Not too sore, are you?"

The ropes creaked as Will dropped onto the bed. "Ask me again on the morrow. You?"

She rubbed her hip and stretched her torso, feeling her abdominal muscles protest. It had been hard work holding herself upright in the ridiculous sidesaddle all day. "I am of half a mind to don breeches on the morrow. We would arrive sooner if I rode astride."

Unable to put it off any longer, she untied the lace at the front of her bodice.

The room grew still.

"Have you need of any assistance?"

His voice was low and silky. If the serpent spoke like that, she would have eaten the apple, too.

"I chose this frock so I could dress and undress myself," she said.

He was gazing hungrily at her, his skin glowing gold in the lamplight, his collar parted to reveal the dark hair scattered across his chest.

She took pity on herself. "I brought another, though, that will require aid."

"Your servant, my lady." He leaned back, supporting himself with his hands behind him. The collar of his shirt parted further. "I hesitate to call you the more miserly of us two, but at least there is a benefit to your frugality."

As he spoke, she tossed the lace and bodice on the table and draped her skirts over a chair. "In addition to saving coin, you mean?"

"No maidservant. No one to uphold the rules of propriety."

There was nothing proper about the way his eyes raked over her. She came to stand between his knees and traced her fingers over his bare collarbone, as she had wanted to do all day. His eyes were level with her chest, but he craned his neck to look up at her.

"Who will protect my virtue?" he murmured.

"What virtue?"

He fell back on the bed, pulling her atop him and kissing her while still laughing. She set herself to the business at hand, but after only a moment, he put his hands on her shoulders and held her at bay.

"That is five."

She gazed at him in confusion before she remembered the conversation from this morning. "I am a generous mistress."

He rolled her onto her back, pinning her under him. "That is bad business, my lady. You must have me earn my fee."

"Must I?"

"Set me a task. Give me a command."

"What if you find the task distasteful?"

"For you, I would do anything."

She squirmed beneath him. "You must not speak in such poetic terms, lest I believe you."

"Believe me." He took her mouth in one breathless kiss. When he pulled back, his eyes were dark, ravenous, wicked. "Set me a task, and I will tell you my fee."

A sharp, surprised laugh escaped her throat. "You cannot demand employment and set your own wages! *That* is bad business."

He ignored her, instead ducking his head and feathering kisses along her jaw while his hand went to cup her breast. Within seconds, he had changed her mind.

In a small, tight voice, she said, "Peace! Do you wish to hear my command or no?"

With a final tug of her earlobe with his teeth, he lifted his head. His fingers toyed with the taut peak of her breast as he looked down at her. "What is your pleasure?"

She was about to make a fool of herself, and she nearly backed down, but desire made her bold and his tantalizing fingers made her desperate. "Tell me a story. A fairytale." He raised an eyebrow, skeptical, and she explained. "Tell me how it would be if I took you inside me. If you cannot show me, you must tell me."

Will stared down at her, the hand at her breast stilling. Her stomach fluttered as the corner of his mouth turned up in a wicked smile. "This is your command?"

"It is. What fee do you require?"

"The standard rate, methinks: my name, eked out from between these perfect lips..." He rubbed his thumb across her bottom lip, tugging it down. She couldn't resist closing her mouth around his finger, eliciting from him a sharp breath. "My name, spoken as a prayer when I make you come."

The sensual timbre of his voice, dropping to a growl on the final words, was her undoing. She fisted her hand in his hair, and their mouths crashed together, tongues wet, teeth sharp, his mustache a still-foreign, ever-alluring texture that scratched at her skin. He pushed her shirt up past her waist, over her breasts, and she helped him pull it off and cast it aside.

His doublet and shirt came next, but he stopped before taking off his breeches, instead pausing to look down at her where she lay naked on the unfamiliar bed. "God-a-mercy," he muttered. "A painter would sell his soul for this view."

She blushed, covering her breasts with her arm.

Will smiled. "Forgive me—I am distracted. Once upon a time..."

"Now I feel foolish. Prithee, do not start it so."

"No? How am I to start?" He slid his hand up her thigh, grazing the curls between her legs, and came down to stretch out beside her. "Shall I tell you how I would touch you? How I would coax your legs apart and slide my finger along your seam?" He performed each action as he said it, and she trembled at the way his entrancing voice augmented each touch. "I would find you wet for me, of course, for you are a generous mistress. I would swell at the thought of it."

A demanding voice she didn't recognize interrupted him. "Show me," she said.

When he untied the front of his breeches, his erection sprang loose, its head ruddy and weeping. She watched him as he finished undressing, remembering the satisfying sensation of it against her tongue, smooth and firm and musky. If only he would touch her again now, feel how much wetter she was at the thought of him, so she could prove the power he wielded over her.

"I would kneel between your legs..." He crept onto the bed, and she opened her knees, unashamed. "And worship at your altar..." The humming sound he made when his fingers found her was like a hymn.

Somehow, while he stroked her slick folds, she managed to find her voice. "'Thou shalt have no other gods,'" she teased.

"Yours are the only commandments I obey." He slid his hands under her, cupping a cheek in each palm. "This?" Ducking his head, he dragged his tongue through her folds, making her clench and twitch. "This is my eucharist."

"*God's death,*" she groaned.

"Then I would stand before your gates, and your heavenly cunt would welcome me, inch by inch." He slid two fingers inside her, and she squirmed, taking them deeper. "I would watch us joining and marvel at how deep you took me, how tight you held me. I would withdraw just so I could enter you again, just for the joy of it, and you would sigh and pant and call out my name."

She *was* sighing and panting as he curled his fingers and pumped them into her, so desperate for more that calling out his name wasn't enough. "Will… Prithee, Will…"

"And aye, my cock would give you pleasure as I filled you up over and over, but then I would touch you here…" She jolted at the sudden pleasure and rolled her hips against his thumb as he rubbed her exactly where she wanted him to. "You would ride me until you saw stars, and I would make a home in your hot cunt until you saw God. And even then I wouldn't relent."

His voice was husky and low, his words coming faster as the pace of his hand increased. "Because as soon as you came, I would lay back and set you down onto my hard cock and thrust up into you, and your breasts would sway, so ripe and sweet, and I would raise my head and suckle you until you came again."

Maggie shut her eyes tight and rode his hand, manic with desire. His voice hypnotized her, made her see stars, made her fling her hand out for something to hold on to—and she knew what she wanted to find. She encircled him tightly with her fingers, greedy for his hard girth, and stroked fast, if only to gift him half the agony he gave her.

He leaned down and closed his mouth around the tip of her breast, sucking hungrily, threatening to devour her. Each pull and lick sent a shock through her, each spark feeding the inferno of her desire. Her muscles clenched; the ache was too much to bear.

He tore his face away from her breast, and his voice was tight as he continued his wicked story. "But you are a cruel mistress, and you would go to your hands and knees for yet more, and—God forgive me, but I am a glutton for you—Like an animal, I would take you from behind, and your cunt would be so tight, Maggie—" His voice broke on her name, but he didn't stop the movement of his hand, and neither did she. "So tight, but I would—*fie*—I would fuck your cunt until you begged me to come inside you at last, and by God, Maggie, I would oblige you."

"Christ, Will!" Her orgasm ripped through her, tumbling her helplessly about, the swollen muscles of her sex clenching around his fingers. In her delirium, she felt him thrust into her tightened fist, and she opened her eyes in time to watch him spurt onto her stomach, his face twisted in ecstasy.

After he had cleaned up, Will stretched out on the bed beside her. Maggie hadn't moved, couldn't move, but she attempted to flutter her eyes open when he gathered her against him. The warm press of his skin all along hers, the breeze of his breath on her neck, was enough to lull her to sleep. But before she slipped away, she heard him whisper, "And they lived happily together forever after."

40

AROUND NOON ON the third day, they turned onto the street separating the shops and ordinaries of Bristol from the sparkling green ribbon of the Avon. The Silver Starling was unchanged, the bird on its sign retraced with fresh paint, the windows clean, the roof well thatched.

"Does this not remind you of the night we met?" she sighed, taking his arm as they approached the inn's front door. "You, standing in the moonlight, looking dashing and dangerous. And me, frozen in terror with a knife at my back."

"You are a wicked minx," he muttered as he pushed the door open.

The dining room was warm and smoky, most tables populated by local shopkeepers taking their midday meal. She spotted Stephen Brown setting down a pair of mugs at a patron's table. While she stood in the doorway taking it in, Anne Brown emerged from the kitchen with a tray. The woman glanced up at them and called, "Be with you presently!"

Maggie nudged Will toward an empty table. She peered around the room, seeing ghosts everywhere she looked. That was where the musicians sang the haunting lament for the lover lost at sea. That was where Alinor sat griping about everything and everyone.

She nodded toward the far corner, where even now a card game was being played. "Over there is where Robert Sherman sold me to you."

He rolled his eyes. "Are you enjoying this?"

"I would rather laugh than weep."

Will reached across the table and covered her hand. She entwined their fingers. All it took was the brush of his thumb to set her heart fluttering.

"Good day, sir, madam. Are you needing a room, or just a hot meal?"

Maggie snapped her attention to Anne Brown, who stood beside their table with an empty tray at her side.

The woman's eyes widened. "Lady Sherman!"

"Well met, Mistress Brown." Maggie stood and attempted a smile.

Anne laid the tray on the table, her eyes never leaving Maggie. She examined her from the top of her head to the hem of her skirt, as if to convince herself she was real. "We thought you... We thought not to see you again."

"I imagine I caused a stir the last time I was here."

"Aye, indeed, my lady! You being snatched from under all our noses, 'twas the talk of the city for weeks after."

"I will not claim to have emerged unscathed, but I am as you see me. I hope we may yet be welcome here."

Anne's face softened. "You are most welcome, my lady." She nodded at Will and added, "As are any of milady's friends."

Maggie turned to her sham husband, who was surveying the conversation with his patented half-smile. "Will, this is Anne Brown. Mistress Brown, may I present my husband, Captain William Stokes?"

He stood and bowed his head. "I am glad to know you, Mistress Brown. I understand your friendship was important to my wife while she resided in Bristol."

Maggie mentioned Anne once or twice on the journey, but she had not referred to it as an "important friendship." Yet another detail about her he had filed away for future use.

Anne blushed. "Well, Lady—Mistress, um..."

"Stokes." The easy way he supplied his name for hers made Maggie's stomach flip.

"Mistress Stokes was important to us as well," Anne finished. "Stephen will want to see you. Sit while I fetch you something to eat." She picked up the tray and turned to leave, then pivoted back, looked between Maggie and Will, blushed, and bustled away.

After their meal, which Stephen Brown only grudgingly accepted payment for, Maggie paid a boy to take a message to Master Chauncey letting him know she had arrived in town. While they waited, they walked the city streets, Maggie pointing out her favorite shops and memories. The three years of her marriage had been a difficult period, and the strangest details impressed themselves onto her troubled mind: the ornamental wood carving on that door lintel, or the misshapen branch of that sycamore.

She could not bring herself to take him down the tree-lined road to Sir John's house.

Thomas Chauncey invited them to his home, providing the direction in case Maggie had forgotten it in the year and a half since their last arranged meeting. Following the same path from the Starling to the Chaunceys' residence was surreal. A chill went through her as she passed the spot where Padraig had grabbed her and Will had put a hood over her head. Where would she be now if she had made it safely to her destination?

The door swung wide, and the little steward stared at Maggie, an awed expression on his round face. "Lady Sherman, you are well met!" He looked her up and down, just as Anne had done, and muttered, "God-a-mercy."

As they entered, Maggie introduced Will, neglecting to mention his relation to her out of some superstition it would change the meeting's outcome. A dower didn't vanish when a widow remarried, as far as she understood, but it wasn't worth the risk. Chauncey ushered them into a tidy sitting room, and his wife materialized with three mugs of cider and a word or two about Maggie's miraculous reappearance before he shooed her away.

Leaving his mug forgotten on a side table, Chauncey leaned forward. "I was all amazed to receive your note. You have quite returned from the grave."

"Forsooth, my story is scarce to be believed," Maggie said.

"And you wish to discuss your dower as Sir John Sherman's widow?"

She produced the sealed letter she had brought from town. "I have spoken with a solicitor in London who feels certain the dower payments may resume if I show myself to be the woman I say I am."

He took the letter from her and set it in his lap without opening it. "I would so attest. There is no denying you are Sir John's wife."

"But the managing of the account is yet in my father's hands."

"Not so, madam! No payments have been made, neither to Lord Donwell nor to another soul."

She wrinkled her brow, glancing at Will to check if he had heard the same thing she had.

"The missive your lord father sent me—I have it here..." Chauncey flipped opened a leather folio and withdrew a creased piece of paper. "I fear a signature was not sufficient. Such a request as his lordship's requires the presence of both parties to sign before a witness. The law did not permit me to carry out his wishes."

She stared, hardly daring to breathe.

"Then you vanished within a fortnight, *after* requesting to meet with me to discuss your father's order." He raised his eyebrows and picked up another piece of paper, on which she recognized her own handwriting. "His lordship was forced to declare you deceased, and the dower reverted to Sir Robert. I kept your missive as evid—" He caught himself and gave a sheepish smile. "As a remembrance."

Did he suspect her father of murdering her to keep her from taking the dower back? Or did he think Robert did it out of fear she would make the order official? Chauncey was as animated as she had ever seen him, delighted to discuss what must have been the most sordid tale of his career.

"So you see, no payment was ever made."

"And now?" she said.

"I know only little of the law, but... I would imagine you are owed arrears."

Her face went slack. She glanced up at where Will leaned against the door frame, and his expression of disbelief mirrored hers. One third of Sir John's estate, accumulating since April of last year. More money than she knew what to do with.

"Have you ever discussed this with Sir Robert? The possibility I might return?"

"Nay, madam. That is, I received a note this morning..."

"What did it say?"

He fidgeted with the two papers in his hands before placing them back in the folio, straightening them with careful movements. "I have ever had only one wish," he said. "That on the Judgment Day, I might stand before the Lord and receive my eternal reward." Maggie and Will waited while Chauncey pretended to examine the sealed letter she had brought. He set it atop the other papers in the folio and cleared his throat. "I pray no man will ever tempt me to stray from the path of righteousness."

Will had guessed Robert would go to any length to keep his money. What nefarious thing had he asked his steward to do? She longed to be privy to the intrigue, but Chauncey clasped his hands in his lap and looked openly at his guests, his speech finished.

"You are a good man, Master Chauncey," she said. "I will remember your kindness always."

He shrugged, his cheeks pink. "'Tis my great honor, madam." He picked up his mug. "May God give you health and prosperity." Then, raising the mug in Will's direction, he added, "And a blessed union."

41

THE MOMENT THEY entered the priory grounds, the melancholy of twenty years of memory flooded Maggie's senses. This was her home, however much she pretended otherwise. These were her hills, her trees, her gardens and her stone walls. London was where she lived. This was where she was formed.

Their mounts' shoes crunched on the crushed stone of the long approach, the sound bouncing off the priory's facade. There was no turning back; the household knew they had arrived.

Assuming anyone was at home.

"Mayhap my father and my aunt are at matins," Maggie said, dismounting and gazing around. It was not Sunday, and the family didn't display peak piety, but maybe Alinor was trying to invest in her spiritual cache before she met St. Peter.

She hadn't expected a fanfare, but someone—her father's head of household, at least—should have met them at the entrance. There was no movement behind the leaded glass windows.

Then someone hurried around the south corner of the house.

Ayda, gray-haired and rosy-cheeked, flew across the gravel and barreled into Maggie, smelling of herbs and flour. She stepped away enough to grasp Maggie's face in both hands. "God bless you, child," she said, a crooked smile above her quivering chin. "As beautiful as the day I last laid eyes on you. A little older, mayhap."

"Wiser, too, I hope."

"My master and her ladyship are yet at matins." Ayda glanced behind her at the front door. "Thomas is to admit no one until they return. I would feed you while you await them, but…"

"Never mind. We have broken our fast and are content to wait. I will show Captain Stokes the grounds."

Ayda took in Will for the first time and raised her eyebrows. Maggie recognized the glimmer of appraisal and knew Ayda didn't find him wanting. "Well met, Captain," she said, curtsying. To Maggie, she said, "This is a tale I must hear. Pray do not go away again without telling me all!"

"Do not be troubled! I will find you anon."

Ayda took her hands and squeezed them, nodded at Will, and made a hasty retreat toward the kitchen garden.

"Rather a skittish thing," Will said.

"I am as astonished as you."

She led him around the house to the outbuildings, hoping they could at least stable the horses, unless her father had forbidden that as well. Luckily, the master of the horse didn't show the same reticence as Ayda.

With nothing to do but wander the grounds until the household returned, she decided what she most wanted to show Will.

They passed through the formal garden on their way. It was devoid of any color aside from the browning hedges. The roses were gone, the rocky paths littered with withered petals. She led him around angles and down straightaways until they were free of the garden's geometry, and they stepped out onto the sprawling lawn.

There, fifty yards ahead, was her tree. Its trunk grew straight and tall out of the hill, so wide she couldn't reach her arms halfway around it. The spreading branches pressed tightly against the gray autumn sky. Maybe it was because she was with Will, but it had never looked more like the sail-topped mast of a ship than it did now.

At the top of the hill, she tilted her head back to look straight up into the red-brown canopy until she was dizzy. When her eyes settled back on Will, he was leaning one shoulder against the tree, arms crossed, watching her.

"I used to come here as a child, to play or to read," she said. "Or to avoid my duties."

"I can well imagine that."

He was teasing her, but she felt obliged to clarify. "I was not a wicked child. I did try to mind my aunt—she was my mother, after my mother died. She was always telling me what I *must* do, but she never told me why. I did not like doing anything I knew not the reason for."

"So Osborne told me when you first came aboard. He was astounded when you would not just *count the coins*." He slipped into a thick Yorkshire accent at the end of his speech, grinning at the memory.

She lowered herself to the ground and leaned her back against the trunk. "Poor Osborne. He fair shook when I turned his system on its head."

"You grew on him, just as you grew on the rest of us."

He joined her on the damp earth, knobby with roots. They looked out toward Duntsford Priory, each scanning the horizon, Will thumbing the brim of the hat in his lap.

With his free hand, he pointed toward a little copse of trees. "There is a likely place. Or there." This time, he was gesturing toward the stables. "Even there, mayhap—nay, too near a window…"

"What are you looking for?"

"All the places I would have lain you down, had I been one of your swains."

Their lovemaking was far too cosmopolitan for sleepy old Duntsford Priory, so she decided to be scandalized. When she lifted her hand to whack him, he caught her wrist, kissing her palm before letting her go. "Did I choose well? Where did the lads give you green sleeves?"

"Nowhere! The very thought…"

"Come, you may tell me of them. My pride is in no danger of being damaged, for I am convinced I rank among the best of your lovers."

If he kept using that seductive tone, she would add this hill to his list of likely spots.

"I had no swains. I fell in love with Matthew when I was fourteen, and he left when I was fifteen. There was no one else until I married."

He stared at her. "That was your love affair? You were little more than a child!"

"A child may yet feel."

She realized he only knew what little she had admitted that first summer, and what Luke had divulged that awful day in June. So she told him the story.

"We began our courtship just after my family returned from London for Elizabeth's presentation at court. It had frightened me, I suppose, knowing I would soon be auctioned off to a man I did not know. I knew Matthew, and he seemed to like me well enough. We neither of us truly believed we could marry, but we played at it, inventing futures for ourselves. After my presentation, I confess I grew more desperate. I agreed to run away with him when he asked. And you know the rest.

"After that, I had been struck by Cupid's lead arrow. I felt certain I would never wish to love again. I hated the husband my father chose for me. He was not a good husband, but even if he had been, I would not have grown to love him. And Robert, though he was young and handsome and wanted me… I could not bring myself to love him either. There were pangs of something—longing, ardor, I know not. I was lonely, but I felt no affection for him.

"He called himself Apollo, and I was Daphne, cursed by God to despise men. I fled him every day, and the day I met you was the day I learned I was trapped. I could not keep running, yet I would not be caught. So I chose to sacrifice… everything. Just to be free of him."

It was easier to say all this when she could stare out at the countryside instead of at Will. She was grateful he wasn't looking at her either. It gave her the foolish impression he might not even be listening.

But of course he was. Will Stokes was the only person who had ever really listened to her.

"What happens to Daphne? In the story?"

"She becomes a tree."

"That I ken," he chuckled, nudging her with his shoulder. "But after. Is there more?"

"Apollo vows to honor her by using her wood for his weapons and crowning his champions with her leaves."

"So her new form does not save her?"

"Indeed not."

"Then you are no Daphne. She sacrificed her freedom and lost all the same. When you sacrificed your comfort, you gained your freedom. I do not say it was not a monstrous sacrifice, but you thwarted your Apollo and may put down your roots wherever you please."

It was too great an oversimplification. She was still reeling from that sacrifice, still mending the seams she had torn when she ripped herself away from polite society and became a pirate. She had lost Robert, but she had lost a good deal else as well. And she had gained another Apollo.

She snickered at the irony. "I thwarted Apollo and found Matthew Kent."

"There's the rub."

"The night you played the fiddle, and I danced with him—you remember?" He nodded, and she leaned her head back against the tree. "You warned me then."

"You had known him for years, and me for mere weeks."

"I had known you for mere *minutes* when you told me Robert was a villain, but I trusted your word."

"And why was that?"

"I cannot say for certain. Mayhap I needed him to be a villain, and you to be a hero. I was ready to run, and the moment you gave me a reason, I ran."

It was the only explanation for why she had made such a reckless decision with so little information. If Will hadn't been trustworthy, her story could have ended very differently.

"Why did you allow it?" she said. "Did you take pity on me because I was at my lowest?"

"At your strongest, you mean. You looked at me with such hope, knowing there was no open path but forward. How could I be so cruel as to return you to the path you came from?"

"Do you speak of Bristol or Rotherhithe? You have saved me from wretchedness so many times, I begin to lose track."

"Rotherhithe had nothing to do with pity. That was simple weakness." He pressed his forehead to hers. "God help me, I heeded nary a word after you told me you were free of him. I wanted so fiercely to kiss you, I was poised to leap over the table."

He showed her how he would have done it, and she breathed in the sweet scent of his warm skin to temper the flood of desire his words unleashed. She played with the silken hair at his nape as they parted.

"It was torture being your captain. Knowing how fortunate I was to see you every day—and how cursed. Having to inspect each command I gave you, lest I foolishly abused my authority over you."

She fixed him with a critical look. "Nay, I cannot credit that. You are not cruel."

"I never thought to be cruel, but there were other ways, smaller ways. I wanted to request your presence more often, or require you at supper… I thought of all manner of ways to keep you near me."

"And instead, you ignored me for months."

"For my own sanity," he said, squeezing her hand. "I would never know whether you enjoyed my company or whether you were required to. How often did you declare yourself indebted to me? I would have despised myself for every payment I mistook as a gift."

His gaze was focused on something far away from her. "You require balanced scales, but I cannot keep from heaping more and more onto yours. I delight in it—in granting your requests, in doing all in my power to see you safe and content, with no thought of reward. Yet to you, who cannot bear to leave a debt unsettled… I must be your bane."

"Cease this talk of balance." His words hurt, a tiny sting of truth amid an unbearable swell of affection. "Aye, your kindnesses inspired me to offer kindnesses in return. Whatever I did for the ship or the crew, I did it in aid of you. For love of you."

The word hovered between them in the autumn air, feather-light and precious. Will's eyes widened a fraction, and she worried she had repeated her Blackfriars blunder, but his mustache twitched with a hidden smile.

"Forsooth," he said, voice catching, "I am a novice in the ways of love, but you will find in me a ready pupil."

It only required a slight lean to find his lips, and she tried to infuse this kiss with all the feelings she couldn't yet put into words. She remained pressed against him, not moving, breathing him in.

How could she have allowed her own folly to delay this? How could she ever leave this miraculous hill, where every breath, every touch, every word was a component of some heady witchcraft?

"Heap whatever you wish upon the scales," she said, "and I shall do the same. May they break under the weight."

They sat, hand in hand, against the stout trunk of the tree. She was tempted to call it silence, but silence implied the absence of something, and Maggie could find nothing missing. Will's hand was warm, his body shielding her from the worst of the autumn breeze. While this moment stretched on, nothing could persuade her that she wasn't, perhaps for the first time, content.

Will shifted his position and took a breath. "How do you think Bisset is managing with you gone? I understand you run his entire enterprise, or near enough."

"Nothing like. I am a competent secretary and no more. 'Tis enough for me to make a small mark on the world."

"'Tis a greater mark than you think."

"I am making a mark on the women of Bartholomew Close," she added with a laugh. "Mistress Routledge again asked me when I will marry—by which I was marvelous relieved, for I feared she was to tell me she saw you sneaking away the other night. Half of her neighbors think me a whore, and the other half believe me possessed by the devil. An unmarried woman has no place in society."

"You are still letting society dictate your happiness?"

She screwed up her face. "Of course I am. I have to live among these people. I may counterfeit by signing my business correspondence 'M. Bailey,' but I remain a woman when I leave my rooms. If I am ever to escape the sneers and the gossip, I must needs marry."

"Is that your wish? Is it not better to withstand the gossip and have your freedom, rather than putting yourself in shackles in exchange for a good name?"

"Is there no world in which I may find a man who gives me both respectability and freedom?"

"Most men would not allow a woman the sort of freedom you desire. The husband you seek would need to respect your choices and not be threatened by your success. Nor can he be cowed by public opinion, which you yourself find difficult to ignore."

He had a point. Society hated a businesswoman, regardless of her marital status. Both she and her chosen spouse could expect censure.

"So you believe no such man exists?"

"I believe but one such man exists."

She raised a cool eyebrow at him, while inside her heart pounded. "Where, pray, might I find him?"

"This time of day?" he replied with mock pensiveness. "Under a tree on a hill."

At first, giddy joy made her tremble. It was the most beautiful speech ever given, more magical than a hundred Prosperos, more poignant than a thousand Hamlets.

But it was too good to be true. He masqueraded as a nobleman, but his fiefdom was the sea. Was she so arrogant to tempt a man to uproot his whole life? Was she cruel enough to demand it?

"You have no wish to marry, and I have no wish to search the horizon every day for your return."

She pleaded with him to reply. She loved his wit, even his ridiculous innuendo, but she knew what his flattery could do to a weak-willed individual. If he had been teasing, she had fallen for it.

He cleared his throat. "I enjoyed Treningham's celebration—what I saw of it."

"Oh, Will, forgive me—"

"Nay, I did not mean it in so cruel a way. Only, the small taste of a life of leisure leaves me hungry for more. The *Merrow* is a fine ship, and she has a fine crew, but drinking wine, going to the theater, attending masques and banquets... Those are the pastimes I crave. 'Tis the sort of life that is not like to end in a noose," he added with a grim smile. "And I may take to sea whenever I wish, not whenever I must."

"You are speaking of retiring." It was difficult to envision him anywhere other than on the deck of the *Merrow*.

"I have saved a few coins and made sundry investments. I could live like a gentleman. Keep my feet firmly on land for a change."

"What of the *Merrow*?"

"I could... sell it?"

"Nay, you must not! She is your legacy!"

He sighed. "You are right. I am too proud to cast her aside."

A thought was forming in her mind, but she wasn't sure how he would react. "If you are in earnest..." She scanned his face while she spoke. "You could put her to work while you remain ashore. Maintain ownership, but leave the command of her to another."

"Become a merchant?"

"No, only lease her to the employ of a shipping company. She runs the cargo, and you are compensated for the use of her. Over time, 'tis like to be more lucrative than selling outright, anyway."

He looked at her, a smile of understanding beginning on his lips. "Indeed? And have you a shipping company in mind for such a task?"

"As it happens, Bisset is seeking to expand..."

"And shall I address my correspondence to Monsieur Bisset or Master Bailey?"

With a grin, Maggie linked her arm with Will's and leaned her head on his shoulder. Even curled up against him—knowing he was here not because she had asked, but because he had wanted to be—doubt lingered in the back of her mind. Doubt he could be sincere when she knew flattery was a second language to him. Doubt the feelings he admitted would last into the new year.

Doubt was not necessarily her enemy. She needed a certain amount of it as she learned to trust herself, to question what she felt and heard and saw, and to file each away as a lesson in being Maggie.

"Do not give up sailing unless it is what you want," she said. "I am not worthy of such a sacrifice."

"That old refrain about your unworthiness is perilous. Take care who hears it."

"I cry your pardon?" she said, snickering at his ominous tone.

"Anyone who speaks ill of the woman I love will suffer a most painful death. I give no quarter."

She looked up at him, his eyes laughing, his head ringed by the high-above leaves of the oak tree. His lips covered hers, soft but steady, the sensation still novel, the heady pleasure of it still enough to leave her senseless. Over the beating of her mending heart, his words echoed without end: *the woman I love, the woman I love.*

Far away, she spotted the shapes of the returning mass-goers coming up the drive on foot. Alinor had set a slow pace, hanging on Lord Donwell's arm. They trailed a small entourage of personal attendants and pious household staff. Will nodded toward the group.

"Are you ready?"

It was generous of him to assume she ever would be. She untethered herself from the comfort of the oak tree and descended the hill to meet her fate.

42

MAGGIE MOUNTED THE priory steps.

The ancient wooden door swung open before she could extend her hand to lift the knocker. Thomas, her father's head of household, jumped at finding her so close.

They stared at each other.

"Well met, Thomas."

He bowed. "Lord Donwell awaits you in the great hall."

The great hall? What of the comfortable family sitting room? It felt ridiculous to be treated with such cold formality. Thomas was about to ask them to enter through the kitchen like vagabonds, she was sure of it.

But he opened the door and stood aside. Arm in arm with Will, she stepped into the jaws of Duntsford Priory.

It was all unchanged. The same tapestries covered the walls, the same sconces and lamps spilled light over the same rugs. And yet, a niggling thought in the back of her mind told her it wasn't the home she had left, but a replica, with every post and chair and lintel shifted one half-inch south.

Thomas ushered them into the great hall, the formal reception space for honored guests. "My lord," he said, his voice resonating in the tall ceiling. And that was all. He left them stranded in the empty archway.

Something told her to turn around and walk out, that she wasn't welcome here. She focused on the figures sitting before the fire, the gray head of her aunt Alinor, the lined face of her father, and gathered her courage.

Lord Donwell stood and approached, the only sound his leather slippers padding on the stone floor.

She curtsied. "My lord Father."

"Let me look at you."

She raised her face for his inspection.

Alinor turned in her seat. "Is it she?"

Donwell didn't answer, only looked past Maggie to where Will lingered in the corridor.

"Captain William Stokes, sir," she said, voice wavering. "Captain, may I present to you Henry Donwell, the third Baron Donwell."

Will executed his finest bow, bending with beautiful grace, and when he righted himself, his expression was neutral, pleasant. Unthreatening.

An observer would have assumed Lord Donwell was a duke from all the pomp they heaped on him. She had the mad notion she shouldn't have to work so hard to earn the respect of her own father.

"Are you to thank for ensuring my daughter's safety on the road from London?" Donwell said.

"No thanks are needed, my lord. 'Twas my duty and my pleasure."

"Your duty?"

This was the moment she would learn how well she and Will had prepared, and whether they had chosen the right story. Will waited for her approval to begin the charade, but she knew she should be the one to say it.

She sipped in a shallow breath, her chest tight. "Captain Stokes is my husband."

"Why are you whispering in the corridor? Come here where I may see you!" Alinor peered around the edge of her tall chair back, and her shrill voice in the wake of Maggie's announcement made everyone jump.

After a brief hesitation, Donwell swung open like a gate and beckoned Maggie through.

She stood before Alinor, who was thinner and grayer, blue eyes no longer as clear, skin no longer as firm. "So it is you," Alinor said. "Your father was certain an imposter would arrive at the door and wheedle her way into the house."

Had he instructed the household not to engage with her until Lord Donwell could validate her identity? These people knew her: Thomas, Ayda, even the stableboy remembered her from before her marriage. But Lord Donwell's opinion was the only one that mattered.

"You survived, then. Where have you been, girl?"

She had been right about one thing: no one was going to slaughter the fatted calf. Maggie sat opposite her family and placed an inviting hand on the arm of the chair next to her. Will's strength was more essential to her now than it had been at Treningham's party.

"I have been living in London for a time, madam."

"Aye, the messenger came from there," Alinor snapped. "Where have you been since failing to board the ship to France? You did not fall into the harbor, as we all believed."

Alinor was *angry*, Maggie realized with bewilderment. There would be no joyful reunion until she explained herself to everyone's satisfaction.

So, with her head held high and Will by her side, she delivered her speech.

It had all the criteria for a thrilling adventure story. Robert was the villain, and a crew of mercenaries were the monsters. There was a second abduction resulting from an insufficient ransom payment, then a surprise skirmish with a corsair that took Maggie far from home. A storm, of course, and a shipwreck, a blow to the head, and a serendipitous rescue by the gallant Captain Stokes. Maggie lost her memory, as so often happens, and by the time she recalled where she came from, they were too deep in love to imagine life without each other.

When she finished, she took Will's hand and smiled at him, the image of a woman in love. Surely a father would be gratified to see his daughter happy.

A faraway sound reached her ears, movement and clattering and laughter. It grew louder until a tiny figure dashed past the hall entrance, followed by a laughing nursemaid, followed by Elizabeth. She peeled off from the giggling boy and his nanny to enter the hall, and Maggie now saw she was holding a baby in her arms.

"I cry your pardon," Elizabeth said. "I meant to be here when you arrived." She came to stand beside the cluster of chairs. Maggie stared at the baby, a handsome boy, blond and pink. He would have to be a year old already. He stared back at her, blue eyes wide and watching. Elizabeth shifted him higher on her hip. "What have I missed?"

Lord Donwell ignored her, looking at Maggie with such severity, she felt like a child again. "Who else knows of this?"

She frowned, thinking she must have misheard him. "Who knows I was captured? Only my husband and his crew, methinks."

"That is well. Although you showed little regard for your family's good name by marrying this sea captain, I hope you will endeavor to begin now by keeping this sordid tale to yourself."

Will's hand tensed in hers and her blood went cold.

Alinor sniffed and said, "She did finally marry him, Henry. That must figure into it."

Elizabeth, despite missing the performance, looked down at Maggie and Will's joined hands and caught up quickly. "Aye, Father, why do you not wish her joy?"

"Be silent, Elizabeth."

"None of this was my doing," Maggie said.

"Except marrying well below your birth."

Elizabeth snorted, a sound so unexpected, Maggie's head snapped up to gawk at her. "You are a baron, Father, not the Duke of York. At least she is happy—and alive."

"Be silent!"

"If only you had stayed at the inn…" Alinor began.

"If only Robert had not gambled with my life!"

"I cannot have it known my daughter was abducted by brigands not once, but *twice*—"

"She hardly asked for it, Father!"

The little boy in Elizabeth's arms began to cry.

Maggie swiveled her focus between each of her family members, her chest tightening as the clamor increased.

Donwell stood, and everyone but the baby knew to be quiet.

"Ayda will prepare you a meal in the kitchen before you depart."

"Father!" Elizabeth said.

Maggie looked at him, this stranger with whom she shared a name. The best-case scenario had always been out of reach: that he would embrace her with tears in his eyes and welcome her home, thanking God she was alive. She would have settled for a grudging acceptance she was none the worse for wear, even if he could never bless her sham union.

But despite all the thorough planning, all the careful tailoring to answer every question and tug each heart string, she hadn't been able to bring herself to acknowledge one truth: that it might not matter what she told him.

She stood, her legs weak, her mind numb. Curtsying to her father was a habit; she hardly noticed she was doing it. Alinor was grumbling something and Elizabeth stuttered variations of "Father, I pray you."

Will stood and met Donwell's gaze, propelling Maggie from the room with a light touch at the small of her back. He didn't bow. It was a glorious snub; if only she weren't too broken to enjoy it.

43

AYDA COULD MAKE a terrible racket. She slammed the water pitcher, smacked the worktable with her spoon, and swung the stewpot over the fire with such force the spill obliged her to stoke it up again.

Maggie was gratified to know Ayda was angry, but the noise made her jumpy and irritable. She took out her frustration on the dough Ayda let her prepare, tearing it from the work surface, hurling it back down in a puff of flour, and punching it until it was as smooth as a river stone.

Will kept out of the way, leaning the small of his back against the worktable, watching her out of the corner of his eye with a wary expression.

Though she told Ayda that Lord Donwell banished her from the house, she hadn't yet given her the full tale of her adventures, as she had promised. She couldn't decide which story to recount. Ayda deserved the truth, but hadn't she always wished for a happy ending for Maggie? It might be more cruel than kind to reveal the promising young girl Ayda had nurtured had made so many, many mistakes.

With a clatter and a giggle, the fleet-footed little boy she had glimpsed earlier now came flying into the kitchen, startling the bustling staff and eliciting grunts of dismay. The hapless nursemaid followed, shouting empty threats. So this was Elizabeth's firstborn, the future Baron Chichester. Little Henry, the terror. He had been barely walking when she saw him last.

He tore around the room, his nursemaid trailing him, the kitchen staff dodging out of the way. An instant later, his movements so quick and smooth she didn't see it happen, Will lifted the boy into the air and turned him upside down. His blond hair waved like seagrass as Will swiveled about, a puzzled look on his face.

"Did you hear something?" Will asked Maggie. Henry shrieked with delight at finding himself topsy-turvy. "There it is again!"

"Down!" said the boy.

Will turned to Ayda, Henry swaying side to side with each movement. "Mistress, I fear your kitchen may have a fairy infestation."

"Down, down!"

"Methinks the imp is trying to speak to us! I will search the room to see if I may discover it."

Will began a lumbering tour of the kitchen, taking exaggerated, bouncing steps that had the little head bobbing up and down with nauseating frequency. It lent a silly hiccoughing rhythm to the incessant giggles. The kitchen staff smiled and shook their heads with relief. The nursemaid hovered, her hands fluttering as if to be ready for the moment Will dropped the child on his head.

Her life could have been like this, full of joy and close to her family, watching her nephews grow, perhaps even watching them play with their cousins. All she had to do was board that ship to France. The scar from Robert's betrayal would have faded in time. She might have married a man of whom her family approved, boring but comfortable. Or maybe she would have spent the rest of her life a widow, raising Elizabeth's children instead of raising children of her own.

There was one glaring flaw in this otherwise perfect portrait. To have a happy family required the various members to like each other.

Her thoughts summoned Elizabeth a moment later. She still held the baby, his round cheeks red from crying. Elizabeth's face was also red, her mouth pinched.

Maggie prepared for a tongue-lashing. She wasn't sure what the subject would be, but she knew it was coming.

"Prithee, take him," Elizabeth called to Henry's nursemaid, shifting the baby to her other hip. "I fear I have been squeezing him in my anger, the poor babe."

"I will take him." Maggie didn't know she was going to say it until her arms were already outstretched. Elizabeth handed him over without objection and shook out her aching arms.

Maggie gazed down into her nephew's gem-blue eyes. "Well met, little fellow," she murmured to him. He stared and stared, one hand gripping her sleeve.

"Say 'good day' to your Auntie Margie," Elizabeth cooed. She glanced up at her sister and corrected herself. "Maggie. Cry pardon."

The shame of their last meeting, the way Maggie had rebuffed her, resurfaced with a wave of stomach-turning guilt. Maggie hugged the baby to her. "The way I behaved in London—"

"'Tis forgiven. I did not know why or from whom you were concealing yourself, but I would not be so cruel as to expose you. I was distressed, but not fatally wounded." She smoothed the baby's hair and beamed at him. "This is James. I think you two have not been introduced."

"He is a treasure."

Elizabeth leaned against the worktable. "*His highness* recounted to me the story you told him. I assume your performance was more stirring, but I now know the details, at the least. I declared this an unseemly punishment for your crimes, whatever he thought them to be, but he will not yield. I will try again once I cease shaking."

If Maggie had been looking for a champion, she would not have sought one in Elizabeth. Yet here her sister was, furious, an avenging angel Maggie didn't deserve. She laid her cheek on James's soft, warm head and took comfort in feeling his little breaths.

"I have bungled this," Maggie said. "I thought this story was the way into his heart. Methinks I must try again with the truth."

Elizabeth quirked an eyebrow. "In this truth, is your sea captain a prince in disguise?"

They both turned their attention to Will, who had swung Henry onto his back and was accepting commands like the obedient horse he pretended to be. Maggie hid her laugh by burying her face in James's ear. The baby squirmed and held out his arms for his mama.

"I should like to hear the real tale, if you would entrust me with it," Elizabeth said as she dragged the baby across the empty space between them. "And more besides. Come up to the ribbon room."

It was the shorthand they used to identify their shared childhood bedroom. Maggie's eyes darted to the door as if she might find her father hovering in the doorway, waiting to catch them making mischief. "Father sent me away. He will not like me wandering the house."

"Then you will have to step lightly." Elizabeth summoned the nursemaid with a pointed raising of her chin, and the frazzled woman hurried over to take little James.

Maggie caught Ayda on a trip between the stove and the table and said, "Will you take care of the captain for me?"

"'Tis we must take care," Ayda said with a chuckle. "The lasses are in love with him already, and half the lads are on their way."

Maggie glanced around at the staff and discovered more than one girl watching Will and Henry instead of the task before her. She smiled. "I will return anon."

The sisters zig-zagged through the winding priory corridors, peering around each corner before turning. They went up the back way, via the drafty, crumbling steps of the original building. Everyone used the eighty-year-old addition, so there would be less chance of being caught here.

She hadn't been in the ribbon room since the night before her wedding. It got its nickname from the narrow band of painted flowers encircling the room near the ceiling. The bed was the same one she and Elizabeth had slept in their entire lives, and which had belonged to fifty years of other Donwells before them. Without a fire, the stone floors and walls radiated cold, the milky daylight through the narrow windows not enough to brighten the gloom.

Elizabeth picked up a candle and a flint and crawled onto the bed, then got to work untying the heavy red curtains. Maggie watched in bemusement for a moment, wondering who this stranger was.

"I thought to muffle our voices," Elizabeth said, her low tone resonating in the sterile room. "And try to keep warm. Was it always this cold when we were children?"

"Aye. Worse when you left." Maggie tugged on the cords on the other side of the bed before heaving herself up onto the massive piece of furniture. She had chosen to wear the gown from her masquerade at Hattecliff House, as it was the nicest one she owned, but it was stiff and cumbersome and required stays. She sat crunched, pinched, and cross-legged at the foot of the bed.

By the light seeping through the gap in the curtains, Elizabeth lit the candle and twitched the drapes shut. The dancing flame was a beacon in the black, something to anchor her, and Maggie watched it flicker.

"I can well imagine," Elizabeth said, continuing their conversation. "I wondered if you would share Aunt Crane's bed to keep warm."

"Never!" Maggie shuddered. "Nay, we Donwells would rather each suffer alone."

"'Struth. I cannot credit why Father did not take a wife after Mother. Do you think it would have improved his ways? Could we have had a happy family?"

"That depends on the woman."

"It would have been worth it. You needed a mother."

"And you did not?"

"I had more time with Mother than you did. And our dispositions differ, as you well know." Elizabeth raised an amused eyebrow. "Which I believe is the cause of your present..." She waved her hand, a gesture to encompass everything about Maggie.

It was too flippant a motion for someone who knew nothing about her. "My life these many months has been a comedy of errors, certes, but I will own it," Maggie said, her pulse racing as her body came to her defense. She opened her mouth to say more, but Elizabeth broke in.

"Evidently not. You have lied to our father, by your own admission. What of your comedy shames you enough to conceal it? Your second disappearance was not the doing of brigands, I warrant."

She froze. How could Elizabeth know she ran? Even Maggie could admit it was out of character.

"I always supposed you seized the chance to change your fate. You were not yourself when Sir John died. But where did you go? Did your handsome captain promise you adventure?"

She wanted to argue she hadn't allowed a dashing stranger to sweep her away, but there was no way to explain it. That was precisely what she had done, even if it hadn't been a gripping love story or a scandalous exchange of virtue for venture.

"I see now why you wished for a mother for me," she said, her voice sharp with bitterness. "You regard me as some wild creature."

"Then why?"

"Because Robert sold me. He hired mercenaries to take me, then invented a ransom debt that he demanded our father repay."

Elizabeth grappled with this new information for a long time, her face contorting into a dozen expressions, disbelief mingled with concern, mingled with surprise, mingled with fury. She asked all the questions Maggie expected her to ask, and Maggie answered them as they came.

When it came time to defend her choice not to call Robert out, she almost rolled her eyes. "Tell me all who heard the tale would believe me. Tell me they would care."

"But to carry that burden alone... To make the choice you made..."

"I sacrificed security and gained freedom. I cannot regret what I did."

They sat in silence, each thoughtful. The candle flame reached toward the canopy, still in the still air.

"How miraculous the mercenary told you of Robert's treachery. To think you might never have known."

Maggie bit her tongue. She had been on the verge of revealing Will's identity a dozen times as she explained the circumstances, but by some miracle, she kept him out of the story. Everyone was a liar to some degree, but Maggie had needed to become more proficient than most.

"How long did you serve on Captain Stokes's ship? How came you to London?"

So Maggie told her the rest. The music she played and the skills she learned. The mystery at the Dagger and Sheath and her friendship with Ellen. The saga surrounding Matthew, as painful as it was. The way she weaseled her way back onto Will's crew. The threats Driscoll made and how it led her, inexplicably, to Bisset. Will, her friend and supporter and partner in crime.

That last was a euphemism, of course. In this telling of the truth, Will was an honest sea captain and Bisset always paid his taxes.

When she finished, she stared at the stub of candle in its puddle of wax and heaved a sigh. "As you see, the true tale will bring far more shame than the false one."

"'Twill indeed."

"I think I must tell it."

"No, you must return to London and leave Duntsford behind you."

Maggie looked wide-eyed at her sister's frank expression. "How can I? I have come all this way, and my quest remains incomplete."

"Are you a hero of legend? One of Arthur's knights? What binds you to this quest of yours? Abandon it, if 'tis not to your liking."

"I have always walked away from a thing when it became too difficult. 'Tis the coward's way out. I would be better." She clenched her hands into fists in her skirts. "I would see this through."

"To what purpose? What may you gain from him? His love? His blessing? He has already shown his love is conditional, and as for his blessing, what good will it do? If he does not give it, will you uproot yourself to become the dutiful daughter he requires? Will you marry a stranger, birth his heirs, and make yourself small, all for the love of one old man?"

While Elizabeth spoke, Maggie gazed unfocused at the dying candle flame, letting tears trail down her cheeks as they would. She tried to pinpoint the source. It wasn't anger, though her father deserved it. It was neither worthlessness nor despair.

She was disappointed, she realized, and more in herself than in her father. All the running away was because of some misguided notion that her family wanted what was best for her, and she feared betraying them. At the time, she was sure she had made a mess of her life, but if she had stayed, she would have made *nothing* of her life. And no one would ever have asked her if she was happy.

Elizabeth chuckled. "'Tis unfortunate the tale you told our father was a fabrication. It was just the sort of thing you would always read aloud from your plays and books. There is a little of… what is't? Tristan and Isolde?"

"Mayhap," Maggie said, wiping her face. "We drew from the great narratives."

"We? You and your fine captain?" She gave Maggie a knowing smile. "Tell me, did you bring him along because your tale required a love story to be believed?"

Maggie's stomach fluttered as impressions of his smile, his touch, his laugh winged through her mind in a shimmering swarm. "Methinks the love story is the only part that is true."

Elizabeth's face broadened, her eyes filling with tears. "You always swore you were bound for some storybook ending. I despaired of you finding it, but here he is: your Lancelot." She reached out and took Maggie's hand in her cool, slender fingers.

"Do not tell him so, I beg you. His pride needs no encouragement."

Elizabeth snuffed the candle and parted the curtain, letting the sisterly magic disperse into the chill room.

The kitchen was calmer and more industrious than they left it, and before Elizabeth could panic about her missing children, Ayda directed them toward the stables.

The two hired mounts that had brought them from London were grazing in the pasture alongside Lord Donwell's horses. In the foreground, the nursemaid lounged on a blanket while the baby bounced and flapped his arms beside her. Two mismatched swashbucklers battled with tree branches nearby, the taller one parrying each energetic swing with careful grace.

Will crouched down to Henry's eye level and said something. The little boy's blond head whipped around, and he dropped his stick as he dashed toward his mother.

Elizabeth scooped him up with a groan, and Henry explained in the stammering, roundabout language of a toddler that he was about to vanquish the evil pirate captain and he wanted them to watch. At least, that was the translation Elizabeth gave Maggie after seeing her expression.

Will gave Maggie a tired smile as they approached each other. How long had he been forced to entertain this tiny warrior?

"I cry your pardon, captain," Elizabeth said, setting Henry down again. "We were absent longer than I intended. You should have left him with his nurse and taken your ease."

Will shrugged, and the corners of his eyes crinkled. "'Twas no hardship, my lady. You've a fine, brave lad."

Henry was already halfway across the field, looking for his dropped stick. Elizabeth watched him for a moment before returning her gaze to Will. "Do you have children?"

"I have never been married, madam."

"That is not always a requirement, I understand. Is a family on the horizon for you?"

Maggie wanted to throttle her.

"That depends," Will said, unruffled as usual. "Your sister, as you know, is the mistress of her own mind."

"How!" Maggie blushed scarlet, and her stomach gave a nauseating flip. "We have no understanding. Do not tease her!"

Will and Elizabeth had the same smug expression on their face. Either Will really was an aristocrat at his core, or Elizabeth had some pirate in her.

"My father is not like to change his mind," Elizabeth said. "I am sorry to tell you that you will not be welcomed at Duntsford Priory after this. But I hope you will come to Cheltenham often. Henry will be overjoyed, and my Lord Chichester will not share my father's opinion—once I tell him what his opinion should be."

Maggie had never known what kind of woman her sister was. Or perhaps the woman she had once thought her to be had transformed over the years. Those unfinished versions of themselves struggled to love each other then, but now, Maggie could see a path.

She wrapped her arms around Elizabeth's slim, rigid form. Her sister's posture softened as she embraced her back, her chin sharp in Maggie's shoulder.

"Write to me of your news. The happier, the better."

Maggie nodded. "Be well," she said, her voice thick.

The priory grounds receded, the tree on the hill a smudge on the horizon, as Maggie and Will squelched along the muddy road to London. She didn't speak, and he didn't make her. There was nothing about the morning's trial she wanted to explain or justify, neither to him nor to her own disjointed mind. She had suffered a loss, and she would mourn it in time. The anger and sadness would diminish.

That night, she lay awake on the inn's lumpy mattress, Will's arm a comforting weight on her waist, his breath caressing her neck.

Eighteen months ago, she had stood alone at her husband's graveside, unmoored and frightened. Margie Sherman could never have imagined a transformation so sublime, so fantastical, so complete. It could be more change was still to come: an expanded career, an improved outlook, maybe even a new name.

But Maggie was beginning to like this form, and the more she grew into it, the stronger she would become.

Epilogue

THE EVENING SUN generously set behind Maggie as she gazed east, where the Thames curved away from the land on its stalwart trek toward the sea. Each ship to round the bend made her heart race. She had considered traveling all the way to the coast, even wondering if she should try to spot the ship from Sandwich, but she had to remain near enough to London to meet it when it docked. That was why she chose this scrubby stretch of beach near West Tilbury, far enough from the blockhouse the soldiers stationed there wouldn't question her presence.

She stretched out her tired legs on the blanket and leaned back on her aching wrists, certain the ship would sail into view any moment.

She had been saying that for nearly two days.

The Thames lapped against the sandy shore, its lullaby as soothing this evening as it had been all day. She had walked the shoreline when she was antsy and dropped back onto the blanket when she was tired. The books she had brought were discarded in the basket beside her, already plumbed of their stories and no more use to her until she grew bored enough to read them again.

The ship was supposed to arrive today. Maggie only began her vigil as early as she had because she couldn't bear the thought of missing it. Now, it appeared she would repeat the process tomorrow.

The usual visions bubbled up from the deep well of her dreams—storms, pirates, submerged rocks, sea monsters. It killed her, the waiting, the not knowing. The anxiety might fade in time, as the ship completed more voyages and returned with cargo and crew intact, but she suspected that was wishful thinking. She would always be waiting, always training her eyes on the horizon.

What had once been the *Merrow* was rechristened *Phoebe*, after the legendary huntress. Her crew of criminals was now a crew of honest sailors, even if the roster retained a few familiar names. They were generous with the men who didn't wish to stay, and they offered a competitive wage to those who did. Bisset liked knowing the first ship in his fleet belonged to someone he trusted, and so the pirate ship became a merchant vessel.

The cargo did not much change, nor did the number of customs officials they listed among their friends.

The sky above the river was deep blue. Overhead, purple faded to pink. Behind her, the sun settled onto the horizon, with the spires of London silhouetted against it.

Finally, there she was.

Many ships had passed by today, but Maggie knew those sails, that hull, that bowsprit. It glowed orange in the light of the setting sun, and soon she would make out the figurehead's feminine curves, the masts' green and yellow patterns, the flag's newfangled crest.

She scrambled to her knees, tangling herself in her skirts. The rocky ground was bruising, but she didn't care. Eyes fixed on the *Phoebe*, she begged Will to hurry.

There was a clatter behind her, metal on metal.

"Why did you not say the goblets were wrapped in your cloak? I have been searching for an age."

Will dropped to his knees on the blanket beside her and got to work on the wine bottle, glancing up to track the *Phoebe*'s progress up the river. "She is a wonder, is she not?" he said.

"Hurry, she is almost upon us."

He got the cork out and poured two generous portions of wine, handing one to her before helping her to her feet. She leaned into him, overcome by the beauty of the evening and the marvel of the thing she had accomplished. He pressed his lips to her temple as his arm curled around her waist.

The ship sped closer, magnificent and sleek, its sails swelling with a favorable wind.

"Look at her," she said, voice taut with suppressed glee. "My ship."

"*My* ship."

She jabbed her elbow into his side. "Very well. But 'tis my cargo."

"Only if Padraig has kept it intact. The man has a troubling habit of trying to outmaneuver a storm."

"The cargo is all there, I know it. See, she has nary a scratch."

It was true: no holes in the sails, no splintered yardarms, no breaches to the hull that she could see. It looked like the grueling voyage to Arabia and back had been as uneventful as Maggie had prayed it would be.

As the *Phoebe* passed before them, miniature sailors scurried across the deck and up the ratlines. One bright blond head caught her eye, the only crew member she could identify from so far away. Maggie raised her cup and shouted her joy, hardly knowing what she said, and a line of tiny heads appeared at the railing to shout back. She and Will offered up huzzahs and blessings until the *Phoebe* was past and their voices were hoarse.

Will held out his goblet. "To the *Phoebe*, the flagship of the fleet."

"To her crew of miscreants!"

"To Jules Bisset."

She knew by the twinkle in his eye he was goading her, but she didn't mind being predictable. "And?"

He stepped closer and appraised the dregs of wine in his goblet. "And this excellent vintage."

Chuckling, she tugged one side of the open collar of his shirt, bringing them nose to nose. "*And?*"

With a sigh, he conceded. "And to the cleverest businessman in London…" He raised his goblet to head height and tipped it in her direction. "My wife."

Grinning, Maggie swallowed the last of her wine and handed Will the empty goblet. "We must make haste if we are to meet her at the Pool."

To the west, the sky was light, but night followed hard on the *Phoebe*'s stern. The Tilbury blockhouse braziers flared to life as Maggie and Will traipsed over the grassy dunes to where the horses grazed.

As she secured her saddle bag, Will snaked his arms around her and propped his chin on her shoulder. She brought her hand up to stroke his hair as the usual warmth blossomed in her belly.

"Are you content?"

She took in a breath. "What if the crew suffered losses?"

"'Tis a venture not without risk, as you knew." With his hands on her waist, he turned her until she faced him. "But you will accomplish your aim this day. Tell me, does it bring you such joy as you hoped it would?"

The swell of pride when the *Phoebe* rounded the river bend nearly overwhelmed her, but it swelled in tandem with paralyzing relief. She lived in uncertainty for so many weeks, the anxiety had become part of her.

"I am happy. And proud." Resting her hands on his chest, she sighed. "But I was sore afraid."

"A child must climb a tree, betimes, even if you cannot bear to let him fall."

She shot him a sharp look.

His shoulders sagged, and he touched his forehead to hers. "Forgive me. I will take better care."

"Nay," she said, softening. "I must strengthen my defenses. I cannot avoid children altogether. I only…"

"I know. It will come."

"What if it does not? I was wed to Sir John for three years."

"Then it seems to me we have two years yet before we may despair." His adorable laugh lines reappeared as he squeezed her waist. "When it comes, I will love it, for 'twill be made of you. And if it does not, then I will have only you to love, and I think that a fine thing."

Out of habit, she caught herself dismissing his sentimental speech even before he had finished. It remained a novelty to be loved this fiercely, and she despaired of ever feeling worthy of such an honor.

"And in the meanwhile," he continued, "there is Ned, and Katherine, and…" He furrowed his brow.

"Azalaïs."

He grunted. "'Tis too big a name for so small a babe."

"And Ellen should not have let Bisset have the choosing of it—aye, your views are well known."

With a low chuckle, he closed her in the circle of his arms. "You have ne'er spared much patience for my foolishness."

"How can you say so? I spare all I have!"

"Forsooth? *That* is the sum of your indulgence?"

"A man as vexing as you should feel fortunate to receive any indulgence at all," she replied primly, forcing the corners of her mouth down. "If you discover a woman who will suffer you, you must take care never to let her go."

"I mean not to."

He was smiling, so she kissed him.

She loved to kiss him when he smiled.

About the Author

Emma Golding grew up going to the Renaissance faire, which is where her fascination with daily life in 16th- and 17th-century England began. A degree in English literature seemed like a good excuse to read Shakespeare and take some creative writing classes, and now in her professional life, she divides her time between music and theater. It is a mystery how she got lucky enough to include so many of her favorite things in one book. Emma also loves crafts, calligraphy, Jane Austen film adaptations, and her piano students. She lives in Chicagoland with her pets and her spouse in her very own Happily Ever After.

Find out more at emmagoldingwrites.com.

Playlist

Music and sailing are as entwined with each other as the fibers of a rope, and I have a soft spot for British folk tunes, so it felt natural to weave music into the action of *Rooted*. All the songs mentioned throughout the book are real songs appropriate to the period, from Robert's irritating rendition of "When Daphne from Phoebus Did Fly," to the innuendo-filled popular tune "Come Again," to the "Heart's Ease" Maggie and Will dance together.

The only exception is the lament of the lover lost at sea that Maggie hears at the Silver Starling. "I'll Lay in the Heather" is one of my own compositions, inspired by Renaissance ballads, and as of this publication, it hasn't been recorded. Seems like the kind of thing that might show up in a newsletter, though! You can explore the *Rooted* playlist and subscribe to my email newsletter at emmagoldingwrites.com/about.

Acknowledgments

Writing this book is the hardest and most rewarding thing I've ever done, and like Maggie, I owe a debt I can never repay to all those who helped me along the way.

To my wonderful beta readers, especially Regina, Hunter, and Cybil, and to my supportive writing groups, thank you all for the insightful feedback, the incessant cheerleading, and the occasional tough love. I learned so much from you.

To my parents, thanks for sharing your wisdom as both parents and publishers. Some authors head into self-publishing without a clue, and I'm fortunate I had your guidance.

To my husband, thank you for sharing me with this project for as long as it took. Thank you for all the times you engaged with me when I needed to gush or rant, and for pretending to engage when I went on too long. Thanks for covering for me, for cheering me on, and for being my real-life book boyfriend. And thank you in advance: this won't be the last time I neglect chores in favor of fictional characters.

All the beautiful epigraphs are from *Ovid's Metamorphoses: The Arthur Golding Translation (1567)*, edited by John Frederick Nims and published by The Macmillan Company, 1965. The text has been edited for the benefit of modern readers, with updated spellings and translations of obscure terms, while attempting to maintain the integrity of the poetry.